I0662866

Watersmeet

A Novel of the Twelve Baronies

by
Rachel Cotterill

Copyright © 2014 Rachel Cotterill

1 3 5 7 9 0 8 6 4 2

Published in the United Kingdom by Rachel Cotterill.

Cover art by Jessica Soria Gázquez.

All rights reserved. No part of this publication may be reproduced without prior permission of the copyright holder. The right of Rachel Cotterill to be identified as the author of this work has been asserted by her in accordance with the Copyright, Designs and Patents Act 1988.

A CIP catalogue record for this book is available from the British Library.

ISBN-13: 9781910331040

Chapter One

"Savash and Oelum!"

Ailith stepped back just in time as the jug shattered on the flagstones at her feet, splashing ale across her boots.

"Sorry, Nana." She held up the orphaned handle, which had come away from the pot so suddenly that she couldn't stop it falling. "I think you'll be needing a new jug."

"It's my fault, dear," Nana said. "I take all your father's rejects while the apprentices are learning. And handles are difficult."

"No, you can't blame the boys, I know exactly whose mistake this was."

"Well, it's a lovely design, you might just need to work on your handles. Although you've probably mastered it by now, haven't you? I've had that one for a while."

"Ailith's better than Papa now," Aidith said, not managing to keep the amusement from her tone. Ailith rolled her eyes at her twin before bending to collect the broken pieces; Aidith had never understood how much she enjoyed making things. She would have stayed in the pottery forever if she could.

"But when I grow up I'm going to be the best of all," Edeva piped up.

"Perhaps I can get another of yours then, Ailith, love," Nana said. "Since that one served me so well."

Ailith, however, had stopped listening. On her knees, she examined the broken pot, as oblivious to her family's chatter as to the ale now soaking into her skirt. The bottom third of the jug had split away, forming a neat bowl, and the break ran around precisely where the jug had been dipped in decorative green glaze. The top, meanwhile, had shattered. Ailith laid the remaining sherds out on the floor and sorted the biggest pieces. From the back, there was nothing remarkable about the pattern of the breaks, but as she turned them over one thing became obvious: wherever she'd painted green patterns the break skirted the edge of the decoration, and the glaze remained smooth and glassy. The base white, meanwhile, had crazed and cracked.

"I'm going to borrow these," Ailith said, scooping the sherds into the bowl and setting them by her plate.

"Whatever for, dear?"

"I just want to try something. It's no use to you now, and I'll get Papa to find you a new jug as soon as we get home."

"Whatever you're thinking, promise me you won't start until after the wedding," Aidith said. When Ailith didn't respond at once, she picked up the pot and held it behind her back. "Promise me. I don't care what you do once I'm married, but you will not spoil the next two days with your tinkering."

"I promise, I promise."

"Good."

"We won't have a moment spare before the wedding as it is. Eddy, go and fetch some more ale, Grandpa hasn't got a drink."

Edeva hopped down from her chair and almost skipped across the room to fill her grandfather's tumbler straight from the barrel. If there was one advantage to having a six-year-old sister, it was that she was still young enough to do chores and think she was playing. She'd filled it a little too full, and walked ever so slowly back across the room, tumbler clutched tightly in both hands, ale sloshing over her fingers with every cautious step.

"Eddy, be careful!" Sunneva snipped.

"Leave her be," Ailith said. "She's trying her best."

"She's so mucky, she makes a mess of everything."

"Do not!" Edeva protested.

"Do so."

"Children are messy," Nana said. "At least with a little sister, you can get used to it before you've got your own."

"My children will never get away with being so sloppy," Sunneva said. At fourteen, she knew precisely everything about being a grown-up. "Papa should hide her until she learns to steady her hands."

"You must be the only child to wish her father was quicker with the cane," Grandpa said, taking the tumbler from Edeva's sticky fingers. "Thank you, dear. And given the stubborn streak you girls got from your mother, I don't think you'd like it if he was."

"I'm a good girl."

Ailith laughed. "You just don't remember being younger, Sun. I bet Drefan has some tales to tell of both of us."

After they'd eaten their fill of cold beef and flatbread and salad, Ailith and Sunneva returned to loading the cart. Aidith was excused from chores, and stayed in the kitchen sipping tea while the others gathered provisions for her wedding feast. They couldn't waste time if they were to get home before dark. Mama had sent them to the farm to fetch flour, milk, and meat, while she and Papa and Drefan cleared and decorated the clearing where the feast would take place. They'd spend the evening making dough for the wedding buns so the levain could do its work overnight, and in the morning they would have to set the hogs roasting before dawn. Even with the whole family working around the clock, it would be a struggle to get everything ready in time.

Ailith hefted sacks of flour from the barn, while Sunneva fetched milk from the dairy. Edeva's only job was to hold the reins and steady the horses, but she was still too young to attend to her task without becoming distracted by every passing butterfly.

"I do love a good wedding, don't you, m'dear?"

Ailith turned in surprise to the old man who had come up behind her in the barn. He wasn't anyone she recognised, and she thought she knew everyone in Bracklea, at least by sight. Meeting a stranger at her grandparents' farm was particularly unlikely.

"You must be so pleased," he went on.

"I'm sorry," she said, dusting her hands on her skirt. "I don't think we've met. I'm Ailith. Do you know my sister?"

"I know your family," the man said, kissing the back of her hand despite the remaining flour. "Although it has been some time since I paid a visit, and I haven't seen you or Aidith since you were both knee-high. My name is Malachi."

"Pleased to meet you." Unsure what else she should say, Ailith turned her attention back to the stores.

"I dare say you've an eye open for potential matches of your own. A feast like this should be a perfect opportunity — you mustn't be shy."

Ailith nodded mutely. There was nothing to be achieved by arguing with a stranger; he couldn't know that most of the town's eligible men had rejected her already.

"No?" He raised an eyebrow. "Could it be that a girl of your age has something on her mind more important than marriage? That would be a novelty."

"I don't… I mean, I'd like to meet the right man, of course."

"Naturally. But in the meantime…"

She shook her head. "It's nothing. I haven't much luck, that's all."

"Ah, well, it will come at the right time. Now, your grandmother said I might find some willowherb out here," he said. "I hoped you could point me in the right direction."

"I didn't think she kept any," Ailith said. "It grows so well it's a pest, in the fields, so you can always find some when you need it. But she's got racks of herbs over here… hang on, I'll have a look."

Ailith turned to the shelves behind her, where Nana kept her ingredients in a row of mismatched pots, and glanced over the faded labels. She didn't think she would find any, but there was a small brown jar at the front of the shelf: the writing was difficult to decipher, slanted and spidery, but if it didn't say 'willowherb' then there must be something of an uncannily similar name.

"Here," she said, picking it up. "Is there anything else you need?"

He took the jar, and placed it gently down on a nearby surface.

"Thank you," he said, a strange smile playing on his lips. "That was what I wanted."

"What?"

"It's unusual to find a young woman who can read. Who taught you letters?"

She blushed, ashamed to have been caught out so easily. "Nana showed me."

"Well, well. What a coincidence," he said, and something in his tone told her that it was no coincidence at all. "It happens that I taught your grandmother to write, many years ago. What else did your grandmother teach you, I wonder?"

He picked up a fragment of the broken jug, and smacked it hard against the corner of the bench before dropping it back into the bowl.

"Walk with me," he said. "We have important matters to discuss, and those sisters of yours will be back any moment."

"Oh?" Ailith couldn't imagine anyone needing to have an important discussion with her, let alone an old man she'd just met, but he looked terribly serious as he led her out into the fields behind the barn.

"Your grandmother taught you more than just reading, didn't she?"

"What do you mean?"

"Here, let me show you something."

He pulled a leather pouch from his pocket, dipped his fingers into it, and removed a pinch of black powder. With a flick of the wrist he sent the powder arcing through the air, and as it flew, it ignited into a series of tiny white sparks.

Ailith couldn't help smiling. "That's beautiful."

"Your turn."

He proffered the pouch, and she nervously pinched up a little powder. It was coarse, and felt like rough sand between her fingers. She was afraid it might flare up at any moment, and if there was one thing she was absolutely sure of, it was that she didn't want it to explode in her hand. And what if a little of the powder got caught beneath her nails, or stuck to her skin? She could lose a finger. No, she would quite prefer it to stay as safe black sand until it was as far away from her as possible.

"Now throw it," he said.

She flicked her wrist the way he had done, but there were no sparks. The powder floated harmlessly to the ground.

"What do I need to do to light it?" she said, thinking of fires and flints. Perhaps he'd done some sleight of hand when she wasn't looking.

"Try again," he said. "But as you throw it, try to visualise the sparks cascading down the way they did before. Don't worry, it's not going to hurt you."

She took another pinch of powder and threw it, imagining the result just as he'd suggested, and this time the air sparkled with a thousand tiny fires.

"As I thought." Malachi nodded. "You have a knack for this."

"Me?" She prodded curiously at the powder. "You made it, though. I don't even know what's in here."

"I made it, but not anyone could use it. It's a hard thing to explain. Think of when you add water to clay to make it workable. It burns off in the kiln, but if you didn't have any water, you wouldn't get very far. By itself, the powder is harmless. It can only burn when you add your intention to it."

"My intention?"

"Yes. You have to want it to burn, and you have to know how to project your intention into the powder. Then it sparkles."

"That sounds like black magic." Ailith crossed her palm with the symbols of the Pantheon to ward away the attention of the gods. Even talking about such things was a heresy that could put her on the wrong side of the Temple Law, and she didn't know this man.

"Some people call it that way — usually the fearful ones, the ones who can't do it. You're a mage, it's a natural ability. Nothing to be afraid of. Some people can sing, others can play the flute, you..."

"I can do *magic*?"

"You can touch the world with your thoughts. And you've already learnt to do it. Most people would take a day or a week on their first attempt with shimmering powder. You've already mastered it."

"That's…" She shook her head, unable to think of a suitable word. "I don't understand at all. You think Nana taught me this?"

"Your grandmother is extremely talented. She might not have explained all this to you, but if you've ever seen her make anything, then you've doubtless seen her project her intentions. It's not impossible that you've picked it up quite by accident."

Her eyes lighted on a dead tree at the edge of the next field. "Can I set anything on fire?"

He laughed. "That isn't how it works. The powder burns because of its ingredients; you're just providing the spark it needs to get started. But I realised when I saw that pot that I needed to test you."

Suddenly she understood what he was driving at. "Because the green parts didn't break," she said. "You think I did something to the green glaze while I was making it. But why would I do that, and not the white?"

"I suppose you just stumbled on a formula that works. It could be that whatever ingredient makes it green also makes it amenable to your power, or maybe you were distracted when you mixed the white — I won't know that unless you tell me the two sets of ingredients."

"They're basically the same, but the green has copper and the white has tin."

"Well, I do think it's important that you try again, m'dear. Don't you?"

"I'm not sure."

She'd already been thinking about the tests she could try with the glazes, of course, but this was different. This was dangerous.

"You're a mage who knows her letters, girl. You're half way to being an alchemist already."

"Yes, I can read, but what good does it do me? It's just something I have to hide from Papa, and from anyone who might want to marry me. I'll never have access to a library."

"A library, is it? Well, that is a rare dream. There's precious few libraries that aren't attached to castles. Maybe one or two of the larger manor houses."

"Exactly. And even Mama wouldn't look to make that kind of match for me, so what was the point? Numbers are good for keeping ledgers, but people round here are suspicious of letters, and there's no work for a scribe. I'm not sure this alchemy business sounds any more useful, to someone like me."

A smile spread across his face. "You seem like you're in need of a little guidance. Perhaps you'd allow me to read your stones."

Ailith hesitated, and before she had chance to express her doubts he had pulled a second, much larger leather pouch from his pocket. Bracklea was a large enough town to have all eight deities of the Major Pantheon represented, and a person might go to seek out the appropriate priest to ask if a date was auspicious or a match well-made, but never before had she seen a reader of the ancient stones. It had been an age since the tokens were relegated, for the most part, to being counters in a children's game. He emptied the pouch into her hands.

"Is this magic, too?"

"Of a different kind." He knelt, using a stick to flatten a patch of soil, and scratched out a grid of three squares by three. "Now, you don't want to use them all or the reading will take forever. Close your eyes, and set aside around half of them."

She squatted beside him and dropped a few of the stones back into the pouch.

"Now, throw the rest onto the grid."

Ailith shook the stones lightly between her fingers, and scattered them across the ground. Malachi turned the stones which had landed face-down, deftly switching the places of two of them as he did so. Then he traced a line in the dirt, joining five of the stones into a single winding path which crossed the middle three squares.

"This is your life's journey," he said, indicating the wavy line. "It starts with the Earthquake — that's Savash in her elemental aspect, not so uncommon as a beginning. She signifies fear and disruption. And see, here, Joy comes much later, signified by Keyif in his human aspect. Only after War."

"Why did you swap Death and War?"

He blinked up at her through wrinkled, half-blind eyes. "Did I, m'dear?"

"Don't pretend. I know you didn't mean me to see, but look, your War stone has a slightly flat edge. And it landed over there." She pointed to the spot where the Death stone now rested, in the top left-hand square.

"Well, well. You are observant. But you can't overcome Death in the middle of the story, where would be the sense in that? It makes more sense in the sphere of Character, where the stone can be interpreted as showing Oelum's strength and wisdom."

"The stones lie where they fall, though. Isn't that where the phrase comes from?"

"I can trust you, I think." The old man leaned forward conspiratorially, his voice barely above a whisper. "Then let me tell you a secret. Telling fortunes, there's less to read in the stones than in the face of the person in front of you."

"What do you mean?"

"I can read a little of your story, but it's not from rocks on the ground." As if to prove his point, he scooped up the stones and tucked them out of sight. "Take that young lad at the Temple of the Twins. Between you and me, he deserves a closer look. What can you tell me about him?"

Ailith thought for a moment, chewing on her lower lip as she tried to picture him. She spent as little time as she could get away with in the temples, unless it was a feast day: you didn't want the gods' eyes to light on you any more than was strictly necessary. "He's tall," she said at last. "Skinny. Hair a bit darker than mine, skin a bit lighter. And he's got a really, really long nose."

Malachi nodded. "What else?"

"He's a few years older than me, I think. Maybe closer to Ingrith's age."

"Ah, now that is interesting."

"Is it? Why?"

"I'll let you think about that. What else have you noticed?"

"I'm not sure. I don't really know him."

"Well, keep an eye open, and think on it. There's more to that one than appearances suggest, and he won't stay an altar boy for long."

"What do you mean?"

"Oh, no, that wouldn't be half as much fun. You should talk to him, though. See if you think he might make you a suitable husband."

"Ailith? Ailith!" Edeva's voice rang out across the yard. "Where are you?"

"Ah, you're being summoned," Malachi said. "And I had better tell your grandparents that I'm here. Do see what you think about that boy when next you see him... hush hush, though. Not a word."

"Not a word," Ailith agreed. What could she say to anyone, anyway? Some strange old man had told her she was a mage, and should consider marrying a temple orphan? Mama would have a fit.

He pressed the pouch of powder into her hand. "Keep this," he said. "And practice. You never know when you might find it useful."

Chapter Two

There was nothing remarkable in the rattling of the temple door at midnight. Men could injure themselves at any ungodly hour, trying to finish a job by candlelight, and when Eadweard the blacksmith caught himself on the furnace or Brun the carpenter put a nail through his hand, it was to the temple of Saaluk and Bereket they would come, asking the Twins for blessings and their priest for salves.

If it was somewhat out of the ordinary to have a second visitor arrive while Garrick and his master were already tending to the burns of Godwine the potter, well, it probably would have passed without notice if not for the fact that Selwyn turned as white as a sheet and let the stack of papers slip from his hands, knocking over the ink pot. Thick black ink ran in rivers across the desk, dripping and pooling on the floor as Selwyn hurried to lift his most important documents clear of the mess. In the three months of his apprenticeship to date, Garrick had never known Selwyn to misplace as much as a pin, although he'd suffered a couple of beatings for his own carelessness in the beginning. Now the old man looked as if he'd seen a ghost.

"Get this mess cleared up, boy," Selwyn barked, flicking out at Garrick with his cane before the youth had chance to turn and see whose arrival had caused such a ruckus. "No, finish that first, you lackwit. Just finish it quickly."

Garrick tied the bandages around Godwine's arm, testing to make sure they were secure before he hurried for a mop and bucket. Sometimes he was sure it was all a game to Selwyn: how much abuse would the spoiled brat put up with before running home to Father? But two could play that game, and Garrick had resolved to tolerate almost any indignity for the sake of knowledge. He certainly wouldn't take any part but that of the meek and obedient apprentice with gossiping peasants like Godwine present, let alone this mysterious stranger. He began to wash the ink from the flagstones, taking the opportunity to examine the newcomer as he worked the mop back and forth. Selwyn was old but this man was ancient, his skin dark and etched with deep wrinkles, his hair white as ash.

"Can your friend excuse us?" the stranger asked, looking pointedly at Godwine.

"I'm waiting for a sacrifice," Godwine said, his voice sharp with pain and annoyance. He'd come for Selwyn's salves, as they all did, but he too had a part to play lest they all be accused of heresy. It was particularly important with strangers present. "If we could just…"

"Yes, yes," the old man interrupted. "A sacrifice, indeed. I'm sure your priest will not forget you, but in the meantime you have some good ointment on your wounds. You'll heal in no time."

"Garrick will prepare the rites at once," Selwyn said, forestalling any further argument. "And he'll be sure to offer a few extra words for your sweet daughter's wedding tomorrow, won't you, boy?"

"As you say." Garrick opened the door to empty his bucket of inky water into the gutter, and held it as Godwine stomped sullenly from the temple apartments. As he made his way back to the inner sanctum, Selwyn and the stranger watched one another in silence. It was only as he closed the door on them that Selwyn spoke.

"Why are you here?" There was no mistaking his tone. Garrick had never heard such anger in the voice of his mentor, and something in the sound of it held him close against the door. "I told you never to darken my door again. Savash and Oelum, I told you never to set foot in this town again."

"I need to talk to you," the old man replied.

"There is nothing for us to talk about. You made sure of that forty years ago."

The old man snorted. "So you think. You always did think you knew best."

"You took the only thing that mattered to me," Selwyn said.

Garrick held his breath. He knew he shouldn't be hearing this, and if Selwyn realised he was there it would mean a beating for certain, possibly even the untimely end of his apprenticeship. But knowledge was power, he'd learnt that at his grandfather's knee, and he would need all the power he could get to make up for his father's failures. He was here to learn Selwyn's arts, but if the priest had a secret then that was another kind of knowledge worth possessing.

"No amount of talking will make this better."

"I think he's still alive," the old man said.

"You told me he was dead. It's been thirty-six years and seven months — how can you possibly bring news after all this time?"

"It seemed almost certain, when I couldn't find him. But word has reached me, lately, that forces me to consider an alternative course of events."

There was a long pause. Garrick could hear his heart thudding in his chest, and the whistling of the wind through the eaves, but in the next room both men were completely silent.

"I think," Selwyn said, after a painfully long silence, "that you had better sit down and tell me exactly what you're talking about."

"I was never pleased with the way things turned out," the old man said. "If it makes any difference. Whatever you might think, I didn't take him to spite you. I had hoped, being your son, he would prove stronger than he was."

"That doesn't change what happened."

"No, but my assessment of what happened might have been wrong. When Anselm left me he took all my notes, and emptied a bottle of a very particular amalgam I'd been working on. I doubt he realised precisely what he was doing, he just knew it was important to me. I assumed he'd attempted to use it himself, which would soon have proved fatal… under any normal circumstances."

Selwyn waited without comment for the old man to lay out his alternative theory; on the other side of the door, Garrick's burning curiosity held him in place against his better judgement.

"If he had found himself in the company a suitably talented alchemist, however," the old man went on, "things could have gone a different way. There are hints that perhaps he found himself in the company of a man named Leofwin, once a student of mine. Now Lord Baron of Watersmeet."

Garrick barely managed to suppress a gasp of shock. Leofwin wasn't just one of the Twelve, he was probably the most infamous man in the Twelve Baronies. He skirted along the very edge of social respectability, regarding even his fellow barons as beneath his notice, their lives below his consideration. Garrick had never expected Selwyn's path to cross with that of such a great and fearsome man.

It was, apparently, equally surprising to Selwyn. "The Lord Baron of Watersmeet is an alchemist?"

"One of the very best."

Garrick edged away from the door. He didn't need some itinerant commoner to tell him about Leofwin, and if he took much longer over the sacrifices, Selwyn would become suspicious. That Selwyn had a son, though: that was news. He hadn't known the old man had even been married. And what had the boy stolen that might — but might not — have killed him?

Chapter Three

Ailith ran her fingers through her sister's straw-coloured hair, pulling and twisting, weaving the strands together into a complex braid of her own design. Ever since she'd been old enough to be entrusted with a hairbrush, Ailith had amused herself creating ever more intricate patterns. She divided sections and united them with well-practised fingers, twisting and weaving, until the pattern began to match the one in her mind's eye. This would be her masterpiece… but it would also be the last time she indulged in this simple pleasure with her twin. Tomorrow Aidith would wear her hair loose for the wedding blessings, in beautiful curls set by today's pattern of knots. And after that she would be gone, sleeping in Uchtred's bed instead of with her sisters.

Aidith sat cross-legged on the sleeping pallet they'd shared since they were toddlers, teeth gritted, but though Ailith tried to be gentle it was impossible to make braid-work of this detail without occasionally catching a stray hair. And when she tugged the ends to attach beads and tiny bells, Aidith gasped aloud.

"There," Ailith said, rocking back onto her heels to admire her handiwork. "Shake your head."

Aidith did as she was told. The bells jangled prettily around her neck, but of the knots and plaits which crowned her head, not one strand moved from where Ailith's fingers had set it.

"Perfect. You look stunning, and you'll be able to dance with every man at the feast without a hair falling out of place."

"Your turn," Aidith said, turning to face her sister. "After all, you need to be just as pretty as me tonight. You don't know whose eye you might catch — and you need to get on with it."

Ailith grabbed the nearest pillow and hit her sister squarely in the chest.

"What?"

"You sound like Mama. Just because you're getting married before me, that doesn't mean I'm never going to find a husband."

"If you can learn to shut up, you might, but you're running late. We were always supposed to wed on the same day."

Ailith shrugged, and wished she could cast off her family's expectations as easily as she could suppress the frown that threatened to twist her lips. The night was Aidith's, though, and she wouldn't ruin it for her sister by sulking. There would be time enough to argue with Mama another day. Instead she tossed the pillow aside and shook her hair out of its demure plait so Aidith could brush it out. She would have to train Sunneva to make braids; the stiffness in her right shoulder meant she'd never be able to reach up and do it for herself, although she'd learnt to put a basic plait in one-handed.

"How do you want it?" Aidith asked.

"Do something simple," Ailith said. "Maybe six braids, linked in a rose at the back?"

"Only you would call that simple." Aidith shook her head, causing the bells to tinkle in time with her laughter. "Really, only you even have names for these things."

"Make up something else if you prefer," Ailith said, but she knew she was safe. Aidith's fingers might be almost as nimble as Ailith's own, and she had a wonderful imagination, but she didn't have the knack for designing new patterns that would hold. Whenever she tried something a little out of the ordinary, however pretty, it would collapse on itself and fall out before the evening was through.

"No, I'll do my best, but you might have to remind me how to make the rose secure."

"Of course."

Once the rose of braids was whipped tightly against the crown of her head, Ailith slipped into her best party frock and helped Aidith into the red wedding gown. The dress had been taken in to fit

Aidith's slim frame, and adjusted for height; Ingrith, who'd worn it last, was broader in the shoulders and a good three inches taller. If there was one advantage in Ailith's failure to find a husband, it was that the twins hadn't needed to fight over who got to wear their sisters' dress.

Mama was in the kitchen with Eddy when they came downstairs, ferrying fresh buns from the oven while trying to avoid getting flour on her own finest dress.

"Oh, my baby girl!" she exclaimed when she saw Aidith. "So grown up."

Aidith gave a slow twirl to show off her gown and her hair. "Do you like it?"

"You're beautiful." Mama dabbed tears from her eyes. "Now, Uchtred is bringing his carriage to take you to the party, isn't he, dear? You'd better make sure you're ready to leave as soon as he gets here, but we'll need to go ahead of you and get everything set up for the feast."

"No problem." Aidith folded her hands demurely in front of her, standing stiffly in the swathes of heavy fabric. The wedding gown was easily three times the weight of the girls' other party dresses, let alone the light and practical frocks they usually wore when the kilns were hot.

"I hear old Malachi's taken an interest in you," Mama said, as Ailith helped her with the next tray of buns.

Ailith started. If that news had already made it across from the farm, she wondered what else. Had someone seen them in the field? Was she already in trouble for a heresy not of her own making?

"That man's a hundred if he's a day," Mama went on. "An impossible heretic, of course, but he usually has some wise words despite it all. You should listen to him if he's giving you the time of day."

"I always listen to my elders," Ailith said, hoping her mother would miss the irony. Since none of her elders seemed to want anything beyond marrying her off to the first eligible bachelor, whether she liked him or not, she wasn't sure why listening to them was to be so highly recommended.

"He's quite the matchmaker, too. He introduced me to your father. Did he make any suggestions as to a match for you?"

"No," Ailith said, because the alternative was to explain exactly who he'd suggested. "But I'll bear that in mind if I see him again."

"Good girl." Mama patted her on the shoulder, and moved off again to attend to Edeva, who had somehow managed to twine the thin laces of her party frock into a complex knot. "Oh, Eddy, I don't know how you do it, but I think we'll have to cut this mess out. You might need new laces."

"No, Mama, don't cut it. I can work it out," Ailith said. "Come here, Eddy, and hold still."

"Thank you, sweetheart." Mama kissed her lightly on the cheek, and hurried off to start loading the cart.

Ailith crouched in front of her little sister and studied the knotted threads. It wasn't as straightforward as unfastening braids, which at least had a logic governing their interlocking patterns, but in many ways the same principles applied. She just had to tease the threads apart enough to see what was going on, and after that it was simply a matter of un-weaving the knot that Eddy's careless fingers should never have woven. If only everything in life were so simple.

Chapter Four

"Good evening, young Highfort."

Garrick swung around in surprise, only to find himself face to face with the old man from the temple. By the time he'd returned from preparing the sacrificial offerings the night before, the man had gone, leaving only a bad-tempered Selwyn in his wake. He didn't know he'd been recognised.

"I don't know what you mean," he said coolly, drawing his shoulders back and straightening to his full height so that he stood a good half-head above the stranger.

"Yes, you do." The old man met his gaze without a moment's wavering. "Do you think I wouldn't know a child of Oeric's when I saw them? It's a wonder your disguise has taken anyone in, with a nose like that. I suppose most of the town have never set eyes on their liege lord, though, so how could they hope to recognise his likeness?"

"I do rather depend on that," Garrick said, with forced levity. The old man knew too much; there was no point making more unnecessary fuss with hopeless denials. At least their conversation wouldn't be heard over the music. "You know my father?"

"I know a good many people across the Twelve Baronies."

"I see. And you are?"

"Malachi." He said it as if the name alone should be enough of an introduction. "And although you may not know me, rest assured, I know enough for the both of us. Knowing things is rather my business, in fact, that's why I wanted to talk to you. There's a fine young lady here who I think you should meet."

"Here?" Garrick looked around in disbelief. "At some peasant's feast?"

"Here."

"A girl?"

"A young woman you should consider most seriously. After all, what's a little thing like ancestry when your future is at stake?"

"You sound just like Father, with all his talk of love matches." Garrick shook his head. "Such follies are fine for younger sons, but for those of us due to inherit…"

"Quite so, m'boy. Quite so. The heir to a barony can't for a moment consider wedding for something as frivolous as love."

"So you see, I don't think…"

"That's precisely why you must meet this woman," Malachi continued, undeterred. He clamped a surprisingly firm hand down on Garrick's shoulder and turned him away from the crowd. "It hasn't escaped my notice that you've apprenticed yourself to the only priest within thirty leagues who also does a fine line in alchemical cures. And for a young lord to debase himself with an apprenticeship, when he could be out hunting all day and dancing all night, that says something about a man, don't you think? You're a sly one, and no mistake."

Garrick glanced around, uncomfortable enough to be discussing his lineage in such open surroundings, let alone these hints at his motives. But the only way to get rid of the old man without making a scene was to hear him out, as quickly and quietly as possible. "I don't see what this has to do with my marriage prospects."

"You don't need a decorative wife to hang off your arm," Malachi said. "You need a girl who knows her letters, not one who can play twelve-dozen sonatas on the flute. You need a partner who will be your equal, if not your better, in the business you wish to pursue."

No, what he *needed* was a woman who could offer a solid military alliance, and a sufficient dowry to refill the treasury from years of Father's excesses. But he could hardly say as much to this stranger.

"I thank you for your advice." Garrick offered a small bow, and turned his attention deliberately back towards the party, but Malachi hadn't finished.

"If you don't want me to tell your master that you were listening at the door yesterday, you'll at least give her a dance. She's the sister of the bride and they're quite identical, so you shouldn't have any trouble picking her out."

"As you say." Garrick didn't much like being forced to do anything, but if there was one thing he needed to avoid, it was having Selwyn dragged into this. Being scolded by a common priest was embarrassing at the best of times. To have tales told by this stranger, when the gods only knew what history lay between them… he couldn't allow that.

"Her name's Ailith," Malachi added, and offered a conspiratorial wink. "Interesting young woman. I think you'll like her."

Garrick paced around the clearing, watching the dancers spin beneath the trees. After that conversation he needed a stiff drink, though he'd found nothing stronger than ale since he moved to Bracklea. He'd become rather partial to the brewer's darkest, though, so he headed for the barrels stacked at the edge of the clearing. A couple of friendly words with the brewer's boy, one apprentice to another, and he had himself a secluded spot to sit behind the barrels, within reach of a tap of his favourite. The plan worked even better than he'd hoped, and he sat undisturbed until the evening started to draw in, sipping the sweet black ale.

He'd spotted the girl easily enough, sitting with her friends beneath the splayed branches of a copper beech tree, but she hadn't been alone for a moment. He squinted between the barrels to watch her, but he couldn't interrupt without drawing attention to himself, and his privacy was too important. Surely the old man would understand that. The band moved on from love songs to more bawdy rhymes. Ailith and her friends clapped in time, and she sang along with the chorus at the top of her voice.

"Someone caught your eye?" the brewer's boy asked, noticing where his attention was directed.

Garrick was about to brush it off, but the lad seemed nice, and perhaps he could help. "I was hoping to talk to Ailith," he said. "But she's busy with her friends, and word would get around if I went to ask her."

"And you wouldn't want to get on the wrong side of her mam." The boy nodded sympathetically. "Leave it to me."

Garrick watched as he walked across to the group of girls, chatting easily and making them laugh as he gathered their tankards for refills. And a moment later he was striding back towards the barrels, Ailith two steps behind him, both of their hands laden with flagons.

"Actually, I didn't just want your help with the carrying," the brewer's boy said as they returned. "My friend here was hoping to talk to you."

"Oh, hello." She spotted Garrick and smiled, dropping to the ground beside him and tucking her hands beneath her legs. "I don't think we've been introduced."

"My name's Garrick. I'm apprenticed to Selwyn at the temple of the Twins."

"The orphan," she said. "Of course. I'm Ailith."

"Pleased to meet you, Ailith. Shall we dance?"

She shook her head. "I don't, really."

Garrick bit back the first half-dozen retorts that rose to his lips. She didn't know who he was, and if he was to persist in this mummery he'd have to get used to the idea that a girl might refuse an nameless priest's boy in ways that no-one would ever refuse Garrick son of Oeric. It was more than a girl of her standing had any right to expect, and she threw it in his face when she should be honoured to dance even a single step with a partner of his nobility. The indignity was worth it for the skills he was learning... but at times it still stung.

She patted the ground beside her. "Couldn't we just talk?"

"That's what dances are for," he started, and then realised that was his old self speaking. In his world, a man needed an excuse to talk to a woman, but things were different in the provinces. No-one would think anything of it here if he sat beside a girl and made idle conversation.

"What a funny idea," she said. "Dances are for dancing. I'm not sure there's much time to converse while you're stripping the willow. I might like it better if there were."

He glanced over to where two dozen dancers, young and old alike, were weaving back and forth in a lively jig that saw them changing partners every few beats.

"Maybe not. But why don't you dance, Ailith?"

"Why don't you? I haven't even seen you twirl my sister round the oak, and everyone dances with the bride at least once."

He studied her for a moment. She had an open, honest face, and he almost wondered if he should just tell the truth, but everything depended on his anonymity. She might look trustworthy, but what could you really tell from a face?

She already knew he was a stranger: if he'd always lived in Bracklea they would doubtless already be acquainted. Most probably they would have spent their childhood years chasing each other through the fields, or climbing trees, or whatever it was that peasant children did to pass the time of day. He couldn't quite imagine it, himself.

"I didn't grow up here," he said, settling on something between the truth and his usual slew of lies. "I don't know your customs — or your dances."

Finally, she smiled. "I can see that."

"What's your excuse?"

"Oh, I hurt myself when I was little." She patted her right shoulder. "I can't get my arm to do half the things it should."

Garrick wondered why the old alchemist was pushing him towards a girl who was not only a commoner but a cripple. "But you can read?"

"I can." She laughed. "Did that meddlesome old man tell you that? It's one of my better-kept secrets, usually."

"It doesn't seem a very good secret."

A sudden seriousness came over her face, and she gripped his hand. "It's important. You mustn't tell my father."

"Why?"

"It's not becoming for a young woman, is it? What if I end up marrying a man who doesn't know his letters? My husband will think I'm writing all kinds of secrets, and it's a short step from there to shouts of heresy and witchcraft. Or what if word gets out, and I can't find a husband at all?"

Somehow while he was looking into her worried blue eyes, she'd managed to entwine her fingers with his. He wasn't sure how he could extricate himself from her grasp without causing a scene, but the prolonged contact embarrassed him. It wasn't like a formal dance, where there were layers of dress fabric to contend with, and where the young ladies wore gloves even in the heat of summer. Her fingers were bare and surprisingly warm, and her skin was soft as silk, quite unlike the serving girls he'd fumbled with back home.

"You should marry someone literate, then," Garrick said, stroking her fingers in what he hoped was a reassuring way. Her hands really were very soft. Maybe he needn't be in such a rush to pry himself free. "That much seems obvious."

"Oh, yes, because Bracklea is overflowing with literate, eligible men, and all of them just clamouring for my hand," she said, pulling sharply away and wrapping her arms around her legs. "Aidith's younger by a head, you know, so I'm already marked an old maid."

"Perhaps that's because you're this charming to any man who tries to talk with you."

He'd meant only to tease, but she looked up at him with sad eyes.

"Maybe it is. I don't mean to, you know. The words just come out." She shrugged, seeming to cheer a little. "So I don't think I'm in much position for picking and choosing a man of letters, do you? At the moment my only choice seems to be whether to run away before Mama foists me onto someone against both our wishes."

"You wouldn't."

"I might. Mama's getting desperate. She even said I should listen to Malachi, though he suggested you, and I wouldn't have thought an orphaned altar boy would meet her requirements for wealth or status."

Garrick snorted with laughter, managing at the last moment to turn it into a cough.

"Don't be offended," Ailith said before he could recover enough to respond. "I don't think any less of you, it's just that Mama is obsessed by all that. You'd think the only purpose of a daughter was to marry up, and why? Just to turn out a better class of baby?"

"It's a transaction like any other," Garrick said. "What's marriage for, if not to acquire some benefits for your family? Your sister weds the alderman, he gets a pretty girl half his age…"

"More like a third."

"A half, a third. What difference does it make? He gets a charming young bride, your father gets the best spot on market day, and everyone is happy."

"What about Aidith?"

"She gets a comfortable house, a man who will look after her — and the eternal gratitude of her parents."

"You know an awful lot about families, for an orphan."

He shrugged. "It's common sense."

"Where did you come from, anyway?"

The question hit Garrick like a jousting blow. "Has the old wizard been spilling my secrets, too?"

"I just pay attention. He said you might be interesting — I haven't made my mind up about that, yet."

Garrick laughed.

"But you've got my secret, it's only fair I should have one of yours."

"If I even have a secret."

"Temple boys don't usually spring from nowhere as near-grown men, and the callouses have barely formed on your hands. I think you're hiding more than one thing."

"You are observant." Garrick didn't for a moment take seriously Malachi's suggestion that he might wed this one, but she was diverting company, and seemed to have more wits about her than the air-headed sons and daughters of his father's courtiers. He smiled. "Maybe if you'll dance with me, I'll tell you something worth knowing."

Her hand went to her shoulder, and her face fell. "I thought I'd explained…"

"I know a dance or two that you could manage."

He got to his feet, and this time he took her hand without waiting for her to offer it and pulled her by her good arm until she was standing beside him. It was risky, but the free-flowing ale had made him bold. Besides, they were hidden away at the side of the clearing, and the townspeople were preoccupied with their own dancing and drinking. And it was mostly drinking, by this stage. Nonetheless, he steered her a couple of steps further into the shade of the trees before he guided her hands to his waist.

"What dance is this?" she asked, as he stepped closer and took hold of her shoulders. Her dress was a light cotton and his fingers traced the lines of her muscles beneath the fabric.

"This is one of my secrets," he said. In the back of his mind, a little voice warned against this, but he'd drunk enough that the immediate appeal of a young woman's arms could overwhelm his longer-term goals. "Promise you won't tell."

"I'll keep your secrets as long as you keep mine."

He smiled, and started to hum an ancient melody that was slower and more stately than that being drummed out by the players in the clearing. Studiously ignoring the more raucous tune, he started to step in time to his own beat, gently pulling her closer so that her body had no choice but to follow his movements. He'd deliberately chosen a sequence with simple steps, but she moved awkwardly, and he could feel the tension in her arms.

"Relax," he breathed into her hair. "It's easy… but it's easier if you can relax."

Chapter Five

Of the three traditional wedding blessings, the most important was always saved for last. The blessing of Saaluk and Bereket, twin gods of health and fertility, was the most crucial to any marriage. Aidith and Uchtred had already been to the temples of Refah and Keyif, so by the time the wedding party traipsed across town to the temple of the Twins they were all growing somewhat weary of prayers and sacrifices.

Or Ailith was, at least.

She suspected Aidith was still walking on air, and Mama was so pleased with the match that she had happily devoted months to the wedding arrangements — one more day was neither here nor there, in her complete dedication to the task of marrying off her daughter.

The priest had cleared the temple of casual visitors, so they had the inner sanctum to themselves, although the space around the altar was still crowded. Even in a town the size of Bracklea, almost everyone was a distant cousin on one side or another, and weddings brought those remote connections out in force. They'd all wanted to enjoy the family's hospitality at the feast, and most had the decency to turn up the following afternoon and pretend the blessings were of just as much interest to them.

Ailith caught Garrick's eye across the room and he pulled a face, making her bite her lip to stifle a giggle. Surely this was inappropriate behaviour for a priest's boy during what should have been a very serious rite of blessing. But he grinned at her, and her heart fluttered in her chest.

"Meet me later," he mouthed.

"Why?"

He shook his head, and just mouthed "Later. Behind the temple."

She shrugged. Maybe she could escape from her family for long enough to see him, or maybe not. Now that their wedding had been witnessed by the community and blessed by the gods, Aidith and Uchtred would be expected to go straight home to their marriage bed, hoping to conceive a thrice-blessed child. Everyone else would enjoy a rare day off before resuming their normal lives tomorrow, but that didn't mean Mama wouldn't have chores in mind for her remaining daughters. A day when the kilns were cold was a day for catching up with all the other jobs that tended to fall by the wayside when there were glazes to be mixed and pots to be fired.

Ailith watched as Aidith's hand was bound to Uchtred's with the green cord that represented Saaluk's power. The priest wove the rope loosely in with the red and yellow they still wore from the previous blessings, making a three-shaded plait which looped around the couple's wrists.

A few more murmured words of prayer, a short chorus echoed by all the guests, and they were released, blinking, into the early springtime sun. Uchtred's carriage awaited the newlyweds, and Ailith rushed forwards to embrace her twin before they embarked. She nodded politely to Uchtred, too, but neither of them would soon forget that he'd first attempted to court the older twin. The less said about that disaster, the better. At least Aidith seemed to have taken it all in stride.

Ailith dabbed tears from her eyes, and hugged Edeva to her side as they waved the carriage away.

"Why are you crying?" Edeva asked. "It's not a sad day. Is it?"

"His gain is our loss," Ailith said. "I'm happy for her, but I'll miss my sister."

Edeva looked solemnly up at her. "You'll always have me."

"That I will," Ailith agreed, and kissed her little sister lightly on the forehead. "Where's Mama?"

Eddy shrugged, and Ailith spotted her opportunity.

"Will you find her for me? Tell her I needed to buy a couple of things at the market. I won't be out late."

"Okay."

"Thank you, sweetheart."

Edeva hopped away, and Ailith walked down the hill towards the market square, just in case anyone was watching her go. Then she turned into a side street and made her way towards the back of the temple complex.

Garrick was waiting in the alley behind the temple, leaning nonchalantly against the wall. He looked so casual that Ailith wondered if he was really waiting for her, but as she approached he looked up and winked at her.

"You came."

"I came to see what you want."

"Can't I just want to see you?"

She shook her head, laughing. "You only met me last night. You cannot want to see me."

"I met you last night and you intrigued me, with your little secrets and your constant questions. Being a temple boy is lonely work, you know."

"Hmm."

"And I wanted to show you something."

"What?"

"You'll have to come with me, and it's a bit of a way. How long have you got?"

"I told Mama that I needed to do some shopping, but she won't worry until it gets close to sundown."

"I can get you home before dark. Come on, then." He took her arm to steer her through the streets. "Can you ride?"

"No, I've never tried. I can drive a wagon, though."

"That won't be necessary." He ushered her through a gate into a walled courtyard, where horses stomped and whinnied in their stalls. "This is the temple's stable, no-one will notice if we borrow Chestnut for the afternoon."

Garrick saddled a huge bay stallion and led him over to the stepped mounting block by the gate. He helped Ailith up first, and swung himself up behind her before she had time to worry about being alone on the giant horse.

Ailith looked around her constantly as they clopped through the streets, feeling a thrill of fear at the idea that she might be spotted by a stray relative. She had no way to explain her lies if she was caught out. She only started to relax as they rode out towards the southern forests, leaving the town behind them.

They must have ridden for over an hour before Garrick tied the horse to a tree and lifted Ailith down.

"We have to walk from here," he said, detaching the saddle bag and looping the strap over his shoulder. "It's not much further."

They followed a narrow path between the trees, walking in silence, accompanied only by occasional bursts of birdsong or the scuttling of a small animal disturbed by their footfalls. Dappled sunlight fell through the branches, catching the first bright green shoots of spring and making the woods sparkle with a magical light. Beneath their feet, white anemones and yellow celandines struggled to break through the covering of last year's leaves.

"This way," Garrick said, cutting away from the path and along the side of a steep gully which clearly hadn't seen a stream in some years. "Here."

Ailith wasn't sure what she was supposed to be looking at, until Garrick scrambled up the bank and vanished entirely from view. She followed, and found a flight of steps that disappeared into a hole in the ground.

"Wait there," he called up from somewhere out of sight. A moment later, a flickering candle cut through the gloom. "Do you want me to come back for you?" he asked, but she was already making her way down the rough-hewn stairs to join him.

"What is this place?"

Garrick grinned at her with childlike glee. He looked like a little boy showing off his favourite toy, and Ailith couldn't help smiling back, although she still wasn't quite sure what was going on. At the bottom of the steps they had to drop to their knees to crawl through a low entrance, and then the space opened out into a small chamber where they could stand again, although Garrick had to bow his head to avoid the ceiling. The air was cold, with an earthy smell. He took her hand and pulled her across to the side wall.

"Look," he said, holding the candle up to the stone.

At first, she thought the wall was simply blotched with moss and lichen, but as her eyes adjusted she realised that there were letters underneath the years' accumulations. She reached out to trace the lines of the aged paint.

"What does it say?"

"I only found this place a few days ago," he said. "I've started transcribing it, but it's old, and I don't recognise all the words. I thought you might want to help me work it out."

"Oh, yes, I'd love to." She started to read across the wall. *This tale concerns Ealhwyn and the garden elix…* No, it wasn't garden. Golden. *This tale concerns Ealhwyn and the golden elixir…* "Did you bring paper?"

"Of course. And cake — are you hungry?"

"Let's make a start on this first, then we can think about what we've learnt, while we eat."

They soon fell into a natural rhythm: Ailith would trace the letters and read out words, while Garrick inscribed whatever she told him. From time to time she would hit a patch that was ill-preserved or simply unfamiliar, and they would puzzle over it together until they decided what to write down.

They worked until the guttering candles threatened to burn their fingers, or worse, the papers. Garrick lit a fresh candle from his stub, wedged it upright with a few stones from the ground, and laid out a thick blanket. It wasn't the most comfortable place to sit, but by unspoken agreement they opted to stay inside the mysterious chamber rather than taking their picnic up to the softer, warmer ground of the forest floor.

As well as a slab of dense fruit cake, Garrick had brought apples and cheese, which he laid out on a wooden platter, and a small pot of honey. He handed her a leather flask, which proved to be full of the brewer's darkest, most expensive ale.

"When did you have time to pack all this?" Ailith asked.

"I got everything ready before the blessings. I just hoped you'd agree to come."

"You're crazy." She shook her head. "It's great, though. How did you find this place?"

"I stumbled across an old map. I didn't really know what I'd find — I'm still not sure what this is."

"No. It must be ancient, though." The words had made vague references to mages and elixirs; words Ailith hadn't heard used outside of the sagas, until Malachi came along. She wasn't quite ready to mention that experience to a temple apprentice, even if he did have secrets of his own. "Could it be a saga? It's not one I've heard."

"It sounds like it should be. Selwyn has a written copy of the sagas, though, and there's nothing there about a golden elixir, although the draught of life crops up a few times in passing."

"But it could be a new one. I mean, an old saga, but one nobody knows? Imagine if you've found a piece of forgotten history. What do you think it means? *The golden elixir, the draught of unending life…* It's awfully cryptic."

Garrick packed away the remnants of their lunch and took a final swig of ale. He reached out and brushed away a crumb from Ailith's chin, his thumb trailing across her lips in a gesture that could almost have been accidental in its intimacy if his hand hadn't continued smoothly round to the back of her neck.

He pulled her towards him until their noses bumped, making her giggle with embarrassment, and she planted her mouth firmly on his to try and stem the badly-timed laughter. His lips were soft, his beard tickled her chin, and he tasted of apples and ale and treacle. As he pressed forwards with renewed enthusiasm for a second kiss, she put her arms awkwardly around his waist. She shuffled to try and get comfortable on the stony ground, losing her balance slightly and kicking over the candle.

"It doesn't matter," Garrick said as she tried to reach the extinguished candle before the wick stopped glowing. "We can kiss just as well in the dark. Better, maybe."

"We shouldn't," she said, brushing his hand away as he reached for her bodice laces. "It must be getting late already."

The interruption had given her just the shock she needed to remember herself. There were herbs, of course, if she wanted to make sure she didn't fall pregnant — Nana would help her — but they barely knew one another. And kissing temple orphans didn't feature prominently in Mama's strategy for arranging a good marriage. Snatched kisses and whispered flirtations were all very well, but it could never come to anything. She'd been soundly thrashed a couple of years earlier when it had come to light that she was taking too many walks with one of the hands who worked at her grandparents' farm, and that had been nothing more than a childhood friendship.

"I'm in so much trouble," Ailith said as they rejoined the path, thinking of the kisses as much as the hour, though the light was already fading.

"Me too," Garrick agreed. "It was worth it, though, wasn't it?"

They rode back in companionable silence. Ailith tried to concentrate on the way the horse rose and fell beneath them, or the wind in her hair, or the silhouetted trees against the skyline… anything to take her mind off the way Garrick's arm clamped tightly around her waist. On the way here she'd imagined it a completely innocent gesture: he was just holding her upright, something that was indeed perfectly essential to her staying on the horse. But after that kiss, the way his fingers splayed across her hip felt positively obscene, and she couldn't tear her attention away from the feel of his hand.

Chapter Six

"What are you doing?"

Ailith started, almost dropping the tray of small jars she'd prepared for the kiln. "What? Nothing."

"I didn't ask you to make green pots."

"No, I was just trying something out."

Papa waited in silence for an explanation, arms crossed in front of his chest, and Ailith realised she should have thought about this before she started. There was no space in Papa's life for making things that weren't saleable. She set the tray down, and looked about for the broken jug.

"I wasn't going to bother you with it until I knew if it worked," she said. "Here, look what happened to Nana's jug. The green glaze must be stronger than the white, but it isn't like that on the normal pots, so I wanted to try… um… firing these at a higher temperature."

It was a clumsy excuse — Papa would know straight away that a higher temperature would do nothing but risk explosions in the kiln — but she could hardly admit that she'd just made a batch of glaze while thinking about it really hard. It sounded stupid enough in her head, but Malachi's words had stayed with her, stewing in her mind over the course of the week, and she'd been compelled to try.

"Throw those away, and get back to work."

"But I thought you'd be pleased. If we can improve our production, then…"

"You can't make an unbreakable pot." He swiped his arm across the tray, sending the unfired pots to shatter on the ground. "You spend too long at that farm, child. You shouldn't even attempt such things."

"Why not?"

"It's against the natural order. Pottery breaks. Next you'll be saying that people shouldn't die."

"And why should they?" As soon as the words were out of her mouth, Ailith knew she'd made a grave mistake. "I don't mean trying to cheat the gods," she added quickly, trying to smooth over her error with more words. "But if it was offered, if Oelum herself turned up at your doorstep offering you a longer life, why would you say no?"

"The gods are not to be trifled with, Ailith. Even in the days of the sagas, no gift was given without strings, and no daughter of mine will flirt with such heresy. Clear up this mess and come straight to the kitchen."

Ailith swept up the pieces and dumped most of them into the bin, although she slipped a couple of the larger fragments into her skirt pockets. Perhaps she could sneak them into the kiln when her father was busy. Now, though, she knew he would be waiting for her with his cane.

It wasn't the first time she'd spoken out of turn, letting accidental heresies pass her lips. It felt different, though. This was the first time she had something else to focus on as she bared her back for her father's lashes. His furious reaction made her more determined than ever: she would fire what remained of the pots, somehow, and then she would try with some other glazes, but this time she would be absolutely sure to do it in secret.

The planning helped her to keep her mind from the pain. Briefly she wondered whether she could use her magic to stop her back from hurting or to weaken the cane itself, but Malachi had been quite clear: it was in the realm of alchemical changes that she could exert her influence. She could push powder into flame, and maybe change the formulation of a glaze, but there was nothing she could do to stop her own nerves from screaming.

Papa set the cane aside after thirty lashes, and ordered her to go straight to the temple of Saaluk and Bereket to confess her sins.

The temple was on the outskirts of town, almost as far as it was possible to get from Godwine's pottery workshop. With every painful step up the hill, Ailith wondered if that was why her father had chosen Saaluk, of all the gods he could have asked to punish her for her insolence. It certainly didn't have much to do with Saaluk's remit of health; Oelum, Lady of Death, would have been a more logical choice. Ailith shuddered. That had been a narrow escape. No-one wanted to be sent to the Temple of Oelum for penance.

Eventually she came to the gates of the temple complex. The arched gateway towered over her, with intricate woodcarvings decorating the inside of the curve: heavily pregnant women vied with war-wounded soldiers for the attention of Saaluk and Bereket, who posed surrounded by their attendant dryad youths. Feeling more than a little nervous, Ailith crossed the first courtyard and knocked at the door of the priest's apartments.

It was Garrick who opened the door, and Ailith wasn't sure if she was pleased to see him again or humiliated to have him witness her predicament. He grinned at her. She wasn't sure she could bear it if he decided to take upon himself the job of beating some sense into her.

"Good afternoon," she said, forcing herself to smile. "I, um, my father sent me to see the priest. Is he at home?"

"He's out making his rounds, but he shouldn't be long. Come and sit down."

Ailith followed him into the sparsely-furnished room. He waved her towards the low pallets that probably served for sleeping as well as seating. She couldn't help wincing as she lowered herself to the floor.

"Are you injured?" Garrick asked. "We shouldn't wait for Selwyn to come back if you're hurting. Let me see."

She shook her head. "That's not why I'm here. I asked an impertinent question, and Papa sent me to confess."

"He beat you?"

Garrick lifted down a heavy jar from a shelf by the door. Ailith recognised the pot as one of her father's best, probably donated as part of their tithes.

"Just thirty lashes. He said the priest would want to add some more, once I told him what I'd been saying."

"And what were you saying?"

"I'd been experimenting with the glazes." She wrung her hands together, wishing she could avoid answering, but word would surely get back to Papa if she didn't properly atone for her mistakes. Garrick seemed nice enough, but he wasn't on her side. Not today. "This sounds so silly. Something happened with one of the firings, and I thought maybe we could make a pot that didn't break. And somehow… somehow we got from there to immortality, and I know it's heresy, but why would you say no if it was offered? That's all I said. How much do you think the priest will want to beat me?"

"Selwyn's a healer — I think I'm the only one he beats." The boy winked at her as he spoke, and she wondered if maybe things might be alright after all. "Now, let me see that."

Garrick set the jar on the floor and prised out the cork, releasing a pungent smell of peppercorns and lavender. Ailith hesitated. She might share a sleeping pallet with her sisters, and sometimes with female cousins who squeezed in when they were visiting, but she wasn't in the habit of baring her back to young men. Most certainly not to the mysterious and handsome kind who kissed you in secret caves, and mere days after someone had suggested they might marry you, at that.

"It's fine," he said, and she blushed at the idea that he'd sensed her thoughts. He turned his back on her. "Tell me when you're ready, and I won't look anywhere I don't need to."

She eyed him suspiciously for a moment, but the smarting of her back outweighed any concerns of modesty. Besides, he was the priest's apprentice, even if he wasn't quite what he pretended to be. She was still trying to work her way through that particular mystery, but now wasn't the time to ask. She unlaced her dress down to her waist, and lifted her under-tunic to her shoulders.

"Ready," she said, holding the dress fabric bunched against her breasts.

The ointment was cool on his fingers, and it stung and soothed at the same time as he spread it across her back, gradually warming and numbing her skin. Garrick rubbed the cream into her wounds with slender, well-practised fingers, and she shivered.

"You must get to see all the girls in their smallclothes," she said, trying to lighten the awkwardness of the moment.

"It's mostly been carpenters," Garrick said, trailing his fingers across her back. "It isn't usually girls who put nails through their hands, and you'd never guess how common a problem that is."

"And most girls aren't stupid enough to tempt their fathers to the cane. I know. But I'm sure he didn't send me here for ointment, he doesn't hold with creams and poultices."

"Your father found himself in need of a salve for some burns a few nights ago, actually. Just before the wedding."

"Papa would have come for a sacrifice to keep the blood sickness at bay, perhaps."

"It's amazing how a man's beliefs can change when his skin is peeling off."

The door opened before Ailith could think that one through, and the old priest came in, his cane tapping on the flagstones. Ailith pulled her tunic hurriedly back into place, and started to lace up her bodice.

"What have we here?" he asked, peering at Ailith. "Has our newest bride angered her husband so soon?"

"This is her sister," Garrick explained.

"Ah, yes, I see it now," Selwyn said, although clearly he saw nothing of the kind. "Are you hurt, child?"

"My father caned me," Ailith said. "But he sent me here for punishment, not healing."

"Why?"

"I said some heretical things." The telling was easier the second time, and Garrick's relaxed response had calmed her nerves a little. Selwyn's interest appeared to grow as she told her story, he asked several probing questions, but he didn't look like the avatar of a furious deity. By the end he was almost smiling.

"I don't suppose a potter would think much of an unbreakable pot," he said.

"What?"

"Never mind. It would seem counterproductive to beat you, after the boy has patched you up," Selwyn said. "But if you must have some penance, you can clean the temple complex. That should take you long enough."

Garrick grinned. "Let me show you where things are."

"Don't think this gets you out of your duties, boy," Selwyn said. "You can show her how it's done. Between the two of you I'll expect the stones to be sparkling by sunset. And Garrick?"

"Yes?"

"While you're cleaning, you can tell the child something about your studies."

Chapter Seven

Garrick wasn't sure what he'd been expecting when Ailith turned up at the temple, but he certainly hadn't guessed that by the evening they would be walking hand in hand across Bracklea as he quietly explained about the meeting they were about to attend. As well as being smart, and charming in an unpolished kind of way, the girl was a mage. Of course she was. Nothing had been remotely normal since the night before the wedding, and the strangeness showed no sign of abating.

He was only disappointed not to have spotted it himself. He'd had all the clues before Selwyn got back, but he simply hadn't been looking. And why would he? No-one knew how much latent talent there was in the population — except that it was rare enough to be interesting. But meeting a mage who had learnt to use her powers without tuition was positively unheard of. Perhaps that was why Malachi had pointed him towards her in the first place.

Selwyn had spotted her talents, kept her busy with cleaning and temple maintenance until it was time for the Guild meeting, and ordered Garrick to see her safely there. Theirs wasn't a registered Guild, of course, as he'd already had to explain. You could never put an Alchemists' Guild on the ledgers at the Guild Hall, but it was a useful shorthand and the group did adopt some of the same functions as the Guilds of merchants and artificers.

He led the way through the darkened streets, all the while trying to convey the dynamics of their group as simply as possible. She was still having some difficulty grasping how a priest and his apprentice could be part of a group of magi who met secretly and always after dark, in obvious contravention of the Temple Laws, but frankly

Garrick wasn't quite sure he understood that part himself. Selwyn had studied alchemy for years, using his position in the temple to offer remedies to the sick despite the heresy of it. Fortunately the people of Bracklea found his cures too useful for anyone to want to make a fuss, the other alchemists had accepted him into their circle of trust, and the idea of temple mysteries could cover a multitude of sins.

"And this is all in Bracklea?" Ailith asked, disbelieving. "How many of them... of you are there?"

"Sometimes six, sometimes eight. More if we have visitors from out of town, which seems to happen fairly regularly." Garrick wondered whether Malachi would turn up. The old man was a puzzle, but he'd clearly known something. "Tonight we're meeting at Ebba's house. She was widowed two years back, so she has the dower house at the Manor."

"I've never been to the Manor," Ailith said. "I mean, I've snuck into the orchard like every child does in apple season, but I've never been invited."

"Ebba's is only the dower house, though. Her son has the main house."

"Same thing. Alchemists and aristocrats... this is all foreign to me. So now we know I'm a mage, is there more you can tell me about that place we visited? About the golden elixir?"

Ah. He'd forgotten about that. He wondered idly whether he would have taken her there, if he'd known what was coming next.

"I'm afraid you already know as much as I do," he said. "There's no golden elixir in any of the texts I've studied."

"And none of the others have any ideas?"

"I, uh, I haven't told the Guild about it. And I'd rather not start today, so if you could just keep it to yourself while we're there..."

"Why haven't you told them?"

"It's complicated. There are things Selwyn won't allow me to study. And the people we're going to see... they're not bad people, but they're not ambitious, either. They're happy to settle for what they already know."

"But you want to know everything." She squeezed his hand. "I understand. I think I'd want that, too."

"If?"

"You know. If I could take this whole thing seriously. It's all very well sneaking out here for one evening, but Papa would kill me if he knew. If I proved one thing this morning it's that I'm no good at trying things out in secret. Clearly I can't be any kind of alchemist without Papa's say-so, and he'd never agree."

"We'll see about that. If there's one advantage to Selwyn's position in the temple, it's that he can get away with a lot more than most. He might be able to reason with your father."

"I'm not sure anyone can reason with him," Ailith said. "A trade isn't what he wants for me — even if it were a respectable one. Not before I find myself a husband. Gods, he won't even countenance the idea that I might stay and take over the pottery with Drefan."

They turned onto a small path which lead through the grounds of the Manor, and approached the glowing windows of the dower house.

"Ebba, this is Ailith," Garrick said as they let themselves in to the kitchen. "Selwyn just discovered her."

"Oh!" Ebba opened her arms and pulled Ailith into a warm embrace. "Welcome, child. Welcome. There's tea on the stove, Garrick will pour for you both. Selwyn didn't warn me we'd have a newcomer."

"We only found out today," Garrick said before Ailith could speak. "She appears to be self-taught."

"Oh, that is special! Usually the talent runs in families," Ebba explained. "So we test our children, once they're of an age for it. It's rare we find a mage any other way."

"It was all an accident," Ailith said. "I didn't know, either."

"No, I suppose you wouldn't, without a family tradition to guide you."

Garrick poured two mugs of tea, and pressed one into Ailith's hands. "Come and sit down," he said. "The others should be here soon."

"Are we expecting Selwyn to join us, or did he send you on your own?" Ebba asked.

"He had a couple of errands to attend to in town, but he'll be here."

The others arrived in ones and twos while they were sipping their tea. Garrick made polite introductions, with occasional whispered asides to make Ailith laugh. Morwrei was Ebba's apprentice, but devoted too much time to railing ineffectively against the Temple Law, and not enough time studying. Penda was an elderly man with a worrying penchant for love potions, and never mind that everyone knew no such thing was possible with magic; his repeated attempts had never worked to secure him a woman. Orvyn and Totte arrived late, looking windswept and harried from their ride into town, but then they were newlyweds.

"I trust everyone has met Ailith," Ebba said once they were all assembled. "She should be our first order of business, I think."

"Oh no," Ailith said. "You don't need to worry about me, I'm happy to listen. And Garrick will whisper in my ear if I lose the thread."

"It's our job to concern ourselves," Ebba said. "That's what makes us a Guild. And ours is a difficult path to walk alone. When our children show promise, we try to arrange marriages and professions that will give them the freedom to pursue their studies."

"But you're too young to retire into convenient spinsterhood," Totte said. "And too old to be adopted or formally apprenticed."

"It's fine," Ailith insisted. "I didn't come here to ask you for anything. I didn't know where I was coming, at all."

"You say that now," Ebba said, her friendly tone hardening a little. "But one wild mage puts all of our safety at risk. If you've started to use your abilities, even by accident, then you're living with the danger that someone invokes the Temple Laws, and that kind of attention would be bad for all of us. We can't have an untrained power loose in the town."

"My father would never let anyone teach me. Never."

"We could circulate a message," Totte suggested. "Maybe one of the other guilds has a bachelor who'd wed you, though you shouldn't pin your hopes on it — the talent runs stronger in women."

Selwyn leaned forward. "I think we should leave this discussion for another time. The girl is still in shock, and I may be able to assist with her family."

"How long would you leave it?" Ebba eyed him uncertainly. "Every day is a risk, if she's running about unsupervised."

"It's a risk, but not a large one. If we're to talk about risk, your girl's far more likely to bring the wrath of the temples upon us, since she's so determined to share her views every time he gets half a cup of wine into her."

Morwrei flushed to the roots of her hair, but made no move to deny it.

"Present us with a solution at the next meeting," Ebba said. "Or we will have to consider our options."

As the Guild moved on to discuss the latest news and rumours from similar groups, near and far, Ailith leaned over to whisper in Garrick's ear. "Is she in charge?"

"Ebba? She has a tendency to take the lead if she thinks it's necessary. Selwyn, too. They don't always get along."

Ailith smirked behind her hand. "I can tell."

The conversation turned to take in an improved formula for treating infections of the blood, developed by a solitary mage in Wulfsberg's lands, and news of a trial under the Temple Law in some far corner of the White Marches.

"One more thing," Selwyn said as the gossip started to dry up. "I had a visitor. Anselm may be alive."

The room fell uncharacteristically silent.

"Anselm?" Morwrei asked.

"His son," Ebba said. "It was before your time."

From the expressions around the table, Garrick gathered that this was news to everyone else around the table. Only Ebba and Penda seemed unsurprised. Since he wasn't supposed to have been eavesdropping, Garrick added his own quiet murmurs of astonishment.

"It was a long time ago," Selwyn said. "He ran off to apprentice himself to some charlatan, and we all thought he was dead, but now... there's a chance he's still alive, held captive at Watersmeet."

"Watersmeet?" Orvyn said. "That's Leofwin's seat."

"And he's an alchemist himself," Totte added.

"One of us should go to investigate," Ebba said. "One of you younger ones."

Totte frowned. "Leofwin would recognise us. Everyone knows he sends out spies, and Bracklea has one of the bigger Guilds."

"Garrick may be new enough to pass without notice," Penda said.

Garrick wasn't sure whether Leofwin knew his father, but it seemed more than likely. Most of the Twelve had met, at some function or other, and though Leofwin was famously reclusive he could hardly neglect his baronial duties altogether. He was trying to think of a way to demur without raising suspicions when Selwyn spoke up.

"I was thinking about this, and praying on it." Selwyn steepled his fingers, and looked around the room. "It seems the gods have already sent the answer to my prayers. Ailith is perfectly suited to go."

"No." In an attempt to keep his apprentice persona intact, Garrick tended to treat the alchemists' gatherings as opportunities to practise his silence and forbearance, but he couldn't keep quiet this time.

Everyone turned to stare.

"Leofwin has the worst reputation in all the Twelve Baronies," he went on. "You can't send a girl alone into that kind of danger."

"Danger?"

"He's a murderer. He's the only one of the Twelve to have gained his seat by bloodshed."

"In this generation," Selwyn said, just as Ebba added, "Discounting those who got the temples to do their dirty work for them."

"And that's not the end of it." Garrick was standing now, his fists drilling into the table. "You're saying he's held a captive for years, and you want to give him another hostage. That's bad strategy, pure and simple."

"But Ailith looks young for her years: young enough to put herself forwards as an apprentice," Selwyn said. "He'd never know there was a connection."

"He might suspect."

"Do I get a say in any of this?" Ailith asked.

Garrick caught her eye and smiled, hoping to reassure her. "Of course. The decision should be yours, you mustn't feel pressured."

She nodded once. "Then I'll do it. Tell me what you need."

It wasn't the response he'd been hoping for. "You don't understand. He's a sadistic tyrant, we don't know what he's capable of."

"Yes, so if he's already taken Selwyn's son captive, we just have to try whatever we can, don't we? Gods, there's nothing I wouldn't do if someone snatched Sun or Eddy."

"Bless you, dear child." Selwyn reached across the table and clutched her hand. "I knew the gods had sent you to me for a reason. Ebba, lass, there's your answer. The girl won't be here to bring the wrath of the temples down on us."

"I hope you know what you're doing," was all she said.

"If we can get you horses, can you ride?" Selwyn asked, returning his attention to Ailith.

"I don't know how. But Watersmeet is east, isn't it? I'll be going as far as Combeford with Mama on the morrow, if that isn't too soon."

It would take her ten days at least to reach the quay at Catchstone Gorge, and that was if she was always lucky enough to find wagons going the right way. Garrick was already making the calculations as Selwyn took Ailith to one side to swear an oath to the Twins. He could get home to the Highfort within two days, and back in a day and a half if he rode hard and changed horses at every tavern, by which time she should be getting into Watersmeet's lands. Then, if he hurried on, he should be able to catch her at Sixlanes or

Oakridge.

It was just as well the girl couldn't ride, or he'd never make up the distance.

"May the gods watch over you," he said as he left her outside the pottery, not wanting to give any hint that his path might cross hers again before she returned. No sense raising her expectations when his plan might not work out. "Travel safely."

"I will." She smiled at him, not looking half as afraid as she should; his warnings about Leofwin could hardly have fallen on less willing ears. He'd thought it worth breaking his usual silence to keep the girl from this, but if she wouldn't heed his words, well, he would simply have to look out for her more directly. A letter of introduction with Highfort's seal would at least see her safely through the gates.

"I can get her into Watersmeet," he told Selwyn as soon as he got back to the temple. "It will require a trip home, but my father's name would open doors that might otherwise be closed to her."

Selwyn didn't like to be reminded of his apprentice's origins, but on this occasion he skipped the usual warnings against pride. "Do it," he said without hesitation.

Garrick nodded. "I'll leave at dawn."

He had little to pack; in the temple he slept on a hard pallet and wore the same cotton tunics for days at a time. He could take a change of clothes in case of rain, but beyond that his options were limited. A small pot of salve for the inevitable saddle sores, some hard biscuits to make up for the meals he was bound to miss, and he was ready. A good night's sleep was the only other thing he needed, and with the worries running riot in his head, that was vanishingly unlikely.

Chapter Eight

Ailith returned home after dark, clutching a short note with a Temple seal. Her father couldn't spell his own name, and her mother would never admit to the little she'd learnt of reading and writing, but they both recognised the forest-green wax of Selwyn's seal. Ailith still had to explain the contents twice before it seemed to sink in.

"A pilgrimage?" Papa spluttered with indignation. "I'll be having words with that man. An unmarried girl can't be expected to make a pilgrimage all alone."

"You sent her, Godwine," Mama said, tapping the seal with her fingernail. "You could have just caned her yourself, but no. You wanted to teach the girl a lesson."

"It was heresy, and heresy must be punished by the temples. The Temple Law is quite clear on that point. But he didn't have to send her away."

"Perhaps he did. Perhaps that's what his Law dictates."

"Poppycock! There's nothing says he has to send her halfway across the world. Nothing."

"It's okay," Ailith said, trying soothe her parents without raising their suspicions. "It sounds less painful than another thirty lashes."

She'd known it wasn't the most usual of punishments. The priest had framed it as a pilgrimage to demonstrate her dedication to the faith, an archaic form of penance that would typically see the pilgrim travel to the High Temples, though Selwyn had been deliberately vague in his wording. It wasn't unheard-of, but sending a girl off, alone, to travel across the Twelve Baronies was bound to raise questions.

"You can't go."

"She can, and she must," Mama said. "It is written."

"I'll have it unwritten, you just wait," Papa said, but Mama was already packing a travel sack with food from the kitchen shelves.

"I'm to travel with you to Combeford," Ailith said. "So I can help you and Sun at the market before I look for a cart going east."

"Go and get some sleep, then." Mama kissed her lightly on the forehead. "You'll want to be fresh in the morning."

Sunneva was crouched, listening, at the top of the stairs, although she darted back into the girls' bedroom as soon as Ailith started up the steps. Ailith stomped loudly to the bedroom door, then turned and tiptoed back to the top of the stairs to take the spot Sun had vacated.

"This could be perfect," Mama said. "She can't go ruining every possible match when she's not here."

"But the roads are dangerous."

"No-one would dare to touch a woman on a pilgrimage. Who would risk the wrath of the gods when there are so many easier targets? No, she'll be fine. That priest's got it right, it'll be good for her to have to think of something but herself for a change."

Papa grunted unhappily, but he didn't insist again on going to settle things with Selwyn, and they fell into silence. Ailith tiptoed back to her room.

"You missed supper," Sunneva said. "What's happening? Where are you going?"

"You were listening, weren't you? Papa sent me up to the Twins for punishment, and the priest is sending me on a pilgrimage. So Papa's furious, of course."

"Are you really going away?" Edeva asked. "Is is like a quest?"

"Don't be silly, Eddy," Sunneva chided. "Girls don't go on quests."

"Of course they do," Ailith said, gathering together a couple of spare outfits. The bedroom felt strangely empty without Aidith's joyous laughter punctuating the girls' every conversation. "Even in the oldest sagas: think of Oia, she had to rescue her sister."

"She had to dress up as a boy, though." Sunneva pulled a face.

"It's hardly respectable."

"It is a bit like a quest," Ailith told Edeva. "I have to go on a journey, but it won't be dangerous like in the sagas."

At least, she hoped not. Garrick's words didn't exactly reassure her, for all that his objections had hardened her resolve. But there was no backing out now: she'd sworn before the Twins that she would do everything in her power to rescue Anselm, if he was there to be rescued. Selwyn had told her that the vow would secure the gods' protection and guidance for her, as well as binding her to the cause, but she had no illusions about whose interests were best served by such an oath. She'd spent her life trying to avoid the gods' attention, as any sane person would, but now she was enmeshed in something far bigger than herself.

She packed a couple of spare dresses while Sunneva peppered her with questions and Edeva bounced around the room. Along with the note for her parents, Selwyn had given her a green armband to wear to show she was on temple business, with the interlocking symbols of the Twin Gods embroidered in golden thread. That obviously wouldn't help with the baron himself, but until she reached Watersmeet it would be useful: inns and lodging-houses should feed her for a symbolic penny, and wouldn't dare cheat her when she needed to bargain for lodgings. And in a couple of the larger towns along the way, there would be temples where she could stay and be fed in exchange for assisting with the rites.

Ailith hardly slept that night, though she wrapped her arms around her youngest sister and held her tight against her chest. At the idea of leaving her parents and their expectations she felt nothing but relief, but she would miss the girls. As the middle of seven children, and with more cousins than she could count, Ailith had never been anywhere that she wasn't surrounded by family. Losing Aidith had been hard enough. Being apart from them all would be almost unbearable. And Edeva might be excited by the idea of a quest, but she was bound to cry when her most indulgent sister didn't come home for weeks on end.

Chapter Nine

It was his first return to the Highfort since taking up the apprenticeship, and Garrick hadn't thought through the consequences of returning in commoners' garb and riding a borrowed mount. And bearded, of course, for no true apprentice boy could afford to keep a blade sharp enough to shave with, let alone regular visits to the barber. He wasn't sure if it was an achievement or a humiliation to ride unrecognised up to the gates of his own seat, but the result was that he crossed the bridge unnoticed behind a peasant girl driving a small herd of goats, and had to look about for someone to attend him.

He swung down from his horse and loosed his hair, straightening his shoulders from the slump he'd so deliberately adopted in Bracklea. "Have I been gone so long that you don't recognise me, coz?" he asked the nearest pikeman, whose eye had followed the girl as she crossed the Great Yard.

"My lord!" The young squire snapped to attention. Five years younger than Garrick, and the eldest son of his mother's younger brother, the boy had always been in awe of his older cousin. "What brings you home without heralds? And dressed as…" The boy's voice trailed off as he found himself unable to form a description that was accurate without being offensive.

"It has been a long ride," Garrick said. "And I shan't be back for long, I fear. Tell me, Wymark, is my lord father at home?"

"The day is fine, and the leaves are still buds on the trees," Wymark said. "Where do you think you might find your lord father?"

Garrick handed his reins to the stableboy who had darted over, as word of the young lord's arrival spread through the castle with the speed Keyif's fire.

"And my sister?"

"Likewise, my lord."

"I may ride out and join them later," Garrick said, although he had no intention of hunting on this visit. "First, I must refresh myself. Send word to the kitchens that I will require a late lunch in my father's solar, as soon as Cook can muster some bread and cheese."

He strode across the yard, brushing away noisome pedlars. Once he changed into a gold-embroidered doublet and combed his hair, they would be falling over themselves to gift him their wares, but while he went unrecognised he was a target for all manner of hawkers who thought to part him from his money.

His old apartments were shut up and unattended in his absence, and he shivered as he looked through a dusty chest for some clean breeches. He wouldn't be staying long enough to make it worth taking the chill off the rooms, though, so once he'd picked out a few suitable garments he headed straight to his father's quarters. For tonight he would take a guest room. He sent the butler to lay the table for his lunch, and ate hurriedly while one of the housemaids drew him a bath.

She was pretty enough, but he dismissed her as soon as the water was ready. Today he had no time to waste. He stripped and sank into the hot water, wishing he could spare long enough to luxuriate and soak away his saddle sores, but he'd been on the road for most of the day and his father could hunt only until the sun dipped below the horizon. He had time to bathe before attending to his errands, but only if he was quick about it.

He scrubbed the past days' accumulated dirt from his skin, and stepped dripping from the tub to shave at the looking glass. Removing the beard was straightforward, and a blessed relief. Working all the knots from his tangled, shoulder-length hair would be another matter entirely. The comb handle was inset with jewels that chafed his water-softened hands as he attacked the task. After his months in the temple, the idea of encrusting a simple tool in rubies struck him as too ridiculous for words. It wasn't just unnecessary, it was uncomfortable. He jerked his arm in frustration, which only made things worse, but he couldn't afford to summon servants, not when his haste would appear suspicious. Word could get back to his father if he slipped up in the smallest way. He settled for slashing out the worst knots with the razor blade, which helped, although he nicked his ear in the process.

Once he was confident that he looked like the lord he was rather than an anonymous stranger whose will could be challenged, he strode to his father's study, waving away servants whenever they crossed his path.

His father favoured the dramatic, slamming a seal the size of his palm into a lake of wax. It was the Highfort tradition. But somewhere in here, disused and tucked away out of sight, would be the signet ring. Less impressive, perhaps, but just as official. Once Garrick had that in his possession, he would have most of the power of Highfort at his fingertips, and certainly the small part he needed to prepare a letter of introduction for Ailith. Father used the ring so infrequently that he would never miss it.

The study had never been tidy, but Garrick fancied it had become worse than ever in his absence. It was the one room Father forbade the servants from cleaning, and that meant that nothing was ever cleared or even rearranged. It wouldn't make it any easier to find the ring, but it did mean Garrick could search without fearing he'd upset the order of the room — and it guaranteed the loss would go unnoticed, just as long as he was quick about it. He pulled trinket boxes and filing boxes down from the shelves, opening them as he went, rifling through piles of papers and collections of junk.

He eventually found the ring in a battered, iron-bound box, jumbled in with a couple of candles, the straggly end of a ball of twine, and a handful of copper coins. He slid the ring onto his thumb, then reconsidered and tucked it safely out of sight beneath his shirt. Wearing the thing here would make a mockery of his efforts to acquire it in secret. He piled everything back to roughly where he thought it had come from, and went to lounge around like a proper lord until Father came in from the hunt.

The servants brought a steady supply of wine and cakes, and young nobles crowded him, overflowing with gossip and questions. He kept his answers brief and haughty; the story of his extended absence wouldn't stand much scrutiny, but nor would the tolerance of a spoiled baron-in-waiting. In this, at least, his position was an advantage. Meanwhile, he learnt a few interesting snippets from the court: rumours of a new alliance in the west between Saerima and Torkfast; Wulfsberg recalling their stewards from the Highfort in protest over some perceived slight; a black-skinned princess from across the seas, turning heads wherever she went but by some miracle not yet betrothed.

Mayda came straight in from stabling her horse, splattered with mud and flushed from the chilly air. "I wasn't sure whether to believe it," she said as she embraced her brother, placing polite kisses on both cheeks. "We weren't expecting you home so soon."

"Just passing by," he said lightly, as if the Highfort were sensibly on the way to anywhere. But like the others, she was too polite or too discomfited to question him.

By the time Garrick and his friends reached the dining hall, Father was already well into his cups, and although he demanded an explanation for Garrick's unexpected visit he clearly didn't expect an answer. As ever, he was more interested in the goblet that was constantly refilled with fine wine, the succession of dishes that crossed the table, and the pandering courtiers who surrounded him.

Garrick took his expected place at his father's right hand, laughing and smiling as if he hadn't a care in the world. If he could play a commoner for the sake of Selwyn's tuition, he could certainly play this part well enough to get through one more vapid evening. Things would be very different once he was in charge, but until then it was important to keep his father distracted. It would never do for Oeric to pay too much attention to his son's affairs.

There was one other thing he could usefully do while he was here. After he'd put on a sufficient show of feasting he summoned Wymark, who had always managed to make himself popular with the young ladies of the court.

"Is fashion as fickle as ever, coz?" he asked. "Do the girls still change their dresses with every change of the winds?"

"Why, naturally, my lord."

"Excellent. I need to find some clothes," he said. "Women's clothes."

The boy gaped at him.

"Don't stare at me like that, you half-witted fool. I'm not going to wear them."

"I didn't for one moment think it," Wymark said, blushing to his ears.

"I need to find a suitable travelling outfit for a young woman," Garrick went on. "Nothing too rich or fashionable, just... imagine the sort of thing your sister might wear for a long journey. Do you think any of your young lady friends might have such a thing to spare?"

"Possibly, my lord, but could you not more easily summon a dressmaker? Then you would be assured of getting precisely what you want."

"I don't have time for arguing with tailors tonight, and I need something by the morning. Might any of the young ladies be discarding something they've outgrown? My friend is on the skinny side, else I'd ask Mayda."

"The ladies are always putting perfectly good dresses aside as the fashions change. Mayhap there's something tucked away in an old trunk somewhere, if your friend doesn't mind being out of style."

"Ask around, would you?"

Wymark nodded, and went to do so. Within the hour he'd returned with two dark-coloured dresses and a smart blue riding coat which would be substantially nicer than anything Ailith possessed, although the thick fabric was better suited to the winter weather they were leaving behind. First impressions mattered, and this would improve her appearance significantly. Perhaps she yet had a chance of slipping past Leofwin's defences.

Chapter Ten

Ailith reached Sixlanes on the eve of the equinox. Everyone on the
road had been coming into town for the spring festival: newlyweds
heading to the temple; farmers in need of blessings over their fields;
traders hoping to sell their wares to enthusiastic and tipsy revellers.
There would be no chance of finding a wagon heading out again until
the day after the festivities. All the inns and taverns were full, too, so
she was especially glad of Selwyn's armband. The temple of Saaluk
and Bereket here occupied a much smaller premises than the one in
Bracklea, but the priest shared a simple meal of bread and cold beef
with her, and showed her to a crawlspace under the eaves where she
could sleep in privacy if not comfort.

She woke with a stiff neck feeling anything but festive, but as
befitted her role as a religious pilgrim, she joined the priest at his
daybreak prayers. The temple of the Twins was a focus for the whole
town's celebrations, and it would raise any number of unwelcome
questions if she didn't participate. She hadn't given a thought to the
impending feast day when she was packing, but fortunately she had a
simple moss-green dress that was just about appropriate.

It was a little before dawn, and every couple who'd wed in or
near Sixlanes this spring would be on their way to throw a handful of
grain into the sacred brook as they cast their matrimonial wishes.
Ailith had to swipe a tear from her eye as she thought of Aidith and
Uchtred performing the same rites in Bracklea. She'd always assumed
she would be there with Aidith, as she had been with Hilde and
Ingrith on their wishing-days. Saaluk's hands, until a year or so back
she'd assumed that she and her own husband would be standing
there at the same time. It had never crossed her mind that she might

be spending the day alone, in a little town far from home, not even yet betrothed while her younger sister was married.

Gods damn her quick tongue for ruining her chances — and thrice damn the men whose infuriating tendencies pushed her into speaking her mind. Perhaps Mama would actually find someone tolerable while she was away, but she didn't dare hope for it.

She stepped outside into the cool morning air and gathered up an armful of the flowers which had already been brought as offerings to the temple door. At the priest's instruction she arranged generous bouquets to fill all the urns around the courtyard, and scattered whatever blooms remained on the floor around the altar. No doubt there would be more on the way once the newlyweds returned from their wish-casting.

As the priest of Saaluk and Bereket had no assistants of his own, two teenaged acolytes of Refah had been borrowed for the day and put in charge of accepting the food offerings. A small amount would be burnt as propitiation, but most would be served as a huge noontide feast. Ailith helped herself to a fruit bun as she flitted around the temple, picking up small jobs and answering the queries of passing townsfolk.

Chapter Eleven

It had taken Garrick longer than he'd hoped, with bad weather and a couple of slow horses delaying him, so by the time he rode into Wicker's Cross he was starting to fear he might have lost too much time. Ailith had been at the temple in Sixlanes for the Feast of Bereket, but that had been three days ago. Then the trail had gone cold.

Wicker's Cross was a tiny village with only one coaching inn, and his enquiries brought him no news of the young woman who was travelling ahead of him. Perhaps her party had passed through without stopping earlier in the day, and would be overnighting at the halfway house. If she beat him to Catchstone Gorge and took a barge downriver, he'd never be able to gain on her on horseback. The sun was setting, though, and Garrick had no choice but to stable his horse here and take a room for the night.

He was picking the meat from the bones of a roast quail when a small band of rag-tag merchants came in through the back door. Ailith was wrapped up so tightly in her woollen cloak that he almost didn't notice her, but as soon as he did he shoved back the table and called to her across the room. She looked past him as she searched for a familiar face in the crowded inn, and he had to wave before she finally recognised him.

"Bring more bread and cheese, and another bird," he ordered the taverner. This far from Bracklea, he didn't care who knew he was nobility, and nothing ensured good service like an imperious tone. Ailith's place was set with an empty plate and a jug of small beer before she managed to elbow her way across to him. Garrick cut a few thick slices from the fresh loaf and quartered the roundel of waxed cheese.

"Hello!" He couldn't quite tell if she was pleased to see him, through her evident confusion. "What are you doing all the way out here? And... you look different?"

"Eat first," he said, skewering the juiciest piece of quail-meat with his knife and lifting it from his plate onto hers. "We can't talk in here, but the food isn't bad."

She slid onto the bench across from him, and he continued to load her plate with cheese, bread, and salad leaves. A moment later, the taverner deposited a second platter with another steaming quail and a pile of roasted onions.

"I can carve," Ailith said as he reached for the knife. "You keep eating, I've interrupted your meal."

"A most welcome interruption," Garrick said, but he let her attack the bird, a task she took to with enthusiasm. "Tell me about your journey. Were your family happy with the pilgrimage idea?"

"Happy would be too strong a word, but Mama persuaded Papa that I'd be safe under the temple's protection. Which I have been, of course."

"I'm glad to hear it."

"And Mama's hoping to find someone to marry me off to, while I'm not there to spoil it for her by actually being myself. It'd be funny if it wasn't my whole life she's going to ruin."

"I'm sure she only wants what's best for you."

Ailith shook her head. "It's like you said. She wants the most profitable arrangement."

"Well, you can't blame her for wanting to see you comfortably settled."

"And your Guild was hardly better, ready to send word across the barony and match me up with some stranger."

Garrick shrugged. Marrying a stranger was normal, in his world, but he could hardly say as much. "They mean well," he said.

After they'd cleared their plates of all but bones and cheese rinds and onion skins, Garrick led Ailith out into the stable yard. He unhooked one of the lanterns and walked away from the road.

"Where are we going?" she asked, but when he didn't answer she followed a few paces behind him. He stopped when they reached the wall separating the inn from the surrounding fields, and rested the lantern on the stones.

"Sit down," he said, perching on the edge of the wall. "I wanted to get away from any prying eyes."

"We're at a tavern in a town the size of a penny. Who could possibly be interested in our business?"

"I wanted to talk with you about Leofwin," Garrick said. "And we're within his lands now. Many a gossip-monger would be interested to hear where you're going, and why."

"Maybe."

"What's your grandfather's name, on your father's side?"

"Cuthwine. Why?"

"It's the easiest way to answer if he asks who you are. Your father is Godwine son of Cuthwine. Give no more detail and if you're lucky he'll assume you're from a family of some minor nobility. And you should always call him 'my lord', and make a habit of saying it — only not too often, or you'll sound like you've never met anyone of status before."

"I haven't."

"Better he doesn't realise that."

"Why are you telling me this?"

"Leofwin isn't known for welcoming visitors. You'll have to take care not to upset him."

"But you didn't ride all this way to give me lessons in etiquette that you could have given at home."

"No." He reached into his pocket and drew out the oiled leather pouch containing his hastily-written letter. Muttering thanks to Refah that the spring rains had briefly abated, he handed it to her. She spread the paper beside the lantern, smoothed it against the rock, and squinted at the words.

"What is this?"

"I thought you could read?"

"I can read the words." She glared at him. "It just doesn't make any sense. Oeric of Highfort sends his most cordial greetings to Leofwin of Watersmeet, and hereby requests… why would some lord I've never met be vouching for me? What does that even mean?"

"It means Leofwin, Lord Baron of Watersmeet, most difficult and deadly man in all the Twelve Baronies, might see you and let you live to tell the tale. But you don't have to thank me."

"How did you get this? Is it forged, is that why you didn't mention it earlier? Did you tell the others that you were planning to do this?"

"It's not a fake." Well, only insofar as it bore the name of a lord who had never seen it — but Garrick felt no pressing need to mention that little detail. "It does need sealing, though, if you've finished reading."

He folded the page into three, leaving a generous overlap for the seal, and unlatched the door of the lantern to melt his stick of red sealing wax. As she watched, he brought out his father's signet ring and pressed it into the pool of wax.

"Garrick son of Oeric," she murmured suddenly, as if recalling some long-forgotten fragment of her oral histories. "Oeric, Lord Baron of Highfort… that's the one, isn't it? Heir to the whole barony. But in that case, why in Refah's name didn't you take a false name for your apprenticeship?"

"Garrick's common enough to pass without notice," he said, sliding the letter back into its protective pouch. "And the people of Bracklea aren't exactly looking for lords on every corner. You hadn't guessed, and you've had more clues than anyone."

She shook her head. "And now I feel very stupid," she said.

He put his arm around her shoulders and squeezed her to his chest. "You're far from stupid."

"I knew there was something strange, but I thought perhaps you were the fifth son of some minor house, or an unacknowledged bastard in need of a profession. Not the heir to Highfort playing at being a commoner. Never that."

He could tell that she was barely suppressing tears, but he couldn't begin to guess why. "You're upset," he tried, but that only made her wrench herself away from him and stride back towards the light of the inn. He left lantern and letter alike, and ran to catch her hand. She tried to pull away but he was stronger.

"At least tell me what I've done wrong," he said, tugging her back towards the wall. "I don't understand. I'm only trying to help you on this damn fool quest."

"Of course you don't understand." Tears glistened at the corners of her eyes. "This is all just a game to you. My lord." She spat the words out as though they had a bitter taste.

"It isn't a game."

"You're just playing at being normal. You can pretend for a month or a year, and then it's back to your castle to laugh at all the poor sods you fooled. And just when I thought we could be friends!"

"It isn't a game," he repeated. This time he was the one who twined their fingers together. "I've never been more serious about anything, but Father would kill me if he knew I was associating with alchemists. It's heresy. A position at the temple is almost approaching respectable, or rather he can't refuse it, but I'm safe only as long as no-one knows who I am."

She nodded, though she didn't look much cheered. He dabbed at the corners of her eyes with his shirt-sleeve.

"And do you think I would have ridden all the way home, and raced to catch up with you, if you weren't my friend? Now, come, let's sit by the fire and drink a toast to friendship before we say farewell again."

He handed her the pouch, and she loosed the front lacing of her dress to tuck it securely beneath her shirt. Garrick had to look away sharply to preserve her modesty, although she didn't seem to think anything of it. Her manners unnerved him. He wasn't used to the ways of these peasant girls.

Back inside, he found seats by the fire and ordered spiced ale to warm their fingers. Ailith was unusually quiet, and stared into the flames as she sipped her drink, until he fetched across a Fortunes board and proceeded to narrowly beat her. Her play was erratic, and she kept none of the conventions he was familiar with, but she was no denying she was naturally skilful at spotting the patterns which mattered in the unfolding game. If she hadn't been distracted by whatever was going on in her head, he feared he'd be in danger of losing.

Once they'd finished their drinks the taverner's young servant led them up the stairs and showed them into a room overlooking the courtyard.

"Is this my room, or the lady's?" Garrick asked as the boy started to unload their bags from his shoulders.

"Sir?" The child's voice quivered.

"The lady should have whichever is the better room, it's only proper. And besides, she has a long way to travel on the morrow."

"There's only this one room, sir. For the both of you, ain't it?"

"Oh, no," Ailith shook her head, laughing. "You've misunderstood, we're not together, not like that. Never mind. You'll just have to get another room ready."

"There is no other rooms, miss. It's a busy night, Master Fulbric is turning men away."

"It's my fault," Ailith said, turning to look at Garrick over the child's head. "I should've seen about a room before joining you for dinner, but I can find somewhere else to sleep."

Garrick barked at the boy to leave them and he scurried off, clearly relieved to be out of it. He turned back to Ailith. "You make yourself comfortable here. I'll have a quiet word, and no doubt another room will suddenly become vacant."

"You can't kick someone else out of bed," she said. The revelation of his status certainly hadn't done anything to make her less vocal in her opinions. "It's fine, I'll shelter in the stables, or find a doorway. I've slept in stranger places."

"I will not have you out there with this perfectly good room available. If there's sleeping in stables to be done, I'll be the one to do it."

"Well, I'm not staying in here if there's half a chance you might decide to use your powers of lordly persuasion to make some poor traveller give up his room." Ailith stepped towards him, looking like she might try to physically force him out of her way, though he was a head taller.

"This is ridiculous." Garrick put his arms up to block her way to the door. "As your liege lord I command you to sleep here and be comfortable."

"You command me?" She stopped short, staring at him with eyes wide.

He shrugged. "If it's the only way to make you see reason."

"Is that how you treat your friends, then? Is that what it means to be a lord? Because that's not what friendship looks like to me."

He'd thought only to tease her, but the look she levelled at him made him think twice before reassuring her.

"If you speak like that to Leofwin you will anger him, and he will expel you if he doesn't kill you," he said. "Letter or no letter."

She might hate him for saying it, but better that she lived hating him than died because some part of him wanted to coddle her.

"I am your friend, but I came here to help you. If you can't learn to hold your tongue then you would be safer to turn around and ride home, and take your chances with breaking your vow."

"It's not the same," she insisted. "I can bow and scrape to some strange baron, but I shouldn't have to take orders from a friend."

"I just hope you can keep quiet when you need to."

"I'm the middle of seven children," Ailith said. "I know how to shut up when it matters."

"As long as you remember that he's no friend of yours." Garrick leaned against the doorframe, suddenly weary of the argument. "What do you think we should do about this pickle, then, if you won't let me negotiate for another room?"

She looked about. "There's plenty of space on the floor," she said. "If you don't want me to camp in the stables, I can just curl up in a corner."

"If you don't mind the scandal," he said. It would have been quite impossible for him to suggest such an arrangement, but he found himself more than happy with the idea.

"There is no scandal. We're a long way from home, and we've

enough secrets between us that keeping one more won't hurt. I certainly won't be telling anyone."

"You should have the bed, though. With a fair wind you'll be sleeping tomorrow night in the hold of a trading barge."

"Fine." Apparently she was also tired of fighting. "Wait outside while I undress."

Garrick stepped outside and pushed the door closed, standing with his back to the door to avoid the temptations of the keyhole. Malachi had been right when he noted that this was no ordinary girl. Marrying her was out of the question, but she fascinated him, especially when she forgot his status — or chose to ignore it. He rather wished they could share the bed, but he'd just given her a document that, while it didn't stop her being a potter's daughter from some nowhere town, certainly meant she was no longer quite *just* a potter's daughter. If nothing else it put her under his protection, and he couldn't take advantage of that even after — especially after — that kiss.

Besides, he wasn't quite sure that she wouldn't push her way past him and go to sleep in the hay loft after all.

Chapter Twelve

Ailith had been travelling for the past day and a half with a train of three farm wagons from Millbridge district, and she rejoined her travelling companions at breakfast after wishing Garrick an awkward farewell. Part of her wanted to apologise for their spat the night before, but she wasn't entirely convinced it had been her fault so she settled for thanking him for his letter and wishing him a safe journey home. He'd given her some clothes that were nicer than anything she owned, and a solid pair of boots which fit well enough once she padded the toes with rags.

The farmers made much of the way she'd disappeared the night before, but though she blushed and tried to dismiss their gossip, she couldn't deny the facts. The others had huddled in one small room, and they'd noticed her failure to return to their company… and after being summoned to eat with a mysterious young gentleman, at that. They remarked upon Garrick's noble bearing and aristocratic tone, but she refused to say anything that would identify him, and soon enough they moved on to other topics, no doubt carrying the conviction that she was the mistress of some minor lord. Their gentle mocking was friendly enough, even slightly envious, but it reminded her all over again why there was no way that she could get involved with someone like him. She could cope with misunderstandings from people she'd never meet again. But if she made the same mistake in Bracklea, word would spread like Keyif's fire, and her reputation would be ruined forever.

It was late afternoon when their wagons pulled up at the riverside quay in Catchstone Gorge. The farmers hoped to sell their produce at the lively market which gathered in the dockside square, and then they could turn for home. Ailith's only goal was to find a barge sailing down to the harbour at Watersmeet.

As she started along the quay, looking for sailors to ask, someone grabbed her roughly by the arm and pulled her into a narrow alley. It came as such a shock that she didn't even try to fight him off as he pushed her through the door of a small warehouse.

"Malachi!" she said, relieved to recognise him as he led her into a narrow aisle between towering crates. "You've come to help me as well, have you? Everyone seems to think I need it."

"Garrick," Malachi said.

Ailith looked up, trying to figure out how he'd guessed so quickly and assuredly.

"It's no great mystery. The boy's soft on you, no doubting that, so of course with his connections he'd think to smooth your way. Besides, that dress isn't yours."

With his connections. Ailith's temper rose as the implications of that phrase sank in. "You knew?"

"I know many things."

"Then how could you possibly think I should look to him for a husband? And him a baron-in-waiting!"

"He's the most like to give you your library," Malachi said. "You can't argue with that."

"But he's a lord."

Mama was ambitious for her daughters, but even she wouldn't think of such a thing. In three or four generations, if they kept making good marriages, maybe a descendent of her line would be in a position to marry into the lowest ranks of the nobility. But that would be some distant cousin or great-nephew-by-marriage, never one of the Twelve. Ailith's ears rang with the memory of words oft quoted by parents and priests alike: respecting the social order was important, because it was knowing your place that allowed you to feel comfortable. Everyone tried to stretch a little beyond their birthright, but this was a reach beyond her furthest dreams.

"He may take a little persuading that a girl of your background is fit for marriage, not just bedding while he waits for some better alliance," Malachi said. "But that's down to you. I'd say you've made a good start."

Ailith flushed at the memory of the night they'd shared in the Wicker's Cross tavern. They'd done nothing improper, but she wasn't sure what she might have done if she hadn't been so incensed by his deception. "Even if he was interested in me that way, what makes you think his father would ever consent? What lord would choose an artificer's daughter for his son?"

"An old man hears things. It's the only advantage of this old body — people imagine you're deaf as well as blind. If there's one thing Oeric believes, it's that his son should marry for love."

"Really?"

Love was a popular idea amongst the lowest class of peasant, where there was little else to affect a couple's choices, but Mama had told Ailith a thousand times that women of their station should have loftier goals. It amused her no end that opinions in the nobility might swing back the other way.

"Garrick, of course, considers this just another example of his father's poor judgement. The lad's cut from his grandfather's cloth. But not to worry, you'll soon show him you're more than just a pretty face — you've more talent than he has. First, though, I do believe Selwyn has given you a job to do."

"How do you know about that?" It was as if he'd been watching over her shoulder, but he'd as much as admitted that the stones didn't give him that kind of sight.

Malachi shrugged. "It was the sort of path Selwyn would take. But we'll get on better if you stop worrying about how I know things. They've asked you to find the captive and get him out, I assume. Did they give you any indication of how you might achieve that?"

"Selwyn said the gods are on our side."

"The gods take no side in mortal struggles — I, on the other hand, have come to help you. Let me tell you a story."

"Okay." Ailith wasn't quite sure that a story qualified as 'help' in any meaningful sense, but Malachi seemed to frown on her asking questions, so she would wait and see what he offered her.

"Once upon a time — almost forty years ago, now — I had a couple of very enthusiastic students," Malachi began. "They were excited to get away from home, they were enticed by the promises and the power of alchemy, and they were thoroughly infatuated with each other in the way that young people so often are. The young woman had promise, but the young man… well, he would never be great. I was younger myself, naïve in these matters, and I thought he'd be happy just to see her succeed. Instead he grew jealous. I should never have allowed him to stay, but I thought she'd follow him if he left, and I wanted more than anything to see what she could become. One morning, though, we woke to find him gone off alone, along with most of my notes and some valuable preparations."

"Anselm," Ailith said, the light suddenly dawning.

"Anselm, yes. But his is only one half of this story. The girl he left behind, we soon discovered, was carrying his child. She returned to Bracklea and found a husband who didn't ask too many questions, but her eldest girl never did look much like the children who came along later. The girl's name was Millie… Mildred. Though you know her better as—"

"Nana."

"Your grandmother, yes. So, you see, this story is also yours."

"And my mother is the eldest," Ailith said slowly. "So I'm going to rescue my grandfather. I see. My grandfather by blood, who abandoned Mama before she was even born, and never came back to see how Nana was doing, let alone his child. How could he be so heartless?"

"It was my fault, m'dear. He thought I was holding back on him, and since I was trying to avoid telling him to go home, you could say that I was not entirely truthful. I don't suppose he knew Millie was pregnant, and as far as I can tell, he went straight from me to Leofwin. He has not been seen since."

"Leofwin has held him captive for forty years?"

"Give or take. We don't know exactly how it happened. I had assumed he was dead, until strange rumours drew my attention to this other possibility."

"What rumours?"

"Never you mind about gossip, m'dear, you let me concern myself with that. You concentrate on finding out what actually happened, if you can glean it without risk to yourself. You mustn't do anything rash."

"I don't think I can avoid risk, in a business like this."

"Yes, and I'm not sure your so-called Guild have thought this through properly. How are you to get word to them, if you learn something?"

"We didn't really discuss that."

"Do you think you can put something like this on paper, and trust a messenger with a letter? Or do you think you can break a prisoner out by yourself?"

Ailith was starting to feel slightly sick. "Right."

"You understand me, I see. Good girl."

"What should I do, then?"

"There's a market in the Outer Court, every other morning. Get into the habit of visiting, make a few innocuous purchases. I'll be there once a month, after each full moon. I'll be well hidden, but I'll find you."

"And meanwhile…"

"Take the opportunity to learn something," Malachi said. "The man has skill, there's no denying that, and if you can get past his pride then he'll relish an opportunity to show off. I suspect he could be a fair teacher."

He pressed a piece of broken pottery into her hand.

"I picked this out of the gutter and had your sister fire it for you," he said. "If you needed any more proof of your abilities."

She flexed the sherd between her fingers, then dropped it to the ground and stepped on it. Nothing happened.

"Have you tried to break it?" she asked as she picked it up again.

"I've driven a cart over it," he said. "Does that satisfy your curiosity?"

She nodded, although her curiosity was far from sated. She looked hard at the fragment, trying to find any clue as to what had really happened in the glaze, but it appeared perfectly normal. It was all very well being a mage, but what was the use of having a power if she didn't understand how it worked? She tucked the sherd into her pocket. She was on her way to persuade an infamous alchemist to apprentice her; perhaps she could make a little time to learn something while she was there.

"Oh, and if Anselm did go to him, then I'd thank you if you could keep your ears open," Malachi said, his tone suspiciously casual. "I need to find out what happened to the work he stole."

Chapter Thirteen

Watersmeet stood at the confluence of two great rivers, providing a natural moat of raging force. Even Ailith could immediately see that it held a strong defensive position with the Keth to the northwest and the Brim to the south of the castle. She stood in the prow of the barge and watched the silhouette of the castle slowly growing on the horizon.

The archers patrolling the ramparts looked like ants, but they were fire ants with the worst kind of sting. Ailith had found herself on the wrong side of her brother's first hunting bow when they were both much younger, and though the toy was barely good for bringing down squirrels, her shoulder had never quite been the same. She didn't fancy her chances against anyone armed with a real weapon.

At the quay she hopped ashore and wove through the winding streets of the town, turning wherever she could in the direction of the looming castle. The town seemed to huddle beneath the hulking walls, sheltered and overshadowed by the great fortress. She followed a small band of peasants across the drawbridge and through the narrow barbican. A steep cobbled road led up to the gatehouse, where the crowd formed two parallel lines for the guards to inspect and tax the traders' goods.

She gripped her bag tightly to her chest, and thanked the gods for the letter Garrick had brought for her. Not that she was about to forgive him for being the heir to Highfort. No, not when she'd thought they could have a real friendship, and maybe something more. She found herself wiping tears from the corners of her eyes, and gritted her teeth in grim determination. She was here to do a job, not to mope about some stupid boy.

When her turn came she proffered the letter, sure she didn't look the sort of person likely to be paying a casual visit to a lord in his castle. Though she'd tried to neaten herself up a bit, and put on the clothes that Garrick had brought her, her hair was matted and tangled and there was nothing she could do about the creases in her dress or the mud that had caked around the hem.

"What's your business?" the guard asked, admiring the seal without breaking it.

"I'm here to see the Lord Baron."

He hesitated, clearly measuring the impressive seal against her dirty clothing.

"Maybe you could deliver my letter of introduction to his lordship," she said, hoping to speed matters along. "Let him decide if he wishes to see me." Hopefully Oeric's name would get her at least far enough to make her own impression on Leofwin.

"No, you can deliver it yourself. Entrance toll's a ha'penny if you're not selling."

She fished out a coin and pressed it into his palm. She wasn't quite sure if she was being conned, but she didn't want to jeopardise the little progress she'd made by arguing. And it was a small enough fee.

"You'll be wanting to cross the yard and go through to the Inner Court," the guard explained. "Speak to the men at the gate, there, they'll direct you."

"Thank you."

But the guard had already moved on to the next visitor, leaving her quite alone in the crowd. The traders were setting up in the Outer Court, and Ailith had to dodge the attentions of numerous merchants offering their wares as she made her way to the inner gatehouse. The main gate was closed, but two armed guards stood to attention beside the wicket gate. Ailith took a moment to gather her nerves, and prepared to present her credentials again.

"His lordship doesn't have many guests," the guard said when she handed over the letter. "What do you want?"

"That's private."

"We can't let you in unless you have legitimate business at the castle."

"I have," she said firmly.

The guard stepped across to confer in whispers with his colleague. Ailith strained to hear what they were saying, but over all the commotion in the yard she couldn't make out the words. For a moment she lost sight of her letter, which sent her spiralling through a series of worst-case imaginings until the guard returned his attentions to her.

"Listen," she said haughtily, emboldened by her success at the outer gate. "I don't have time for this nonsense. If you don't believe me, and Oeric's seal doesn't convince you, then just go and fetch his lordship — he'll be glad to see me."

A look of absolute horror crossed both their faces; clearly the idea of disturbing the baron and bringing him to the Outer Court, with a market in full swing, was not a prospect that appealed.

"It's highly irregular, but we'll send you through," he said, placing the paper back in her hands. "Go round to the right of the stronghold, there's a door just out of sight. His lordship's chamberlain will see to you there, he'll find a maid to run you a bath, and a room where you can change — you can't expect an audience with mud on your skirts."

"Of course not," Ailith agreed, wishing she had the first idea what the rules were for this kind of thing. Perhaps she should have taken advantage of the opportunity to interrogate Garrick about the finer points of baronial etiquette, rather than just getting cross with him for interfering. And she wasn't sure she had any clothes left that weren't muddy.

Relieved that the guards hadn't called her bluff, Ailith walked out of the gatehouse without looking back. That, surely, was the hardest part out of the way. The yard of the Inner Court was almost empty, save for a young lad scattering fresh straw across the cobbles. She got a whiff of fresh bread from the bakeries, and passed an open kitchen where three whole pigs were turning slowly on iron spits above a fire pit.

At the top of a short flight of stone steps, an oak door barred her way into the stronghold. It was small compared to the huge gateways she'd already passed through, but still stood at easily twice her height. She gripped the iron handle in both hands. It turned stiffly, and she had to put her whole weight behind it before she managed to push the door open. There was no need to call out to announce her arrival; the deafening creak could have woken the newly dead.

Before she even had chance to admire the wall hangings, a tall, well-built man stepped out from a side door and intercepted her.

"Are you lost?"

"No, sir." For the third time, she held her letter in front of her like a shield. "I'm here to see the baron."

"His lordship doesn't like to be disturbed," the chamberlain said, not deigning to take her papers. "He won't take visitors when he's working."

"I can wait."

He shook his head. "I'm sorry, miss. His lordship simply doesn't take unexpected visitors. I can arrange a room for you, and a little supper, but that's the best I can do."

"I'm not here because I need somewhere to stay," Ailith said, a sharp edge creeping into her voice because she knew that to the sort of man who lived in a castle and controlled access to a powerful lord, she must look like she needed exactly that kind of charity, borrowed clothes or no. "I'm here to see the baron. I'll wait until he's available."

She reached into her pocket and punctuated her words by sending a stream of shimmering powder arcing above her head. The trick worked perfectly — she'd practised a few times, when she was sure no-one was watching her, and could do it smoothly now — but it didn't have the desired effect. The chamberlain's face remained impassive.

"If his lordship wanted to see party tricks, I'm sure he would have sent for an illusionist," he said. "Now if you please, miss, I'll have someone show you to a guest room."

"Not so fast."

The voice was smooth, with an edge of iron that made Ailith's blood run cold. She turned to face him; she hadn't heard him enter the room behind her, and moreover, he stood before a blank wall with no obvious doorway.

The man who studied her didn't quite have the aristocratic look that Ailith had expected. He was tall, that much matched her imagination, with a stern, handsome face and long, white-blond hair which flowed over his shoulders. But he was dressed plainly, in clothes that wouldn't look out of place at the market: a crumpled linen tunic under a weather-beaten leather jerkin, and a belt around his waist that held tools and vials and the sheath of a missing dagger. And he was younger than she'd expected, maybe in his thirties, though she'd never been good at judging such things. Certainly he looked a few years younger than Papa or Uchtred. His voice, however, packed more assured authority into those three words than she had ever heard in her life.

"Leave us, Rethar, and see we're not disturbed."

The chamberlain gave a silent bow and removed himself at once.

"Now then, young lady," Leofwin continued, addressing Ailith directly now.

"My lord." She ducked into what she hoped was a passable curtsey, as low as she could manage, and bowed her head.

"That's enough of that. Stand up straight where I can see you. Why are you trying to dazzle your way past my servants?"

"Would my lord like to see?" Her hand moved towards her pocket.

He shook his head. "There's no need. I've seen shimmering powder enough times."

"Were you watching?" she asked, glancing around for a gallery or overlooking window. The words were out of her mouth before she realised this was exactly the sort of impudent question Garrick had warned her about.

"I often do," he said, apparently taking no offence. "But that's beside the point. What is it you want with me? What's that you're holding?"

"It's…"

He stepped across and snatched the letter from her fingers.

"Highfort, is it?" he said, examining the seal before snapping it open. "Highfort isn't in the habit of sending me girls with magic tricks. This doesn't say why you're here."

"I was hoping," she said, "that you might consider taking an apprentice. My lord."

"Me?"

"Everyone says you're very talented, but that you've never taken anyone on, so I thought maybe…"

"You thought that was a good sign?" he asked, raising one blond eyebrow. But a smile came to his lips as he asked, his eyes crinkled, and Ailith's heart fluttered. He might not be what she'd expected, but when the icy mask slipped, he suddenly proved to be a very attractive man.

"I hoped," she said, realising as she spoke how silly that must sound. When the suggestion had come up, sitting at Ebba's kitchen table, she'd been too preoccupied to even think of the possibility that he might turn her away. It had been a cunning plan, worthy of a saga or at least a song, and Selwyn insisted the gods were smiling on them. How could they fail?

"You hoped," he said drily. "And unlike everyone else with hopes, you just happen to have connections who can write you a charming letter of introduction. Alright, then, let's see what you can do."

"My lord? I mean… truly?"

"Did you want it to be more difficult? You'll have to prove you're capable, naturally, but I'm happy for you to try." Leofwin took a heavy key which hung from his belt, and unlocked one of the doors which led out from the antechamber. "Come along, then, before I change my mind."

"Yes, my lord."

The steps were uneven beneath her feet, and more than once Ailith narrowly avoided tripping on the hem of her skirts as she trailed behind him. At the top of the stairs, the passage opened out into a broad corridor, and he led her to a door at the far end.

"This will be your room," he said, indicating a heavy door. "This wing has the best views over the Keth. I'll have one of the servants sort you out, and once you've cleaned up you can get some rest. You look like you need it. Someone will bring you to the dining hall in time for supper."

"Thank you." Ailith didn't know what else to say, but he swept back along the corridor without waiting for her to find any more words. She pushed at the door, but found it locked. A couple of minutes later, a brown-skinned woman of about her own age appeared with a bunch of keys.

"Milady," she said, dropping into a brief curtsey before unlocking the door. "This is the Red Room — it's to be yours, and I'm to attend you."

"Thank you... what's your name?"

"Frida, milady."

"Thank you, Frida."

A little too awestruck to make intelligent conversation, Ailith allowed herself to be guided into the room. She'd wondered how the guest quarters here would compare to the rooms of the taverns and temples she'd lodged in on her journey but there was, frankly, no comparison.

For starters, the Red Room was really a pair of adjoining rooms connected by a large, arched doorway. Frida took her bag and helped her out of the borrowed coat.

The first room had a low table, a couple of stuffed chairs, and large bay windows set into the three-foot thick wall, looking out over the churning water where the two rivers met. One of the niches was occupied by a small writing desk. A large fireplace was set into the opposite wall, the fire already laid in the grate, and a healthy stack of dry kindling and firewood which meant she wouldn't be cold even if the temperature dropped at night.

A four-poster bed took pride of place in the second room, with red velvet curtains which dropped from ceiling to floor. It was easily large enough to sleep four. The mattress yielded softly to the touch, nothing like the stuffed straw she was used to, and the sheets were smooth as silk. Perhaps they *were* silk. The dressing table — easily the size of Mama's kitchen table — looked diminutive at the side of the bed.

While she'd been looking around the room Frida had unpacked the entire contents of her bags, stuffed her dirty clothes into a laundry sack, and excused herself. Another servant brought in two large jugs of warm water to fill the washbasin. Ailith shook her head. This was going to take some getting used to. She loosed her hair from its braid, and turned to consider her appearance in the gold-framed mirror which hung above the dressing table.

A moment later Frida returned with couple of simple dresses.

"Milord apologises that there isn't anything more suitable." She presented the clothes with a shy smile. "These are mine but they should fit you, I think. If you'll change now, I'll have your own dresses sent straight to the laundry."

"That's very kind — are you sure?"

"Milady?"

Ailith swallowed past the lump in her throat. How could she begin to explain that she was just a normal girl herself, when she'd arrived with a letter of introduction from a neighbouring barony?

"Never mind. Thank you for your help."

"Would you like me to comb your hair?"

Ailith had been trying to ease the knots out with her fingers, but the idea of letting someone else struggle with it was definitely appealing. Might as well make the most of this luxury while she could. She nodded. "Thank you."

"You don't have to thank me, milady, this is my job."

"That doesn't mean you shouldn't be thanked for it."

Frida's swift work had most of the tangles out in minutes, and she put in a loose braid without waiting to be asked. Ailith washed, and changed into one of the spare dresses. The maid had a fuller figure so the fit was a little loose, but that was better than the alternative.

"That's better," Frida said. "Do you need anything else?"

"No, thank you. Unless… do you have time to talk?"

"I've been assigned to you. I've got time to do whatever you want me to."

"Could you tell me about him?"

"About his lordship, milady?"

"Yes." Ailith sank into one of the chairs, and waved at Frida to join her. "I only met him for a couple of minutes, and he seems friendly enough, but he doesn't have the nicest reputation. I wondered what it was like for you, working here."

"Well, his lordship keeps himself to himself, I've never met him in person. Most of us haven't, we get orders from Rethar — his lordship's chamberlain — and that's as close as we get. But I couldn't hardly complain about a little thing like that, could I? Not when he took me in and gave me a job."

"How long have you been here?"

"Since I was six, milady."

"Six?" That was young to start work, even as an apprentice.

"When my parents died. My uncle couldn't afford to care for me. Coming to the castle is, well, it's a lifeline such as a lady like you wouldn't understand."

"I'm not really a lady, you know."

Frida smiled indulgently. "As you wish. Now, you get some rest, milady, and I'll fetch you when it's time for supper."

Chapter Fourteen

The first course was a whole trout smothered in creamy parsley sauce. Leofwin helped his new charge to a slice of fish and poured rich red wine into her goblet. She thanked him and tucked into her food in silence. Her hand trembled a little as she scooped up a large forkful of trout, using the fork like a spoon, balancing her food all the way to her mouth. The fish knife lay neglected on the table.

He studied her as she ate, and wondered what impulse he'd given in to. Why had he agreed to even consider apprenticing her? She'd shown a smidgen of natural talent with her use of the shimmering powder, but that didn't prove much. It wouldn't usually have swayed him. And while the letter from Highfort was a nice touch, it hardly constituted an obligation. He could have fed her supper, given her a bed for the night, and sent her on her way with the guest-right satisfied. He could have allowed his chamberlain to do all that and never even met the girl, without breaking a single precept of the Twelve's unspoken codes. He wasn't sure how she'd snared his interest, yet somehow she had.

She took one sip of the wine and started to cough. Once she'd recovered, she set the goblet aside and continued eating as if nothing had happened.

"Would you prefer something different to drink?" he asked.

"This is fine, thank you, my lord," she said. "It's all delicious. Thank you for your hospitality."

"It's a good wine," he said. "But it can be overpowering if you're not used to it. You'd prefer ale, perhaps, or apple juice? It's no trouble."

She smiled. "Juice would be perfect, if you have some."

Leofwin summoned the chamberlain, dispatched him to send word to the kitchens, and returned to his seat. Nothing about this woman made sense. She had a letter from the Highfort, but she wasn't accustomed to drinking wine or using cutlery. She'd arrived wearing an expensive tailored coat, but her boots fitted her poorly. She'd brought little enough luggage, no entourage to attend to her, looked overwhelmed by her surroundings… and yet the letter was genuine.

And the talent couldn't be faked.

"You'd be more comfortable using your own knife," he said, thinking back to his own younger days. The array of cutlery on a noble table had at first struck him as absurd, nothing more than a vessel for showing off gems and pretty engravings. She might come with references but she was obviously a commoner, and as such she was bound to be carrying a utility knife in her boot or at her belt. The servants, doing a discreet sweep for weapons in her luggage or concealed about her person, would have allowed her to keep such a basic necessity.

She glanced down at the silver utensils. "I wouldn't want to be rude, my lord."

"It wouldn't be rude. Besides, who's here to be offended? I doubt Rethar will mind."

"No, my lord." She reached down and pulled out a wooden-handled knife. "Thank you."

"I would prefer you to be comfortable."

He'd invited her into his private quarters to dine, so they sat at one end of a table which could seat only a dozen, and which seldom saw a guest at all. Normally he would accept visitors only in the public rooms, but she'd already seemed overawed. He could hardly imagine how she'd feel if he made her eat in the austere surroundings of the Great Hall. It was one thing to assess her abilities, but if she was too nervous then it wouldn't be a fair test. For the same reason he was reluctant to press her with too many personal questions, despite the inconsistencies in her story. Her skill mattered more than her history.

He'd cancelled and rearranged his usual commitments, and spent the afternoon carefully preparing a series of tests. By this time tomorrow, he should know exactly what she could — and more importantly couldn't — do. His remaining decision was the difficult one: exactly how good did he need her to be?

It was a solitary business, being an alchemist, and part of him already wanted her to stay. Even if she wasn't much good, there were moments when she forgot where she was, and then she let out an innocent enthusiasm that warmed the room. But the more cautious side of him knew that liking her just meant he would have to test her more thoroughly. If he pushed her harder, he could prove to himself that he wasn't being soft just because he was lonely. And as much as he hoped she'd be good enough to stay, he didn't dare expect it. He was accustomed to disappointment. More than likely he'd be sending her away before lunchtime.

And if not, he would have to find out where she'd come from.

He folded his arms across his chest, and watched her eat for a moment. "So, why did you come here?"

"I was hoping you could teach me more about alchemy," she said. "And how to use my… skills. The unusual ones."

"And what made you think I'd be a good teacher?"

"I just…" She stopped, and shrugged. "Why wouldn't you be, my lord?"

"Who told you about me?"

"Told me? But you're well known, my lord. You're quite famous, even in the West."

"Someone taught you to make shimmering powder," he tried. "Or gave it to you. And I don't think it was Oeric of Highfort."

"Oh! No, that was a wandering fortune teller who came to my sister's wedding. He read something in my stones, and he had me try with the powder."

"Was he by chance a very old man?"

"As old as any I've seen."

"Malachi."

He wasn't sure how Malachi would have managed to acquire a

letter from Highfort, but perhaps the girl really was that well-connected in her own right. The rest made sense. The old man was always meddling in things that didn't concern him. It would be just his style to decide that Leofwin needed an apprentice, whether he wanted one or not, and if that were the case then there was a slightly higher chance that she'd meet the necessary standard.

Ailith was nodding. "That name sounds familiar."

"Well, if he thinks you've got it, you probably have. Though you need to be careful when he starts spouting prophecies."

"You mean the stones?"

"The stones, and the rest. That man will use promises of your future to get whatever he wants of your present."

"Anyway, he gave me some of the powder. I don't know how to make it."

"You'll soon learn, if you stay."

"Of course I'll stay," she said, looking at him earnestly across the platter of fish.

"I don't think that's your decision to make, is it? Since this is my castle."

His words startled her, at which he couldn't help laughing. He wasn't doing a very good job of playing the haughty lord, with her, but if she did stay then he wouldn't be able to hold up that kind of pretence for long anyway. It was an attitude he managed to adopt for occasional visitors, but he couldn't very well persist in acting a part for days or weeks on end. Easier to let her see a little something of the man she'd actually be spending her days with.

"Sorry, my lord. I didn't mean to presume."

"I'm not putting you out into the street tonight, don't fret. But in the morning we'll see what you're made of."

He wasn't sure, but he thought she attacked her food with more gusto after that. Perhaps the thought of the long journey back to Highfort — or wherever she'd actually come from — made her hungry.

"I'd offer you a second helping," he said, noting her empty plate and the way she tried to avoid staring hungrily at the remaining fish.

"But Cook will be so excited at the prospect of visitors, the kitchens have probably prepared twenty courses."

Her eyes widened. "All for me?"

"Well, maybe not twenty. It would be inauspicious to serve fewer than nine dishes, though."

As if it had been prompted by his words, the rattling in the walls started up again as someone down in the kitchens hauled on the ropes to hoist their next course up to the dining room. Rethar replaced the trout with a fresh platter, piled high with steamed greens and boiled barley, and set the carafe of apple juice at Ailith's side.

"We won't be able to eat all this," she said. "Even if it's only nine."

"No, we're not supposed to. Not between the two of us. But whatever we leave will be shared out to all the household staff — that's why they'll be so happy you're here."

"That sounds expensive, if you have to feed everyone just because I arrived."

"They're my responsibility. I have to feed them one way or another, you're just giving them an excuse to enjoy a little more variety. But it's sweet of you to care about my expenses."

She blushed. "I didn't mean to imply you can't afford it. You're a baron, you have a castle. Obviously you could afford to lay on a feast every day of the year."

"Obviously," he said with a slight smirk, but she didn't notice that he was teasing. "Running a castle is a somewhat expensive business. Something else you'll learn, if you stay."

"Is it relevant to alchemy?"

"Everything is connected. If you aspire to be my student, I hope you're ready to learn all I can teach you, not only the narrowest of academics."

Chapter Fifteen

The following morning Ailith was woken by Frida, who brought a jug of hot water for her ablutions and insisted on helping her to dress, although Ailith said she could manage by herself just as well as she had every other day of her life. Frida wouldn't hear of it, and at least it meant her hair was competently braided. As soon as she was dressed Frida led her back along the corridor to Leofwin's private quarters. The guards on the door were expecting her, and the chamberlain led her along a couple of corridors and directed her up a steep flight of stairs. She emerged, blinking, into a rooftop garden that occupied the top of the keep's widest tower. A small table was laid with an assortment of breads and fruits, meats and cheeses. The baron himself arrived just as she was considering the spread.

"Breakfast," he said. "Help yourself. I thought we could talk about your studies while we eat."

Ailith filled a plate, and sat on a low bench beneath an arbour of trailing vines which shaded them from the bright early morning sun. He pulled up a chair across the table from her and dipped a slice of apple into honey. The fragrance of spring flowers filled her nose, and she could almost have forgotten that this particular idyllic garden was tucked away within the walls of an immense stronghold. Could almost forget that the teacher she was trying to win over was a lord better known for his harsh judgements and unforgiving nature.

"There are two things you need to be a successful alchemist," Leofwin began as she took her first mouthful of bread and cheese. "There's the basic talent, and you've already shown with the shimmering powder that you have some of that. And then there's the theory you'll need to master if you're to create your own powders and potions."

"I see."

"If you've spent any time around artificers, you know that training an apprentice is an investment of time you can never get back."

She nodded, feeling a little queasy. Was he hinting that he knew where she'd come from? But if he was, he didn't say it.

"It's only worth my while if one day you're going to be smart enough to help me develop new formulae — and powerful enough to use them. You'll have to excel in both aspects if you're to be any use, so I think we should start by exploring the limits of your abilities."

"How can we find anything near the limit? My lord, I'm only just beginning."

"This isn't like learning to read, you know. Your skill level isn't determined by experience. Most people have no ability whatsoever, and no amount of teaching will help them. You have something — you can use the shimmering powder — but until we've done some more tests we won't know how much you could achieve. I intend to find out before I make any decisions."

"Malachi said most people would take days or weeks to get the hang of the powder, the first time."

"That is true."

"So you might give me something that I can't do straight away, but that doesn't mean I couldn't manage it with practice."

He set his plate down and turned to study her, causing her to take a sudden interest in the last crust of her bread. "You're becoming defensive already, and we haven't even started yet. If you're to be my student, we'll both have to learn exactly what you're capable of, and that means accepting your limits. It also means trusting me to help you find them. Do you trust me?"

"Of course."

"You do realise that I'm a powerful lord with a truly horrific reputation? Look at me."

She looked up. She'd been sent here to find evidence of that same reputation, and if he knew what she was really up to then she almost certainly should be afraid for her life. Yet his expression was nowhere near as hard as his words, and as she met his eyes she realised she didn't even doubt that she could trust him. The challenge would be to avoid trusting him too far.

"If you had any sense you'd probably be terrified of being alone with me," he said. "And I've brought you to a secluded garden where we won't be disturbed, no matter what might happen. That was no accident. Now, look me in the eye and tell me that you trust me to help you."

"I trust you, my lord. Are we ready to make a start?"

"Better." He leaned back in the chair and allowed himself a smile. "You'll excuse my caution, but I've attempted to teach a student only once before, and he proved a great disappointment. Have you had enough to eat?"

She nodded.

"Then we'll begin."

There were six pots on the table, which Ailith had assumed contained condiments of some kind, though when she'd uncorked one to investigate it the pungent smell had put her off. It wasn't unpleasant, but it certainly didn't make her want to put it in her mouth. She'd wondered if it was some kind of acquired taste, like last night's wine, but now Leofwin reached for one of the pots and removed the lid.

"These are the raw ingredients of Payne's balm," he said. "I'm lucky that every one of these herbs grows well in this very garden, and you're lucky that I've picked them for you already. It's an extremely simple preparation, so this will be your first test."

"Payne's balm? But that's not alchemy, it's just herbs. Self-heal and lavender."

"Oh, anyone can mix up a nice soothing lotion that feels good on your skin, and it might even help. But if you want it to really heal, you need to amalgamate it properly."

Ailith was about to point out that her grandmother had certainly patched her up with Payne's balm enough times, until she remembered what Malachi had said: Nana had magic. In the rush of everything that had happened since, that fact had apparently failed to sink in.

Leofwin handed her a pestle and mortar, then passed across the pot, which contained pieces of self-heal root, green peppercorns, mallow seeds, and lavender leaves.

"Do I get any guidance?" she asked. "If it's not just a matter of grinding everything together, then what do I need to do?"

"You need to grind everything together while projecting your intentions into the mixture, but how you achieve that is something only you can know. Some people like to visualise the end result. Some people use a physical focus, like the way the pestle feels in your hand, though relying on that kind of prop can cause problems later. I find it easiest to close my eyes, so I can empty my mind of everything except my purpose." He placed a small bottle on the table. "You can add a few drops of oil if you need it, to help bring everything together, though the purists wouldn't like it. You've seen real Payne's balm before, I assume, so you know what you're aiming for."

Ailith emptied the contents of the pot into the mortar, and started to crush the ingredients. She watched as the seed husks cracked, the leaves wilted, and the roots gave up their sap into the mixture. It was blending nicely, and if she'd been making the base for a stock or stew she would have been perfectly happy with her progress, but she needed something more. Something like magic.

Intention.

That was the word she kept hearing: from Malachi, the Guild, and now Leofwin. She could change the world with her intention, if only she could learn to direct it correctly.

Her eyes drifted closed, and she continued to work the pestle back and forth. The vibrations soaked into her fingers as the rock scraped over the ingredients. She pushed her awareness down through her hands, down to the gradually homogenising mash of herbs. It was mixed well enough, but she needed it to change, to become the silky smooth ointment that Nana would use if she scalded herself in the farmhouse kitchen.

Purpose. Focus. Intent.

She could feel the ingredients, inches away from her fingers, with a sense that wasn't quite touch… and she pushed with the same awareness, encouraging the substances to knot together until something felt different. She opened her eyes and studied the mixture for a moment before offering the bowl to Leofwin.

"Has it worked?" he asked.

Ailith prodded the mixture with her little finger. "Well, it's changed. I think it looks about right."

"There's only one way to find out." He pulled a short, wickedly sharp dagger from the sheath on his belt. "Give me your hand."

She flinched, but extended her hand. As he gripped her fingers and turned her palm towards the knife, her muscles tightened of their own accord and tried to escape his grip.

"You said you trusted me."

"I do," she squeaked, holding still though every fibre of her being told her to pull away.

"Then trust me."

The blade was keen and slid through her skin like it was butter, and he was sheathing the dagger again before she realised she was bleeding. Leofwin dabbed at the welling blood, then scooped up a glob of what she hoped was Payne's balm and spread it gently across the wound. He massaged it into her skin until the initial stinging pain subsided, to be replaced by a spreading warmth that numbed her whole hand.

He pulled a small rag from one of the many pouches on his belt, and wiped the remaining balm from her hand. The skin underneath was unbroken, without a scar or even a scratch to show where the cut had been. Only the pinkness of her skin suggested that the whole thing hadn't been an illusion. She ran her finger across her palm, not quite believing the evidence of her own eyes. Nana had always bound her up with so many bandages that she wouldn't see for days how a scrape had healed, so she'd never suspected magic in the ointment.

"I'll ask you once more: did it work?"

"Yes, my lord," she said, more confidently this time.

"Good." He nodded. "You knew that before I proved it to you.

Trust yourself, and I hope I won't have to do that again. And we'll have no more of this 'my lord' nonsense from you, either. If you're to be my guest and my student, you had better learn to use my name."

While she turned her hand this way and that to try and see some ghost of a mark on her skin, Leofwin scraped the balm into the empty pot, and cleaned out the pestle and mortar.

"Next, lemontyne salve."

"Another familiar name." She opened the lid of the second pot, and sniffed at its contents.

"That's not entirely coincidental. We needn't worry about it within these walls, but out there, it's very useful to have folk remedies with similar ingredients to alchemical cures. That way it looks much less suspicious for the heretic healer whose potions just happen to work a little better than her neighbour's."

"Or a lot better," she said, glancing at her palm again.

"Yes, although your average healer will also have a set of less potent mixtures ready to go, just in case someone from one of the temples comes along to stick their nose in where it doesn't belong."

"I don't understand how the temples can do this, just for the sake of their own power. If there are better cures, for more ailments, why is alchemy a heresy?"

"You've understood it perfectly. Power. The Temple Law is a compromise between factions who hate each other, but they hate nothing more than ordinary people having power. Now, lemontyne salve the way commoners make it is just lemon balm, honey, and ginger, but there you've also got extract of peppermint, amber, and sand."

"Sand?"

"Yes, which makes this a much harder amalgam to get right. You'll need a lot more focus to transform minerals, so this is a good test of your skills."

"Right."

"Not every mage has the strength to use mineral ingredients, but those without it are little more than hedge-healers dabbling in herbal cures. Any alchemist worthy of the name needs to command a range of materials."

"Hence the tests." Ailith took back the mortar and pestle. "What did the shimmering powder tell you?"

"If you'd made it, that would be informative. It's a volatile mixture, though, and it takes only the merest nudge of intent to set it off."

"So I'd better get this right."

She was starting to understand the way she had to work, filling her mind with the feel of the blending ingredients until those thoughts forced out all distractions. Then she pushed with her mind, focusing into the bowl, mentally weaving the ingredients together and concentrating on the result she needed until something shifted in the air and she knew with an inexplicable certainty that the necessary change had happened. She had to push a little harder to force the lemontyne salve to amalgamate, but the feeling of completion was exactly the same.

"Done."

She offered the bowl to Leofwin, but he set it aside without examining the contents. "You know?" he asked.

"I know."

"Better. No, keep that out, we may need it. You're going to try something a little bit different, now, and it might hurt."

"More than when you cut my hand open?"

"This is different. You've made up a couple of basic cures, but now I need to see what you can do with an existing formulation. I'm going to poison you."

The blood drained from Ailith's face. "You're going to do what?"

"Don't worry, it won't be fatal. The worst case is I use a little of this lemontyne salve to revive you."

He didn't have to prompt her this time: "It's fine. I trust you."

"This is mousebane." He pressed a small bottle into her hands. "As you might guess from the name, it's often used for vermin. Have a look."

She took a tentative sniff, but she didn't want to get too close to something poisonous, even if it wasn't deadly. It smelled of bitter almonds, and something acerbic that she couldn't place.

"I'm going to break your skin again, and put a drop of this liquid into the wound. That's the quickest way to get the poison into your system, and you'll know exactly where to focus your attention. You'll have about fifty heartbeats before it weakens you too much."

"What do I need to do?"

"Mousebane is an alchemical preparation. If you know how to make it, you know how to unmake it, and take it back to its harmless ingredients."

"But I don't know how to make it."

"Actually, that was going to be my third test. I'd planned to have you prepare your own batch, first, but you're doing so well that I thought we could skip ahead. If this doesn't work we'll go back to the other way, but I suspect you'll be fine."

"Let's get it over with, then."

She offered her hand, and this time he just pricked the tip of her finger with his dagger. He dipped a fine rod into the bottle and drew out a single drop of mousebane.

As it touched her skin, Ailith fought to see past the searing pain and into the heart of the poison. Though she had no difficulty focusing on her finger — she could think of nothing else — she couldn't force the pain aside to find the alchemy. The searing fire of the poison, the creeping dizziness, the heat that flushed her cheeks... she was beset by pain and uncertainty and fading awareness of...

She awoke to find herself lying on the warm flagstones, her head cradled in Leofwin's lap. His fingers rested at her temples, sticky with the residue of lemontyne salve, and her clothes were soaked with sweat. When she opened her eyes she found his concerned face looking down at her, framed by white-gold hair that shone in the morning sunlight. She pushed herself up on her elbows, still feeling slightly sick.

"Ugh, what happened? Did I faint?"

"I pushed you too hard."

"I failed."

"It wasn't a fair test. We'll go back to my original plan, and you can make some mousebane before you try to counter it again."

"Let me have one more go." She scrambled to her feet and grabbed the bottle from the table. "Could you?"

"Are you sure?"

"Certain," she said, determined to get on with it before she lost her nerve. She held out her hand and reopened the wound on her finger.

This time the pain didn't come as a surprise, and instead of struggling against it, she used the feeling to funnel her attention directly into her finger. Trying to suppress the pain had been a fast route to failure so this time she embraced it, allowing the feeling to flood her awareness until the world was reduced to pure sensation. It was agony, but alongside the agony were other feelings: her pulse throbbed in her finger, sweat beaded on her forehead, a trail of blood snaked across her skin. And something foreign crept into her veins. There. She pushed against it with every screaming nerve, every stab of pain strengthening her resolve to rip apart the bonds of poison. Her knees buckled, strong arms caught her as she fell, but she didn't lose consciousness this time.

"I'm okay," she murmured as he helped her to the bench.

She slumped into a heap and he sat beside her, checking her pulse and her temperature. She blinked at him, trying to shake the blurriness from her vision.

"Really. I'm okay."

"You did it." He beamed at her, looking almost as triumphant as she felt. He pulled a small bottle of silvery liquid from an inside pocket, considered it for a moment, and then tucked it back out of sight. "That will do for now. There are bigger challenges to come, but you look exhausted."

"I'm fine."

"You'll be better once you get some lunch inside you."

"So… did I pass? Do I get to stay?"

His face became serious. "That was a good start, and you clearly have a reasonable aptitude, so I'm going to give you a trial period to make sure you can apply yourself properly. We'll see how you're doing after a month."

"Just one month?"

She wasn't sure if a month would be long enough to figure out whether Anselm was here, but she could hardly say as much to him. And it was better than being thrown out this afternoon.

"One month," he said. "That should be long enough for you to show your potential. You'll spend your mornings on theory, and afternoons on practice. Not today, though. You've done quite enough for today."

He pulled a silver chain from his pocket and looped it around her neck. A heavy coin settled cold between her breasts.

"This will let you come and go without paying the toll," he said. "But you'll need something more to persuade the guards that you're allowed into my private wing. Only Rethar has that distinction."

He took a sheet of blank parchment, wrote *Ailith may go anywhere she pleases within the castle*, and slid the signet ring from his thumb to add his seal.

"There. Not all the guards can read, mind you, but I'll make sure they know what to expect."

Ailith blinked and reread the words, expecting to find she'd made some mistake, but she hadn't. He'd written that she could go anywhere.

"Thank you," she said, tucking the paper safely out of sight.

Chapter Sixteen

Ailith was left to her own devices after lunch. Leofwin insisted that being poisoned entitled her to some recovery time, and besides, he wanted to tidy up before he showed her the rooms where he worked. Afraid this meant he would be hiding away all the interesting secrets, she'd tried to insist on a lesson, arguing that if she had only a month to make her case then she wanted to use every minute of it — but he'd simply agreed to start counting from the next day, instead. His pragmatism was infuriating, but she had no argument to counter that move.

With nothing better to do, Ailith started the search for Anselm under the guise of a casual stroll around the castle. She might not have many days here, and if Leofwin had a prisoner then surely he would be hidden away, well out of sight of passing visitors.

The thought of hidden places gave her an idea. She made her way back down the dingy corridor, which was nearly dark despite the blinding sunlight outside, and retraced her steps back towards the entrance. She was stopped once by the chamberlain, who wanted to know how he could assist her, but she'd made the first use of her token and explained that she wanted only to take a walk and get her bearings in her new home. If he was surprised to hear that she was staying, he hid it well. Eventually she found her way back to the entrance hall where she'd first met Leofwin.

She turned to consider the spot where he had appeared. A second look confirmed her first impressions: there was no obvious door on that side of the room. He'd been on the wrong side of her to have entered by the main door, and besides, it creaked like a wonky waterwheel. And he certainly hadn't arrived by the door they'd left through, which had been in her line of sight the whole time. There was, however, a heavy tapestry covering part of the wall. Given the slight curve of the walls, and the relative straightness of the hanging rods, there was a space that would be just about large enough to conceal a man of Leofwin's build.

After checking there was no-one around to stop her or report back on her movements, Ailith pulled the edge of the tapestry away from the wall and slipped into the gap. She moved to the wider section as quickly as she could, fighting against the heavy fabric which pressed her into the wall. There was definitely space to stand here out of sight, but unless there was a gap in the weave somewhere the thick, musty tapestry would block any view of the room beyond. She edged a little further into the gap, and stumbled as the wall gave way beneath her hands.

She caught herself on the corner of the stone and felt around in the dark, gradually realising that she stood at the entrance to a narrow passageway that was barely the width of her shoulders. She had to turn sideways to make her way inside. Going back to her room to fetch a lamp was out of the question; instead, she shuffled along in the pitch black, keeping her hands on both walls to guide her way. After only a couple of paces, the passage turned sharply to the left and deep steps climbed up within the wall. There were no forks in the path, no choices to make or opportunities to get lost, so she just kept moving slowly forwards and upwards, struggling to keep her balance on the uneven stairs.

As the ground levelled out, a thin shaft of light came into view a few paces ahead. As she'd suspected, there was a peep-hole overlooking the entrance hall. She looked down, past the dusty tapestry rail and to the floor where she'd been standing only a moment before. Leofwin must have watched her from here as she argued with his chamberlain.

The passage didn't end here, though. It wasn't a dead end with a viewpoint, and more than likely the baron hadn't been waiting here all day just in case an interesting visitor showed up. That implied that she could get back to his apartments by way of this secret passage.

Just as long as she didn't accidentally emerge in his bedroom — that would be awfully difficult to explain.

She left the peep-hole behind and continued to shuffle along, one awkward step at a time. The passage curved slightly, following the line of the antechamber wall, until she came to a junction where another tunnel branched off to the right. It was, she judged, about in line with the door they'd used. Did that mean this was the right direction to get to Leofwin's rooms — or her own? Without anything else to go on, it seemed as good a choice as any. At least she would be moving back into the heart of the castle.

She counted her steps as she walked. After twenty paces, she came to another peep-hole, this one overlooking a grand chamber, its vaulted ceiling painted with an arrangement of creeping roses and ivy. Another thirty, and from the other side of the passage she was looking down into a huge banqueting hall that must have been at least twice the size of Bracklea's tithe barn.

The rooms were furnished but currently deserted; it was strange to see so much empty space indoors. And since Leofwin was known to be a recluse, probably these public rooms never saw much use.

She chose the right-hand branch next time she had a choice. After a couple more turns she emerged into a musty store cupboard, and picked her way over piles of neglected linen to reach the door. She found herself in a corridor she didn't recognise. She tried a few of the nearby doors, but all were locked. Brushing the cobwebs from her skirts, she set out to hunt for her bedroom.

Once she was safely back in her room she sketched out a plan of the castle from memory. She started from the antechamber, drawing in the corridors Leofwin had taken her along to reach her bedroom, and the route up to his private apartments and garden. Then she added the passages she'd explored by herself, marking such entrances and peep-holes as she'd discovered.

And then, because she feared such a map might be the death of her, she folded the paper and stuffed it beneath the mattress. Even out of sight, the knowledge of it gnawed at her.

In her nervousness, she began to wonder why Leofwin had

chosen to accept her into his castle in the first place. It surely couldn't be because he thought she was an aristocrat; whatever Garrick's letter subtly implied, she was obviously a fish out of water here. And until this morning's tests he'd had no reason to believe she would even be a competent mage. She worried, in the back of her mind, that he might know exactly why she was there. Perhaps he just wanted to find out what exactly the Guild knew, before doing away with her in her sleep.

In that case, though, she could do nothing to save herself. She curled up on the bed feeling sick to her stomach, and by the time Frida came to fetch her for supper she was fast asleep.

Chapter Seventeen

"Let me show you the library and store room, and then we'll go to my workshop for your first lesson," Leofwin said. They had breakfasted in the garden again, though he was saving a proper tour of the rooftop space until he'd taught her more about the plants he grew here. Until she understood what each was used for, there was little sense teaching her to distinguish hemlock from chervil, and he simply had to trust she'd have the good sense not to start eating unfamiliar leaves and berries when he wasn't there. If she was that foolish, she deserved whatever she got, didn't she? But she seemed to have her wits about her.

He led her down the steps and into his private apartments. His personal rooms in the castle spanned the upper floors of two towers, and the corridors and chambers which connected them, but unlike his predecessor he never entertained visitors in this wing, so he had less need of the space. To reach the library, they passed by several doors that had been sealed up ever since he took command of the castle.

He unlocked the library door, and Ailith gaped at the room beyond. Shelves lined the walls from floor to ceiling, stacked with leather-bound tomes, piles of ancient scrolls, and towers of loose-leaf papers. He didn't want his new student to repeat the mistakes of the last, so Leofwin had moved his most sensitive notes to a locked chest in his bedroom, well out of the way of prying eyes. But that was a tiny fraction of the material he owned, and what remained was more than enough to render Ailith speechless.

"Don't be shy," he said as she hesitated on the threshold. "Come in and have a look around."

She walked across to the desk by the window, where he'd weighted open a couple of scrolls he'd been studying before breakfast. Keeping her finger carefully aloft from the aged papyrus, she slowly traced her way along a couple of lines.

"I know most of the words," she said, "but I don't understand."

"You will, in time."

"If I stay," she finished for him. "I know, you might not keep me."

He didn't quite trust himself to answer that, so he plucked Givold's *Botanical Compendium* from the shelf and laid it open in front of her. "This might be a better place to start," he said. "You need to know what things are before you worry about what they do, and herbs are the easiest place to start."

"That's not how you did the tests."

"No, I was trying to get the quickest possible assessment of your abilities. We can afford to be more systematic, now, and you'll need as much theory as practice."

She dropped into the only chair — he would need to equip the library with a second — and skimmed the page, which contained everything anyone might ever wish to know on the subject of purple sage. There were diagrams, preparation notes, and exemplar formulae. It wasn't the world's most exciting ingredient, but it nicely illustrated the way that even a common plant could be put to extraordinary uses.

"Can I borrow this?" she asked.

"You can come to the library any time you like. You have your token and your letter, and I've told the guards to let you through."

"Yes, but…" She hesitated. "I might like to take it to the garden. I'd be very careful, and I wouldn't take books outside if it was raining, only on sunny days like today."

"You may take this one to the garden," he said. "And you may take whatever you wish to the workshop, or elsewhere within my apartments, if you find a more comfortable spot to read. Will that do for now?"

She thanked him with obvious delight, and it was only with

difficulty that he persuaded her to leave the *Compendium* in the library while they continued their tour.

Crossing back out into the corridor, they came next to the store room, which was equipped with almost as many shelves as the library. These were crowded with all manner of dried leaves and chopped roots, mineral powders and bottled liquids. Although the shelves were cluttered, he knew roughly where everything lived. Small labels named every powder and potion, as well as noting the season when each had been prepared.

"You shouldn't have made me leave the book behind," Ailith said, marvelling at the range of ingredients. She might have stood there for hours reading the labels, although many of the words surely meant nothing to her, but he hurried her onwards. There would be plenty of time later for her to explore his collections.

The workshop lacked the meticulous organisation of the library, or even the ordered chaos of the store room. One huge table occupied the centre of the room, variously serving as desk and workbench, and frequently even a dining table when Leofwin ate alone. He'd cleared the usual clutter, so today it stood strangely empty. Ailith went straight to examine the shelves, which ran around the walls and held an assortment of tools and trinkets. Those, he had not had chance to tidy.

"Have a seat," he said, pulling out a chair for her. "And let us talk a little about the foundations of alchemy. Have you ever baked bread?"

"Of course."

"Then you're already familiar with the idea of taking a number of raw substances, and following detailed instructions that result in a drastic transformation. Think of the application of your intent as something akin to the oven: if you ate levain and flour and salt without baking it, you'd probably be sick."

She nodded her understanding.

"But you also need to get the quantities right in the first place, and for that you need a recipe. A lot of the scrolls you saw in the library contain what we call formulae, the alchemical equivalent of recipes."

"That makes the store room your pantry," she said. "And this must be the kitchen."

"That's a good analogy. The only difference really is that your mind takes the place of the stove, and you carry your power with you wherever you go."

"So why haven't you had a constant stream of apprentices?" she asked. "Every kitchen needs someone to scrub the carrots."

"I didn't agree to teach you so you can do the boring bits for me," he said. "That form of apprenticeship might work in the kitchens, but it won't work for me."

"You're avoiding the question."

He looked her straight in the eye. "Do you really want the honest answer?"

"Absolutely."

"I'm rich and powerful, and it's a well-known fact that getting too close to someone who is neither is a mistake you only make once." He hated saying it, especially with his background, but there could hardly be a clearer truth for someone in his position. And even at this early stage, if she was brave enough to ask the question — and insist on an answer, meeting his gaze with an impressive steadiness — then she'd earned it. "Bringing such a person into my home and teaching them everything they'd need to destroy me is a huge stride further along the road of stupidity."

"Then why now? Why me?"

"I wish I knew. To be honest, not many have dared to ask. But here we are, so we'd better make the most of it, don't you think?" He fetched a few pots from the shelf, and set them out on the table. "I told you yesterday that minerals were harder to work with than plants. That's generally true, but it's also a simplification. Not all plants are straightforward to work with, some metals are easier than others, and that isn't the only thing to affect how challenging a formula is. We'll start with basic preparations using simple ingredients, and gradually introduce more complexity as you get stronger."

"You said I can't control my strength."

"I said it's an absolute limit. You can't be better than your body allows — but if you don't take care, you could easily be worse."

"How does that work?"

"Think back to just before you discovered you were a mage. You had all the raw potential that you have now, but you didn't know how to use that talent." He thought for a moment, reaching for another analogy. "Imagine if I challenged you to a simple contest of strength, where each of us would hoist a sack of flour over our heads and see who could hold it there the longest. You wouldn't accept, because I'm taller and stronger."

"And because I can't lift my right arm above my chest, let alone my head," Ailith said, raising both arms as she spoke to display her limited range of motion: while her left arm continued in a smooth arc above her head, her right froze stiffly before it reached the horizontal.

"I chose a bad example, then," he said, eyeing her with concern, though he didn't feel comfortable asking how or when she'd been injured. At least the demonstration didn't seem to cause her any pain. "I didn't know. Think instead of the baker's apprentice. He's a strapping young lad who hefts sacks of flour around every day, whereas I'm lazy and seldom lift more than a pen, so I would be a fool to take him on if he challenged me. Agreed?"

"Agreed."

"Yet if he had to set his time today, and I could take weeks or months to train my muscles, then I might yet succeed in outdoing him at a time of my choosing. I am, in my present state, very far from the best I could be when it comes to hoisting sacks of flour. You train your mental strength just as you would any other part of your body, by using it more often, and for harder tasks."

"But you tested me without giving me chance to train."

"A little." Admittedly he'd poisoned her, but in alchemical terms it was minor. "But I gave you the easiest formula I could think of, for each class of problem. Over the next few days we should be able to push you further, and maybe we'll find some things you can't do.

And of course, one day you might realise that you can hoist a sack of flour far more easily with rope and a series of pulleys, and that you barely need the strength of your arms at all… but by then we're talking about alchemy, for learning to ask a better question is a different art entirely."

"I see."

"Returning to the kitchen analogy, increasing your strength is like building a better oven, but at the same time a good cook — rather than a kitchen skivvy — should also know how to adapt and create new recipes. My job is to help you with both these things."

And as she'd already noted, he had little experience of teaching, and no real idea of where to start. He tried to think back to the early days of his own apprenticeship but he'd been very young, and Malachi had been an impatient tutor whose ways he had no wish to mimic. No, in this as in so many things, he was going to have to make it up as he went along. He only hoped she'd have the patience to make it through these first few days.

Chapter Eighteen

When Garrick returned to the temple, it was as though nothing had changed. Selwyn was perhaps a little edgy, a little more bad-tempered than usual, a little quicker with the cane. But if he hadn't known, Garrick wouldn't have guessed that the events of the past two weeks had been so monumental. Surely sending a girl into the jaws of a dragon should demand a little more attention?

"You succeeded?" was all Selwyn asked, and when Garrick confirmed it he put him straight back to work without another word on the subject. Garrick resumed his studies and temple duties without complaint, and although a quiet impatience burned in his chest he couldn't think what he would gain from forcing the issue.

It wasn't until the next Guild meeting that Ailith's name was mentioned again.

"Any word from that girl of yours?" Ebba asked, after an evening where everyone had talked earnestly of everything and nothing, while carefully avoiding the most important question.

"No news as yet," Selwyn said. "Garrick went part of the way with her, so we know she made it as far as Wicker's Cross."

"And if Leofwin hadn't taken her in, she'd be home by now," Totte said.

"If he let her leave." Orvyn frowned. "For all we know, she could be locked in the dungeons of Watersmeet by now."

Garrick nodded, glad that at least one of their group had taken his warnings to heart.

"I pray for the girl, every night," Selwyn said. "The gods will lead her where she is most needed. If the best course is for her to be imprisoned beside my son, then who are we to question the ways of the gods?"

"You sent her under the auspices of the temple," Garrick said. "That gives us a responsibility."

"And the Guild," Penta said. "The Guild looks after its own."

"She is not part of our Guild," Ebba said firmly. "Not unless the Lord Baron of Watersmeet truly shapes her into a responsible member of the community before she returns to us. And from what little we know of him, I doubt that."

"We will lend her what assistance we can," Selwyn said. "Naturally. But since we cannot reach her, our best hope lies in constant entreaty to the Pantheon. The gods may accomplish what we cannot."

"The gods don't care for our petty human struggles," Morwrei said. "I pity the girl if that's her only hope."

Garrick shared most of that sentiment, but he knew better than to voice it in such company as this. Selwyn fixed Morwrei with a cold glare, but he would leave it to Ebba to chastise her apprentice as she saw fit.

"Whatever our personal views on gods and barons, there's little we can do until Ailith sends word," Totte said. "It's too soon to conclude that she's in trouble."

But it was much too late to assume she wasn't. They had sent her. And whatever Selwyn said, they held the responsibility for her safety.

Chapter Nineteen

On her fifth morning in Watersmeet Ailith woke a little before dawn, and a couple of hours earlier than she'd be expected for breakfast. Despite the enveloping warmth of the soft mattress, she tossed and turned fruitlessly between the silk sheets, unable to get back to sleep. She pulled on a clean dress and went to explore the castle. She'd been taking whatever opportunities she could to learn her way around, and the quiet of the early morning was one of the best times to wander undisturbed.

After investigating a couple of branches of a secret passage, she found herself close to Leofwin's rooftop garden and decided to get a little fresh air. But unlike the corridors of the keep, the garden wasn't empty: Leofwin was pruning back the dead growth behind the arbour. She stopped a few paces away and watched for a while without words, not sure if he knew she was there. His attention appeared to be entirely focused on his knife and his plants. Perhaps she should sneak away again before he noticed her, but she couldn't seem to stop watching him.

"You're really not what I imagined," she said at last.

"Oh?" He cut through another stem, dropping the dead wood to the ground. "What did you imagine?"

"An old man in a dusty library," she said, casting her mind back to when the Guild had first told her about him, everyone chipping in with their own disconnected snippets of information. None of what they'd said seemed to have any relation to the man standing before her.

"I don't think you can claim to have been wrong about that."

"You're not old, even if the library is dusty. And…" She

blushed. "I'm afraid I pictured you as rather stern and unforgiving. And with a host of servants on hand to attend to your every whim, not one to do your own gardening."

"Ah, but the garden is my space." He tucked the pruning knife back into its sheath and picked his way back across to the path, wiping his hands on his breeches. "No servants. No responsibilities. No interruptions. Even Rethar knows not to trouble me here. I think, for the sake of a little weeding, it's worth it."

"Will you tell me more about the plants? There are some here I don't recognise, even from the books."

He favoured her with a broad and genuine smile. "We can take your theory lesson in the form of a walk, if you'd like."

The sun was shining, the birds singing as they flitted between the shrubs. Ailith could think of nothing she would enjoy more than to take an educational stroll around the garden.

"Do you want me to come back after breakfast?" she asked, not wanting to sound too eager. "I didn't mean to disturb you."

"You're not disturbing me, I was just enjoying the morning air. I can do that as well in your company. Can you talk me through this border? You'll recognise most of the culinary herbs, I imagine, and hopefully the *Compendium* has given you some new ideas about their uses."

She started with the woody, shoulder-height rosemary bush which occupied the corner between two branches of the path. Once she'd given a brief summary of its alchemical properties and uses, he prompted her to explain the steps she'd take to preserve the delicate blue flowers which dotted the stems. As they meandered slowly along the path, she continued to provide an account of everything she'd learnt about the herbs they passed, although she knew she was missing a lot of detail. Staying up every night with a lantern, she'd made her way through the *Compendium* twice over, but not everything had stuck in her mind. Still, she did her best, and Leofwin added details when she hesitated.

Thyme, which grew low to the ground and clambered over rocks and paths alike. Lavender, with fresh grey-green shoots that were just emerging from between the bare sticks of last year's dead growth. Sage, the first entry he'd shown her, which had particularly varied uses in alchemy. Mint, which self-seeded and sprung up wherever there was a bare inch of soil. Chervil, which was good in salads, and hemlock, which would poison you if you confused the two, although their alchemical uses were closer. Leofwin seemed surprised that she would so easily know the difference, but then he'd probably never had to forage for wild food.

She broke off a sprig of fennel and chewed it as they walked. In between the theory, he interspersed comments on more practical matters: which plants died back in the winter; which seeds needed to be harvested at what times; what needed pruning or staking or watering; which grew like weeds and which needed more careful tending.

They ducked beneath an arch of trailing jasmine, and emerged in a small yard by the tower wall. A narrow alley ran between a row of wooden sheds, which abutted the curving wall, and an opposite, near-parallel row of glass-houses. Ailith stared at the way the panes of glass had been fitted together to make buildings almost entirely constructed of windows.

"How?" she asked, aware that she was gaping like an idiot, but unable to tear her eyes away. "And why?"

Leofwin pulled aside the curtain of glass beads which covered the entrance to the first glass-house. "Step inside."

She did, and was surprised to find the air was warmer, and humid. A row of grey flagstones provided a clear path through the middle of the glass-house, flanked on both sides by busy herbaceous borders.

"I can grow things in here that won't survive outside," he explained as she took it all in. "I've managed to buy all kinds of seeds from traders who thought they were only selling exotic spices, and would never guess they could be coaxed back into life in these climes. Not all of them germinate, of course."

She knelt on the rough stones to get a closer look at the unfamiliar plants, some of which had grown to only inches above the ground.

"Be careful," he said, reaching out to stay her hand as she went to touch the bright red fruits of a nearby shrub. "Those ones can burn your skin."

"What are they?" she asked, rocking back on her heels.

"The traders call them red scorpions because of the sting. They're sold as a seasoning, and I haven't found an alchemical use for them yet, but I'm sure something will turn up."

"This is a lot of work for something that might not even be useful."

"I enjoy it," he said, simply. "Sometimes it's nice to take a break from the books and do something a little more practical. And until you arrived, I had little enough else to occupy my days."

He showed her inside the wooden sheds, next, which contained racks of tools, pots of seeds, trays of seedlings, and bunches of air-drying herbs. One, tucked into the shadow of the wall, had a shelf full of ledgers which enumerated planting instructions and harvest seasons for every part of every plant. When Ailith asked why the books weren't sequestered in the library, he shrugged and said they'd seemed more useful here. The casual disregard for valuable paper made her squirm. He laughed at her discomfort and said he'd hire a scribe to make copies for the library if it would make her feel better, though the idea of someone being hired at her request was ridiculous in its incongruity.

"Is it time for breakfast?"

He glanced up at the sun, which had sailed high overhead as they'd explored the garden. "More like lunch," he said. "Shall we go and see what the kitchens have got for us?"

As they made their way back towards the stairs he gathered a small bunch of some of the garden's more abundant flowers: forget-me-nots, miniature daffodils, snowdrops, and bluebells. Ailith wondered if there was a formula that called for all of them, or whether he was just going to dry them for future use. Then he cut a couple of spikes of lilac flowers from the bush by the door, and handed her the impromptu bouquet.

"Stop off at your room on the way to lunch and have your maid put these in water," he said. "It'll brighten things up a bit."

"Oh, I… thank you," she managed, too surprised to come up with anything more eloquent.

When she presented Frida with the flowers she got a raised eyebrow and a promise that it would be handled at once.

"They're from his lordship's garden," Ailith offered up by way of an explanation, but apparently Leofwin's little sanctuary was so well hidden that even his household staff didn't know about it.

"Well, isn't he just full of surprises?" Frida said, sniffing appreciatively at the lilac blossoms. "And very pretty they are too, milady. I'll get a vase out at once."

Ailith left her to it and hurried on to lunch, and thence to an afternoon of alchemical weight-training.

That night, alone in her room, she sat with a borrowed scroll spread on the table in front of her, weighted down by a glass lantern on one corner and the vase of flowers on the other. The lilac fragrance mingled with the scent of ancient paper. She'd told Leofwin that she wanted to make sure she succeeded in her month of probation, but more than that, she wanted to squeeze everything she could from every moment of this experience. If she found Anselm before the full moon she could report as much to Malachi, and she didn't know whether he'd want her to stay beyond that point, even if she'd done well enough to impress Leofwin into keeping her on.

Meanwhile, there was a library full of texts that demanded her attention, and she had a gorgeous suite — in a castle, no less — where she could study them while she should be sleeping.

The library had been like nothing she'd ever seen or even imagined, even though for years she thought she'd dreamed of libraries. The tiny collections held by the local temples hardly deserved the name. She remembered her flippant comment to Malachi on the subject… now this, with its vaulted ceilings and shelves which extended up beyond the reach of her fingers, this was a library she would marry for. And, more surprisingly, its owner would make an unexpectedly fine husband to share it with. She shook her head as if to shake out such foolish thoughts, and tried to concentrate on the page before her. It was no good to be tempting fate with childish dreams of a match so far above her station, even if he did behave with startling normality.

And picked her flowers from the garden he tended himself.

Given the way Frida had looked at her when she'd brought in the bouquet, she was afraid she might already need to quash rumours amongst the staff, as well as stamping down on her own imagination. She was lucky enough that Leofwin had taken her in as an apprentice, and maybe even that was only because she had papers that hinted at something more than her actual position. She simply had to make the most of it while she could. And if he had no wife, in his position, it could only be because he had no interest in marrying: there couldn't be a shortage of beautiful women with hefty dowries for him to choose from.

She pored over the elegant, looped handwriting. At home she'd had little to read that she hadn't written out for herself, giving her the dual advantages of reading her own careful script and already knowing what it said. This was quite a different challenge. Even if the writing had been clearer, there were words in these texts that she simply didn't know. Leofwin had supplied her with a leather-bound journal for her own notes, and she'd started making a list of the terms she didn't recognise. It was clear from the context that some were ingredients, but other words seemed to refer to techniques or equipment. If one thing had become abundantly clear already, it was that being a mage was only one tiny part of being an alchemist.

First, you had to know your ingredients. Leofwin had spent their first three mornings running through common plants, their properties and uses. She'd started to notice the different herbs growing in the borders of his rooftop garden, recognising leaves and flowers alike from the manuscript illustrations, and she'd learnt a lot more this morning when they'd left the dry pages of the *Compendium* behind.

Once you knew what you needed, you had to apply the correct techniques for preparation. Here, too, they had so far concentrated mainly on botanical techniques. From any plant you might choose leaves, roots, seeds, or petals. From a tree you might take a strip of bark, or tap the trunk for sap. You could use the ingredients fresh, or dry them, or distill their essence. The uses would be similar, yet the effects could be subtly different.

Then, the combinations of ingredients offered an endless number of possibilities. Ailith already realised that she'd never be able to memorise every formula for every amalgam she might ever wish to make, quite aside from the fact that no amount of memorisation would help her to create her own formulae. It was only by understanding the theory underlying the interactions that she could hope to master this most complex part of the process. This was also the area where they'd done the least work, since Leofwin insisted she should stick to established recipes while she was learning the basic principles and honing her strength. Even without his guidance, though, she was starting to sketch out links and patterns that she thought might help in that regard.

Preparing the amalgam itself was another art altogether. Some mixtures, like Payne's balm, required only a light touch of the mind to come together. Others needed heat to speed up the amalgamation process, or ice to slow it down. Some, like Malachi's shimmering powder, involved a two-stage process: first to form the amalgam, and secondly to activate it. She'd even read about substances, usually poisons, that could be formed only within a living body. And the amount of intention that the mage needed to apply varied with the nature of the ingredients and the complexity of the formula.

All in all, there was a vast world of information to discover. Sleep was of secondary importance, and the search for Anselm was also slipping to the back of her mind. She scratched a couple more words onto the end of her list. If he'd really been trapped here for thirty years already, he would surely forgive her a few extra days for the sake of her studies, and she prayed the gods would overlook her lack of urgency so long as she eventually succeeded. She might never have another opportunity like this.

Chapter Twenty

Leofwin hobbled back across town from the shabby tavern where he'd shared watery ale and snippets of gossip with his informants. His usual attire was plain and practical, and he had an ample collection of finery for those inescapable times that the occasion demanded it, but he kept one more set of clothing. He kept it, for that matter, under lock and key in an iron-bound treasure chest which he alone could open. Now he was dressed in a worn tunic and plain breeches, and a ratty woollen cloak that wouldn't look out of place on a beggar. These clothes might be the least valuable in his possession, on the open market, but the privacy afforded by the disguise was a treasure beyond price.

At the end of the road, he limped into the damp cellar beneath a carpentry workshop, leaving the door hanging half off its hinges behind him. Securing such a place would look suspicious, and besides, even the best locks could be broken off by a suitably determined intruder. Obscurity gave a greater protection. He'd had taken care to purchase these buildings as soon as he inherited the castle, and had rented them back to himself through a series of intermediaries who had no idea at either end that they were dealing with their own liege lord. The workshop above was let on to a legitimate woodworker, while Leofwin held the lease for the cellar in the guise of a struggling rag merchant.

He scrambled out of the shuttered window in the back of the cellar and onto the ancient smugglers' path which traced around the headland in a deep ditch, giving a sheltered route between town and castle which never raised its user's head above the sight-line of the opposite bank. He was making his way home when he spotted the light at Ailith's window. It had been less than two weeks, and she was making remarkable progress, so he wasn't exactly surprised to discover that she'd been putting in extra hours.

The postern gate was tucked into a narrow crack in the outer wall. From across the river the gap was almost imperceptible, looking like nothing more than a seam in the rock, but it was just large enough for a man to squeeze through. Leofwin let himself in and wound his way through the secret passageway that led up to his private quarters. He'd chosen his bedroom for its proximity to this particular route, but the five strides between the doors always felt dangerously long. There was always a risk his chamberlain would see him… but chamberlains were replaceable if one ever happened to be in the wrong place at the wrong time. The concealed route out of the castle, however, was one of his most closely guarded secrets: any way he could slip out, there was a slim chance an enemy could get in.

He washed and changed, and went to call on Ailith.

She opened the door looking puzzled but not sleepy, despite the hour. As he'd suspected, she had papers spread across the desk, and a small lantern flickered against the wall, reflecting in the window glass.

"Is something wrong?"

"I saw your lamp," he explained. "It's silly for both of us to be quietly studying into the night, alone, on opposite sides of the castle, so I thought I'd pay you a visit. What are you working on?"

"I was going over what I've learned these past few days."

He picked up the top sheet of her notes and skimmed it. "Where did you copy these charts from?"

"Oh, that? It's nothing. Just a few notes I made to aid my memory."

"But why have you grouped them like this?" he asked, afraid to hope it was more than chance. Surely she'd seen the tables in a book somewhere, even if it was half-remembered now. "You've got crops together with wildherbs, even poisons…"

"It's not about what they're for. It's how they feel, when you nudge them."

"Savash and Oelum." Would this woman never cease to amaze

him? "It took me months to sense the difference between hemlock and chervil, and that was practising nothing else. And you just happened to notice all these relationships?"

"I see patterns." She shrugged. "It's like Fortunes pieces, they just sort of fall naturally into sets. See, this page matches that one, only it covers a different set. I have some gaps, and some things that don't seem to fit, but you've only taught me about fifty herbs."

"I think we can dispense with the idea that you might not be good enough at this. Your trial period is over. That is, assuming you still want to be an alchemist?"

He was suddenly stricken by the idea that he might have pushed her too hard and put her off entirely. She was, after all, losing sleep to her studies. Perhaps she would prefer to return to a less demanding existence.

She nodded, eyes wide. "Absolutely, yes."

"Then we're agreed." It had been only half of the proposed trial period, but spinning things out seemed ludicrous. "Speaking of Fortunes, are you a good player?"

"I enjoy it well enough. Every few weeks one of my sisters threatens to stop playing with me, but there's little enough else to do if we're at market on a quiet day, so they always relent."

"You usually win, then? I suppose you would, with a mind like that."

"You'd be an interesting opponent. Do you think you might play me, sometime?"

"How about now? Since it appears neither of us is sleeping."

"If you like." Ailith shuffled her notes into a rough stack, and tucked them under her arm.

"Are you bringing those with you?"

"I've a lot to learn, and I may as well have something to do between turns."

"Between turns." His mouth quirked into a smile. "I realise you're accustomed to players of significantly lower skill, but I hope to give you enough of a fight to require all your attention."

"Perhaps," she said, but she kept hold of the papers.

They went up to the rooftop garden, and Leofwin lit the storm-lamps which he kept there for just this kind of insomniac evening. He left Ailith marvelling at the faerie grotto effect while he went to hunt out his Fortunes board. It had been some time since he'd had anyone to challenge his wits against.

The board he eventually set upon the table was a slab he'd cut from a fallen oak, and the Fortunes stones were wooden tokens he'd carved himself back in the early days of his apprenticeship. The edges were smoothed by years of use, and the paint had begun to fade, but the old set felt more comfortable than the expensive, blown-glass pieces he'd inherited along with the castle. He brought a bottle of his favourite blackberry wine, as well, and two large glass goblets.

He sat beneath the arbour, poured wine for both of them, and passed one glass across the table to her.

"Do you play red or black?" Ailith asked, scooping up the two Justice tokens.

"You can choose."

"I'll have red, then." She shook the pieces lightly together, and extended her two closed fists in front of her. "Pick for who goes first."

He tapped lightly on the knuckles of her left hand, and she opened her fingers to show the red piece.

"I win," she said, dropping his black token in front of him. "Though I'm not sure going first is a real advantage."

"We can play two games," he said. "That would even it out, if it matters."

Ailith gathered the red pieces in front of her and studied them for a moment, flipping the Justice token casually between her fingers before laying it down near the middle of the board.

"To my new apprentice," he said, raising his glass in a toast. "Long may she outsmart me."

She mirrored the gesture. "To me," she said, beaming, and took a cautious sip. She was still nervous about wine, but he was determined to give her enough chances to decide whether she enjoyed it once the unfamiliarity wore off.

Leofwin reached out and placed his Death token carefully on the board.

There were conventional starting patterns that would have left them both in safe, predictable positions, but Ailith either didn't know or didn't care for them. Her starting move had been standard enough, and he'd matched in the expected manner, but after that she laid down her pieces in a sequence that bore no relation to any of the forms he'd studied.

"Have you played with many people, aside from your family?"

"Only occasionally." She laid down her Storm token between Drought and Prosperity. "Sometimes on market days, if I find another player at a near enough stall. Sometimes my sisters only want to play scuttle."

"And you're not a fan of dice?" he asked as he played his own piece. He was determined not to give her the time to read, even if she was making unpredictable moves.

"It's silly fun, but it's more of a drinking game. You wouldn't want to play all day. But why do you ask who I've played with? Am I doing dreadfully?"

"I wondered if you knew how many conventions most people play, that's all. Standard openings, and response patterns, and what have you."

"I don't know of any."

"There may be a few books in the library, if you're interested."

"I am playing dreadfully, then, aren't I?" She took a long swallow of her wine. "You needn't go easy on me."

"No, you're not doing badly, not at all. But that doesn't mean that you couldn't play better with study. After all, I carved these tokens when I was eight, and I've been studying the game ever since — yet I'm no master of Fortunes."

She picked up one of her unplayed pieces and turned it carefully in her fingers. "You made these yourself?"

"I did."

"That doesn't seem a very lordly activity, even for a child."

He could almost convince himself that she was asking the right question, even as he knew she wasn't. To her, if there was a question to be asked, it was as an opportunity to learn about the lives of young barons. She couldn't be expected to guess that he'd had quite a different start in life. So although he dearly longed to tell her that he'd been no lord at eight, he held his tongue, and instead offered, "I'll show you my other board tomorrow, and you'll see why lordly Fortunes sets aren't well suited to child's play."

They played for a few minutes in silence, the gaps between their turns decreasing as Leofwin tried to keep his promise that she wouldn't have time to read and Ailith, he was sure, sped up to match his pace in an attempt to prove him wrong.

"No, no!" She shook her head, half-covered his hand with her own smaller fingers, and curled his fingers to pick up the piece he'd just laid. "That's silly, because I can push here, and you don't have a matching piece to stop me. If you want to play there, you should play the Flood."

"Even if you're right, if I make a mistake you should let me lose. It's only my own foolishness." He studied the board as he spoke. She *was* right, of course. The Flood would be a much stronger play.

She stood, poured a little more wine into both of their glasses, and moved to sit beside him under the arbour. "It's easier to make mistakes after a few drinks. And this… what did you call it?"

"Blackberry wine."

She took a long drink. "This is potent stuff. I'm not sure it's what I'd choose if I wanted to keep my wits about me."

"Do you like it?"

"It's delicious. Where does it come from?"

"They make it in the villages. Brambles grow wild along the riverbanks, so there's no shortage."

"Oh, blackberries are just brambles? We put bramble-fruit in pies." She sipped her next mouthful carefully, as if trying to recognise the familiar flavour through the alcohol. She closed her eyes and he felt the brief flare of her magic.

"What are you doing?"

"I was just exploring it." She blushed. "How did you know?"

"I felt it." He thought for a moment about the best way to explain, then asked: "How many senses do you have?"

"I always supposed it was five." She looked at him as if she suspected a trick. "But if that was all the answer there was, you wouldn't be asking. Would you say it's a sixth one, the way we feel the ingredients when we're making up an amalgam?"

"The answer is more than five, I'll give you that. But it's quite a few more. Let me show you."

He pulled out his dagger, took her hand, and pressed the flat of the blade against her palm. Though she still flinched a little, she didn't try to pull away as she had during their first lesson.

"What do you feel?"

"It's cold."

"And?"

"Scary." She laughed. "Last time you did this, you put a hole in my hand."

"Only for a moment, and I won't do it again." He concentrated on keeping his hand steady despite the alcohol in his veins. "Tell me what else you feel."

"I can feel the knife pressing into my skin, across my hand. The metal is cold, like I said, and it's hard. Even the blunt edge is kind of sharp."

"And if I cut you, it would hurt."

"Yes. Please don't."

"Is that all one kind of touch?"

"I'm not sure. I can feel it all at the same time."

"Can you feel the warmth of this lantern?"

"Of course."

"How about in the same place as you can feel the chill of the knife?"

"No... No, I don't think so..." Her eyes wandered off into the garden as she fell into her thoughts, seemingly oblivious now to the blade against her skin. "Are you saying that things I can feel distinctly at the same time are different, and things I can't — like heat and cold — might be the same?"

"It sounds reasonable, doesn't it?"

"But is it the right answer?"

"Ah." He smiled and sheathed the knife. "You've got me there. This isn't really a question where there's a right answer. But I think it's worth giving it some thought. Now, stand up, and close your eyes."

She did, and he stepped up behind her, taking her shoulders and spinning her first one way, and then the other. He brought her to a stop with her face to his, her eyes still squeezed shut.

"What do you feel?"

"Dizzy."

"And?"

"Can I open my eyes yet?"

"Not yet." He let go of her shoulders. "Can you balance on one leg?"

She lifted her left foot from the ground, wobbled, and almost fell. He slid his hands beneath her arms to steady her, holding her body upright even as he felt himself becoming increasingly lightheaded.

"No," she said. "Not after this much wine."

"No, that wasn't fair of me. I'll hold you up. Keep your eyes closed, and touch your left forefinger to your nose."

She managed that one easily enough.

"And my nose?"

She pushed a clumsy finger into the flesh of his cheek, and giggled as she traced her way across his cheekbone to rest on the bridge of his nose. "Why?" she asked, her eyelids fluttering open as she looked up at him, her face mere inches from his own.

"I wanted to show you. You always know where your own body is, even with your eyes closed. That's another kind of sense. And a bit like all of these ones have been things you might have called touch, if I hadn't made you pick them apart, your magical senses give you another whole set. You can learn to use them even when you're not doing alchemy."

He released her, somewhat reluctantly, and plucked a couple of leaves from a nearby shrub.

"What am I holding?"

He felt her mind reach out. "Is it yarrow?"

Although she phrased it as a question, he could tell there was no real doubt there.

"Good. Keep concentrating."

He pushed his own focus into the leaves, just lightly, but it was enough to make her jump. Her attention fell away and she stepped physically away from him, looking at him in awe.

"That's what I felt when you prodded at the wine," he explained. "Once you've had enough practice, you'll always notice when someone nearby uses their power. It's instinctive, the way you can't help hearing if someone sings a familiar ditty or calls your name."

"It's magic," she said, reaching out gingerly to touch the herb again, and finding his mind still there. "It's really magic."

Chapter Twenty-One

The woman was tall and willowy, with greying, straw-coloured hair pulled back into a sensible plait. Her right hand held a basket full of leafy vegetables and her left clutched the arm of a small girl, who for her part was trying to hide in her mother's skirts.

People came to the temple for any number of reasons: to celebrate feasts and holy days; to seek blessings; to beg forgiveness or penance; to request healing potions and prayers. They did not typically look as though they had simply been passing the temple on their way home from the market. For that matter, the temple of Saaluk and Bereket was not well positioned for anyone to be casually dropping in on their way past. That, however, was exactly the impression the woman projected.

"Can I help you?" Garrick asked.

"I was hoping to see the priest," she said, glancing around the room. "But I can come back another time."

"Selwyn has gone out for the day, I'm afraid. I don't expect him back before nightfall, but I'm at your service."

She looked him up and down, uncertain. There was something familiar about her manner that Garrick couldn't quite put his finger on.

"It's a delicate matter," she said at last. "My daughter…"

"This charming young lady?" Garrick asked when she faltered. He shelled a cobnut and offered it to the shy youngster, who snatched it from his hand before disappearing again behind her mother's leg.

"No, one of my older girls. I'm not sure… perhaps I should come back another day."

"Please, have a seat." Garrick adopted his most soothing tone, a skill Selwyn had forced him to practice endlessly since he'd come to the temple, and guided her to a chair. The child sat at her feet, still clutching at her mother's skirts until Garrick gave her another handful of nuts. "Some matters are best dealt with sooner rather than later. If your daughter has taken a careless tumble and needs a tonic to…"

"No!" The woman's vehemence took him by surprise. "That's not it at all. Gods, none of my girls would dare get herself into that kind of mess."

"Then surely it's nothing to trouble your heart. Let me see if I can assist you."

"The thing is, Ailith — that's my middle daughter, the one I'm here for — has a bit of a difficult streak."

Garrick studied her with renewed interest as she spoke. This was Ailith's mother, then. No wonder she'd struck him as familiar. He must have seen her at the wedding. He tried to imagine Ailith growing into a formidable woman like this, and found it remarkably easy to picture. He wondered what she'd say if she knew half of what Ailith had been up to over the past few days, but he wasn't going to mention the magic… or the kissing.

"You're here about her penance," he said, steering himself quickly to safer ground.

"Oh, you know about it?" For the first time she smiled at him, relief clear on her face. "Ailith's not a bad girl. Whatever she said, she didn't mean anything by it. Edeva, stop fidgeting! The thing is, it's been over a month, and we were wondering when we might expect her home again."

"Ailith has a long journey ahead of her. And you must know that a pilgrimage is about more than the miles travelled." It was the sort of nonsense Selwyn would come out with, and Garrick was inordinately pleased with himself for thinking of it. "The length of her road cannot be measured in such simple terms. The gods will bring her home when she's ready, and not a day before."

"And when she wins at her quest," Edeva added.

"Hush, child."

"She's not wrong," Garrick said. "A pilgrimage is a lot like a quest, but in the sagas the gods weren't always on the side of the traveller. A pilgrim should expect better fortune."

"Has she been in touch?" Ailith's mother asked. "I thought she would have sent word, by now."

"You know how unreliable letters can be," Garrick said, though the look on her face suggested that she had no idea. And why would she? These illiterate peasants never went far enough from home to worry about such things. "She could have written from her destination, and still make it home herself before anyone manages to deliver her note."

"And she'd have to find a scribe and a messenger, I suppose, and to pay for their services." The woman shook her head, increasingly agitated. "I knew we should have given her more money."

"She passed safely through Sixlanes," Garrick said. "I can tell you that much. She was there for the spring festival."

"But you would know, wouldn't you? If there was a problem?"

Garrick hesitated. There was a fine line between making the most of temple mysticism and being downright misleading, and Selwyn would thrash him soundly if he crossed to the wrong side of it.

"Isn't that the sort of thing you can divine?"

"I'll make an offering," he said at last. "And I'll put the question. Unfortunately, when dealing with the gods, there can be no guarantee of an immediate or straightforward answer."

Indeed, the only thing he could guarantee was that there would be nine times nine possible omens between now and sundown, and nine times as many interpretations that could be drawn from each event. An answer from the gods was promised by their faith, but it was less than certain that the questioner would spot it, or could read it correctly. Such oversights were the stuff of sagas, but no less so, they were the modern curse of anyone who tried their hand at divination. It was a messy business that Garrick tried his best to avoid.

"We live above the pottery workshop, at the bottom of the hill," she said. "Please, if you have news, at any time of day or night…"

"Of course," Garrick said. "Of course. If anything comes to us, be it letter or omen, someone will be with you in all haste."

"Thank you."

She made a donation in cash, nervously expressing her fear that it wasn't enough, although he made the usual comforting noises. There was no tariff of fixed fees for such services, and no amount of money would make it easier for him to read the wretched signs. Then she left, carrying her shopping and her child, leaving Garrick with an uneasy feeling in the pit of his stomach. He couldn't vouch for Ailith's safety; he hadn't even wanted her to go into such danger, but he could hardly have explained his fears to her mother. Not when he was supposed to be a poor orphan, knowing nothing of courts and castles, nor when Ailith's journey was supposed to have more to do with gods than mortals.

He would prepare the sacrifice and ask the question.

And then he would wait.

Chapter Twenty-Two

Ailith had done as Malachi suggested, and taken to wandering in the market square whenever she had time to spare. Usually, like today, she went out before breakfast, coming back with fruit or freshly-baked pastries to add to the breakfast table. Leofwin had teased her for it at first, and offered to instruct his servants to stock the kitchen with whatever her heart desired, but she'd identified a purveyor of sweet, spiced buns that he was particularly fond of, and he eventually seemed to accept the idea that she enjoyed the act of shopping. He'd even given her a small stipend for buying new clothes, once he realised her own purse wasn't up to the task of replenishing her wardrobe.

Well, he'd called it small. To Ailith it was a minor fortune, and spending it all on new dresses felt wasteful beyond belief, but she wanted to look like she belonged in the castle. Even though Leofwin usually wore plain, practical clothes, she felt out of place in her hand-me-down, patched-up dresses. The things Garrick had fetched her were more appropriate, but didn't quite fit properly, and were too warm when the sun came out.

This morning she was due to collect half a dozen new dresses from the itinerant tailor who'd taken her measurements the week before. She'd haggled hard, and agreed to buy eight new outfits for a total of just over half of the money Leofwin had given her. He would have the everyday dresses ready for her today, and two fancy gowns in two weeks' time. She'd ordered a pair of smart new boots from the shoemaker, and stashed away the rest of the coins in her room. There was nothing wrong with being prepared, she told herself, and she didn't know what else she might need money for.

Malachi had claimed he'd be in disguise, but although he'd tucked his little fortune-telling stall away in a quiet corner of the market, he himself looked just the same as he had the day he'd stopped her by the river.

"Tell your fortune, miss?" he offered, and she smiled and allowed him to usher her through the faded curtain, behind which he'd set up a folding table and two chairs. The fortune telling grid had been painted on the table's surface, along with a number of symbols she didn't recognise.

"Sit down," he said. "Maybe we'll finally have time to finish reading your stones."

"Must we?" Ailith wasn't sure that was a good use of her time. "I just came to give you an update."

"It's important you know where you're going, don't you think? And a proper telling takes time, it would look strange if you wandered on too soon."

"Don't cheat this time, then."

"Don't cheat? Dear child, I thought I'd explained. If I don't cheat, you might as well read off the patterns yourself."

He passed her the stones. She set a few to one side, and shuffled the remainder briefly between her fingers before casting them onto the tabletop.

"At least show me how it should be done," she said, flipping the stones which had landed face-down before Malachi could rearrange them. "I'm curious about the traditional ways, even if they don't work."

"There's never been a tradition of fortune telling without a fortune teller," Malachi said. "But the basics are simple. You scatter the stones across the nine squares. The top row represents the character, fears, and desires of the querent."

"Querent?"

"The one with the query. That's you."

"Okay."

"The bottom row represents gods, obstacles, and friends with a part to play. And the path across the middle row, that's your timeline.

The life story: past, present, and future. See, here, the square representing your present is empty. That's rare, and it signifies a time of great upheaval, where everything is changing too fast for the stones to keep up."

"What happens at the end?" she asked, pointing to where the future square contained three stones in a neat triangle.

"This is a classic example of a forked path, where the future hangs balanced on one or two key decisions." He chalked in a Y-shaped line which connected the timeline stones. "With these stones, your path could be there, or it could be here. There's bound to be War — that just means conflict, not an actual war. And then your path is open. You can choose Justice, or you can take the path of the Earthquake — which stands for fear and uncertainty. A classic opposition."

She shook her head. "You're doing it again."

"Sorry, m'dear, it's a habit. But the forked path is no invention of mine."

"No, but I'm sure it helps you spin your yarns."

"True enough."

"And a choice between the path of fear or the path of justice, that's straight from a saga."

"It does have a classical ring to it," he said. "Rather wonderful, isn't it?"

"Is that all there is to it?"

"The next stage is all in the interpretation of the timeline, m'dear, but I fear you'd call that part cheating. It's an art to weave a story from the stones."

"Let's skip that bit, then," Ailith said, spinning one of the uncast stones between her fingers.

"Look at the top of the board, then. Here we see the internal factors. First, signifying your character, you have the Harvest. That's Hasat in his human aspect, where he stands for productivity and an industrious nature. Qualities that will serve you well as an alchemist, no doubt."

Ailith laughed, causing him to stop and look up at her with a puzzled frown.

"You just can't stop, can you? You're physically incapable of keeping things simple."

"Perhaps," he said. "Or perhaps it is simply that a woman with such a turbulent present should heed all the advice she can find from other quarters."

"I didn't come here for advice. You wanted to see me."

"Very well." He sighed, and scooped up the stones. "I thought I should carry some news to your friends, since it's hardly safe for you to write. Far better to meet in person, at least as long as his lordship allows you out to the market."

"I'm not a captive, you know. I can come and go as I please."

"So you believe."

She pulled the token from around her neck and slammed it onto the table. "This says I can."

"This?" He picked up the coin and examined its markings. "I think you'll find this little trinket merely excuses you from the tolls. Nothing about a servant's marker says you're free to leave."

"Well, I am," Ailith said, though some instinct kept her from showing him the other paper Leofwin had given her. "His lordship hasn't put any restrictions on me."

"And yet, though you didn't let me get so far as to explain it to you, you had Prosperity and Storm in the area representing the obstacles in your path. That's both aspects of the goddess Refah in one place, making as clear a sign as any you might hope for."

"I'll think I'll trust in my experiences over your stones. He lets me wander freely in the castle, even to his private apartments, which hardly seems the way you'd treat a prisoner."

"Though you haven't found Anselm, yet."

It wasn't a question, as such, but she answered it anyway. "No."

"I thought as much. Nor any, ah… indications of the work he stole from me?"

"His lordship's library is twice the size of my house. Even if I knew what I was looking for, it would take months to find anything."

"Ah, well." Malachi smiled knowingly. "You did want a library.

Perhaps we will simply have to wait until he trusts you."

"He does trust me." Even if he shouldn't.

"That's doubtless what he wants you to think," Malachi said. "But you'll know, for sure, if he starts to tell you secrets. Describe him to me."

"What do you mean?"

"I'd like to know what he looks like, this adversary of ours. He's a famous recluse. No-one ever sees him."

"Oh! Of course." Ailith found she could bring a picture of Leofwin to her mind quite easily. Thinking of him as an adversary was much harder. "Well, he's tall — much taller than I am. Blond hair, almost white."

"How old?"

"I didn't ask."

"Guess."

"Maybe around Uchtred's age, or perhaps a little younger. Thirty-something, perhaps forty."

Malachi nodded, muttering to himself. "And have you learnt much?"

Ailith thought of the hours of discussion, the late nights hunched over the scrolls, and the subtly different vibrations of every substance she touched with her mind. She had learnt three thousand little things, but mostly she'd learnt how much more there was that she didn't know. Even when she'd sketched the charts that had made Leofwin wave away her trial period as an unnecessary formality, she'd been drawing in gaps and predictions.

"I'm learning," she said. "But slowly."

"Such things are always slow in the start," he said. "But are you enjoying the process?"

She nodded. *Too much*, she wanted but was afraid to say. So much so that looking for Anselm was of only secondary importance. But she couldn't say it. Saying it would force her to face up to things she'd been trying to push down. Instead, she changed the subject. "Does Nana know where I am? And why?"

Malachi shook his head. "She doesn't keep up with the Guild, these days."

"So she doesn't know that we're doing this for Anselm? I think someone should tell her."

"You'd like me to visit her when I'm next in Bracklea."

"Please. I want my family to know I'm okay, and Nana at least should know the real reason why I'm here."

They said their goodbyes, and Ailith went on to collect her dresses. The parcels were heavier and much more unwieldy than she'd expected, but the nobility weren't known for moderation in the designs of their clothing. She'd have to get used to the extra bulk.

She hired a couple of nearby children to heft the bulky packages up to her rooms, and summoned Frida to help her try the dresses on before she put them away. Her utility knife needed sharpening, but with a little effort she managed to work it through the strings securing the first parcel, and at least a dozen dresses cascaded onto the bed.

"Oh no." Ailith frowned at the swathes of coloured fabric, which she would somehow have to cram back inside the wrappings. "There's been a mistake — this must be someone else's order."

"You haven't tried them on yet, milady."

"No, but there's much more here than I ordered, and I only asked for blue and brown linen."

"Oh, that's no mistake. I took the liberty of talking with the tailor."

"You did what? How?"

"He already had your measurements, I just added to your order."

"To the tune of…" Ailith started to work out an estimate based on the prices she'd agreed, but Frida interrupted her thoughts.

"A lot less than you think — I negotiate better than you. You should have taken me with you in the first place, milady."

"But I haven't paid for these. You might have got the price down, but I've still nowhere near enough money."

"It's settled. I charged the balance to his lordship's account."

"You…" Ailith's mouth dropped open and she shook her head, momentarily speechless.

"It's fine," Frida said, but it wasn't.

"You spent all this on my behalf. If I can't send them back, I need to go and explain. Wait here."

Frida tried to protest, but Ailith wasn't listening. She almost ran through the corridors until she found Leofwin in his workshop, hunched over the pestle and mortar. She didn't need to use magic to identify the fennel seeds he was grinding; the scent made her mouth water.

"You're early today," he said, sparing her only a brief glance. "Can you wait a little longer for breakfast?"

"Actually, that's not why I came. I just learned that Frida increased my order with the tailor, and I wanted to apologise. I'll find a way to repay you."

"Repay me? There's no need."

"She didn't just add a couple of extra frocks, she must have made it five times the amount. It'll come to much more than you gave me."

"Was the allowance too mean?" He looked genuinely concerned, which made her feel worse. "I'm unfamiliar with the cost of women's garments."

"You gave me more than enough." He couldn't know that she'd kept back some of the coins to make herself an emergency fund. Could he? "The silk was expensive, of course, but how often will I need fancy gowns like that? And I got a good pair of boots, too. It was just... Frida overstepped herself. It won't happen again."

"I ordered her to take care of you. She's doing exactly as I asked."

"You gave me a full purse, which was more than generous, but she can't go charging things to your treasury on my behalf."

"I gave you money because I sensed you'd be more comfortable spending coin you could hold. It's not that I wanted to constrain what you could buy." He shuffled for a moment, and brought out a couple of gold guineas from his pocket. "Here. If you need something else, don't hesitate."

She pushed the coins back across the table. They were

surprisingly small for their value: each one was worth more than Papa made in a year. "I didn't come here to ask you for money, I came to say I'm sorry. If I need something, I'll ask you — but I've never needed a gold coin before, and I doubt I will again."

"As you wish." He scooped up the coins. "But you mustn't blame Frida for doing her job."

Chapter Twenty-Three

Leofwin was tallying his accounts when his chamberlain slipped almost silently into the workshop, with only a single light tap at the door to announce his arrival.

"You have a visitor, milord," Rethar said.

Leofwin frowned. He'd set Ailith up in the library, and given strict instructions that he was not under any circumstances to be disturbed while he was examining the figures. It was his least favoured part of his duties, and he needed peace to get it out of the way.

"A gentleman calling himself Malachi, milord," the chamberlain went on before he could object. "He's most insistent that you would wish to see him at once, but he refused to state his business. He sent a note."

Leofwin glanced over the scrap of paper, gave a heavy sigh, and set his papers aside. "I'll come to the Lower Hall. Have him wait for me there."

The chamberlain nodded and backed from the room.

It had been a short enough missive, but Malachi had always known how to stack ten layers of meaning into fewer than ten words. It was ambiguous enough to mean nothing to Rethar, but to Leofwin's eyes, there was no doubting the message behind the words.

He shrugged a fine cloak on over his work clothes for the sake of appearances, though he had little enough to hide from Malachi. If anyone knew exactly where he had come from, it was the wandering alchemist who'd apprenticed him away from his ruined family when he was only a scrawny, half-starved child. Leofwin had given up asking where, exactly, he'd been born. His family was long lost to him, if they'd even survived that harsh northern winter; all that he had of them was the spark of magic that had brought him to the position he now held.

"Malachi." Leofwin examined his visitor; the old man had barely changed since the last time their paths had crossed. Though his face was etched with deep wrinkles, they were familiar lines. "What a surprise."

"Not really."

"No. Not really." It had been longer than he'd expected, in truth. "Tell me what you want."

With Malachi, it was always business; there was no sense dithering on small talk.

"You have the boy?" Malachi asked.

"What boy?"

"Don't play me for a fool," Malachi said. "There's only one boy whose story connects us, since you left my charge. He did come to you, didn't he?"

"And what if he did?"

"You wouldn't have taken him in, if not for what he stole from me. And looking at you, I can't doubt the truth of the rumours."

Leofwin tried to keep the frown from reaching his face, but if rumours had reached Malachi, they could have fallen on more dangerous ears. Discovery was the stuff of his worst nightmares.

"You haven't told me what you want from me."

"What I've always wanted," Malachi said quietly. "Co-operation. We're on the same side. It's us against the gods, and we can't afford to fail."

"But we've never agreed," Leofwin said, thinking back to the many philosophical arguments they'd at first enjoyed, and he'd later grown to hate, when he'd been Malachi's apprentice all those years ago.

"Still, even you cannot hope to succeed alone. Ours is an art that grows best in the space between minds."

"Speaking of which, did you send me a student?"

"Do you like her? I thought there was something there worth

cultivating."

"There is. But I wasn't looking for an apprentice."

There was no need to make this too easy. Malachi was already looking smug and self-satisfied; he didn't need to know that Ailith was everything Leofwin had ever hoped for, and something he'd never thought he'd find.

"Not looking, perhaps, but needing. I always have known you better than you know yourself."

"You've always had a knack for manipulating people, I'll give you that. How did you find her?"

"Her grandmother has a rare talent, and her mother showed promise, too, though she never had the interest. But finding a good teacher was the least I could do for the girl. She told you I'd discovered her?"

"She told me of an old, itinerant fortune-teller, and you were the obvious candidate. Though how you got a letter from Oeric of Highfort…"

"That was nothing to do with me." The old man pulled a face. "I thought I'd given her a good enough calling card, but how was the girl to guess you'd be more interested in talent than in titles?"

"What, shimmering powder? That's hardly a mark of distinction."

"Ah." Malachi steepled his fingers and gave a knowing smile. "She did not use it, then."

"Didn't use what?"

"No, no. It is not for me to spill her secrets."

As much as he wanted to press for details, it would be easier to get blood from a stone. If Malachi decided something was not for sharing, then he could not be made to share it. The old man held secrets closer than gold.

"So you wanted me to take her in, and… what? You think she will already have come along enough to improve your formula? She has a natural talent, it's true, but less than a month of study behind her."

"I think my days are running out, and I know your

perfectionism. You would never have used it yourself, had you not succeeded in making certain improvements already."

"I made some minor adjustments, yes."

"Will you take pity on an old man?"

Leofwin had been sure the question would come up, so he'd made his way to the Lower Hall by way of his bedroom to retrieve the notes he'd locked away from Ailith's curious gaze. He and Malachi might not always see eye to eye, but he could hardly deny his old mentor's plea. The adjustments he'd made to the formula were subtle, but by trial and error he'd managed to suppress a couple of the more insidious defects of an ageing body. Without the corrections, it was no surprise a man of Malachi's years was beginning to falter. He passed across a copy of his latest refinement.

Malachi glanced over it, nodded, and returned the page.

"Keep it, if you like," Leofwin said. "I have other copies."

"My memory doesn't yet fail me. And I've rather lost my affinity for paper, since that boy."

"If he hadn't brought your work to me, I wouldn't have been able to improve it for you. Gods, you would never have trusted me with it yourself."

"I've spent half my life looking for someone I could trust with this. For what it's worth, you were one of a mere half-dozen who came close… but I was right not to trust you, if what they say is true. Is it? The Lord Baron of Watersmeet has made alchemy into a commodity?"

"I learned my trade from a wandering merchant," Leofwin said, hoping to gloss over the discomfort those words had lodged in his stomach. "What would you expect?"

"A little more discretion," Malachi said. "If word has reached me, how can it fail to reach the temples?"

Leofwin shrugged. There was nothing to say. He'd chosen a risky path, but as a young man shouldering an inheritance he hadn't been born to, the alternatives had all been far worse.

"And the boy's father knows he's here. You might expect to hear from him."

"He's one of us, is he not?"

"He's a priest first, alchemist second. I'm not sure where being a father falls, on the scale of his priorities."

Chapter Twenty-Four

It wasn't the first time she had seen Leofwin talking with a richly-dressed man in the Lower Hall. She'd never gathered anything interesting from their conversations, and generally preferred to use the time to continue her search for Anselm, but this one made her stop and look twice. He was older, and rather rounder, but he was unmistakably related to Garrick. She pressed her ear to the peep-hole, anxious to hear what was being discussed.

"You could give me a little more time," snapped the man who must have been Oeric of Highfort. "It grows tiresome, this obligation. And you needn't pretend you enjoy my visits."

"I told you what to expect before we began," Leofwin said, and there was an iron in his voice to which Ailith was unaccustomed. He was dressed, too, in a rather more lordly fashion than was usual for him. She wasn't sure she liked the transformation. "Was I not perfectly clear? There can be no negotiating."

"And what if I simply did not return? What then?"

"Then you would die."

The words hung in the air. Ailith realised she was holding her breath, and let it out slowly, afraid they would hear her through the heavy silence.

"We are not debating the price of butter," Leofwin said flatly, when Oeric didn't respond. "You're asking the impossible. I could not do it, even if I wished to."

"Let us get this tawdry business over with, then."

Ailith watched as the man held out his hand. Leofwin pricked a finger, brought out a small vial, and applied something to Oeric's skin. Then he bowed his head in the way he always did when he worked on a difficult amalgam. Ailith smiled with sympathy, and wondered what formula he was amalgamating. It must be something that required the living blood, else he would never have allowed a fellow lord to see him at work. She was surprised he'd chance it in any circumstances. Stretching her attention as far as she could, straining at the edges of her consciousness, she hoped to catch a glimpse of the ingredients if not the whole pattern... but it was beyond her reach. As it was, she could only guess from Leofwin's words that it must be some kind of cure. For what, she had no inkling.

Within a couple of minutes he was finished, and Oeric passed him a heavy purse.

Leofwin weighed it in his palm, and nodded. "Until next time, then."

"Until next time."

Leofwin swept from the room, and Ailith scrambled through the secret passages, determined to be hard at work in the library if he should come to seek her out. He didn't, though. She was a little disappointed. It wasn't that she was short of tomes to study, and he'd given her plenty of ideas to keep her busy, but the time passed more easily in his company, even when he was just quietly working on his own projects. By herself it was easy to get distracted into following up anything that intrigued or puzzled her, but when Leofwin was there she could usually get a quick answer from him without needing to search the library. Or, on those occasions that she asked about something he didn't know, he'd invariably be interested enough to look it up for her while she continued her original train of thought. Without him, she spent half of her time wondering what he was up to.

In the end he called on her just in time for supper, and after a brief meal and even briefer apology he left her to her own devices and disappeared back into his bedroom. His unusual reserve left her feeling uncomfortable, and she returned early to her rooms.

"You didn't feel like attending the feast, milady?" Frida asked as she brushed out Ailith's hair ready for bed.

"What feast?"

"For the Lord Baron of Highfort. We have guests, that always means a feast."

"But Leofwin ate with me," Ailith said, puzzled. "We had supper in the workshop."

"His lordship doesn't go to these things, but you could if you wished it. I could prepare your clothes for you."

"Oh."

"Next time, perhaps?"

"I think I prefer to eat with his lordship, but thank you." Ailith thought for a moment. "Will you be going down soon to get your share of the leftovers?"

"Yes, milady, there's usually a group of us meets in the kitchen on feast nights."

"Well, I don't really want to attend a feast for some lord I don't know, but perhaps I could come with you?"

"I'm not sure that would be a good idea."

"Why not?"

Frida blushed. "It's not right, is it? A lady like you shouldn't be eating in the kitchen. What would folks say?"

"I hope they'd say 'nice to meet you, Ailith, pull up a chair.' I'm not a noblewoman, Frida, you've surely noticed that."

"I don't know what you are, milady. You mightn't be noble, but you're not one of us, neither."

"Please? It's a bit lonely here, just books for company when his lordship's busy. It would be nice to have some friends."

"I can't call you milady if you come down to the kitchens," Frida said, her voice uncertain, and Ailith knew she was close to winning. "And you can't be expecting the others to bow and whatnot. It'll have to be your name."

"That's fine. I like my name well enough."

So instead of getting ready for bed, Ailith dressed in the simplest of her new dresses, pulled on her old boots, and followed Frida down through the servants' passages to the kitchen.

At the centre of the kitchen was a large table, its surface made from one huge slab of oak. During the day it was used for all the chopping and kneading and rolling that was required to feed staff and guests alike, but now it was covered in half-empty platters and surrounded by a cheerful, chattering crowd. Frida led Ailith down to the far end, where a few of the younger staff were gambling with dice.

"I brought someone," she said. "This is Ailith. From upstairs."

"What, 'is lordship's young lady?" one of the older girls asked around a mouthful of cabbage.

Frida gave her a look that said 'I told you so', but she reached for some beef and onions without another word, leaving Ailith to answer for herself.

"I'm staying in the castle," Ailith said. "But I'm no lady."

"Ain't you?" The girl was still staring incredulously across the table.

Ailith slid into an empty chair and picked up the dice. "I don't think noblewomen play scuttle. What's the stake?"

"Half-penny a round," said the lad to Ailith's right. With flour in his hair and his sleeves rolled up to show off muscular forearms, he obviously worked in the bakery.

"Double if you're noble," the dark-haired girl said.

"I'll pay double on any losses this round," Ailith said, and placed a penny firmly on the table in front of her. "But if I win, you don't call me noble again. Deal?"

The girl shrugged. "Deal."

"What's your names?" Ailith asked as she rolled.

The dark-haired girl was Ymma, and usually worked in the kitchens, though she'd spent much of the evening serving at the feast. The baker's apprentice was Wig, and the other players were a scullery maid called Lily and a trainee pikeman called Ulf. Frida didn't join the game at once, although she did fill enough wooden tankards of ale for everyone to have a drink. Ailith took a hearty swig just to show her lack of decorum.

Scuttle had just enough skill to it that she could usually scrape a victory by figuring the odds on each roll, while involving enough chance that her sisters would still play with her. She didn't imagine there would be much of a challenge in beating a group of half-drunk servants, but she'd reckoned without the happy hours they spent on the game every other night, and she was three pennies down before luck and logic finally brought her a win.

"If you're not a proper lady," Lily started, then shook her head. "Sorry, I don't mean it like that. If you're not noble-born, though, what are you here for?"

"An accident took my parents," she said, crossing her palm three times beneath the table to keep the gods from hearing her lie. The last thing she needed was to tempt Oelum into looking at her family. "But I can write well enough, so I came looking for work."

"You're a scribe?" Ulf asked.

"Yes, I'm a kind of scribe." Ailith jumped on the description with enthusiasm. It neatly explained the stacks of papers in her room, and was close enough to the truth that no-one would catch her in the lie. At least, not unless they could read.

"But she stays in guest rooms, and Frida has to comb 'er hair," Ymma chipped in.

"She could do it herself, though," Frida said. "That's the difference. Not like these half-wits tonight."

"That fat one's so far gone, he won't get to bed without someone to hold 'is hand," Ymma agreed. "I'm glad I got away when I did."

"Speaking of drinking," Ailith said, and drained her mug. "Who wants a top-up?"

Everyone did, so she gathered their tankards and headed for the barrel. It was going fairly well, and taking her turn at fetching the beer would only help her to prove she wasn't as stuck-up as Ymma suspected. Having friends would be nice. Having friends who flitted about the castle and listened could also be extremely useful. She balanced the now-overflowing tankards between her hands, and took careful steps back to her place at the table.

The evening passed quickly in a pleasant haze of ale and dice and gossip. Ailith listened and laughed and drank, and didn't try too hard to keep the coins on her side of the table. She still had a chunk of money left from the purse that Leofwin had given her for clothes, and it was well worth investing a few pennies in new friendships. Along the table others came and left, but most of them had trickled away by the time the last couple of serving girls came in from the Hall.

"That's all them lords out the way," the taller girl said, collapsing into the chair next to Frida and stretching out her legs. "Gods, we thought we'd miss you, they stayed for so much drinking."

"You should have missed me," Wig said, getting to his feet. "I'd best turn in, or I'll be up lighting the ovens before I've ever gone to bed."

"'S good bread tonight," Lily said through a mouthful of the same. "Make some more with raisins, will you?"

"For a feast, I can, but not any old day. D'you think raisins grow on trees?"

"'Course they grow on trees, you daft fool."

"What if Ailith asks you to make it?" Ymma asked, looking hard at Ailith in a way that dared her to say she wouldn't.

Ailith nodded. "If I ask you for a raisin loaf for breakfast, we'll only eat a couple of slices, won't we? And you'd better bake two loaves in case one burns."

"I never burnt a thing!" Wig said hotly. "Well, not in a year or more."

"She means that's more for us," Lily said, grinning. "She's a clever'un. I like her, Frid, she can come again."

"Raisin bread for breakfast, then," Ailith said. "And you could put a bit of nutmeg in, and ginger."

Wig shook his head, bemused. "Raisins and spices. Alright. I'll tell the master you asked for it 'specially."

"Just make sure Lily gets a good thick slice."

Once Wig had gone to bed, and the newcomers had been introduced as Lufe — the taller — and Nia, Ulf brought out a shepherd's pipe. He offered it to Ailith. "Do you play?"

"No, I've never learnt. I can sing a little, if you want."

Ulf stuck the pipe between his teeth and blew a couple of exploratory notes. "Do you know *The Sailor's Heart?*"

Ailith shook her head, but Lily knew the first three verses, and they all joined in on the chorus. Then Nia asked for *Pretty Harlot*, and since there seemed to be a bawdy theme developing, Ailith did a rousing rendition of *Under The Willows*. Ulf blushed to the roots of his hair when she sang the part about the guard and his pike, and when she got on to the baker and his buns they all agreed it was best that Wig had already gone to bed.

"He's a sweet boy," Nia said. "But he's too sweet, sometimes."

"Ada likes him that way," Lily said.

"You sing different words to the version I know," Frida said.

"You know it better with women? *My love tends a garden, all verdant and lush...* that sort of thing?"

"That's it."

"That's the original," Ailith said. "A sailor's ditty. But as a woman, I'd rather send up the men. Wouldn't you?"

"Gods, yes," Lufe said with a little too much enthusiasm. Ulf shuffled on his chair, still looking deeply uncomfortable.

"You rewrote it?" Ymma asked.

"With one of my cousins." She'd been lashed until she could hardly stand when Papa had found out they'd written a verse about a potter to wind up his apprentice, but it had been worth it.

"You should put in a verse for 'is lordship," Ymma said. "My lover's a baron..."

"*My lover's a baron, he's rich as ten men,*" Nia started. "Well, I suppose it's more like a thousand really, if not more, but that don't scan..."

Ailith took a deep breath and launched back into the song with a new verse of her own, the words of which had started to form even as the others discussed the possibility:

> *My love is a baron,*
> *he makes all the rules,*
> *but twas under the willows*

he showed off his jewels.

He lives in a castle
And his word is law,
but twas under the willows
he gave me what for.

"How's that for a first try?" she asked.

The girls cheered and hammered on the table, hooting with laughter.

"And another one!" Ymma demanded.

"Another?"

"He's the baron. Don't you reckon he deserves more than one verse?"

"And you're clearly a natural," Lily added, making Ailith blush, but she couldn't resist the challenge and promised to see what she could come up with.

A dozen songs later, and having downed almost as many mugs of ale, they eventually said their goodnights. As Ailith stumbled to her feet, even Ymma agreed she'd be welcome to join them any night of the year.

"You takes your turn and you pays your debts," she said. "That's good enough for me."

Frida and Ailith walked back together to the corridor where they both slept. The servants' routes were surprisingly direct, and Ailith made a mental note to explore them more thoroughly when she was sober. Perhaps she could find her way to other parts of the castle, that way.

There was a guard outside her bedroom who looked more than a little surprised to see his charge on the wrong side of the door, never mind that she was weaving along arm in arm with her maid.

"Milady returns," Frida said with a drunken flourish. "You won't tell his lordship, now will you, Brict? I can't imagine you want to admit to standing guard over an empty room for half the night."

"I won't tell if you won't," he agreed, and unlocked the door for them.

"Why is the door guarded?" Ailith asked as Frida helped her to undress. It felt stranger than ever to have the other girl serving her after they'd spent the evening as friends. "And locked. It was locked."

"Milady?"

"Frida." Ailith gripped Frida's shoulders, hard, and forced the other girl to meet her eyes. "Don't 'milady' me. I'd much rather be your friend."

"Me too, but I still have to…"

"I know, you're being paid to look after me." And to spy on her? Ailith wondered. The unexpected guard had put her on edge, and Malachi's words echoed in her mind. But it didn't matter. "That doesn't make any difference. I won't stop you doing your job."

"Alright." Frida nodded.

"I won't even ask you difficult questions." Ailith turned and stumbled back across the room, throwing the door open hard enough to slam it against the wall. "Brict — was that your name? Why are you guarding my door?"

"Milady?" He gaped at her.

"It's an easy enough question."

"I'm a guard, milady."

"I know, I know, it's your job. But are you there to keep me safe or keep me trapped?"

"He can't answer that. And you're not decent." Frida took her arm and pulled her back into the bedroom, tugging the door closed behind them.

Ailith looked down at her knee-length cotton tunic, surprised to find that she was no longer wearing her dress over the top. "Oops."

"Come on, get yourself into bed. You're going to have quite the headache come morning. And I suspect the answer is both, but you didn't hear that from me."

Chapter Twenty-Five

The Guild turned as one body when the parlour door creaked open. Everyone expected was already present, and the evening's business almost concluded. Orvyn's staff should have deflected any unexpected visitors at the door, and the servants themselves had been ordered not to disturb the meeting.

Malachi stood in the doorway, wrapped in a well-worn riding cloak and leaning heavily on his cane.

"You don't make yourselves easy to find, do you?" he said as he limped into the room.

"That's rather the idea," Selwyn said. "What brings you here?"

"Do you know this man?" Orvyn asked, with a skeptical examination of his unexpected guest. Garrick could only imagine what he made of the sight. With the exception of Selwyn, most of the Guild came from moderately wealthy families. Even playing the part of a temple orphan, Garrick dressed smartly for the Guild meetings. The sudden appearance of a scruffy nomad would raise all sorts of questions in town.

"He is an alchemist," Selwyn said. "If a somewhat disreputable one."

"This disreputable alchemist has news from your pilgrim, should you wish to hear it," Malachi said. "If not, I shall be on my way."

"You'll excuse my poor manners," Orvyn said. "I was not expecting an unfamiliar face. Would you care for a drink while you share your news?"

"I would care for a large measure of the strongest spirits you have," Malachi said as Totte helped him into the nearest chair. "Travel is hard on these old bones."

"Of course." Orvyn went to fetch a bottle of brandy, while the others watched the visitor with a mixture of curiosity and thinly-veiled distaste. Malachi looked a little less composed than the last time Garrick had seen him, but he was very old, and perhaps he wasn't lying about the hardships of travel, if he had truly been to Watersmeet and back.

"Have you been to the castle?" Selwyn asked. Malachi nodded.

"He'll still see you, then?"

"He wouldn't turn me away, even now."

Garrick was sure he was missing something, but he already knew Selwyn and Malachi had some complicated history behind them. The implication that Leofwin's story intersected with theirs in some way was an interesting twist, but if it meant someone had access to Ailith then he could manage to hold his tongue about how nice it would have been for them to mention it when they were making their plans in the first place. He could not, however, muster the patience to keep silent. "What do you know?" he asked.

"Ailith is well, if that's your concern," Malachi said, giving Garrick a knowing look that he prayed the others would miss.

"Are you prepared to take his word for that?"

"No, I saw her myself. She seems happy, and she believes herself free to come and go as she pleases."

"And what has she learned?" Selwyn asked.

"She was still settling in, when I saw her," Malachi said. "She hadn't yet found any sign of Anselm, but Watersmeet is a substantial fortress, and she can't afford to act suspiciously."

"The gods will lead her." Selwyn folded his hands into his lap, and bowed his head as if in prayer. "She will find him, if he's there to be found."

"If Malachi managed to visit her, then we can send help," Garrick said. "We sent her off in such a rush, there wasn't time to make a proper plan."

"The gods will guide her," Selwyn repeated. "She has no need of our meddling."

Malachi rolled his eyes heavenwards. "You haven't learnt, have you? The gods won't watch over Ailith, any more than they watched over Anselm, and the boy's right: you sent her off without a hint of a plan."

"If she finds Anselm, the gods will show her how to save him," Selwyn said. "That much is clear to me. If she fails to read the signs, we can discuss how to help her, but until then we must have patience. And faith."

Malachi shook his head. "You're a fool, but it's no concern of mine."

But it was, Garrick feared, fast becoming something he needed to concern himself with. He'd taken responsibility for Ailith's wellbeing with a letter, and compounded it with promises to the girl's mother. If no-one else was looking out for her then he would have to step up, even if it meant going against his teacher's wishes.

"If you came here to insult me, you can leave right now," Selwyn said.

"I came to update you on the progress of your plan, such updates being just one of the many things you failed to plan for. And I came, if you wish, to help you find a way forwards."

"We're grateful for the news," Orvyn said. "But I don't imagine a man like you has anything further to contribute here."

"No." Malachi downed the last of his drink and got to his feet. "I suppose you wouldn't. Fare well, then. Good night."

Garrick stared at the door long after it had closed, as the others returned to subdued conversation. As much as he hated to admit it, Malachi had a point. Their failure to plan was humiliating, pure and simple. They'd been thoughtless and lazy, and a girl's life could have been forfeit. Why had it taken a stranger — and the lowest kind of commoner, at that — to even make sure they kept in contact with Ailith while she was off doing their dirty work for them? Selwyn might place his heartfelt trust in the gods, but Garrick had no such excuse for overlooking the more mundane requirements.

And Malachi's words echoed in his mind. She *believed* herself free. What was that, if not an indication that the old man believed otherwise?

Chapter Twenty-Six

It was the day after the Feast of Saaluk. Leofwin hadn't been interested in attending the festivities in town, so Ailith had gone down to the temple with Frida. After the sacrifices they'd met up with Ymma, Lily and Nia in a nearby tavern, and it had been almost dawn when they'd stumbled back across the drawbridge. With only a couple of hours of sleep behind her, and still a little drunk, it had been no wonder that Leofwin had deemed her unfit for her studies and insisted she go back to bed rather than joining him for breakfast.

Now, if the light streaming through her windows was anything to judge by, it was probably after midday. She yawned and stretched out in the luxurious bed, wondering if this would be a pattern that held for every feast day. She knew Leofwin thought little enough of the gods, and she'd had a marvellous time with her friends… But no. None of this was real. What chance she would even be here for another festival? Her friends would likely be celebrating Keyif's Night without her at midsummer.

She felt a pang of sadness at the idea, but thinking of it reminded her why she was at Watersmeet in the first place. With an unexpectedly free day, she had another chance to search for Anselm. She dressed quickly without disturbing Frida, leaving her hair in its nighttime plait, and made her way into the secret passages.

She would have hurried past the public halls without a second glance, but Leofwin's voice caught her as she passed the Lower Hall. He sounded unhappy. Curious, she pressed her eye to the peep-hole.

Beneath the rose murals, he stood beside another lord, but it was Rethar who was the focus of his anger.

"You were not to disturb us. Which part of my instructions were unclear?"

Rethar bowed his head. "Nothing, milord. My apologies."

"Your apologies are insufficient. Send Thurstan to me."

"The captain of the night watch, milord? You would have me wake him?"

"Don't question me, just do it."

"Yes, milord."

Once Rethar was gone from the room, Leofwin returned his attention to the stranger who stood beside him, apparently administering an alchemical cure just as he had with Oeric. They said their goodbyes cordially enough, and Leofwin paced the room as he waited for his captain.

Thurstan was an older man, smartly dressed and balding. "You summoned me, milord?"

"You will replace Rethar with immediate effect," Leofwin said without preamble.

The new chamberlain nodded. If the promotion surprised him, he didn't show it.

"Your first job is to deal with him. Report to me in my library once you've made the necessary arrangements."

Ailith knew it was a bad idea, but somehow she couldn't stop her feet. It was all very well coming here to save Anselm, who might not even be in the castle, but how could she stand here and watch an innocent man condemned? The moment Thurstan was gone from the room, she pushed past the tapestry and into the hall.

"You can't have him killed," she said. "He didn't do anything wrong."

Leofwin stared at her, and then his eyes moved up towards the peep-hole. "Have you been watching me?"

"You do it."

"It's my castle. Only I'm supposed to know what can be seen from where."

She cursed silently. Had she ruined her chances by her carelessness? Could she not have taken the long way round, and pretended to have heard something from outside the door? But it was too late now to do anything except brazen it out.

"You did give me a piece of paper that says I can go anywhere," she said.

"I see now that that may have been foolish. Remind me to think a little longer, next time I'm tempted to such folly."

"And I'm your apprentice. I don't see why you would trust me with poisons, but not with the layout of your house."

He nodded, a smile creasing his eyes. "You may be right about that."

"I mean it, though," she said. "You can't have Rethar killed for something that's not his fault. You can't."

"He saw something he shouldn't have seen. How would you protect us?"

"Your staff are loyal," she said. "I think I'd try trusting them."

"You can't rely on loyalty. To succeed in any war you have to make sure your men are more scared of you than they are of the enemy, and when the enemy is the Temple Law, that's a lot of fear to outdo."

"You really don't get it, do you? While everyone in other baronies thinks you're a murdering bastard, here they think you're a hero for giving homes and livelihoods to starving orphans. They love you. They don't need to fear you."

"You'd gamble your life on that?"

"I would."

"Well. I wouldn't."

"Give him to me, then."

"Give him to you?" Leofwin stopped pacing and met her eyes for the first time. "Since when does a potter's daughter have men of her own?"

It was the specificity that floored her. If he'd levelled some vague accusation of pretence and plotting, she might have thought to laugh it off, but this? If he knew that much, then he knew other things. Perhaps everything. She expected him to continue, but he was waiting for her response.

"How long have you known?" she asked.

"Do you think I'd take someone into my home without finding out a little about them? You speak well, but there's no disguising that accent. And you may come bearing a letter with the seal of Highfort, but Oeric has never heard of you. An intriguing puzzle, is it not?"

"It isn't… I mean… it's not what you think."

"You didn't write it yourself, I know that. Your writing is much neater, every stroke its own considered work of art. No, whoever wrote that letter has had far more practice at writing, enough to become quite lazy at it. Yet it wasn't the Lord Baron of Highfort, was it?"

She mumbled her agreement.

"Say that again. I couldn't hear you."

"No, my lord. I'm a potter's daughter, like you say. I've never met Oeric of Highfort."

"Ah." Leofwin smiled. "Then it remains only to ask how, precisely, you have encountered his son and heir. No-one else has access to that seal. No-one else would dare to use it."

Ailith swallowed, and forced herself to look at him. "If you know Garrick, you must know he's away from home. Studying."

"Studying."

"He's learning alchemy, though I think he keeps that from his father. When Malachi told me I had talent, and I said I was interested in learning more, he offered to help me make your acquaintance."

"How very generous of him."

"What?"

"Do you think he'd do something like that out of the goodness of his heart? Or do you think, just maybe, he's hoping for something in return?"

Ailith frowned. "He's my friend."

"Dear one, he's heir to Highfort. Men like that don't make friends with potters' daughters."

"What else could he possibly want from someone like me?"

"Nothing, perhaps, from the woman you were when you left. But I'm sure he could find a use for a fully-trained alchemist, educated by one of the most talented and elusive teachers in all the

Twelve Baronies. After all, I neglected to answer his letters."

"He wrote to you?"

"Of course. If you were a noble brat with a flare of power, who else would you approach? But he's a self-important, pompous little lordling, and I saw no need to reply."

"I don't understand. I thought you'd only let me in because of that letter."

"An apprenticeship is about more than just passing the time of day, but you do have to like someone if you're to spend hours every day in their company."

"You knew who I was, though... who I wasn't. And you still chose to let me stay."

"It was a minor deception, and I understood your reasons. But when I know you've lied to me already, why would I give you a man's life?"

"I didn't lie. I just... didn't tell you everything." She still couldn't tell him everything; not even close. She would trust him with her own life, but she couldn't make that decision for Anselm. "I didn't think you'd want me if you knew I was a commoner."

"I'm far more interested in who you are than where you've come from. Your talent is real enough."

"Then what is it you want from me? If the heir to Highfort wouldn't befriend me out of the goodness of his heart, I don't see why you would, either."

"I've never made any secret of what I want. That's why I tested you on day one, and why I've been testing you ever since. I need a partner who's strong enough and smart enough to help me."

"As an equal?"

"That would be my ideal."

"Then why wouldn't you let me have staff of my own?"

He laughed, and she knew she'd won.

"What would you do with him?"

"I know you like to post a guard outside my door. Let's imagine that's for my own protection. Don't you think I'd prefer to have a man of my own there?"

"Rethar is no guard."

"He was, before you promoted him to be your chamberlain. I'm sure he remembers the basics."

"And how would you pay him?"

"If his alternative is execution, I think he'd work for nothing, don't you?" Though she still had a little left in her savings, enough to ease him through the first few weeks.

"What about his wife and children?"

"His wife works in the laundry, doesn't she? Aelm is almost old enough to take up a trade of his own, and Ada's looking set to follow in her father's footsteps."

"How in Refah's name do you know all that?"

"I'm friends with Wig — the baker's apprentice. He's courting Ada." She'd played scuttle with him half a dozen times now, and that was six times as many as she'd need to, to know the depth of regard he held for Ada.

"Are you, now?" Leofwin raised an amused eyebrow. "You're a very unusual woman, Ailith."

"So I've heard."

"Most people, finding themselves an honoured guest in a baronial castle, would cultivate friends amongst the local nobility, not in the kitchens."

"I understood that most commoners seldom found themselves in such circumstances, outside of songs and sagas."

"True enough."

"And most lords wouldn't take in a potter's daughter, even if she did come with references. These facts may not be unrelated."

"Alright, then." He nodded slowly. "If you can reach an arrangement with Rethar, you may have him. But if he does anything to endanger us, it will be on your head."

"He won't."

Chapter Twenty-Seven

It wasn't the first time Leofwin had found her in the garden at an ungodly hour of the night. He'd set guards to watch her room around the clock, but there was nothing they could do when she smiled sweetly at them and let them know she was on her way to his private apartments — where she was known to be welcome and they could not follow. Now she had Rethar at her disposal, she was even more inclined to do as she pleased. Only the gods knew what the staff made of her midnight visits, although he could guess at the sort of rumours that must be spreading.

Ailith had been at the castle for only six weeks but already she would often get up in the middle of the night, obsessed with some new idea that had come to her in half-waking moments. Nothing he'd said had gone any way to persuading her that she'd lose nothing if she made a note, went back to sleep, and tested her theories in the morning.

It probably didn't help that he struggled to sleep, himself, and more often than not he came upon her in the course of his own midnight strolls, in the garden or the workshop or the library. While he tried to discourage her, it must have been obvious that his heart wasn't really in it. There was something companionable about the way they would often end up sitting beneath the arbour and talking informally of anything and nothing. Under the cover of darkness the years and titles that separated them seemed to dissolve into simple friendship, and she relaxed in a way she seldom did in their lessons.

Tonight she was sitting cross-legged on a secluded section of the path, her hands outstretched between the leaves of nearby shrubs. He reached out until he could sense the way her mind followed her fingers.

She jumped as though he'd laid a hand on her shoulder.

"Sorry," she said, scrambling to her feet, the lantern swaying in her hand. "Did I wake you on my way up? I didn't mean to."

"It wasn't you. What are you working on?"

"I was just thinking," she said. "Testing."

He knew a dismissal when he heard it. She would tell him once she was ready, and not a moment before.

"I'm going to do a lap of the battlements and then I'll be in the usual spot," he said. "If you feel like company."

"Okay." She settled herself back on the floor, extending her arms into the bushes again.

He smiled to himself, watching her for a long moment before he started his walk. Her enthusiasm was enchanting, and her dedication impressive. Never before had he had the company of a fellow alchemist who seemed as curious as he was. Well, Malachi, perhaps, but he hadn't found it easy to exchange ideas with his teacher. Politics and philosophy had got in the way of learning, and there had been too many other apprentices who came and went and distracted their attention. And although Ailith was a beginner, the innocent questions she asked often pointed towards bigger issues that he hadn't even thought about.

After a short circuit of the walls he made his way back into the garden, scratching absently at his arm as something brushed against him in the darkness. He'd just check whether Ailith was still up, and if not, he'd try once more to sleep.

"Got you." Her voice was so soft that he wasn't sure if she was talking to herself.

He rounded the corner and found her lying on her back on the bench, eyes closed. She'd extinguished her lantern, and only the moonlight illuminated her face. As he stepped towards her, she propped herself up on her elbows and looked up at him.

"I knew it."

He leaned against the arbour. "Knew what?"

"I knew I'd found you. How far away were you?"

His confusion must have shown plain on his face.

"Didn't you feel it?" she asked, swinging round to make space for him to sit beside her. "I was sure you would."

"Tell me."

"I was trying to… no, this is no good, I should start at the beginning. Earlier, when you found me, I was trying to see how far I could reach. You know, to see how far away something has to be before I stop being able to feel it."

"I see."

"Well, it was hard." She frowned. "I need to do some better experiments. I thought I could do it by just seeing which plants I could sense, and how far away they were. But it gets all muddled, further out, and some of the plants are really similar, and the directions are difficult."

"Directions?"

"You know when someone drops a plate, and you can tell if it was to your left or right, behind you or in front, even if you're not looking? I don't think I can do that, with these senses. I can tell when things are close to each other, but not where they are compared to me."

"I've never tried that." He probed the leaves of nearby bushes as she spoke, trying to see if he could get a sense of direction or even distance. She was right; it was challenging.

"But then I thought, the books all say there are some things you can only make in living blood, you see? So blood must be an ingredient in its own right, and maybe if I could feel my own blood, I could at least tell what was close to there. That's why I had my hands in the bushes. It helps a bit, but not enough. But once I'd thought of blood, I decided I'd wait for you and see if I couldn't feel you come close. Blood feels different to everything else, so it's easier."

"So that's what touched against my arm. I did feel something, but it was very light — I thought it was an insect, or a leaf."

"If you'd been paying attention, you would have known it was me," she said, with an absolute certainty he didn't share. "Where were you?"

"Just around the corner."

She hopped to her feet and paced out the distance. "About here?"

"Maybe another step back."

She took the step, and then he felt her mind brush against him again. Another step, another touch, light as a feather. If he hadn't been on the alert for it, he might not even have felt her. Another step, but this time he felt nothing.

"Too far," she said, inching back towards him. "But it's somewhere around here that it stops working. What's that, five yards?"

"Nearer six, I'd say."

He stretched out his own mind towards her, and she shivered at the touch. As she walked back to the bench she rubbed her arms as if she were actually cold, though the night was mild.

"Stand up," she said. "And face me."

He did, and seeing that she'd closed her eyes, told her that he'd done it.

"Now keep still." With a slow and deliberate motion, she lifted her finger and rested it gently on the tip of his nose. "There."

"By feeling the blood?" he asked, and she nodded.

He knew then that he had to introduce her to the mice.

"Are you tired?" he asked. "Or would you like to see something interesting?"

"Both."

"If you come downstairs with me now, I'll let you sleep in tomorrow morning. I'd like to show you this tonight."

The room he led her to was accessible only by a small door in the corner of the workshop. It looked like it should lead to a cupboard, though the space on the other side was actually almost the same size again. He kept the door locked, and the key was always about his person. Books gave away little, to an illiterate servant, and could safely be left on show. But even though Thurstan must have realised by now that his master had unusual interests, he'd find it strange indeed to see this.

It felt like an eternity since the last time he'd stunned Ailith into silence, but she stared wordlessly at the cages of mice. He was definitely glad he'd brought her here at night, while the tiny critters were at their most active.

"I thought it was time you met our little assistants," he said. "If you're going to start getting interested in blood."

She turned her puzzled stare on him, at that. "Why do you have mice?"

He unlatched the nearest door, and allowed one of the mice to scramble onto his hand. "Would you like to hold her?"

Ailith cupped her hands in front of her chest, although she didn't look completely convinced.

"They're tame," he said. "They've grown up in here, not out in the wild. She won't bite."

"You haven't told me why you have them." She held the mouse at eye level and stroked it lightly between the ears.

"It's a funny thing," he said. "But a mouse is more like a person than you might imagine. If you want a good test of whether something will amalgamate in a human bloodstream, this is it. And mice grow up and grow older more quickly, which can also be useful."

"Really? You can use them to test new formulae?"

"Really. I'd prefer you not to hurt them, of course, but if you're going to wake up in the night with ideas, I'd rather you not try every theory on yourself. I'll have a spare key made for this room."

The mouse had climbed up to Ailith's shoulder and was sniffing at the end of one of her braids, her whiskers twitching. When she started to chew at her collar, Ailith reached up and scooped the tiny creature back into her hands.

"They are quite cute," Ailith conceded, letting her hop back into the cage. "But why so many?"

"They breed, if you let them." Well… most of them. As far as he could tell, the subjects in his most important experiment were barren. Thinking of which… "The cages on the back wall there are involved in my current trials. Obviously, I'd prefer you to leave them alone."

"Oh, of course."

"I mean, you can feed them or get them out to play, you just need to make sure they always go back into the cage they came out of."

She nodded. "Got it."

"And if you want to test something over a longer period yourself, you can use one of the empty cages to separate off a different group, but keep at least three or four together. They like to have company."

Chapter Twenty-Eight

Over the years of his childhood Garrick had discovered a number of ancient documents hidden away in dark and dusty corners of his own ancestral seat. Whether tucked inside the covers of harmless tomes in the library, or locked away in strong boxes, or tucked into hidey-holes in the walls, the Highfort had yielded a fair number of alchemical manuscripts.

It had been while attempting to follow their directions that Garrick had learnt he had some aptitude for the work of alchemy. And once he knew that, he had hoarded the papers with a kind of desperate selfishness known only to young lords jealously protecting their birthright.

Sharing such things with the priest had been too obvious a folly, but he hadn't liked to leave his collection behind. Finding a hiding place for his own secrets had been almost his first act upon reaching the temple. He'd moved things around a couple of times since then, as he'd discovered ever better, more thoroughly hidden spots within the temple complex.

Now he made his way to the corner of the stable yard, where a mounting block made it possible to climb up onto the surrounding wall. He took this route only when the stables were deserted, but he'd quickly learnt the stable boys' habits and he knew the boys regularly sneaked off together, leaving the place conveniently deserted. Crouched atop the wall, he could then pull himself over onto the roof of the neighbouring building. A couple of loose bricks in a disused chimney stack pulled out to give him access to the best hiding place he'd found to date. Better still, he could scramble over the peak of the roof and sit hidden, out of sight of the road. A slight overhang from a neighbouring building even gave the spot some shelter on rainy days. For a young man with secrets of the paper variety, it was perfect.

He kept the papers in a waxed leather wallet to protect them from the elements. Today, though, the weather was fine. He sorted through the pile with careful fingers, looking for a slim treatise that had stuck in his mind. The papers covered all manner of subjects, but this one distinguished itself by claiming to outline the eight most virulent poisons in the world.

Selwyn had forbidden the study of poisons, of course, but that was just the sort of compromise Garrick had had to make in order to get an apprenticeship. There had been no way to avoid agreeing to the old man's terms, and making a fuss would have raised suspicions, but he didn't take the injunction terribly seriously. It certainly hadn't stopped him from reading the temple's forbidden texts whenever the opportunity presented itself. Thankfully, a respect for history kept the old man from burning even those documents whose contents he abhorred.

Still, he had found nothing in Selwyn's collections to rival the promises of this little gem. It was an archaic document, and knowledge would now have moved on beyond what was known to the alchemists of its time, but he was sure that one of these eight would serve his purpose.

The booklet felt even more fragile than he'd remembered, and he flicked past the introduction to the first formula. The first entry in the book, fate's hand, was described as a subtle weapon, bringing the victim to a slow yet inexorable end over a period of weeks. That wasn't what he was after at all. The second entry sounded little better, and the third, rather heretically named Oelum's balm, relied on the transformation of copper, an advanced technique he'd yet to master.

The fourth entry, however, held promise. False awakening. The ingredients were simple, and the result promised to be quick. That was just what Ailith would need if she was to get out of the castle unharmed.

The thought of her girded his resolve. He was playing with fire, but what was the alternative? What if Leofwin had seen straight through their charade? Ailith was many things, but she was obviously no noblewoman. His letter, with everything it left unsaid but obviously implied, could have made things worse for her. He needed to get her out of danger, and the sooner the better.

He skimmed the second half of the booklet, but false awakening remained the most likely to do what he needed. Garrick scratched out a copy of the directions, and returned the original to its protective sleeve. It would be safer not to take the booklet itself back to the temple. He suspected that Selwyn could piece things together just from the list of ingredients, but one slip of paper was easier to hide, as well as being replaceable in a way the original certainly was not.

Buying the ingredients would be another matter entirely. Possession of even a couple of the constituent poisons would be enough to hang him, if he weren't a lord. No respectable alchemist kept stocks of such things, nor could he ask anyone in the Guild to help him source them. He would have to find someone more disreputable.

As he lowered himself back into the stable yard, his thoughts turned to Malachi. Whatever the itinerant alchemist was, he wasn't quite a part of their community, and something in the way he spoke made it clear that danger was an old bedfellow. He'd brought the news to Selwyn in the first place, and seemed to be keeping tabs on Ailith, so he evidently had something invested in this… though it would be better to know what, before getting into the old man's debt.

He couldn't be trusted, but perhaps he could help.

The only question was how to find a wanderer.

Chapter Twenty-Nine

Ailith was exploring the passages at the far end of the castle when she thought she heard Leofwin's voice. She snuffed her lantern and flattened herself against the wall. It hadn't been solely down to luck that she'd never encountered him in the tunnels, but she certainly had been lucky. She'd tried to tip the balance in her favour by keeping her explorations to the evenings, after dinner, times when she knew he was invariably busy.

Ever since the incident with Rethar, she'd been especially watchful. Leofwin had seemed more amused than angry with her, but he obviously hadn't been pleased, either. She didn't want to risk his displeasure a second time.

She was in an unfamiliar part of the castle, and it had been some time since she'd passed a turning. There was nowhere to hide if he was coming this way.

"What have you learnt today?" he asked.

Her breath caught. What could she say that would adequately justify her post-prandial wanderings within the walls? She couldn't afford to let him know why she was interested in secret passages. She caught herself from speaking just in time, as a second voice responded to the question.

"The volume you brought me last week has some interesting new fingerings," the voice said. "I'm growing rather fond of the harp."

"And it of you, I think. It suits you."

Ailith edged a little closer to the sound. If Leofwin was in conversation with a stranger, he couldn't be in the secret passages with her; he must be in some unknown room beyond the walls. And in that case, she'd be interested to see who it was that had him discussing music. It wasn't a side of Leofwin that she'd ever seen; unlike her, he didn't seem to sing or even hum to himself as he worked.

"Are your new tricks ready for an audience, yet?"

"I'm not sure." The second voice was comparatively young, and uncertain. Ailith wondered to whom it belonged, and why they hadn't been introduced. The castle had few enough permanent inhabitants — besides the two of them, it was all staff and servants. Leofwin had said something about never having married, but that didn't preclude a string of mistresses and bastard children — was this some secret son he'd tucked away in a far corner of the castle?

"Try," Leofwin said, with a tone she recognised all too well from their lessons together. Did he teach music as well as alchemy? She felt an inexplicable flare of jealousy at the very idea. She didn't want to share his attentions.

The boy had started to pluck out notes on what she assumed was the harp. Ailith couldn't find a peep-hole with a view into the room, but with a little trial and error she found the point in the corridor where the sound was clearest, and held still to listen as strains of music floated through the air. The tune was like nothing she recognised; it rose and fell in complex patterns that spelled out melancholy and joy in turn. It held her captivated until the player's fingers slipped, twanging against the strings and bringing her back down to earth with a jolt.

"Once more."

The musician damped the vibrating strings and started again, picking out single notes at first, gradually building up the interlocking rhythms of the piece. This time he managed to keep his composure as he picked up the pace, until the dramatic crescendo that signalled the end.

"Better." She could hear the smile in Leofwin's voice; could picture the crinkling of his eyes that always accompanied that one word.

"I've a long way to go before I'll be half as good as I am at the flute, but you're right. The harp has more possibilities."

"And leaves you your voice for singing."

"Right. That's an instrument I've yet to master."

"One with fewer instructional manuscripts, I fear, but I'll see what I can find for you."

"What I need," the musician said wistfully, "is a teacher."

"You know it can't be arranged."

"I can dream."

Leofwin tsked. "I thought you'd understood the futility of living in your imagination."

"I've days enough to fill." His voice was bitter, and Ailith wondered at the story behind his words. "I can afford to waste some of my time."

"As you wish." Something in Leofwin's tone told her this was a discussion they'd had before.

"Would you like to hear the other piece I've been practising?"

"Not tonight," Leofwin said. "It's getting late, and you should eat your supper. You can play it for me tomorrow."

"Tomorrow, then. Goodnight."

"Goodnight, Anselm."

Anselm?

Perhaps she'd been wrong about the age of the musician: he sounded young, but Anselm must be nearing fifty. And she'd been expecting to find her quarry locked in a dungeon rather than plucking on a harp. But unless Leofwin just happened to have a different captive of the same name as her grandfather... well, that wasn't impossible. She could easily imagine how, in the telling and retelling of rumours, such a confusion could have arisen. And if it wasn't the right Anselm, she could tell Malachi there was nothing to be done, and perhaps then she could continue her studies here.

She felt guilty at how much she hoped for it.

Yet if this Anselm was held prisoner, didn't she have just as much responsibility to him? Why did it matter whose son or father he was? With instruments like that, it didn't sound like he was imprisoned. But if he wasn't shut away, she wondered why she hadn't met him.

She searched again for a peep-hole, finding nothing that would give her a view over the room. There were a couple of promising indents in the wall, but when she inserted a curious finger into one it was met by a layer of thick tapestry. No wonder she couldn't see through.

Ailith snuck back the next night, and the next. It was something of a relief to know where Leofwin always vanished to after dinner. From what she could work out, he always took a hot meal to Anselm's quarters, along with a platter of cold cuts for Anselm's breakfast and lunch, reinforcing the idea that the boy was in some way captive. But their meetings were cordial: Leofwin would ask the boy about his progress, and Anselm would play some music by way of response. Usually it was the harp, but occasionally he would take up his flute instead. Neither of them said anything to help her discern the history of their relationship, and despite her continued searching of the castle, she couldn't find her way around to the door.

Chapter Thirty

It had taken a little effort to track Malachi down, but once found, the ancient alchemist proved useful for more than just the procurement of obscure ingredients. Garrick had been in the process of elaborating a complex plan to get Selwyn out of the temple for long enough that he could prepare his amalgam, when Malachi had revealed a little secret of his own. The back of his fortune teller's cart opened up to display a compact but fully-equipped alchemist's laboratory.

"So I don't think you need make this in the temple, m'boy," Malachi said, laughing at Garrick's surprise. "Best not be waving such things in the gods' faces, eh?"

"Perhaps not," Garrick agreed, although he was far more afraid of Selwyn than of the gods.

"What do you want with an old recipe like this, anyway?"

"I'm going to rescue Ailith," Garrick said. And although he immediately regretted his rash words, he couldn't put them back in his mouth.

"Are you, now? Well, well. There's a thing."

"You mustn't tell Selwyn."

"Mustn't I? You'll need companions, though. Can't go running off on a quest like that all alone, m'boy. That's not how it works at all. Perhaps you'd let me read your stones, see if we can't find a little guidance for you?"

It was superstitious nonsense, of course. The troupes of players and musicians that flowed through the Highfort's gates often brought along a tame fortune teller, and they invariably came up with some witty and inoffensive story to pander to their hosts. Father lapped up every simpering word, while Garrick scowled and made plans to have such charlatans driven from every inch of his lands once the barony was his to command.

But he could tell there was no sense in arguing with Malachi, and he needed to stay on the right side of the old man until his preparations were complete. He allowed the stones to be placed into his hands.

"Keep about half," Malachi instructed, as if he didn't know the game. "Set the others aside. Now, shake those up a bit and spread them here on the table. That'll do. Hmm, what have we here…"

He reached over and turned those stones which had landed the wrong way up, before chalking a line to connect four of the stones across the middle of the board.

"This is your timeline. In the past, the spur of these events, we have Fertility, Bereket in his human aspect." Malachi pointed to the all-too-familiar symbol. "That obviously signifies Ailith, in this instance, with all her youth and innocence. Now in the present, here, you have the Storm and the Hunt. Strong signs, these, and well-fitted to a hero's journey."

"Good." Garrick didn't have to believe in fortune tellers, but every sign in his favour was a reassurance nonetheless. You never knew when the gods would choose to give you an omen, or in what guise.

"And the future is interesting."

"Snow," Garrick said, reading the symbol. An aspect of Oelum, Lady of Death: it wouldn't have been his first choice.

"Yes, and she's a hard one to interpret," Malachi said. "But Oelum in any aspect tends to mean difficult decisions and challenging situations. Now, the rest of the spread is quite unremarkable, but look here. Prosperity and the Earthquake have landed in the sphere of friendships, which suggests you need friends who are strong and wealthy."

"I have wealthy friends," Garrick said, since the old man already knew who he was.

"You should use them. Now," he tapped his fingernail against

Garrick's list. "I'll be occupied for a few days finding your ingredients. Meet me after sundown, three days from now, and you can make your amalgam here."

"And you won't tell Selwyn. Swear it."

"Don't worry, I won't spill your secrets. A man could benefit from a young baron being in his debt, don't you think?"

And that, Garrick realised with a start, was exactly what he should be afraid of. He wasn't the only noble in the game. Perhaps Malachi was right when he said he needed companions, and in Bracklea he had only one acquaintance who might be prevailed upon to help.

Everyone knew that Orvyn's money was dirty, stained as it was with the dust of the mines and smoke of iron foundries, but the family had been rich for just about long enough to pass without comment in polite society. Orvyn had even managed to wed the third daughter of a minor lord. The fact that Orvyn and Totte both had magical talent was surely not irrelevant to the match, although it probably came second to the fact that Totte's father was struggling with ancestral lands that didn't bring much of a profit, forcing him to accept that dirty money was better than no money at all.

Aside from Selwyn, they were also the only members of the Guild to know Garrick's true identity.

Their country manor was an hour's steady ride beyond the outskirts of Bracklea, but Garrick took some of his frustration out on the horse and he made it in half the usual time. A surprised servant started to murmur something about the lateness of the hour, but Garrick's stern gaze cowed him and he was soon settled in the tiny sitting room that served as an antechamber, while his horse was stabled and his hosts informed of his arrival. And before he'd even had chance to demand refreshments, he was being waved through to the drawing room where his friends were enjoying an after-dinner drink.

They both rose to greet him with bows and curtseys as befitted his true station. In private, where there was nothing to be gained by anonymity, it would have been markedly offensive if they hadn't, yet it was strange to receive obeisances while dressed in his apprentice's garb.

"My lord Garrick," Orvyn said, clapping him on the shoulder and leading him to an overstuffed chair that had been decorated with an excess of tasteless embroidery. "What brings you out here so unexpectedly?"

"Let's have a drink, first," Garrick said, sinking into the chair. It was important to handle these things properly, and now that he'd ridden all the way out here he was starting to wonder if he shouldn't after all have waited for a more civilised hour. They wouldn't be leaving for a few days; minutes or hours more would make little enough difference.

"Of course." Orvyn rang the bell to summon his parlour maid. "Bring out the best Wulfsberg icewine. And then prepare a room, our guest won't be wanting to ride all the way back to town tonight."

Garrick nodded. "My thanks."

"It's nothing," Totte said. "But come, tell us why you're here. If it was only for the pleasure of our company then you wouldn't be arriving after nightfall."

"I can only apologise for that," Garrick said, then fell into silence as the maid returned to deliver the wine.

"Tell me what's troubling you."

"We made a mistake letting the girl go to Watersmeet," he said. "And you heard Selwyn at the Guild meeting. He doesn't care what happens to her if there's half a chance she'll bring his son home."

"It was a fool's plan," Orvyn said. "And risky. Everyone knows Watersmeet has a cruel streak."

"Is he really so bad?" Totte asked.

"Worse," Garrick said.

"My sister was offered to him, you know," she said. "But then I think everyone with a daughter to offer has made an attempt to snare him."

It was all Garrick could do not to laugh. Of course every family within a thousand miles would have offered up their daughters, but a family like Totte's would have no chance with one of the Twelve, even one who was more inclined to wed. If you were marrying to cement an alliance, it had better be to a worthy ally. And if you were more interested in the dowry… well, the less said about that, the better.

"I have to do something," Garrick said. "Did you know I wrote a letter of introduction for her? It was a moment of weakness, but you saw how determined she was, and I thought it would be better if she at least had something in her hand."

"In your own name?" Orvyn asked.

"My father's." There seemed little enough point in denying it, now. "But I can't sit around and wait for him to see through her pretence."

"What are you planning?"

"I'll visit. He could hardly refuse me if I turned up at his gate, and it would give me the chance to talk with Ailith. Perhaps these past weeks will have proved that she's out of her depth. Perhaps she can be persuaded to come home."

"You're sweet on her, aren't you?" Totte said gently.

"It's not about that," Garrick said, flustered. "No, that's not it at all. And besides, she's a peasant."

"That means nothing if you love her."

"Love? This has nothing to do with love, and everything to do with responsibility. If I hadn't put my seal on that letter he might have turned her away at the door, and we'd all be the better for it."

"And what of Selywn's wishes?" Orvyn asked. "Does he know what you're doing?"

"He knows nothing of this, and I'd be grateful if it stayed that way."

Orvyn frowned. "I see."

"But if there's anything to learn, the girl should have learnt it by now, and if there isn't then there's no sense leaving her in danger. Selwyn's judgement is clouded by emotion. I'll be going without him, but I need a retinue. I was hoping you could be persuaded to attend me."

"Of course," Totte said before Orvyn could answer. Noble-born herself, she knew full well that they had no choice in the matter when their lord made such a request. "We can take most of our staff, and the road to Watersmeet passes through my father's lands, so you can gather a few more attendants on the way."

Chapter Thirty-One

Ailith knocked, but immediately regretted it as a barrage of curse words came from behind the bedroom door.

"I'll come back later, shall I?" she said, backing away. "No problem."

The door flew open.

"That wasn't directed at you."

Ailith nodded, still poised to retreat.

"I mean it," he said, his voice softening a little. "Come in, tell me what you were after."

The Leofwin who ushered her into the room looked nothing like his usual self, quite aside from the dark look on his face. Gone was the simple linen tunic and worn leather jerkin, replaced by an embroidered silk shirt that was open to halfway down his chest. The thin fabric fluttered as he moved. Ailith averted her eyes as he fiddled to try and close the tiny gold buttons, only to find herself staring at his stockinged feet. She had no idea why he was getting smartened up, but the idea of watching him dress was ridiculously uncomfortable. When Thurstan told her that his lordship was in his bedchamber, she should have known better than to disturb him.

"I just came to ask you about the mice, but you're obviously busy. It can wait."

"*They* can wait."

"Who?"

"Unexpected visitors, some lordling or other with his retinue. They can't see me looking like a peasant worker, can they? So I have to…" He waved his hands to indicate his costume. "I look ridiculous, but no doubt they'll all look ridiculous, too. It's part of the game."

Ailith thought the style rather suited him, but only a fool would have said as much when he was already fuming. Instead, she asked, "Should I make myself scarce?"

"You can stay here, I'll see them in the Lower Hall. Or come, if you want to be bored to tears, but I can't imagine there will be anything of interest to you. Or me. You'll have more fun with the mice. What was it you wanted to know?"

"It's only that one of the girls seems to have put on a lot of weight, and I don't think it's down to anything I've done. I wondered if there was any chance we'd put a boy in with them by mistake."

"Anything is possible." He shrugged. "More mice is a problem we can handle, but it might spoil your experiments if one of your subjects is pregnant."

"Yes, or male. I wanted to keep as many things as possible the same."

"Naturally." As he spoke he emptied the glittering contents of a mahogany box onto the dressing table, and picked out an emerald-encrusted buckle to cinch the belt tightly at his waist. "You might separate the one that's getting heavy into a cage of her own, and check the sex again for the others. That's what I'd do."

He slid a couple of heavy gold rings onto his fingers, lifted an emerald green cloak from its peg, and turned to leave.

"What about your hair?" she asked.

"What about it?"

"It seems a shame to dress up in all this finery but leave your hair hanging loose like a curtain. Even a couple of small braids would make all the difference, neaten it up a bit."

He shook his head. "That's too much like hard work. If they want me to braid my hair, they could at least send a herald ahead to announce themselves before arriving. This kind of impromptu visit doesn't warrant the effort."

"I'll do it. It's a moment's work, nothing more." She placed her hands on his shoulders and pushed him back into the chair at his dressing table. The silk was cool beneath her fingers. "Sit still."

"You?" He looked curiously at her.

"I did my sister's wedding braids." She walked quickly to the back of his chair before he could sense the uncertainty building in her mind. "This is nothing."

"Here." The comb he handed back to her was heavy, the ornamental handle inlaid with an assortment of gems which made it lumpy and difficult to grasp. Fortunately it didn't look like there was much in the way of tangles to be worked out. She pulled his hair behind his ears at both sides, and spread it across his back so she could see what she had to work with.

"Your hair's very soft," she said, running her fingers from the crown of his head down to his shoulders. She knew she was talking to fill the silence, but she couldn't stop her mouth. From the moment she'd taken charge her heart had been pounding in her ears, and though her fingers knew what they were doing her head was suddenly full of wool. "It's aristocratic hair. Nothing like mine or my sisters'."

He laughed. "I wouldn't be a very good alchemist if I couldn't work out how to keep unruly hair under control."

She separated a section at his right temple and started to divide it for the first braid. "Tell me?"

"No, apprentice. You tell me."

"I'd start by cutting a few locks and dipping them in whatever was lying around, but I don't suppose you'll let me do it that way. At least, not with your hair."

"Not right now. Anyway, it's good for you to think about the theory."

"Okay. Let's assume you have to keep the moisture in, to keep it soft." Ailith relaxed as she started to think it through, her concentration shifting away from the man beneath her hands, leaving her fingers to weave as she focused on the puzzle. "My hands are always softer after I've been cooking with butter or oil, so maybe that would be a good place to start."

She leaned forwards a little and sniffed surreptitiously at his head.

"No cheating."

Chastened, she blushed and pulled away. How had he known?

The scent was informative, though: almonds. Was it possible to extract enough oil from those? Her finger brushed his neck and she started, jolted from her analysis by the unexpected warmth of his skin.

"Almonds," she blurted to hide her embarrassment. "You're using oil from almonds. But they're so expensive. There must be a cheaper way, something normal people could afford."

She tucked the first braid out of the way, and moved over to create a mirror image on the other side. This time, however, her attention refused to be distracted by thoughts of alchemy. As hard as she tried, she could focus on nothing but the pressure of his hair against her fingers, the way she tugged against his scalp, and precisely how many hairs' breadths separated her skin from his at every moment — a distance it felt crucial to maximise. She was determined not to brush against his skin again, not when her mouth was still dry from the last time. It was strange enough to have her fingers in his hair. She worked her way down towards his shoulders, drawing the two braids together until she could interleave them at the nape of his neck.

"Done."

"There are pins on the table," Leofwin said.

"You don't need pins. Those won't shake loose, not unless you're planning to dance a lively jig."

She stepped back to get a better view of her work, and he considered his reflection in the looking glass. The looking glass, of course. No wonder he'd spotted her sniffing at his hair.

"Thank you," he said, getting to his feet.

"At least now you look like someone with staff to tidy you up."

She watched as he draped the cloak around his shoulders, using a penannular brooch the size of her palm to fasten it at one side. The diamonds on the pin alone could have bought a small estate.

"Why *don't* you have staff doing this?"

"Apparently, I have you." He shrugged, straightened his shoulders, and set his face into a formal mask. "Now, business awaits."

Swathed in a cascade of green velvet which skimmed the ground as he walked, he suddenly looked thrice three times more intimidating than he ever had in regular clothes. Ailith watched as he strode from the room. Though she knew her own work had contributed to the severity of his appearance, she still wasn't immune to the effect.

And he hadn't answered her question. For a mighty lord, Leofwin seemed to go out of his way to avoid being served by his servants.

Chapter Thirty-Two

"How long will he keep us waiting?"

"As long as it suits him," the young lord replied, a slight pout to his lips.

Leofwin stood in the secret passage which ran above the Lower Hall and observed his uninvited guests through a chink in the wall. The room was opulently decorated, hung with fine tapestries and dotted with elegant statues, but lacking such basic functional furniture as chairs. A cheap trick designed to wear down the resolve of an unwanted guest, but sometimes cheap tricks were all you had at your disposal, and this kind of unheralded imposition deserved nothing better. And he wanted to see a little of Ailith's sponsor before speaking with him.

"If we'd sent a messenger he'd have no excuse for this kind of behaviour," the boy went on. He really did look very like his father, especially when he scowled. "But in the circumstances I thought it was better to have an element of surprise."

"Yes, in the circumstances. Won't it raise questions, though?"

Garrick shrugged. "I can hardly avoid that. I came to speak with him, and I shall."

Leofwin smiled to himself. This was getting more interesting by the minute. Perhaps the boy wouldn't be a complete bore, after all. He made his way down to join them.

"Young Highfort." Leofwin gave a curt nod. "I'm afraid your unheralded arrival has me at a disadvantage. Who are your companions?"

"My cousin Wymark," he said, indicating a scrawny young man flanked by two attendants of his own.

Wymark, whose head was already bowed, straightened just enough to be able to bow again.

"Orvyn, a minor lord of my fief, with Totte, his lady wife."

Leofwin took her hand and placed a polite kiss on her gloved fingers, as Garrick continued to name the host of minor nobles who attended him. Aside from Wymark, who held a distant claim to Highfort, there was no-one whose family would have dared place demands on his hospitality in their own right — divine guest-right or no. He couldn't help feeling Garrick had brought them along merely to add to the inconvenience.

"The rest are your servants?" Leofwin asked, casting a skeptical eye over the assembly. "They would be more comfortable in the servants' quarters, I think. My staff will attend to your needs while you're here, so your people can get some rest before your onward journey."

Garrick nodded. "And perhaps you could arrange rooms for my guests? I would speak with you alone before we dine."

"It will take time to prepare enough rooms, milord," Thurstan murmured in his ear. Leofwin nodded.

But it wasn't their fault the brat had brought them along, so at least he could see Garrick's attendants comfortably seated. He waved over a young serving boy. "See our guests settled in the Drawing Room, and show young Highfort's staff where they can sleep."

Once they were alone in the hall, he turned his attention back to Garrick.

"Did you think I might arrange to be unavailable, if you'd done me the courtesy of sending a herald?" he said. He might have considered it, but the boy didn't know that. This way at least he began with the moral advantage, and he was determined to press it. "I don't for a moment believe you were just passing by."

"No, I came to talk to you."

"On what business?"

"I wanted to see how Ailith's settling in."

"You've come a long way, then, to do what could have been achieved by a letter."

"I trust she reached you safely, but your reputation precedes you," Garrick said stiffly. "I would never forgive myself if she came here in good faith and found herself a hostage or worse."

"If that's what you intended with your charming letter of introduction, I think you might need to work on your phrasing. I took it she was to be my guest."

"She is."

"But you don't trust me." Leofwin nodded. "I understand."

"You can't stop me from seeing her. I sponsored her to come here, she's my responsibility."

"If she wishes to see you, I will permit it, of course."

"Fetch her. If she doesn't come, I have no choice but to assume it's because you've harmed her."

Leofwin raised a skeptical eyebrow. "You share your father's temper, I see."

It was either the best or the worst thing he could have said, and even looking back on the rest of the evening's events, he wasn't quite sure which.

"I share nothing with him! Nothing but a name and an accident of birth!"

"And his seal, apparently." Leofwin pitched his voice soft and low, in deliberate contrast to the boy's outburst. "Tell me, does your lord father know you've already begun to appropriate his power?"

"I haven't…" Garrick spluttered. "I don't… You wouldn't dare."

"You have, and I would. Consider that, before you insult me beneath my own roof. You'll see Ailith at dinner. If she wishes to call on you sooner, it will be her decision."

Chapter Thirty-Three

"It seems you may wish to speak with my visitor, after all," Leofwin said. "He was certainly persistent in his demands to see you."

"Who is it?" Ailith asked, barely glancing up from her papers.

"Do you have so many noble friends that you have to ask? It's your young sponsor from Highfort."

"Oh." She chewed thoughtfully on a stalk of fennel. "Demands, does he?"

"He's waiting in the Lower Hall."

"How does this work?" Ailith asked. "He stands to inherit the barony where I live, but we're not in his fief, and you've chosen to take me in. Must I do as he says?"

"You're really quite something, aren't you?" Leofwin said, barely suppressing a laugh. "I wonder when you'll run out of surprises."

"I like to know where I stand."

"You're my student, and this is my seat. No-one can command you. But the young man would like to see you, and it behoves us to indulge our guests when we can."

"That's fine." Ailith set aside the stalk, straightened her clothes, and smiled at her reflection in the window. "I'll go. I just wanted to know the rules first."

"He has no hold over you," Leofwin repeated. "If he bores you, you can dismiss him with no hard feelings."

"I think he'd take that very hard indeed, but I'm glad to know I'm under no obligation."

As she walked, she wondered what he could want with her. She hadn't spoken to him since Wicker's Cross; she hadn't even written to let him know she'd arrived. And as far as she knew he hadn't sent her any letters, either, but that had been no surprise because she couldn't think of anything he could possibly have to say to her. Not unless he was going to apologise, and he didn't strike her as the apologetic kind.

He was standing beside a bust of Keyif to the left of the Lower Hall, with that air of practised nonchalance which had seemed so charming when she'd thought he was a strangely well-spoken orphan. If his dress and manner in Wicker's Cross had taken her by surprise, then nothing could have prepared her for the finery that now bedecked him. He was every inch the lord, his silk tunic trimmed with cloth of gold and his breeches striped with red brocade. His boots were polished to such a shine that they could have served as mirrors. And if it hadn't been such a ridiculous idea, she would have sworn he'd even dusted his face with some kind of lightly sparkling powder.

"Ailith." He took up both her hands and leaned in to kiss her on the cheek. Yes, there was definitely something strange about the texture of his skin.

"Garrick," she said, forcing a smile and taking a tiny step back. "Or is there another way I should address you, these days?"

He waved away her concerns with a flick of the wrist. "It will be Garrick again once we're both back in Bracklea, so I won't insist on formalities here."

"Well. Good."

They stood awkwardly for a long and painful moment. She thought of asking him what he wanted, but aside from being unutterably rude, she couldn't avoid worrying about all the passages and peep-holes that riddled the walls. If Leofwin was watching them, then one careless word from Garrick could ruin everything she'd worked for.

"This isn't a good place to talk," she said. "Let's take a walk around the yard. Or, no, the battlements would be nicer."

"That's a most inappropriate way to treat a guest," he said. "Not that you would know about such things, but I thought you might have picked up some manners by now. After four days of riding, the last thing I want to do is take a walk."

"I'm not suggesting it to make you uncomfortable. But," Ailith lowered her voice, "I want to be able to talk to you without fear of being overheard. The alternative is to sit here and speak of nothing."

Garrick looked her up and down, taking in the lines of her dress. It was only one of her everyday frocks, but it was tailored to fit her body like none of the hand-me-down dresses she'd lived in at home.

"I can think of plenty of things we could do besides talking," he said.

"Come on." She held the door open. "I'll show you around. Have you been to Watersmeet before?"

"Not that I recall."

"The Lower Hall — that's this one — has the nicest murals, but the Upper Hall is bigger. And the Great Hall has the banqueting table, but I'm sure you've seen enough dining halls. Let's go up on the ramparts, there are some wonderful views over the river."

She usually took a shortcut through the walls, herself, so she had to think for a moment before leading the way to the nearest staircase. There were always archers keeping watch at the front of the castle, where the battlements overlooked the town, but here they were by the river and patrols of scouts walked these walls only a couple of times each day. It should be safe to talk here without fear of being disturbed.

Garrick lounged against the battlement and caught Ailith's hand. "I really hope you wanted to get me alone for something more interesting than admiring the river."

"Please," Ailith said. "Stop pretending. We both know you're not really interested in me."

He ran his hands from her shoulders down to her waist, and pulled her towards him until she was standing between his legs. "I'm very interested in every single inch of you."

"But you're a lord. You can't marry a potter's daughter, even if she is a mage."

"You're right, of course," he said, but didn't release her. "Indeed, for quite some time I can't marry at all — every one of the

Twelve needs to know I could be available for their daughters or granddaughters, so I'd say it's at least twenty years before I can afford to close that door. But I'm sure we could come to a suitable arrangement in the meantime."

"You won't marry me, and I won't be anyone's mistress. I don't think that leaves much space for negotiation."

"Ailith, I don't mean to offend, but you've said it yourself. You have no viable prospects."

"Perhaps not. But I don't need a good marriage, do I? Mama was wrong. With alchemy, I'll have a trade of my own."

"A trade you cannot practice in public."

"People manage."

"But imagine, I could find you a modest hunting lodge somewhere in the forests of Highfort where you could pursue your little hobby without fear of discovery. Maybe even an apartment in the castle, once I inherit." His hand wandered across her back. "You'd get more from being my mistress than from being some merchant's wife."

"We can discuss this another time." Though there was little enough to discuss. Ailith stepped back, forcing him to drop his hands. "You didn't come here to try and seduce me."

"I came to make sure you were okay — and to see if we can get a result a little quicker than all this sneaking around. Selwyn wants to do everything so slowly, putting our progress in the hands of the gods, but if it was my son I wouldn't want him left in the hands of a madman for a day longer than necessary."

"Leofwin isn't mad."

"He's most certainly very dangerous. The fact that he appears to have charmed you is yet more proof of his guile."

"He's been nothing but kind to me."

Garrick shook his head. "You disappoint me. You're assuming he's harmless just because he hasn't hurt you yet. Don't lose sight of why you're here."

"I haven't," Ailith said, although in her heart she feared she had been a bit lax.

"Whatever Leofwin says, don't forget that he's kept Anselm prisoner for some thirty years — if he hasn't killed him."

Ailith bit her lip. "I think he's alive."

"Then you need to get out of here as soon as you can. Here, I brought something to help you."

He reached into a well-hidden pocket and drew out a small leather pouch, from which he pulled a tiny dart.

"What is it?"

"Be careful. That's sharp, and it's drugged."

"Poison?" She held it warily, touching as little of the dart as she could. "I'm not a murderer."

And he was suggesting she kill someone she actually rather liked, though she wasn't about to mention that fact to Garrick. He was being prickly enough already.

"It's a harmless sedative," he said, tucking it smoothly back into the pouch. "And you need it. If you try to break Anselm out of the dungeons without taking any precautions, the only thing you'll achieve is a double execution. This way you can both sneak out while Leofwin sleeps."

"I don't know…"

"Every day you spend here is simply increasing the danger. What if he finds out who you really are? What then?"

Ailith had to bite her tongue to stop herself blurting out that Leofwin already knew exactly who she was, and had been a good deal nicer about it than he was. But it would gain her nothing, and if she annoyed Garrick too much he might start to make things difficult for her.

"Listen," he said, misinterpreting her hesitation. "If you don't want to do this, you're free to leave."

She frowned at him. "What?"

"I mean it. You're safe. He won't dare to stop you leaving with me."

"I've always been free to come and go as I choose."

"What, with that tyrant watching your every step? He might want you to believe you're free, but have you seen the number of guards in this place? You're obviously a prisoner."

"I'm fine." There was nothing to be gained from arguing about semantics. "But I'm here to help Anselm. I won't leave without him, I swore it."

"Then you need to get on with it. I know about your little arrangement with Malachi," he went on, oblivious to her mounting frustration. "If you can drug Leofwin on the full moon, we can help you get Anselm out of the castle before anyone knows there's a problem."

"I'll try," she said. The full moon was only a couple of days away, and she'd been hoping to put Malachi off for another month with the simple news that Anselm was alive. The last thing she wanted was a deadline, but she feared she was being selfish. She tucked the pouch inside her dress and hoped she could forget about it. "Do we have anything else do discuss, or shall I leave you to enjoy the scenery?"

He tried again to persuade her that kissing would be an appropriate pastime, but she wasn't going to fall for that one ever again.

She returned to her room to find Frida waiting. The maid had prepared a tub with steaming, scented water, and laid out a couple of Ailith's beautiful new dresses on the bed.

"For the feast," she explained at Ailith's puzzled expression.

"I don't feel like feasting." She was too incensed by Garrick's behaviour to imagine sitting calmly across from him in the Great Hall.

"His lordship especially requested that you attend him." There was a hint of apology in Frida's voice, but also a tone that said there would be no getting out of it.

"Leofwin is going, this time?"

"Yes, it's most unusual. But you're to dress up nice and join him in the Drawing Room before dinner."

"Aren't you supposed to do as I say?"

"Usually, yes."

"What if I said that I want to read quietly for a bit, and then go to bed?"

"I'm to do as you say as long as I've not been told to do something different, but his lordship has sent for you. I'll be in trouble if you say no."

Ailith reluctantly allowed herself to be bathed and dried, and gave directions for her hair to be braided in one of her favourite designs. She picked a gown of deep purple silk, its bodice embroidered with threads of gold and emerald and lilac. It was just as well she'd been measured for beautiful dresses as well as work clothes, and she was glad in hindsight that Frida had spoken with the tailor, guiding him towards fabrics that would complement the colours of Leofwin's heraldry. The matching silk slippers, which he'd insisted she would need, felt cold and insubstantial on her feet.

"His lordship sent these for you."

Frida lifted a heavy teak box from the sideboard, its lid inlaid with a geometric design of ebony and ivory. Ailith flicked open the clasps and lifted the lid. The box contained three trays which fanned out with the lid, each lined with ancient black velvet and filled with a dazzling array of jewellery. She gasped. Gently, almost afraid that she might break something, she fingered a gold filigree pendant.

"If I might be so bold?"

"Of course."

Frida reached down to the second layer and plucked out a thin necklace. She looped the chain around Ailith's neck, and arranged the trailing jewels before holding up the looking glass. A cascade of emeralds and amethysts hung across her collarbones, suspended from golden threads so light as to be almost invisible. Ailith admired her reflection: it was a good choice, and could have been designed to go with the dress. Frida had woven some gems into her hair, as well, and she positively sparkled in the lamplight.

"Beautiful," she said, as Frida hooked a matching pair of earrings into her ears, and found a ring for her middle finger that was set with a single bold emerald. "Will I meet his lordship's expectations, do you think?"

"I'll say!" Frida giggled. "Can you imagine Ymma's face if she saw you? You've tried so hard to show us you're not a lady, and now this."

Leofwin was alone in the Drawing Room when she arrived, pacing up and down the length of the room, his face set in a grim scowl. She hovered in the doorway, reluctant to announce herself when he was in such an obviously foul mood, but he noticed her before she could work up the courage to speak.

"There you are."

"Yes, my lord." Something about the occasion, the dress, and the impending feast made her lapse into a stiff formality of manners, and she was breathless from the tight lacing of the corset. He glanced up at her, surprised. Then he stopped pacing and really looked, raking his eyes up from the tips of her toes, following the line of her dress up to where the scooped neckline skimmed the top of her breasts. She twisted her fingers anxiously together. Frida had done a fantastic job at making her look like a noblewoman, but were the gemstones too much? Had Leofwin really expected her to pick out such expensive pieces to wear? And this was the first time he'd seen her in one of the fine dresses his money had bought for her.

"You're nervous." He stepped across and took her hands, his expression softening. "Did things go badly with our young guest?"

"He's an idiot, that's all." She could have said more — he'd been rude and presumptive and dismissive all at once, and her anger flared just thinking of what he'd suggested — but she didn't feel like explaining the nature of his offences. Besides, she was struggling to think of anything at that moment beyond the warmth of Leofwin's hands on hers and the intensity of his eyes on her face.

"Ah, well, that gives you the opportunity to learn an important lesson about holding court. Which is to say, there's nothing more satisfying than to have a wonderful time at dinner while ignoring someone who has offended you."

"Couldn't we ignore him better by dining in the garden?"

"I'm glad you like my little garden, and truly, I'd be happier there myself. But tonight I think we will serve ourselves better by ignoring him in public."

"But you never…"

"I prefer not to indulge in these games. From time to time, though, you meet someone who insists on playing, and on those occasions it's important to win. And I know his type — the best way you can needle young Highfort is to make it perfectly clear how happy you are with everyone but him. Stand up straight, curtsey to no-one, and remember you are my equal. He has no hold over you."

Ailith twirled a little, until her skirt filled out with air. Perhaps she could do worse than to show Garrick how much she'd changed over the past few weeks.

"That's better," he said. "A smile is a weapon, as sharp as any sword. Especially on the face of a beautiful woman."

"Oh."

Leofwin offered his arm, and pulled her close as they walked towards the banqueting hall, covering her hand with his own. "Every time you smile at me, you stab him just a little."

Ohhhh. She nodded. The ways of court were a mystery to her, but some things were universal. Leofwin would flirt with her to get under Garrick's skin, and she could have her taste of revenge by flirting right back. She understood that well enough. And it was a strange sort of relief to know why Leofwin was suddenly looking at her like a woman, and holding her with the tender touch of a lover. She'd been afraid it was just a side-effect of the way her dress was cut, and she didn't want to think he was that sort of man.

Chapter Thirty-Four

As they waited for the feast to begin, Totte and Wymark studied the paintings and tapestries which adorned the oak-clad walls of the banqueting hall. Garrick looked on with rather less interest. Avelin, eighth Lord Baron of Watersmeet, looked down on them with a kindly smile, but there was no accompanying portrait of Leofwin. Compared to the Vaulted Hall at the Highfort there was a marked dearth of antlers and stuffed wolf-heads, and the portrait subjects sat demurely in halls and drawing rooms rather than posing with horses and hounds and prey. But then the lands hereabout, while agriculturally rich, were much less suited to hunting. Father would have hated it, but that was why Father had traded away his most productive lands as soon as times got hard.

Then Ailith walked in, taking his breath and his attention away.

He'd seen her only a few short hours earlier, but the transformation was absolute. Then she had been in a practical dress, her cuffs stained with the residue of alchemical experiments, her hair knotted at the nape of her neck. Now she wore a floor-length gown of purple silk, and jewels that were obviously Watersmeet heirlooms. A subtle scattering of diamonds had even been woven into the tight braids of her hair. He wondered if she knew she'd been decorated with gems that could buy the whole town of Bracklea thrice over. She didn't look overwhelmed, though, or out of place in her borrowed finery. She looked… stunning. That was the only word for it. And he was duly stunned.

But the most shocking thing was the way she held herself close to Leofwin's side, her fingers curled comfortably around his arm, as if she belonged there. She murmured something to him as they walked, together, to the centre of the banqueting table.

Garrick thought she could have been designed to vex him. What sort of girl would happily kiss him when she thought he was an orphan, but outright refuse the advances of a lord? It was against the natural order. The way she now presented herself at Leofwin's side just underlined her earlier dismissal. Unless… it would be reprehensible, but he wouldn't put it past Leofwin to make promises he'd no intention of keeping, just to get her into bed. Garrick frowned. At least he'd been nothing but honest.

As a commoner by birth, her status as Leofwin's guest should have gained her at best a seat halfway down the table. By rights she should have been relegated beyond the minor lords and retainers Garrick had brought in his retinue, but instead she took the chair to Leofwin's right. That place should have been his, reserved for the guest of honour. Not that he would expect the girl to know such things, but really, Leofwin should have instructed her. Instead he brushed a stray hair from her forehead and whispered something in her ear, before turning to signal the herald.

The gong echoed through the room.

"Ladies and gentlemen!" the herald proclaimed. "Honoured guests! Please, be seated."

Garrick took the place to Leofwin's left, the second-best spot, and smiled graciously when the baron turned to greet him. Even if the girl had been a wife or a daughter she should have sat to the baron's left, but if the slight had been deliberate he couldn't afford to show any concern. And the slight was always deliberate.

No, insisting on his rank would only make him look weak and desperate. He would bide his time and find a suitable way to retaliate. That was how these courtly games were played, and after his private outburst he was more determined than ever to play the game impeccably in public.

"Your hospitality is much appreciated, my lord," Garrick said as the first platters were brought to the table. "And I can only apologise again for our unexpected arrival."

"It's no trouble," Leofwin said. "As you see, our kitchens are always ready to produce a humble meal for our guests."

"Well, you have my thanks," Garrick said. He should, of course, have contradicted Leofwin's claim that the meal was a humble one — not only because it wasn't, but because good manners demanded it. But he was sufficiently annoyed that subtlety eluded him, and even such a small barb held a certain appeal.

He was only disappointed that Leofwin's studied indifference outmatched his own. It was almost as though he hadn't even noticed, and within a moment he'd returned his attention to Ailith.

Ailith, who hadn't even glanced at Garrick as they entered the room, and still hadn't acknowledged him, smiled and greeted a couple of the serving girls as they poured the wine. Servants! Well, if she was going to act like that she should be eating in the kitchens, not sitting in the best seat and dressed up for dinner in a gown that was worth nine times what she was.

And since she'd commandeered all of Watersmeet's attentions, Garrick had to content himself with listening to Wymark's continued and tiresome appreciation of the decor: a couple of ancient portraits were clearly the work of a famous master, and the more recent work showed an artistic flair that the boy apparently swooned over. He barely stopped for breath as they worked their way through the next three courses.

As the fragrantly spiced ptarmigan was replaced by some confection of hare and stewed figs, Totte leaned in towards Ailith and asked, "How are you settling in? Are you finding it everything you hoped for?"

"Oh, it's been much better than that," Ailith said, her fingers brushing against Leofwin's hand as she reached for her wine. "I'd heard some really quite bothersome rumours, but truly, his lordship has been nothing but charming."

"Your mother came to call on me," Garrick said, taking the opportunity to insert himself into the conversation. "She was very concerned for your welfare. I hope you haven't been too badly inconvenienced by your family's inability to afford a chaperone?"

It was a neat and carefully calculated blow, designed to remind

Ailith of her place and hint in the same breath at the impropriety of an unaccompanied woman taking up residence in the home of an unmarried man.

"Ailith has her own lady-in-waiting to chaperone her," Leofwin said.

Garrick smiled. He'd taken the opportunity for an easy shot, but Leofwin's intervention gave him an opening to transform a mild insult into something far more serious. To Ailith's untrained ears, it should sound like nothing more than a concerned enquiry as to her welfare, but everyone else at the table would recognise the seriousness of his next words. And yet if he wanted to avoid a duel, Leofwin would have no choice but to allow the insult to pass.

"If it were my daughter, I fear I'd find that quite insufficient. A maid in your employ could be just as swiftly employed to look the other way."

"Are you implying I'd ever behave with anything but impeccable honour towards my ward?"

His *ward?*

The room had fallen very, very quiet.

His ward. Garrick took a deep breath. That was an unexpected turn. He'd been so sure that Leofwin would choose to let things slide rather than defending the girl. If he claimed her as his ward, that was no longer an option.

"I could demand you say that again with a sword in your hand," Leofwin went on. "But you're a foolish boy, so on this occasion I think I'll let you live if you'll simply apologise."

"Why should I apologise for a little friendly concern?"

"How dare you?" Ailith jumped to her feet and glared at him over Leofwin's head. Leofwin looked away, smirking into his goblet as the girl spoke. "After everything you said to me this afternoon, how dare you imply that I'm the one who's lacking virtue?"

"My lady, I fear you misunderstand me."

"I've misunderstood nothing!"

Garrick got to his feet, hoping he could soothe her better with his arms than his words. He reached out to take her hand, and she pulled away as sharply as if she'd touched a flame. Then she drew back her arm and slapped him hard across the face.

He stared at her in astonishment as pain blossomed in his cheek. Perhaps she wasn't quite as naïve as she looked. For a moment he thought she might strike him again, but she folded her arms and resumed her seat. Leofwin made no move.

"Aren't you going to do something?" Garrick demanded. "I'm your guest."

"Ailith is my guest, too," Leofwin said mildly. "And if she were a duelist, she could demand satisfaction at sword-point for the slurs you've laid at her door. I think we'll call this an acceptable compromise."

"But…" Garrick started, and stopped, unable to think of anything he could reasonably demand.

"You spoke only to provoke me," Leofwin said. "And believe me, I'm feeling very provoked, but I will not play your games, child. This evening is over, and you will be gone before breakfast if you know what's good for you."

The others in his party were all on their feet before he had chance to protest at this ill-treatment. He should insist that the evening continue in a civilised fashion… with anyone else, he would insist, but Leofwin was dangerously unpredictable. Better to let it go. The girl had the poison. All else would soon cease to be important.

"Come, coz," Wymark said, taking his arm. "It seems we have another early start to look forwards to."

Chapter Thirty-Five

Ailith didn't stop to think, she just bolted through the servants' door into the kitchens, running away almost as soon as Garrick and his retinue had left the Great Hall. Ymma was overseeing a couple of young boys as they wiped down the prep table, while at the end of the table she arranged garnishes on the platters that would have been going out next, had the feast not been interrupted in such a final manner. The boys both stopped to stare, and Ymma scolded them back to work before she even glanced up to see what had caused the interruption.

"Saaluk's hands," she said, taking in Ailith's fine clothes and tear-stained face. "What happened?"

The day had already been so topsy-turvy that collapsing into a kitchen chair in a silk gown seemed almost normal by comparison.

"I said I didn't want to go," Ailith said. "I told Frida. I knew I'd muck it up somehow."

"You were brilliant." Lufe had followed her in from the hall, and crouched at her side, pulling her into a hug. "Gods, I've never seen anything like it."

"And you should've seen his lordship's face," Nia added. "He's never looked so pleased as when you smacked that boy."

"'That boy' is heir to Highfort," Ailith said morosely. "And I've ruined everything."

Ymma set down the mop and bucket. "Let me get this straight," she said, leaning on the table and staring hard at Ailith. "Little miss not-a-lady, all dressed up in silks and diamonds, just smacked some lordling?"

"And his lordship was pleased as anything," Nia said.

"Ha!" Ymma clapped her hands together. "You are most *definitely* not a lady."

But she said it like it was the best compliment in all the Twelve Baronies, and Ailith couldn't help but smile.

"Can I help you clear up?" Ailith asked. "The sooner I can get my hands round a mug of ale, the better."

"You mightn't be no lady, but you're not cleaning in a dress like that," Ymma said. "You'll upset the laundry girls no end."

"I suppose I should get changed anyway. I just didn't want to have to talk to Leofwin."

Lufe looked her up and down. "You're about Lil's size. I'll see if she's got something."

"Someone should go and tell Frida not to wait for me, anyway. She could bring me some normal clothes."

"Nia can run upstairs," Lufe said. "Ymma will finish up in here, and we'll all meet back in the granary. We don't want everyone listening in. Bring us some snacks through, right, Ym?"

"Right."

Lufe stuck her head into the scullery, told Lily what they were doing, and led Ailith through to the granary where Wig was still setting out the morning's bread to prove overnight.

"Lufe?" He looked at them over a tray of loaves. "What's up? And… Ailith, is that you? You look different."

"It's been one of those nights," Lufe said, settling herself on a sack of flour. "We're going to stop in here this evening. Ailith will explain once the others get here."

"Alright." He lifted another tray onto the proving shelf. "I'll fetch some ale in once I've done these, we finished up the last cask."

Nia and Frida arrived a few minutes later, and Wig was ushered from the room so Ailith could change in relative privacy. Frida had even brought an empty laundry sack to keep the gown clean. She kept the jewellery on, at the girls' urging; it felt strange to be wearing jewels with her normal clothes but her friends were right, it was the easiest way to keep track of everything.

When they told Wig he could come back in, he was rolling a cask of ale ahead of him, and he'd gathered Ulf and Lily and Ada along the way.

"What in Refah's name just happened?" Lily asked.

"Wait for Ymma," Ailith said. "I think she'll want to hear this."

"That I do." Ymma had brought a platter of small lemon cakes, and a huge hot water crust pie that hadn't even been cut into. "Out with it, then. And start at the start."

Ailith thought about it for a moment, and decided that the start was probably Garrick's suggestion that she should be his mistress.

"And he made out like it'd be the best thing to ever happen to me," she said, still feeling the outrage simmering. Slapping him had helped, but it hadn't been enough to dissipate her anger. The girls all murmured their sympathy, as Ulf handed round tankards of ale. Ailith downed hers in a couple of anxious gulps.

"They're all like that," Ymma said. "The rich ones."

"We're lucky here, though," Lufe said. "You might get a lord or two ogling you at dinner, but from what I've heard, most lords give out serving girls the way they give out tumblers of wine."

Frida nodded her agreement. "At least his lordship keeps us safe. But Ailith's not quite one of us…" She shrugged apologetically. "You're not. No-one ever demands I get all dressed up like that."

"If he did, though, you'd have to do it," Ailith said. "We're alike in that."

"So, some visiting lord was an idiot," Lily said, trying valiantly to get the conversation back on track. "And Ailith went to the feast?"

"Oh, did she ever," Lufe said. "She got all fancied up, and she was sat with his lordship, and it was all lovely till that idiot lordling tried to start a fight."

"He implied all manner of things about me," Ailith said. "And when Leofwin told him to stop it, he pretended he was just looking out for me."

"So she smacked him a good one," Nia added helpfully.

"I couldn't help myself. I shouldn't have done it, but there you go. It's too late for that now. But Leofwin had to defend me, and he's going to be so disappointed that I failed him."

"I'm telling you, he looked pretty happy," Nia said.

Ailith started to cry again. How could he possibly be happy? He'd told her quite clearly what she needed to do, and they'd been putting on the perfect act. The smiling, the flirting, the shared glances and gentle touches… it had all been going so well that she'd quite forgotten they were acting. But hitting their guest in the face had not been any part of the plan. Even if Leofwin had been secretly pleased to see Garrick embarrassed, she shouldn't have let it happen that way.

Lily put a friendly arm around her shoulders. "Sounds like he deserved it. You shouldn't feel bad."

"It's not him I feel bad for," she said, mopping at her eyes with Frida's handkerchief. "I was supposed to play a role, and I threw it all away in a fit of temper."

Ymma refilled her tankard and pressed a lemon cake into her hands. "Drink until it don't matter any more, then. We'll look after you till morning."

"I shouldn't," Ailith said. "I should go and say I'm sorry, and try to explain myself."

She didn't want to, though. And although she'd sobered up as soon as her fingers connected with Garrick's sharp cheekbone, the three goblets of wine already in her body were trying to re-exert their influence. She took a long, deep swallow of ale. It was a richer, sweeter brew than they usually drank over their dice games. And probably a fair bit stronger.

"You brought us the good stuff, tonight?" she asked Wig.

"Use it in some of the loaves," he said. "So I can sign out a whole cask, if it's not too often."

"Why d'you think we like him?" Ada asked, beaming up at him. He swatted playfully at her head. Their idle flirting just made Ailith's eyes well up again. She set her half-empty tankard on the floor.

"You're all marvellous," she said. "A girl couldn't hope for better friends. But I have to go and sort this out."

"I should come with you," Frida said.

"No, you stay here and enjoy your evening." Ailith picked up the laundry sack and hefted it over her shoulder. "I can put myself to bed."

Leofwin was waiting in her room.

She'd thought she would have time to gather her wits and prepare to face him, but he was sitting at her desk, staring blankly at the wall. She dropped the bag and walked over to rest her hand on his shoulder.

"I'm sorry," she said, trying to read his expression from the window's twisted reflections.

"Don't apologise." He stood and caught her hand, his soft touch at odds with the hard lines of his face. "Don't ever apologise for taking a firm stand against men like him."

"I just… I didn't know what to do, and I got it wrong."

"Shhh." He reached beneath her hair and unfastened her necklace, laying it down carefully atop the papers on her desk. "It's alright now."

"You're not angry?"

"Angry? Why ever would I be angry with you?"

He hooked the earrings out of her ears, and she slid off the beautiful emerald ring, which was now slightly sticky with ale. Her fingers were shaking as she set it down, from some noxious mixture of alcohol and nerves and exhaustion.

"I was worried, though," he said. "When you ran off."

"You could have followed me."

"A couple of the girls went after you, and I'd be as bad as him if I marched in to snatch you away from your friends. No, I figured you'd gone where you needed to be."

"They're good friends." She didn't want to say that she'd fled from the fury she'd projected onto him. "But I am sorry. Your plan was working, he was certainly vexed, but then…"

"He was out of line. Here, sit down." He manoeuvred her gently into the chair and started to unfasten her braids, setting the jewels down on the table as he worked each one free. "I don't know what he said to you beforehand, but no-one speaks like that under my roof. If you hadn't slapped him I might have had to run him through with a sword, and I think we'd all prefer to avoid that kind of thing."

"It sounds messy."

"Yes, and probably one of your friends would have had to clean up the blood, so let's agree that everything worked out for the best. Do you have a comb?"

"On the sideboard."

He'd walked across to fetch it before she realised that she should have gone herself. She hadn't imagined, when she told Frida to stay in the granary, that she'd have the lord of Watersmeet to tease the knots out of her hair instead.

"I can do that," she offered, but he shook his head.

"I made you get all dressed up. The least I can do is help you undress."

There was a moment of awkward silence, and the heat rose in Ailith's cheeks. "Um…"

"That didn't quite come out as I intended," he said, his own face flushing a deep crimson. "I was just thinking of all these unnecessary accoutrements. You don't want to sleep with gemstones in your hair. And I see you've already changed out of your gown."

"Ymma pointed out that silk was hard enough to clean without getting flour and water on it."

"I imagine it is. Were you planning to get covered in flour?"

"It's always a risk when you drink in the kitchens. Not that I mind, but I wouldn't want to spoil such a fine dress."

"You can always order whatever you need, and I'll settle the account."

"No, you mustn't. I have plenty."

"You know, a lot of women would take the opportunity to wear silk dresses every day, and damn the expense if you stain them and have to buy new ones."

"I get the impression I'm not like a lot of women."

"Nor many men. Still, this way is better for my pocketbook."

"And you shouldn't be responsible for my expenses anyway."

"Shouldn't I?" He set down the last of the diamonds and ran the comb gently through her hair. "I'm responsible for everyone who lives in this castle."

"Not for buying their dresses."

"Not directly, perhaps, but the staff are paid for their work. You'd prefer that I gave you an allowance?"

"I'd find a salary less strange than the idea that you own everything I'm wearing."

"I don't consider that I own your clothes just because I paid for them. What would I want with them?" He looked genuinely bemused. "Ailith, I have no use for your dresses, nor for jewels like these. They're yours."

"An apprentice gets food and lodgings, and perhaps a few extra pennies to spend. Silk gowns and diamonds aren't usually part of the deal." She picked up the discarded necklace, running her fingers between the chains. It was wealth beyond measure, and he was so casual about it. "I don't mind borrowing jewels if you want me to wear them for a feast, but you should decide how much my time is worth and pay me for it. I can't wander round charging any little thing I fancy to the castle treasury."

"As you wish."

She could tell that he didn't really understand her concerns, but she was pleased he didn't argue. If Garrick's cruel words had made one thing abundantly clear it was that she needed to avoid any chance that her situation could be misinterpreted. Everyone had to be crystal clear about exactly where she stood. There was one other thing bothering her on that front.

"Back there, when you said I was your ward, what does that mean?"

"It was a convenient shorthand. I had to let the brat know that he should expect me to defend you, with a sword if I must."

"I know why you said it. But what would everyone else take it to mean?"

He waved a dismissive hand. "It's a word that covers a multitude of scenarios, but it gives me the responsibility for your welfare. You could be the daughter of a friend, or a hostage from a rival. I could be planning to take your hand in marriage, for that matter. It's deliberately vague."

"Not an apprentice, though."

"It's fair to say that that would be an unconventional interpretation."

"Nor a scribe, which is what my friends think I am."

"Anyone with a whit of sense can tell you're an honoured guest, not an employee."

She bridled at that. "My friends have plenty of sense."

"And your friends know that you don't work for me. They just don't challenge you because they're good friends, and they know you'll tell them the truth when you're ready."

"What, should I have us all brought up on charges of heresy? I can't tell them the truth."

"You'll find a version of the truth that fits, in time. It's something we all have to do." He set the comb down on the table, and she realised he'd even plaited her hair. "Now, if you're sure you're happy to be alone, I think it would be inappropriate for me to help you any further. I'll make sure your door is well guarded, and our visitors should depart before sunrise."

She stood to face him. "Thank you," she said, hot tears prickling behind her eyelids. He needed to leave before she burst into tears for what felt like the tenth time that night. "For everything. I'll be fine."

"You know where to find me," he said.

She nodded agreeably, but she knew there was no turn of events that could prompt her to further disturb him that night.

Chapter Thirty-Six

Ailith woke the next morning with a blinding headache and a fractured recollection of the evening's events.

"You'll be glad to hear they've gone," Frida said as she poured steaming water into the bowl on the wash stand.

"Did I really hit him?"

"Quite competently, as I understand it."

"Gods help me. I must have drunk too much."

Frida shook her head. "He deserved it. Anyway, it's done now, you can't undo it by wishing harder."

"No, I suppose not. And he did deserve it."

Her fury at Garrick didn't stop him from being right, unfortunately. However little sense she could make of the situation, Anselm was a prisoner, and she'd sworn before all the gods that she'd do whatever she could to free him. Enjoying her studies was no excuse: she'd neglected her duty for too long. And with Malachi due at the castle in two days' time, there was an obvious advantage to getting on with things.

She splashed her face with water and tried to justify giving herself just one more month. But what would she gain from another turn of the moon? She might have gathered a little more knowledge but a month from now she'd still be standing in exactly the same place, feeling equally sick to her stomach and equally reluctant to upset her comfortable life. And meanwhile, Anselm would have spent another month under lock and key.

No, however much she might prefer to close her eyes to it, the problem wasn't going to go away.

She struggled to concentrate on their morning lesson, feeling a stab of guilt as she allowed Leofwin to assume that it was the previous night's events that had her off-balance. But she could hardly explain what was really bothering her. When he sent her back to her rooms after lunch with an injunction to rest and recover, she curled up in a chair and set to planning instead.

The ideal would be to smuggle Anselm out of the castle and hope Leofwin didn't suspect her of playing any part in the escape, but she knew she was a terrible liar. If he even though to ask her whether she'd seen anything, there was no way she could get away with pretending ignorance.

And although her instincts told her Leofwin posed no danger, common sense warned against complete disregard of his reputation. She'd barely saved Rethar from the sword; she'd be a fool indeed to assume she could save herself.

With the most brazen option duly eliminated, it was hard to think of an alternative to using Garrick's sedative, however hard she tried.

First she needed to figure out how to get to Anselm's rooms, though. She couldn't rescue him from the other side of a foot-thick wall. She asked Frida to send a message to Leofwin excusing her from dinner, and refused her friend's offer to stay and keep her company. She needed to be alone tonight.

As far as she could tell, Leofwin delivered food to his captive every evening. Then they talked, and usually Anselm played. She'd crept back a few times to enjoy the music, although she justified it to herself as an opportunity to learn more about Anselm's situation. She found the gentle strains of the harp effective for clearing her mind: a few of her more interesting ideas had come to her while she sat and listened from the cold stone passage. She hoped Leofwin would repeat his usual pattern tonight.

Once she'd allowed enough time for Frida to be out of earshot, Ailith let herself out of her room, nodding to her guards just as she would on any other day and hoping they couldn't see how her heart was hammering in her chest. She went up to the ramparts for a calming breath of fresh air, and when she was sure no-one was following her, she ducked into the abandoned linen closet and entered the maze of passages that riddled the walls of Watersmeet.

She made her way to the passage behind Leofwin's apartments, hoping she was in time. There were peep-holes overlooking the workshop and the library, and she found him studying an ancient book she didn't recognise. She settled down to wait until Thurstan disturbed him with the nightly meal tray. If the chamberlain ever wondered about where the extra food was going, he evidently knew better than to ask, and set the tray down with only a mumbled "milord".

Leofwin waited for him to leave, and Ailith waited in turn. When Leofwin picked up the tray and left the library, she watched as he turned left towards the workshop, then edged softly along the passage to look out through the next peep-hole just as he walked past the open door. Gods damn it. It would have been too much to hope that his secret passage led out of a room she could look into, but worse than that, the only room beyond the workshop was his personal bedchamber. Unlike the library, she'd have a hard time explaining herself if she strolled in there without knocking.

But she had committed herself to finding Anselm, and if this was the path then she had no choice but to follow it.

At the door she held her breath and counted to ten, listening for any hint of movement in the room beyond. All was silent. She patted her pocket to check she still had the sedative dart, and crossed her palm with a prayer to Av to aid her in her search. Her mouth was dry as she turned the handle, but the room was thankfully deserted.

Whoever had raised the walls of Watersmeet had clearly taken security and secrecy very seriously indeed. There wasn't one unified network of interconnected passages: so far, Ailith had found eight separate routes that didn't meet within the walls. And every entrance was different, too, whether it was hidden behind a tapestry or a painting, tucked away in a closet, or built into the side of a fireplace. She hoped Anselm would choose a lengthy sonata for this evening's recital.

She started with the walls, which were fully lined with thick curtains, but behind the drapes she found only cold stone. The fireplace was similarly disappointing.

Leofwin's closet contained several rails of barely-worn fine silks, as well as shelves full of folded linen that constituted his day-to-day wardrobe. Ailith spat on her hands and wiped her fingers clean on her skirts before she started to leaf through the fabric, but the walls of the closet were just as plain as the walls of the main room.

Ailith stood by the door and looked around. She'd examined every inch of every wall but he'd definitely walked in this direction before he disappeared, so she had to be missing something.

The dressing table wasn't hiding anything, and although she couldn't shift the huge iron-bound chest which stood at the foot of the bed, she judged from the surrounding cobwebs that no-one else had moved it, either. She rolled back the heavy rugs and examined the flagstones beneath, finding nothing but woodlice. That only left the bed itself, a sturdy oak frame which dominated the room.

She set her lantern on the floor, lowered herself to her stomach, and shuffled sideways until she was beneath the mattress, exploring the flagstones with her outstretched fingers. It was hard to imagine Leofwin doing this with a tray full of food every day; the undignified image made her giggle, which made her inhale a lungful of dust. The resulting sneeze smacked her forehead hard into the floor.

It was as she was catching her breath that she heard the noise.

She reached out and yanked the lantern under the bed, trusting that the movement would blow out the flame, and pressed herself into the ground, desperately fighting off another sneeze. There. That was definitely the sound of footsteps. With her face flattened against the floor she couldn't even see his feet as he moved around the room, but although she hated having her senses muffled, she clamped down on her alchemical awareness. Nothing would give away her presence more quickly than if she used those skills. She prayed to all the gods that he hadn't heard her sneeze, or the clattering of the lamp.

The bed creaked, and she felt the mattress shift above her. Oh no. No, no, no. Surely he couldn't be going straight to bed. But she'd sent a message asking him to leave her in peace, so of course he wouldn't be coming to call on her this evening. Why wouldn't he have an early night? She turned her head slowly until she could breathe without sucking in more dust. He kicked off his boots and socks, close enough that she'd tickle his toes if she failed to hold back the sneeze that was threatening to escape. The thick ropes supporting the mattress brushed against her hair as he rolled fully onto the bed, and she heard him blow out his lamp before the room went dark.

Well, there was nothing for it but to wait: once he fell asleep, she'd make her escape as swiftly and silently as possible, but she'd have to be absolutely sure he was sleeping soundly before she could make a move. Her shoulder already aching from her strange, prone position, she settled in for what promised to be the most uncomfortable night of her life.

Leofwin tossed and turned above her, evidently as far from sleep as she was, and she wanted nothing more than to tiptoe to the workshop and fetch him a soothing tonic of valerian and chamomile. But she couldn't do that, any more than she could allow herself to doze off as she bided her time.

All this, and she hadn't even found the entrance to Anselm's prison. She was evidently destined to be a complete failure as a spy.

Twice she thought Leofwin might have fallen asleep, but both times he stirred again before she'd even worked up the courage to move. Eventually he gave up on his fitful sleep, lit a candle, and padded out of the room.

Ailith stayed frozen in place a little longer. If he'd just gone to fetch a drink or make himself a sleeping draught, he'd be back too soon, and it could only end badly if she met him in the corridor. Eventually, though, she was satisfied that he must have gone for one of his midnight walks. She hauled herself out from beneath the bed and ran, not stopping until she was safely hidden in the secret passage.

She couldn't go back to her room while it was guarded, not with twenty years' accumulated dust caked onto her dress. Curling up in the old linen closet was tempting, but if she wanted to get Anselm out the next night, she couldn't afford to waste any more time. She couldn't find the door from the outside, but the route out would probably be obvious from Anselm's perspective. She could only think of one way this could work.

After dusting off the worst of the cobwebs, she made her way through the walls until she reached her usual listening post. Anselm was picking out a complicated passage on the harp, or trying to. While she was still plucking up the courage to speak, he fudged his fingering three times and had to start again. On the fourth attempt he managed the short piece without errors, and promptly stepped away from his instrument. Ailith heard liquid sloshing into a glass. There wouldn't be a better time to introduce herself.

"Excuse me." She wished — not for the first time — that she could see into his prison, but she settled for putting her mouth to the covered peep-hole. "Ah, excuse me, can you hear me?"

The room beyond was silent.

"Anselm?"

"Who's there?"

"I'm…"

She paused. She hadn't really thought this through. Who she was, how they were related, who had sent her… any of these things might make him more or less inclined to trust her. But her oath had been to help him: she couldn't let her personal situation get in the way.

"It doesn't matter who I am. I've come to get you out."

"You must be Ailith." His voice was clearer now, as if he'd worked out where she was and turned to face her. "The apprentice. Right?"

"Right." So much for not telling him.

"I've heard a lot about you."

"Have you? Well, that saves me some explaining."

"I'm not sure it does."

Gods, it would be so much easier if she could see him. "What do you mean?"

"I thought things were going well for you. To hear his lordship speak of you, I never would have imagined you'd be the sort to betray him."

"And yet, here I am."

"That's what confuses me. I had the impression that you liked him as much as he likes you."

"Well." She took a deep breath and steadied herself against the wall. "You're not wrong. I'm not doing this because I want to hurt him, but I swore I'd help you get out of here, so… here I am. Helping. If you'll let me."

She fell into silence, waiting awkwardly for him to reply. Should she have risked a lie, claimed to hate Leofwin as much as Anselm must? But she'd always been a terrible liar. Even through the wall, she was sure her voice would betray her. For better or worse, honesty was her only chance.

At last, he spoke: "Thank you, but I think I'm beyond helping."

"But I—"

"Please, go, before he becomes suspicious. You have a good position here, you can't risk his anger on my account."

"At least hear me out. Leofwin is already in bed — he won't disturb us tonight."

"Go on, then. I admit I'm curious to hear how you think you can possibly effect a rescue."

"Right." Suddenly, she had to make this half-baked plan sound plausible. "I've got a dart, here, that I can pass through to you. If you can drug Leofwin when he visits you tomorrow, you can steal his keys and let yourself out. And I've a friend coming with the market, the day after tomorrow, so if we get you out tomorrow night he'll smuggle us straight out of the castle in the morning."

"You've got poison?" He sounded, suddenly, more interested.

"Well, yes, it's—"

"And you're sure it will work on him?"

"Of course." Why wouldn't it?

"Okay."

"Okay?"

"We'll try it."

Chapter Thirty-Seven

Leofwin cut a couple of delphinium stems to add to the bundle in his hand.

He'd been in a bad mood all day. Garrick's visit had unsettled him; it had been an unwelcome intrusion, and he was concerned by how close they'd come to blows. It wasn't impossible to exclude someone from the guest-right but it was uncommon, and to formalise it would mean involving the temples and explaining things he'd prefer to keep to himself. And for the past two nights his usual restlessness had been transformed into serious insomnia.

But he was making excuses for behaviour that couldn't be excused. He'd been short-tempered with Ailith during their lessons and she'd become uncharacteristically wary in return, even after he'd tried to apologise. Her nerves had led to more mistakes, he'd snapped at her again, and in the end he'd dismissed her half-way through a joyless afternoon. He'd regretted it for the rest of the day.

He wasn't stupid enough to think that a few flowers could make everything better, but he would send them along with a half-bottle of her favourite wine, a letter of heartfelt apology, and a request that she join him for dinner. A proper meal in the dining room, rather than perching at the workshop table as they so often did. He'd take Anselm's tray over first, then — assuming she accepted his invitation — he'd have the whole evening to focus on mending bridges he'd never intended to damage.

He tied the bunch of flowers and headed downstairs to give Thurstan the necessary instructions. The chamberlain took it all in without blinking, returning promptly with the tray and confirmation that the kitchens would prepare a suitably fine meal. Ailith hadn't been in her room but the flowers, the wine, and the letter were waiting for her.

Leofwin nodded his thanks and picked up the tray.

"You're early," Anselm said, stopping his fingers mid-phrase as the door opened. "More unexpected visitors?"

"Not exactly." Leofwin lowered himself into a chair. "But I do have to ask you to excuse me, I can't stay. I have an apology to make."

"Oh."

Normally, this would have unleashed a barrage of questions. Anselm made no secret of his longing for the outside world, and although his music kept him occupied, he grasped at any opportunity for gossip. But apparently today was a day of strange behaviours. If he'd been a superstitious man, Leofwin might have put it down to the impending full moon, but more likely the boy was just finally developing some tact.

"I was unkind to Ailith," he said. It wasn't as though he had anyone else to talk to, where she was concerned. "And it wasn't even anything to do with her — it's the Highfort boy who's put me in a temper."

Anselm plucked at a couple of strings, his gaze fixed firmly on his hands.

"I'm hoping a leisurely dinner might give me enough time to persuade her to forgive me."

"You really like her, don't you?"

"I do."

Anselm rocked back on his stool, hands lodged in his pockets. "She's everything you wanted me to be."

Leofwin frowned. It had been a long time since he'd stopped thinking of Anselm as a failed alchemist, and he thought the boy had likewise grown to consider himself primarily as a musician, albeit one who found himself unfairly constrained by fortune. He was trying to put his confusion into words when the boy spoke again.

"Go and fix it, then."

Anselm drew in a sharp breath, and his chair toppled backwards. His head hit the floor with a disturbing crack. Leofwin was across the room in a heartbeat, checking the boy's skull for injuries, but there was something wrong: the way his eyes rolled back in his head was nothing to do with a blow to the head.

Once Leofwin realised he'd been looking with the wrong senses, the poison was easy to spot, and straightforward to unmake. He found the dart wedged beneath Anselm's fingernail, leeching its venom into his bloodstream, and pulled it clear before he finished destroying the amalgam.

The raw ingredients, now dispersed in the boy's veins, weren't exactly innocuous themselves. Leofwin managed to bind most of the castor extract into an almost-harmless amalgam, but the belladonna would have to be treated directly with an antidote. He carried the boy through to the bedroom, propped him up with pillows to keep his airway clear, and went to fetch the things he needed from his stores.

Chapter Thirty-Eight

Ailith read Leofwin's letter with a lump in her throat, and it took her a few minutes to compose herself sufficiently to begin writing a reply. He would feel badly betrayed, of course, but perhaps eventually he'd understand that she'd had no choice. If you went about capturing people you had to expect that, sometimes, someone would want to rescue them. She sealed the note with a blob of candle wax and, for want of a seal, the imprint of her thumb. She left it propped up on her dressing table; by the time Leofwin woke up to read it, she and Anselm should be safely out of the castle.

She settled herself in the workshop with Givold's *Compendium* open in front of her, although she was much too nervous to focus on the words. Wherever the secret entrance was actually hidden, she should see Anselm as soon as he came out of the bedroom.

But when the door opened, it wasn't Anselm who emerged.

Perhaps she'd guessed wrongly, and Leofwin's oblique reference to "a couple of errands" before dinner hadn't actually meant provisioning Anselm's supper. Perhaps she was going to have to sit through a reconciliatory meal after all, and somehow pretend that everything was normal.

But the severe look on Leofwin's face didn't bode well. He swept past without a word and disappeared into the store room, and she could hear the clinking of glass as he started to gather up bottles and jars.

"Don't move," was all he said before he vanished again.

He wasn't gone for all that long, but it gave Ailith more than enough time to imagine a vivid range of unfortunate outcomes. If Anselm had failed her, she could only pray he hadn't also been so stupid as to say anything to incriminate them both… but it wasn't looking good. She considered trying to escape, but although she'd been learning to ride she was far from confident. She could never outrun the whole machinery of Watersmeet, and besides, it wouldn't be fair to leave Anselm to take responsibility for a rescue he hadn't even asked for. Not when she'd had to talk him into it.

Leofwin returned and took a seat across from her, considering her in silence as she forced her eyes to stay on the page. Her attention, however, was completely focused on the man across the room. She felt his magic briefly, and had to rein in her instincts to follow suit and see what he was probing. Yet even as she did, she knew that such restraint was unlike her; the uncharacteristic caution would mark the fact that something was wrong.

There was nothing she could do that wouldn't draw his attention.

Every muscle in her body froze, some ancient instinct recognising that she was now as helpless as a mouse in the claws of a cat. Hardly daring to breathe, she waited for him to make the first move. She watched from the corner of her eye as he reached out and placed the dart on the table between them.

"A sophisticated poison," he said. "Would you like to study it?"

She set the book aside and looked warily at the dart, its tip now stained with blood. What would she say, if she'd never seen such a thing before? How would an innocent woman react? She was suddenly unable to imagine. But… a poison? Was it really, or was it a trap? If she protested that it was just a sedative, that would only prove that she'd been responsible. She probed it briefly with her mind, but what she sensed wasn't anything she recognised.

"Or maybe I should just put that somewhere safe," Leofwin said, scooping it up again. "It's not as though you've never seen it before. Is it?"

"But I didn't—"

"Don't make this worse by lying to me." His expression was hard, his eyes colder than she'd ever seen. "Someone brought a very deadly, very targeted poison into my home, and your face says it was you. What have you got to say for yourself?"

"It wasn't Anselm's idea, okay?"

"That's very noble of you." He laughed hollowly. "Do you think that will help him? And come to that, wouldn't you rather help yourself?"

"I'm just being honest. Besides, you'd know anyway. You always do."

"Okay, so you tried to kill me. What now?"

The implications of his words took only a moment to sink in. Whether or not she'd meant to, she'd almost killed him. Crossing her palm with all the symbols of the Pantheon in a swift and silent prayer, she realised her chances of seeing the morning had suddenly diminished. "Are you going to have me executed?"

"Do you think I should? I thought you were against that kind of thing."

"I am," she said, cautiously, not sure what her views on the matter could really be worth at this stage. "But you do have quite a fearsome reputation. I knew when I came here that there was a risk."

"My reputation is a carefully crafted work of art. It's what makes people leave me alone so I can get on with my studies. Usually, it even works." This time his laugh sounded genuine, and for the first time she allowed herself to believe that he might be able to forgive her.

"You're really not going to kill me?"

"I don't think that's strictly necessary. You are, after all, far and away the most interesting thing to have happened to me this year. We just seem to have had a little misunderstanding: I thought you were my student, you thought you were here to murder me. It's easy to see where we went wrong."

Ailith dropped her eyes to the floor, examining the stones in unwarranted detail so that she wouldn't have to look at him. He'd invited her into his home, treated her well, and become her friend. She felt suddenly ashamed of her deception. She'd never been a good liar; a string of failed courtships attested to her inability even to indulge in the little social lies that kept friendships together. How had she ever thought this was a good idea? How could she have been so stupid as to persist, even once she knew he wasn't the tyrant that people said he was? She'd had one chance to change the course of her life, and she'd thrown it away because she'd listened to Garrick. Well, that and the stupid oath, by which she was still bound if he was going to allow her to live.

"I could so easily let this destroy the mutual trust we need for this relationship to work," he said. "But I'd prefer to find another way."

"But... why?" she asked. "Why would you let me live, when for all you know I might try again?"

"As I said, you've made things more interesting. Besides, real life is seldom as straightforward as it is in the sagas. You don't get to make one choice, hero or villain, and watch your whole life unfold neatly in front of you. You've made a decision — I hope I can convince you it was a poor one — but now you have to keep on choosing, every day, for the rest of your life."

"Choosing what?"

"What to do. Who to be." He shrugged and spread his arms to encompass the world. "Everything."

"You've had people killed for less, though."

"It's almost as if you're trying to persuade me."

She stared in disbelief. How could he be so lighthearted about something so serious?

"You were going to execute Rethar just for walking into a room at the wrong time."

"I wasn't, as it happens."

"So how can you... what? You were, I heard you."

"You heard me give an order, and you interpreted it in the way that made most sense to you. But leaving that aside, it's true that in the past I've made some harsh decisions. I, too, must make new choices every day. Today I choose to be a forgiving sort of friend. Tell me, what would you do next, in my position?"

"I don't know."

"Imagine you have a student. You're fairly sure she's an asset, but she's made an unfortunate decision. How will you handle it?"

"I suppose… I'll curtail her freedom, first. She can't be allowed to run out and tell her friends what's happened, and if she's frightened she might try to flee. I need to take steps to keep her under my control until, I suppose, she's shown her loyalty. Until I'm sure."

"Noted."

She reached into her pocket and drew out a crumpled piece of paper, and looped the pendant from around her neck. In fact she seldom needed to show them these days, the guards and servants usually recognised her, but it felt like the right kind of symbolism. If this was a test, it was one she wanted desperately to pass.

"So I should give these back to you," she said. "Until you're sure."

He took them without comment. "What else would you suggest?"

"Well, the next question is how to test her loyalty — or to secure it. I suppose I'd want to know exactly what she thought she was doing, and why. That might indicate a way forwards."

"I think that sounds like a very good plan. But it's been a strange evening, and I'm tired. Go to bed and we'll talk in the morning."

The last thing Ailith wanted was to be alone in her room, but she wasn't sure if it was a suggestion or an order. She didn't try to clarify, and settled for asking one of the guards to fetch Frida. When she asked why Rethar and Brict weren't on duty, though, she was met with an uncomfortable silence.

"Are you okay?" Frida asked, as soon as she saw the tears streaking Ailith's face. "What happened?"

"I'm a complete fool, that's what happened. Don't," she added, as Frida started to work at her hair. "Please, I need you to devote all your attention to being my friend."

"I can do both," Frida said, but she settled into a chair without further argument.

"I'm giving you the night off," Ailith said. "But I'd be very grateful if you wanted to spend your evening with me, and I'm not sure if I'm allowed out."

"Allowed?"

"It's complicated. If I give you the whole story, will you promise not to tell anyone else? Not even Lil or Ymma?"

"I promise."

She started at the beginning, with the fact that she wasn't an orphan and wasn't exactly a scribe. As Leofwin had predicted, that news didn't come as much of a surprise, although the fact that she was studying alchemy was more of a revelation. And Frida's jaw dropped when Ailith continued on to explain about Anselm and the Guild's rescue operation.

"There must be some mistake," she said, shaking her head. "His lordship wouldn't do something like that."

"I know it sounds ridiculous, but I've spoken to Anselm myself. Anyway, I thought I might be able to help him escape, you know? And someone from home gave me what he said was a sedative to use, but actually it turns out it was poison. Frida, I nearly killed him."

She choked the last words out between sobs. Frida reached for her hand and gave her a reassuring smile.

"You didn't, though. Right? He's not hurt?"

"Right."

"Okay, let me check I've got the whole story. You came here to pretend to be his lordship's student, but you wished you could stay. And you didn't mean to, but you almost poisoned him. He's got a prisoner locked away somewhere. And now you're... what? He wouldn't ask for a trial before the temples, not if he knows it wasn't your fault. Is he sending you home?"

"I don't know. I don't think so. I think he wants me to stay."

"As his student."

"I think so." Ailith blew her nose loudly into her handkerchief, and waved her arms helplessly to try and indicate her general uncertainty. "He sent me to bed and said we could talk about it tomorrow. At least there's going to be a tomorrow, that's something, I suppose."

"Right." Frida nodded. "That's a good sign. So what you need to do is persuade him that you know it was a huge mistake, and you won't do it again."

"Yes, but how? I'm already working as hard as I can."

"No, you're looking at it all backwards."

"What?"

"Studying harder isn't going to help. If you're going to get him to trust you again, it has to be personal — you have to show him that you value him as a person, not just that he's useful as a teacher or patron."

"Oh. Okay."

"Tell me something. If you could wave a magic wand and create another equally comfortable castle, with some other alchemist to apprentice yourself to, would you do it?"

"Of course not." She didn't even have to think about it. Why would she want to be anywhere else?

"Even though you've got some work ahead of you to fix things here?"

"Even so."

"Then you can do this. You won over Ymma, and she really wanted to hate you."

"Yeah, she's hard to impress."

"Do you love him?"

Ailith started. "What?"

"Do you love him?"

"That's not the way things are between us. I thought you, of all people, knew better than to believe the things they say about me."

"I'm not asking if he's carried you off to bed, I'm asking how you feel. Just you. In your heart."

"My heart knows better than to put me in impossible situations. Barons don't marry potters' daughters. He is never, ever going to think of me that way."

"I'm not asking about him."

"Why are you even bringing this up?"

"Someone has to ask you the questions you won't ask yourself."

"You know, this really isn't helping."

"I just mean…"

"Don't."

"But I…"

"Go to bed."

Frida folded her arms across her chest. "Oh no you don't. A friend isn't dismissed so easily as a maid."

"Go back to being my maid, then. Just go."

Frida frowned, but she got up and started towards the door. "For what it's worth," she said from the doorway, "if it helps you work things out — this is a pretty good example of what not to do. Good night."

"Good night," Ailith said quietly, but she'd already gone, the door thudding closed behind her.

Ailith crawled atop the bed and lay there, staring at the wall, trying not to think about the question. Of course she didn't love him. She was a bright, sensible woman who understood what impossibility looked like, and it looked very much like this. It would be meaningless to think about love. No-one could doubt he was a very attractive man, but there was no harm in appreciating the line of his jaw or the warmth of his smile. That didn't mean anything.

But she would *never* be so stupid as to allow herself to fall for him.

Would she?

And yet, she couldn't quite explain her answer to Frida's earlier question. Why wouldn't she swap all this for an easier life somewhere else? Not Garrick's cruel offer of indenture at the Highfort, but if she could dream up her perfect teacher and her perfect home… why couldn't her imagination stretch any further than these walls? Why did it have to be *him*?

And by all the gods, why had she chosen to push away her very best friend over something so stupid?

She started towards Frida's room, but one of the new guards stopped her with an arm across her path as she stepped out of her room.

"Where are you going, milady?"

"I need to see Frida."

He glanced to his colleague for guidance.

This was bad. If they were truly confining her to her room, then this was very bad. Ailith had time to launch herself into a panic before he came to a decision, but he knocked on her behalf at the door across the corridor. A faint voice called out, and the guard stepped aside to let her through.

As she let herself in, Frida propped herself up on the narrow bed. She hadn't been in to Frida's room before. It was a pokey space without a window, but there was enough space for a trunk and a wooden chair beside the cot.

"I came to apologise."

"Go on, then."

"I'm sorry. Truly. I shouldn't have sent you away when you were trying to help me, and…" — she flushed to think of it — "I definitely shouldn't have told you that you can't be my friend. I don't want to be that sort of person."

"Okay." Frida nodded. "I don't want you to be that sort of person, either."

"Will you forgive me?"

"I accept your apology."

"But?"

"Please don't do that again."

"No. And I'll understand if you don't want to help me any more, but if you do have more to say, I'll listen without cavilling this time. I promise."

"I didn't mean to spook you." Frida swung her legs over the side of the bed. "Sit down, then, if you're staying."

"We can go back to the Red Room if you want. It's more comfortable."

"It is, but it'll do you good to see how the other half lives."

Ailith bit back a retort about the crowded sleeping space she'd shared with her sisters growing up, and settled wordlessly on the bed.

"Anyway, I know I scared you, but love doesn't have to be all about marriage — you love your parents, right? And your sisters?"

"Of course."

"And maybe you came back to say sorry because you love your friends, too. You can love him in a way that doesn't lead to terrifying and impossible places."

"Right." Ailith nodded. That made sense. She wouldn't swap Mama and Papa for imaginary parents just because she could imagine them less fussy. She wouldn't swap Sunneva for a less-annoying little sister, and she wouldn't swap Frida for an imaginary friend. In that context, it was obvious why she couldn't imagine replacing Leofwin with some imaginary tutor.

"And as your friend, watching the way you talk about him, it looks to me like you love him. But only you can know."

"I think you could be right." That was as far as she could manage to commit herself, and she couldn't form her lips around the L word, heavy as it was with absurd connotations. "I do care for him. That's why I really want to sort this out."

Frida reached out and squeezed her hand. "And if I'm any judge of anything, then I'd say he cares for you, too. So you just need to be yourself until he sees it."

Chapter Thirty-Nine

Ailith found him sitting beneath the arbour, just as dawn was breaking.

After checking on Anselm's recovery, Leofwin had spent a sleepless night pacing the garden pathways, running the events of the past two months through his mind. Again and again he'd traced a path through his memories, looking for the clues he must have missed. She'd been used, that much was clear. Someone had sent her. But he couldn't believe her whole character had been an act: she was too impulsive, too warm, too enthusiastic. And if she'd truly enjoyed her time here as much as he'd valued her company, then he had high hopes of persuading her to stay despite her betrayal.

It was almost a surprise that she'd waited for daybreak before she came. She must have known she'd find him here, in the one place he could be a man instead of a figurehead, the one place they'd always shared as equals. Surely neither of them had slept. Although if she'd had a night as hard as his, she'd hidden it well behind neatly braided hair and a freshly pressed dress. For his own part, he hadn't changed out of yesterday's clothes.

She dropped into a curtsey. "My lord."

He paused before answering, and looked hard at her. She didn't look as scared as he might have expected, for someone who believed he might wave his hand and have her life. She'd reverted to formality, but she wasn't shaking or crying or begging for mercy. Nor did she look, quite, like someone who regretted her actions. In all, he was impressed.

"Don't," he said, trying to smile but not quite managing to feel it. "Don't make this harder than it already is. We have enough of a chasm to bridge without your adding extra distance."

"I thought you might want to start again. From the beginning."

"I wish yesterday hadn't happened," he said. "But we can only move forwards. That is, assuming you wish to stay?"

"More than anything."

"You don't have another apprenticeship waiting for you?"

"No."

"Then let's start to mend this. Sit down."

She'd brought a plate of his favourite spiced buns from the market, and a carafe of apple juice that she set down on the table before taking a seat. But they were both too preoccupied to eat.

"I just wanted to do the right thing." The uncertainty in her voice made her sound suddenly younger than she was. "I just wanted to help. Do you see? It didn't matter how nice you were or how much I was enjoying myself, because I had to help him. I should have talked to you, I see that now, but I was scared."

"I understand." At least, he thought he did. "We'll come back to Anselm later."

"But I do want to stay, and I want to make this work more than I've ever wanted anything, so tell me what I need to do to win back your trust."

"You can start by answering a few questions."

"Anything."

"Someone sent you, of course. You're learning quickly, but that poison isn't one I have a record of, and you don't have the experience to invent anything so deadly. And while I can believe young Highfort might like to see me harmed, I doubt he'd bother with such subterfuge."

She nodded. "There's a group of alchemists in Bracklea who call themselves the Guild. I've actually only met them once, but one of their number is Selwyn, priest of the Twin Gods. He's the one Garrick's apprenticed to, and he's Anselm's father."

"I see."

"He'd thought for years that Anselm was dead, but then he heard something to suggest he might actually be here. He asked me to come because I was new, so you wouldn't recognise me."

Leofwin smiled to himself. It was all very well maintaining a careful reputation, but people did tend to overestimate his networks. Keeping an eye on a bunch of middle-rank alchemists in another barony wasn't high on his list of priorities. To Ailith, he simply said, "Go on."

"That was the beginning. Selwyn asked me to come and find out if Anselm really was here. He gave me a token so I could travel as a pilgrim. Garrick gave me that letter to get me through the door, and then he showed up last week and gave me the dart, saying he wanted to speed things along."

"The day you hit him."

"I wish I'd hit him twice as hard," Ailith said fiercely. "But he knew I was due to see Malachi today, and he was right. That was the best chance I had to get Anselm out."

Garrick and Malachi. On the surface, that was a strange alliance, but it made sense once you realised that the boy wanted nothing more than he wanted power. And the old man's skill at weaving promises exceeded even his alchemical talents.

"I didn't think it was Malachi who'd put you up to this. He'd know that poison couldn't work, not in your hands and certainly not in Anselm's. And if he thinks you're a piece that he controls, he wouldn't sacrifice you without an obvious gain — though a debt from Highfort might just be enough to tempt him."

Her composure wavered a little as she absorbed the idea that Malachi might also be using her for his own ends. Which, knowing Malachi, he certainly was.

"Anyway, I think you've seen sense now, so as long as you've no more of that stuff tucked away then I think we can move on."

"He only gave me one dose."

"And am I wrong to trust you?"

"No." She met his eyes and folded her arms across her chest, a little of her usual fire returning as she tilted her head to study him. "Am I? Seems to me we've both been keeping secrets."

"And I think this would be a good time for me to try and set your mind at ease. Have you seen Anselm, or just whispered to him through the walls behind the Drawing Room?"

"Behind the Drawing Room," she said. "I couldn't find my way around to the door."

"Come on, then, let me show you where he lives."

She stared at him. "You're very odd."

"How so?"

"I nearly killed you. You can't possibly trust me yet, and suddenly you've decided to share your secrets."

"I'm hoping to persuade you that I'm not the enemy. I want you to devote yourself to your studies, not spend your time worrying about Anselm."

"Oh."

"I think, having gone to so much trouble on his account, you should at least have the chance to see him."

He led her by way of a secret entrance, a thrice-locked door, and two narrow passages to a tower that overlooked the river to the east. Anselm had rooms that spread over the top floor, and access to a small covered terrace on the roof, but for the moment the boy himself was still laid out in bed.

"Not a bad prison, is it?" Leofwin asked as he showed her in. "Now, I don't expect Anselm to wake up for a day or two since he got on the wrong end of that dart, but we'll go and see him."

"Wait, you used it on him?"

"No."

"What?"

"He did it to himself. Perhaps, when he wakes, we'll find out why."

"But he's unconscious? Why are we visiting, then?"

"You'll see."

Even walking a couple of paces behind her, he knew the exact moment that she laid eyes on Anselm's youthful face. She stopped dead in the middle of the room and gaped at him, rendered motionless and unable to speak, until Leofwin took her by the elbow and steered her back out into the corridor.

"But how?" she demanded, her voice returning the moment the door closed behind them.

Leofwin shook his head. "Wait. I know your curiosity is burning, but this may be a long story, and I'd prefer us to be comfortable."

"But that's definitely the same Anselm? Selwyn's son? There hasn't been some kind of mix-up?"

"That's Anselm."

They made their way back to the garden in silence.

"I know you have questions," he said, pouring apple juice into two glasses. "Go ahead."

"Like how you've had a man locked up for thirty-some years, but he looks about fifteen?"

"That's the sort of thing."

"And?"

"He's fifteen. And fifty. But mentally he's just a boy, trapped in that awkward stage between childhood and adulthood."

"Then I'm going right back to my first question. How? How in all the Twelve Baronies is such a thing possible?"

"Have you heard of the draught of life?"

"Of course." Ailith nodded. "But it's a story. You're not saying it's real?"

"The story is a metaphor. There's no spring you can drink from, but there are alchemical reactions that approximate the effect." She'd been too focused on her questions to help herself to food, so he passed her one of the buns. "Here, eat something while I tell you the story of a young apprentice who turned out to be a thief. He stole a formula he couldn't understand, for an amalgam he wasn't strong enough to make."

"I think I've heard this story before."

"You've heard someone else's version, perhaps. Will you listen to a retelling where I'm not the villain?"

She nodded, and broke off a piece of bread.

"Imagine, if you will, an ambitious young man. Skilled, moderately wealthy, but not yet confident in his position. A boy comes to him with a proposition that could make them both richer than the gods, but it's beyond belief, even to an alchemist. The boy, blustering and a little desperate to prove a point, injects the bottle of amalgam that he's stolen, but he's no scholar. He hasn't realised that there's a two-stage process. That in the form he's taken it, the amalgam is a poison. That it's made with ingredients he cannot ever hope to master. Over the next few days he sickens, and the young man has only two options: allow the boy to die, or complete the amalgamation for him."

"To make him immortal."

"Ageless," Leofwin corrected. "He's still mortal, he just isn't getting older in the natural way."

"Okay, so he doesn't get older. That doesn't explain why you've imprisoned him."

She was taking it all remarkably well, but then she'd believed until recently that magic was the stuff of legends. Perhaps this seemed no stranger to her than the fact that she could reach out with her mind and touch him from across the path.

"We haven't yet reached the end," he said. "In the sagas, you need take only one sip from the draught of life, but this amalgam is an imperfect copy. Its effect lasts a little under a month."

"And then you start to get older again?"

"No. Unless you have another dose, you die. Do you begin to see my dilemma?"

It took her a long moment to answer, but when she did, it was obvious she understood. "Anselm wasn't, he isn't, strong enough to make it for himself. Right? But you are."

"I am."

"So you're keeping him alive."

"Yes. He tried to run away, once. That's why he no longer has the freedom of the castle. He can't grow up, so he can't be trusted to take the necessary care for his own safety — he tried to kill himself with your poison. And meanwhile I continue in my attempts to find a better formula, one that will last longer and buy us all a little more time."

Chapter Forty

On the morning of the full moon Malachi went to the castle, leaving Garrick to pace anxiously around his rooms. It was the day of reckoning. He'd sent most of his attendants home ahead of him, along with his belongings, retaining only a couple of essential servants. Even Orvyn had been persuaded to leave. Ailith wouldn't want to see him, but surely even she would realise that she needed all the help she could get. Leaving a dead baron in her wake should shock her back to her senses. He hoped she'd come to see that he'd only been looking out for her.

If he could forgive her for assaulting him, then surely she in turn could forgive the harsh words he'd spoken in his shock. Then he could send her to the Highfort, where his father would be able to protect her from the worst consequences of her actions.

And while she was running, Garrick could step in and assume control here.

It was fortunate that Leofwin was a curmudgeon who had never taken a wife. There were no heirs to seek revenge. There was no line of inheritance, no son to have killed, no daughter to wed. The old fool didn't even keep his court full of minor lords who'd sworn their fealty in hopes of gaining some advantage. As far as he could tell from his earlier visit, he would have nothing to contend with beyond the servants, and he knew well enough how to handle servants.

It was like a dream. There would just be an empty castle, waiting for a suitably high-born voice to issue commands.

Lunchtime came and went, and there was no word from Malachi. Garrick found his appetite had deserted him. The market would close in a couple of hours, and Malachi's excuse to loiter in the castle would be gone along with the traders.

Ailith should have freed Anselm the night before. They should have been out, by now, and well on their way to safety.

When Malachi returned, though, he was alone. Garrick's worst fears coalesced into a nightmare scenario.

"She didn't come?"

"No." Even Malachi, who was chronically implacable, sounded troubled. "I fear the worst."

"She's changed her mind." Garrick scowled. "That bastard's poisoned her against me. Well, if she won't rescue herself, I shall have to see to it."

"What do you intend?"

Garrick straightened his tunic and reached for his riding coat. "I'm going home. You needn't attend me. Alchemy isn't what this situation requires."

"There is one more thing you should know before you dismiss me, m'boy."

"Oh?" Garrick wondered how long it would take the old man to understand that insulting the future Lord Baron of Highfort was a poor plan. At this rate it wouldn't be long before he had outlived his usefulness.

"You've met Leofwin, of course."

"Obviously."

"How many times?"

"What are you hinting at, old man? Speak plainly."

"I am old, am I not? How old, do you think?"

"I said you should speak plainly. Must I command it?"

"Do you think I am yours to command?" There was an infuriating twinkle in the old man's eye. "But if you will not guess, I will tell you. I am past a hundred and thirty years old."

"A hundred and thirty? Preposterous."

"Thirty-seven years ago, Anselm was my student. I was old then, and already I had lived a dozen years without ageing. Do you understand what I'm telling you, boy? This body may look eighty years old, but for the last fifty years, it has not aged."

"You found the elixir of youth."

The first time he'd asked about it, Selwyn had said it was nothing but a fairy story. The second time, he'd thrashed Garrick until he couldn't stand. After that, Garrick had had the sense not to mention it again, even after he'd found the erdstall with its tantalising references. Yet here was a stranger telling him that it might all be true after all.

"I developed a formula," Malachi said. "The amalgam is far from perfect, but it has given me years I might not have had."

"Fifty years without ageing, and you say that isn't perfect?"

"I wouldn't expect you to understand the subtleties, you're not far enough along in your studies. But even you should grasp the implications easily enough when I say that Anselm stole a lot of work from me. Leofwin has a copy of the formula — and I've reason to believe he's started selling it. Ask your father how a man of his age keeps his hair from greying."

It took a moment for Garrick to absorb what the old man was saying, but when he did, it hit him like a blow to the stomach. "He's selling it to my father?"

"Who else but the nobility could afford to buy such a luxury as time?"

Garrick nodded. Naturally, if you had something so valuable to sell, then only a tiny fraction could afford to buy it. Never mind commoners, even minor lords would be priced out of the market. His father, though? His own alchemist-hating, magic-fearing father? The idea of eternal youth would appeal to a man like Oeric, of course, but would he really dabble in the arts he so feared? He didn't even keep decent healers at court.

"This is no time for your dissembling," Garrick said. "Are you truly saying that my father is immortal?"

"Not immortal, but close."

"Close? What does that mean?"

"I told you, the amalgam isn't perfect. You might imagine that the true perfect elixir would last longer than a turn of the moon, but ours is not perfect. That's good for repeat custom, though, if one makes a business of such things."

"I'll need a copy of that formula."

Malachi laughed. He actually dared to laugh. "It would be no use to a boy of your limited experience."

"I'll be the judge of that."

"No." Malachi shook his head, suddenly serious again. "You will not."

"Do you think I'm giving you a choice? You will provide me with the formula, and if I require it, you will interpret it for me."

"This is not your fiefdom, and I am no vassal of yours," Malachi said. Garrick was about to respond, but he held up a hand to silence him. "And I will not, under any circumstances, provide you with a dangerous formula that you are ill-equipped to use. I've made that mistake once before. I won't be guilty of such carelessness again."

"Dangerous? How can the elixir of youth be dangerous?"

"I told you, it lasts only a month. And it doesn't release you back to mortal life, but to a swift and painful death."

"Well, if you won't share the formula itself, then there must be more information you can give me," Garrick said. "Things I'll need to know, if I'm to find a way of defeating Leofwin without starting a war."

But in his heart, it wasn't Leofwin he was thinking of. It was his father, a mere month away from ceding control of Highfort to his first and only son.

Chapter Forty-One

"Today we're going to talk about death."

Leofwin had come to the workshop before breakfast to prepare the necessary ingredients in the required quantities; it wasn't to be a test of her memory. But there was no way to pass on this lesson without practical experience. Gods forbid she would ever need to use it.

"Death?" Ailith looked at him, puzzled, across the workshop table.

"The other day, you tried to kill me. Today, I want you to learn the lessons of that mistake."

"I've already promised I won't—"

"I know, that's not the lesson I'm talking about. But even if Anselm had pricked me with that dart, you would have failed. I want you to understand what you'd have to do differently to succeed."

She gaped at him. "Why? I don't want to succeed."

"You're my student. It's my job to ensure you face up to your weaknesses."

"But... you don't want me to get better at this. Why would you want to make me more of a threat to you?"

"Frankly, if you really wanted to kill me, it would be easier to use old-fashioned methods: a knife to the throat, for instance. But since I've decided to trust you, I should continue your education. Do you remember your experience with the mousebane?"

"I could hardly forget it."

"That was a very weak poison, but it's still poison. And even as a beginner you could unmake it, even as it spread in your own bloodstream. That, in essence, is the problem. Anything made by alchemy can be unmade by the same methods, so there are only two ways to kill an alchemist with alchemy. Can you work out what they are?"

"Catch her by surprise?" Ailith suggested. "If I was sleeping, I wouldn't have time to counter any poisons, not even mousebane."

"I suppose that's a third way. It's not one of the traditional two."

"This is going to be hard work, if you'll only give me credit for traditional answers rather than right ones."

"I'm putting surprise in with non-alchemical methods. If you can surprise me in my sleep, you can surprise me just as well with a sword as with alchemy. The traditional answers relate to the two facets of your studies."

"Theory and practice."

He nodded. "Go on."

"Theory: you could develop something better. A stronger formula."

"Better how?"

"I suppose… it could be something that works a lot more quickly. Or perhaps adding something to confuse the senses or knock out your victim, giving more time for the poison to do its work, while stopping them from breaking it down."

"Excellent."

"But what's the other way?"

"The alternative is simple, though it's almost beyond your control. You'd need to be the stronger mage. To be able to fuse an amalgam even as your opponent tries to force it apart."

"A battle of wills."

"Precisely. A duel. And that's what I intend to demonstrate this morning: you will try to make bloodlace, and I will prevent you."

"But bloodlace can only be synthesised in the body."

"That's why it's a duel. Sadly, it's a duel that only one of us can win: the best I can hope for is to avoid losing."

The look on her face was a picture. It was in these fleeting moments, the times he managed to shock her, that Leofwin wished he could freeze time and study her expression. He wanted to pick apart the nuances of excitement and fear and wonder which flashed across her features. A small part of her was horrified, certainly, but more than that, he thought, she relished the prospect of a new challenge. Just watching her made him feel more alive.

"You actually want me to try to kill you? This morning?"

"Again." He smiled, enjoying the discomfort which framed her face every time he reminded her. He wouldn't ask, and couldn't trust the answer even if he did, but every time she squirmed he took it as her silent reassurance that she didn't really wish him dead. "Yes."

"Why?"

"So you can learn."

"But if I…"

"You won't succeed. You may have more raw talent than I have — I'm not sure about that yet — but you don't have the experience to win this one. I just want you to know what it feels like to try."

"Couldn't we try it with something less dangerous?"

"That would take all the fun out of it. When I was apprenticing we had regular duels — just looking to test our strength, the way youngsters do. No-one ever actually died."

He handed her a bowl of half-formed mixture, along with his dagger.

"Where?" she asked, and he held out his hand, palm upwards. She pressed the blade to his skin and wavered, reluctant to apply the necessary pressure.

"Quickly, if you please, or you'll only hurt me." He wondered if he should have done this part himself, but she needed to stop being squeamish about the human body. A little nick to the palm should be within her powers.

She took a deep, steadying breath, let it out slowly, and drew the dagger across his hand in one smooth, deliberate motion. She had apparently less compunction about the actual poisoning, using her thumb to apply the mixture to the cut before she focused her intentions on forming the amalgam.

Leofwin turned his own attention to the smarting pain in his hand, and beyond that, to the ingredients Ailith was attempting to draw together in his blood. He could feel her mind there, a bright, strong force that fed the amalgamation. Dear gods, but the woman would be unstoppable when she was fully trained. Her focus brushed lightly over him before returning to the job at hand. He wondered briefly whether this exercise had been a mistake after all, but he couldn't afford to be distracted by thoughts of his own mortality. Instead, he focused entirely on preventing the formation of the poison's bonds, pushing where Ailith was pulling, forcing the ingredients apart. Her power flared and for a few heart-stopping moments he thought she was going to get the upper hand, but then it waned just as suddenly.

"I can't do it," she said, and her attention withdrew completely as she slumped onto the bench. "You've won."

"Describe what just happened."

"You felt it, too. You beat me."

"Humour me. Describe it."

"I was making bloodlace, and the ingredients felt the same as ever, but mine wasn't the only mind there. I could feel you, not only your blood but your power, like when you're working or when you reach out to make me jump. I couldn't feel what you were doing, exactly, but obviously you were forcing the amalgam apart. The bit that's your mind doesn't move when I push it, so I can only affect the ingredients, not stop you directly. And you're stronger than me."

"Good. One more try."

"I don't think that will make any difference."

"Let's pretend you've caught me by surprise, and I'll give you a few moments' head start."

It was a dangerous advantage to offer. If she'd already formed the first bonds by the time he started to fight back — and knowing her skill, she would have — he'd have twice the work ahead of him and much less time in which to save himself. But it wasn't the fastest poison, and he could probably still overpower her, if barely.

He promised not to interfere until he'd counted to ten, but a morbid fascination kept him monitoring her progress. She pressed her advantage hard, and by the time he reached eight the first bonds were finished and the poison was spreading. Nine. His arm was beginning to numb. Leofwin closed his eyes and reached out for where she was working.

Ten.

He needed to stop her progress before he could devote the necessary attention to unmaking the existing poison. He started to ease apart the ingredients she was moving, feeling her push back, fighting against him. Once he was sure she was preoccupied with the fight, he divided his attention, keeping up a steady pressure while he turned part of his mind to unpick the existing bonds of bloodlace.

He felt the exact moment when she noticed.

Her focus snapped away from the new formation to clamp around her previous work and maintain the amalgam. Confused, her attention flickered back and forth for a few moments. And then she did something he hadn't predicted: she copied him.

His heart swelled with pride, even as he realised this might make all the difference to the result. The woman was incredible. And she was winning.

She devoted just a small amount of energy to sustaining her existing bloodlace. Meanwhile, she continued to push against him, giving everything she had left to the task of amalgamating more poison. The combination was enough to make his task impossibly difficult. If he pushed harder at the existing amalgam, she would be free to make more, and he would have gained nothing by his efforts. If he concentrated instead on preventing her from progressing further, he would still be slowly poisoned by what she'd already made, until he was too weak to put up any fight at all.

It would be embarrassing to have to ask her to stop, but he could swallow a little pride in exchange for his life. He was about to speak up when he realised that she was now working with him rather than against, unmaking the amalgam she'd been forcing together just a moment before.

"What happened?" he asked as the last of the bonds fell apart under their combined attention.

"I don't want to kill you," she said, breathless with exertion.

"That's sweet of you."

"It's selfish. I like you. And how are you going to teach me if you're dead?"

"Seems to me that you don't need much teaching at all. Tell me what you just did."

"I did... well, I suppose you could say I did two things at once. Exactly as you were doing."

"Indeed."

"You sound a bit surprised — but you showed me exactly how to do it. I assumed that was the point of the lesson."

"Perhaps it should have been, but I admit I was only trying to win. You're very observant."

"So I've been told."

"Good. It makes this process easier."

"This... this new thing. Doing two things at once. Are there other times you might use it? I mean, aside from to try and trick someone in a fight?"

"There are some complex amalgams that require a very similar technique, yes."

"Will you teach me one so I can practise?"

"In light of recent events," Leofwin said, "there is one especially pertinent example, though I'm not sure you'll be practising it any time soon. It's the formula Anselm brought me."

Chapter Forty-Two

He pulled a small bottle from his pocket, and held it aloft in the shaft of sunlight which poured in through the window. The liquid sparkled like molten silver.

"The golden elixir," Ailith said. Except this was a silver elixir.

"What?"

"Nothing. It was just something I read, a fragment of a story, something about transforming the golden elixir."

"Was this in one of my books?"

"No, there were words painted on the walls of a... a place. It was like a cave, but man-made, not natural."

"An erdstall."

"What?"

"A mysterious underground room, built by the ancients, but not obviously a burial chamber?"

She nodded.

"It's called an erdstall. And the tale was about alchemy?"

"We thought perhaps it was an unknown saga. It was about a magician who discovered the golden elixir. The draught of unending life, it said, which sounds awfully like the sort of thing you've been developing."

"Well, it can only be a story. No mage has ever had the power to transform gold."

"What, never?"

"Not that we've known. Very few of us can use silver."

She took the vial from his hand, and tilted it back and forth, watching the flow of the thick liquid. "But you can."

"I can."

"And you've taken this yourself," she said, realisation suddenly dawning. Anselm wasn't the only one who looked younger than his years. "How old does that make you?"

"Fifty-nine."

She cocked her head to one side and studied him. When Malachi had asked her to guess, she'd put him in his thirties, perhaps forty. He had light creases round his eyes, but nothing in the lines of his face suggested he was almost sixty.

"So you've been taking this stuff for, what? Twenty years?"

"More or less." He was watching her almost as closely as she was watching him. "Does that change the way you think of me?"

"I think you're very clever," she said. "But I already knew that."

He looked like he wanted her to say more, but it was just one more strange fact in a sea of strangeness. It already felt like the sands were shifting beneath her feet on a daily basis. Why should she expect to be able to rely on anything, even something so fundamental as age?

She swirled the thick silver liquid again. "When were you going to test me on this?"

"I hadn't decided."

"It matters, though, doesn't it? It matters to you that I can do it, and if I can't, I can't help you and I'll have to leave. Perhaps not today, but eventually."

"I haven't decided that, either." He shook his head, frowning. "You're a good student, better than good. That should be enough."

"Should it? You've always said you needed an equal."

"But now I've got you, and I want that to be enough."

She set the bottle down in front of him. "Let's do the test now."

"Why?"

"Because it might be fine, and then we can both stop worrying. And if I can't do it, then you can start to decide how much that matters to you, but at least you'll know. What's the simplest formula using silver?"

"In theory you can use it almost anywhere you might use copper, just like you can use stabwort in place of sourgrass — the effect will be similar, but stronger. But this isn't fair, you haven't done much work with the metals."

"Don't worry about that part. Copper was my very first transformation."

He stared at her, and she realised she might never have mentioned it.

"Didn't I tell you how this all began? The real version, I mean… not that it's so different. There was still Malachi with his shimmering powder, but there was also a jug I made, which I couldn't really mention when I was pretending to be rather more than a potter's daughter."

"You're a lot more than a potter's daughter, Ailith. You're a mage and an alchemist."

"Well." She blushed. "That's beside the point. My point is that I made a jug, and it was a bit of a pathetic jug because I was just learning to make handles, so when the handle eventually came off the jug smashed. Except it didn't, totally, because it turned out that I'd somehow managed to make a copper glaze that didn't break."

"Alone, and untutored."

It wasn't a question, but she nodded her confirmation regardless.

"Then I don't think there's much to worry about with silver. Perhaps you should just try the gold and be done with it."

"Do you have some?"

"Of course I don't! Not ground up neatly in a little pot and ready to use, not when everyone knows it's impossible."

"Oh. I see."

"But I'm not short of jewellery, if you really want to prove yourself beyond the laws of alchemy."

"I want to know." She took a deep breath, trying to calm her racing heart. "Either way, I want to know. Wouldn't you?"

"I wouldn't be human if I'd never tried to push the boundaries."

"Well, then. It's my turn to be foolish, and it'll serve me right if the gods take away my power to touch as much as a leaf of mint."

"There's no record of anyone's power diminishing over time. Or increasing, for that matter — it seems that whatever talent you've got, you're stuck with it."

"Then we've nothing to lose."

"We'll do silver first, just to be sure." He got to his feet. "Wait here."

It felt like going right back to day one. A sick feeling had lodged in the pit of her stomach when he'd said that the ability to work silver was rare, and it only grew stronger as she waited for him to gather a suitable set of ingredients. She'd thought she was done with tests that could determine her future, at least of the practical kind. She'd thought proving herself loyal and trustworthy was the only barrier that remained.

Logic told her that if copper had been easy, silver should at least be possible, but the nausea wasn't particularly amenable to logic. Besides, that same logic said that someone, somewhere, should be able to use gold. In all the theories she'd read, nothing suggested a reason for it to be otherwise.

Leofwin returned with pots of copper and silver shavings, a bottle of almond oil, and a sprig of thyme.

"This might be the simplest of the copper cures," he said, setting a book down in front of her, open at a very short formula. "It's a remedy against the coughing malady. Start with copper or silver, as you please, and I'll prepare some gold."

He laid a lightweight golden chain on the table, pulled his dagger from its sheath, and prised apart a couple of the tiny rings while she weighed out precise quantities of silver and thyme on the balance. She knew she could work copper; it was better to get the real test over with.

Once she'd measured everything into the bowl and given it a quick stir, she willed it to come together, and a few nerve-wracking moments later she had a smooth amalgam ready to decant into an empty bottle.

Leofwin stopped demolishing his jewellery for long enough to raise an eyebrow. "That easy?"

She attempted a casual shrug, but couldn't stop a grin from creeping across her face as the weight lifted from her shoulders.

"What can I say? You've taught me well."

"I'll have this ready for you in a moment."

She prepared appropriate quantities of thyme and almond oil, and waited. The waiting wasn't so agonising, this time. If he didn't think she could succeed then her future couldn't hinge on whether she could amalgamate gold.

He weighed the gold shavings, and tipped them into her bowl.

She took a steadying breath and pushed her awareness past her fingers, feeling every element of the mixture as they moved together, taking her time to make sure she understood the different qualities of the gold before she tried to change it. And she could definitely feel the gold, right there with everything else… but the sensation was aloof, somehow. She pushed lightly, then steadily harder, until she was expending twice as much force as she'd needed for the silver amalgam. However hard she tried, the gold remained inert, resistant to her direction.

"Don't be too hard on yourself," he said softly, sensing the very moment she withdrew her efforts. "Everyone who ever found they could work silver has tried to progress to gold. It's always in vain."

"It doesn't make any sense. How can it be impossible?"

"Some say there's a secret that was known, once, but is now long forgotten. Others claim the gods became jealous, stripping power from mere mortals. Personally, I tend towards the pragmatic — I can't fly, I can't lift a millstone, why should I be able to transform gold?"

"It's so close, though." She looked morosely down into the bowl. "I can tell it's close. I can feel it."

"You can feel it," Leofwin agreed. "But it can't feel you. It's an immovable object."

"Perhaps," she said, but she knew she wasn't quite ready to accept defeat. Not yet. "I suppose it doesn't matter, when you've already got a perfectly functional elixir of youth."

"Is that what you'd call this?"

"Wouldn't you?"

"I'd call it a suspended death sentence, personally."

Her questions must have been written clear as day across her face, because he answered before she'd managed to shape her thoughts into words.

"It's like having some debilitating disease, and not knowing whether you'll be cured this side of death. You can't afford to mix up the dates, or your blood turns to poison in your veins. You live in fear that some exotic ingredient will stop being available. You can't make friends, or you can't keep them, lest they eventually notice that you don't change the way they do — and because it would take only one betrayal, one person with the power to keep you from your workshop for just a few short weeks, and that would be the end of it. Even the staff can't be permitted to see me over too long a period."

"Then why did you take it?"

"If you'd asked me at the time, I would have said the obvious: to preserve my youth, and stop ageing while I was still in my prime."

"And now?"

"I think I needed to understand it better. And to force myself to commit everything to finding a solution."

He met her eyes for a long, serious moment before a rueful smile crossed his lips.

"But I have had, as you say, twenty years to get used to all that. And almost the same again, before I took the amalgam, to watch Anselm and convince myself I was still making the right decision. I don't mean to burden you with it."

"It's better that I understand the implications." Ailith picked up the bowl and prodded at the failed amalgam. "But that only makes it more important to figure out why gold doesn't work as we'd expect."

When she returned to her room that night, she found her writ and token laid on her pillow.

Chapter Forty-Three

"No."

Garrick's eyes narrowed. "No?"

"That's what I said." Selwyn stood in the temple doorway, cane in hand, his frail form blocking the door. "You walked out. You can't just walk back in."

"I went to help free your son, and this is how you thank me?"

Orvyn had warned him that Selwyn was in a temper, but he'd imagined that at worst it might translate into a beating or extra chores for penance. Refusing him access to the temple was just unreasonable.

"You went to interfere, because you can't put your trust in the gods for five whole minutes," Selwyn said. "How can someone of such little faith hope to succeed as a temple apprentice?"

Garrick snorted. Selwyn hadn't asked too many questions about his faith when he'd arrived with a heavy purse to pay for his tuition. "I believe in discharging my duties."

"The ones that you like the look of, at least. But my answer is still no."

Well, he didn't need the old man anyway. Once he was lord of Highfort he could summon any one of the Guild to teach him everything he needed to know, and if they refused, he could wipe their whole petty group off the map. Selwyn might turn him away now, but even a priest couldn't hope to stand alone against the wrath of one of the Twelve.

"I hope you live to regret this," he muttered as he left.

He didn't need to wait for the stable boys to take their customary break. They gaped at him as he pulled himself up the wall, but it didn't matter: he wouldn't be coming back. Garrick retrieved his papers and stuffed them into his travel bag.

He had one of the lads saddle Chestnut for him. Apparently Selwyn hadn't had the forethought to tell them that he was firing his apprentice. Or perhaps he'd assumed that Garrick would simply never return. Stealing from the gods would probably see him cursed, but he was too angry to care. He needed to get home quickly, and the temple horses were kept in better condition than anything he could pick up from the coaching inn.

As he rode out of Bracklea for the final time, he jerked the reins to the left and took the southern road. It wasn't the most direct route to the Highfort, but there was one more thing he needed to pick up before he left this town for good. He might not have bothered, but Malachi had given him reason to believe that the saga might be more than just a baseless myth. Of course, in that case, he should have the place watched. Ailith had become dangerously unpredictable; there was no way to know if she'd told Malachi or even Leofwin about his discovery. He'd arrange some guards as soon as he got home.

He'd stored his notes in a hollow tree-trunk near the road, so he didn't really need to go as far as the cavern itself, but his feet carried him into the woods before he'd thought it through. He'd found time to come back here only once since the day he'd brought Ailith, and he couldn't help thinking of her as he stood in the cool, dark space where they'd worked and kissed.

And now he'd lost her.

Well, he would see how she liked the sight of armies from her window. Once she understood that she couldn't live safely in Watersmeet, she'd realise that his proposal was her only option. She was proud, that was all. Pride had driven her to slap him, but even pride would have to give way to practicality.

Chapter Forty-Four

Ailith lay on her bed, staring up at the tassels which trimmed the canopy. Ever since her failed attempt at amalgamating gold, odd lines from the erdstall text had been going round in her head, making it harder than ever to sleep.

The golden elixir is made only in the action of pure intent and strength of will.

The words made no sense, even in the context of the study she'd undertaken since first reading them. Of course it could only be made with intent. That was true of all of alchemy; there was nothing about that idea that was specific to gold. Did purity have some special meaning in this context? She'd found nothing else that hinted at such an interpretation, in any of the texts.

Leofwin's imperfect tonic might be close, and the very fact that it used silver was promising, but for whatever reason there was clearly a gulf between silver and gold. She couldn't shake the picture of misery on his face as he'd described the limitations of the imperfect formula. How many mornings had he woken with that terrible sword hanging over his head?

Gold had to be the answer, and she was determined to find whatever key they'd missed to unlock it.

Alchemy was plagued by competing theories offering conflicting explanations for every observation, but whatever their logic, every theory predicted that gold should be stronger than silver, just as silver was stronger than copper. It even *felt* right… except insofar as it failed to amalgamate.

She went up to the garden, hoping the fresh air would at least help her relax enough to rest. Maybe the key was in one of the other ingredients. She thought it through as she paced the paths. It wasn't how things were supposed to work, but maybe they needed to adjust the quantities or even the qualities of the other parts of the formula to make it work. She'd been making and unmaking quantities of the silver amalgam every chance she got, hoping that once it became effortless, the practice alone would lead to some insight. It hadn't.

Eventually she dozed off under the arbour, and woke to find Leofwin sitting across the table, his steady gaze fixed on her.

"You couldn't sleep?" he guessed as she blinked herself awake, the light of the storm lanterns dancing in her bleary eyes.

"No. You neither?"

He shrugged. "I've never slept well. What's troubling you? Are you still worrying about gold?"

Of course: he couldn't have avoided noticing the depth of her new obsession. She'd been virtually unable to work on anything else.

"There's a trick we're not seeing," she said. "It's not possible that it's impossible... not when every theory tells us exactly how it should behave."

"Maybe the theories are wrong."

She shook her head. "That would undermine everything. No, if we don't trust alchemical theory, we can't expect anything to work, and it generally does. But it's clear I can't do it by myself."

"Tell me what you're thinking."

"You know how you made me fight you the other day? I was wondering if we could try the opposite. Is it possible we'd be stronger working together?"

"I don't know that it's ever been tried."

"Then we should at least have a go. Don't you think?"

Back in the workshop, the half-formed cough remedy from the week before was still sitting in a bowl on the shelf. Ailith set it on the table between them.

"It needs to be within reach of us both," she said, prodding at the mixture with a wooden spoon. "Obviously. What else? What have I missed?"

"Let's just try it."

He wrapped his hand around hers, his fingers completely enclosing fist and spoon-handle alike. She shut her eyes and forced her focus down beyond their hands and into the bowl. Everything was the same as yesterday. The gold still resisted her efforts, its inertia silently taunting her. She felt Leofwin's mind join the push, and for a moment she thought that between them they might succeed.

But no.

A long moment later, by some unspoken agreement, they both withdrew their efforts. He released her hand, and she opened her eyes.

"That first morning, do you remember?" she asked. "You told me that I had to accept my limits, and trust you to help me find them."

"I remember."

"I trust you completely — you know that — but as for the other part, I don't think I can. Not while there are things we haven't tried. I'm sorry."

"You don't need to apologise for that. You're an alchemist. You're supposed to be stubborn about looking for answers."

Chapter Forty-Five

It was four days' hard ride to Ailith's home town. Leofwin had worked out the timings carefully, and checked them three times to be sure. If he left the next morning he could spend two or three days there, and still get back before he next needed to attend to Anselm or any of his customers.

He brought the subject up over lunch. "That erdstall you mentioned, with the writing in it. Where exactly was it?"

"It's just a little outside Bracklea."

"Can you be more specific?"

"It was in the forest, south of the town — about an hour on horseback. Why?"

"I think I should visit. If it truly holds a clue to working with gold, then it would be a mistake not to investigate."

"Oh, then that's easy, I should just come with you. It'll be much easier to show you than to describe it."

"I'm afraid you can't come."

He'd reckoned without the disappointment in her eyes. "Why not?"

"Many reasons. Not least of which being that it's four days' ride to Bracklea, and you're not confident on a horse yet."

"What's the rush?"

"It's hard to explain, but I fear we should make what haste we can. If nothing else, the fact that someone thought it was worth asking you to poison me suggests there might be more trouble on the horizon. And however slim it may be, this is the first hope I've had in years of making a real leap forwards. It would be unfortunate to let it slip through our hands."

"Then you should definitely let me come and help. I can share your horse, then my poor riding won't slow you down."

"The extra weight would slow down even the best of horses. Besides, people would recognise you. In my work clothes, I'm just another traveller passing through, but you've lived there all your life. The best way you can help is to look after things here."

"What? How?"

"Nothing too onerous — the household staff know their jobs. We have a good steward, Wynflaeth, who manages the day to day finances, and Thurstan will be your link to her. Between them they'll work out what we need and negotiate with the tradesmen, but someone has to check the ledgers, hear any complaints from the staff, and generally keep the place running. Oh, and make sure there's suitable provision for any visitors."

"But... I don't know how to do any of those things."

"It's often boring, and requires few of the skills we've been honing, but there's nothing likely to present a challenge to a woman of your intelligence. Nonetheless, sometimes an issue can be resolved only by the application of rank."

She hesitated. "Rank which I don't have."

"Surely the servants defer to you?"

"Well, yes. When I ask them to."

"You're obviously here as my guest. What a more worldly woman might have realised by now is that when it comes to the staff, that gives you whatever authority you choose to take."

"I'd never take anything that wasn't mine."

"And I love you for it. But if you're going to survive at court with people like Garrick, then you need to start learning how these things work. Although..." He smiled to remember it. "I think you dealt with him well enough, in your own way. But if you're to manage Watersmeet, you'll need to be confident in your position, especially if there are visitors."

"Speaking of visitors — is it the silver amalgam that you're selling to the other barons?"

"Selling?" He raised an eyebrow. "Have you been spying on me again? Tell me what you saw."

"Now and again you have noble visitors, though they hardly seem to be your friends. You give them some amalgam, and they give you money."

"What makes you think it's the silver?"

"They come on the moon's turn, or thereabouts. You let them see you, so they must know something. And they pay you well, bringing heavy purses that might just contain enough gold to buy a month of ageless life."

He smiled. "If you've been attending that closely to the turns of the moon then you know that whatever I'm selling, they shouldn't trouble you during my absence."

"What if you're delayed?"

"I'll be home as soon as I can, but you're right, we should be prepared for any eventuality. You know how to make the amalgam, and you can practice the final stage on the mice this evening. Oh!" He laughed. How could he have forgotten? "No, you're right, you'll need to keep a lot of beings alive. The mice need a dose of silver every other morning."

"Right." She nodded. "You'll need to tell me which ones."

"And you'll need to give me better directions than 'south a bit'."

"Yes, I'll sketch you a map. Garrick could show you, of course, but I fear he doesn't like you much."

"I don't like him much, either, and I wouldn't choose to put myself in his debt."

Ailith sighed. "I liked him well enough when I thought he was a temple orphan, but he's intolerable as a lord."

Chapter Forty-Six

On her first day alone in the castle, Ailith did a complete stock-take of Leofwin's store room. If he was going to leave her in charge, then she was determined to do a good job of it. She took every jar from the shelves and checked their contents. Some contained ancient and mouldering leaves, which she dumped into the privy. Several pots were almost empty, and a couple contained substances quite unlike what the label indicated.

A number of leaves and seeds could be harvested directly from Leofwin's rooftop gardens. She gathered those that were currently in season and set them to drying, and made a chart of those which should be available to collect in the coming weeks and months. For the minerals, and for plants that didn't grow in the castle grounds or Leofwin's glasshouses, she made a shopping list to pass to Thurstan.

By the time she'd finished, it was past the hour when she should have taken Anselm's tray across. She let herself into the corridor outside his apartments, unlocked the door, and balanced the supper tray with one hand so she could knock.

"Hello… you must be Ailith."

"Sorry it's late." She smiled, suddenly shy. "Did Leofwin tell you, he's travelling?"

"Oh, yes. I… he usually… do you want to come in?"

"If you don't mind."

"Mind? This is the only company I get."

"I was thinking about that." She shuffled past him and set the tray down. "Would you really run off, if you had the freedom of the castle?"

"It would be foolish, but sometimes I'm a fool." Anselm

shrugged. "Sometimes death feels preferable to gaol, though it's a nice enough prison."

"Oh." Ailith sat down and fiddled with her skirts. "Leofwin said you tried to kill yourself, with that dart."

He nodded. "It might not have been the best decision I've ever made, but it was me or him, and he had more to live for. And I thought, if you didn't have me to rescue, you might be able to settle down here."

"Well. Thank you."

"It didn't work, though, did it? I didn't die, and he guessed you were responsible."

"Who else could have brought you poison?"

They fell into an awkward silence while Anselm picked at his food. She toyed with explaining that she'd thought she was misleading him, when she'd allowed him to believe it was deadly, but it seemed an unnecessary complication. And he might be her grandfather — another fact she'd found easier not to share with him — but she didn't really know him.

"How do you spend your time?" she asked, trying to distract herself. "No, I'm sorry, I shouldn't make you talk while you're eating."

"I'd rather talk than eat." He set down his fork. "I'm a musician. I mean, not that I've ever played for anyone besides Leofwin, but it's what I enjoy. I'm learning the harp."

"I heard you, that night we spoke." She was afraid to mention all the other times she'd crept through the walls just to listen. It suddenly felt like an invasion of privacy. "You're good. You could play for me, later," she said. "But eat first, while it's fresh."

Watching Anselm's fingers fly across the harp strings was a revelation. She'd known he was talented, but she'd never seen a harpist at work before. She stared, mesmerised, long after he'd damped the strings at the end of the piece.

"What do you think?" he asked, and she realised she should have said something already.

"Amazing," she said. "You're very talented."

"I have a lot of time to devote to my practice," he said. "So I suppose something good has come of all this. I never would have had the time to learn music, back home, let alone been able to afford an instrument like this."

"Would you like to play for an audience?" she asked, an idea forming in her mind.

"If only it were possible."

"I think something could be arranged," she said. "So long as you promise not to run away. I've already come much too close to being responsible for your death."

The next morning, she asked Frida for a tour of the other rooms in the guest wing. "You know yours is the Red Room," Frida said. "And this next door is the Blue Room, for obvious reasons."

The room was almost a mirror image of hers, but with sky blue drapes that were embroidered with yellow vines.

"Let me guess, there's also a Green Room? Or Yellow?"

"Yes, both. The Green Room is just across the hall here, and Yellow's in the other wing. And Lilac, and Rose. Then there are the smaller rooms for attendants and courtiers, there's at least two dozen of those set up and ready for use. D'you really want to see round them all?"

"I'm more interested in the ones that are standing empty, really. Is there anything here, near my room?"

"A couple of the biggest rooms are empty." She pushed open the door to the other side of Ailith's room. "Like this one. They're a bugger to heat, so we tend not to use them."

The air was musty but the room was gorgeous. Oh, the tapestries were a little moth-eaten, the stone fireplace was home to a giant spider, and dust motes danced in the sunlight. But the sun streamed in through three large windows and there was plenty of space for what she had in mind.

"This will be perfect."

"What are you plotting?"

"Who says I'm plotting?"

"I know that look. You've got some big idea."

"I want to have my own dining room." She certainly couldn't entertain in Leofwin's private apartments. "How long do you think it'll take to get this place tidied up?"

Frida looked around the room, measuring the tasks in her mind. "I'll get someone to beat the tapestries this afternoon. Then it's just a question of mopping the floors and lighting a fire to clear the air. You could use it tonight, if all you wanted was to stand in the middle of the floor."

"I'll need to get hold of some rugs," Ailith mused. "And furniture. I could borrow a few chairs from the guest rooms, but I'll need a table, too."

"I think there are some chairs in storage, and little side-tables, too. His lordship doesn't use a tenth of what he owns. But I don't know about a dining table… and it's a long way from the kitchens. How many people do you want to seat?"

"Let's see. There's you, Ymma, Lily…"

"What?" Frida said.

"Wig and Ada," Ailith went on, counting on her fingers. "Lufe, Nia, Ulf. And me. Seems like we'll need at least nine chairs. A dozen would be better."

"I thought you wanted a dining room?"

"Yes."

"I don't understand you."

Ailith grinned. "Nobody does. But why wouldn't I want to be able to entertain my friends?"

"We're not really dining room people," Frida said uncertainly.

"We could stay up as late as we like, here, and not be disturbing anyone." Ailith tapped her foot on the wooden floorboards. "We could even dance, if Ulf brings his pipe. And if we can't get hot food up from the kitchens, we can ask Cook to make up a cold spread."

"Leave it with me," Frida said. "I'll find you some furnishings."

"Don't tell the others yet. Just… tell them I'll be drinking with them tomorrow. Unless you think we can really have it ready for tonight?"

"Tomorrow is better."

Frida outdid herself. She roped in a couple of boys to help Ailith with the cleaning, and the room sparkled by the time they'd finished. She found a store of disused rugs and chairs, and pieced together a row of small tables to make something that loosely resembled a banqueting table, especially once it had been covered with crisp linen cloths. Cutlery and crockery had been procured from the kitchens, and Cook had agreed to give Ymma the night off.

Ailith helped Anselm to manoeuvre his harp through the secret passages and into the guest wing. By the time her friends arrived, the table was laden with food, and strains of music filled the air. And she'd never seen anyone look happier than Anselm did as his fingers danced across the strings.

Chapter Forty-Seven

Leofwin stopped for supplies in Bracklea, filling his saddlebags with food and ale at the market. The purchase of a significant quantity of lamp oil and charcoal pencils attracted a strange look from the merchant, since he was obviously a traveller, but he offered no explanation and the man wasn't so rude as to ask.

That was the easy part. Next he had to follow Ailith's sketched map, to find a place she'd visited only once and which she'd warned him was well hidden amongst the trees. And that had been early spring: now, the trees were in full leaf and the undergrowth had grown waist-high.

After three false starts and one accidental shredding of his sleeve as he wandered into a patch of brambles, he eventually came upon the gully she'd described. The ground had been disturbed by recent footfalls, and he pulled out his dagger as he scrambled to the top of the bank, but the erdstall was thankfully empty. In the flickering lamplight, the ancient painted words looked more like mystical symbols than letters.

It was getting late, but he didn't dare to sleep within the sheltered walls. Perhaps no-one but Garrick knew of this place, but even that was too much of a risk. He returned to his horse and rode a little further down the road, until he found a suitable spot to tie her within reach of a clear brook and a grassy clearing. For his own improvised lodgings he stretched a canvas sheet between three trees, lashing the corners tightly into the branches. It wouldn't hold off any real weather, but it might keep a summer shower from disturbing his sleep. After a quick supper of ham and hard-boiled eggs, he huddled beneath a blanket and tried not to listen to the insects scuttling through the leaves beside his head. It had been a very long time since he'd slept beneath the stars.

The next morning he left the horse tied up, and walked back to the erdstall carrying nothing but a lantern and his writing equipment.

The erdstall was a long, thin tunnel that ran back into the hillside, and the writing was confined to one of the side walls.

He measured the height and width of the wall, and divided it up with lengths of string until he had a grid to work from. Then, starting with the first section of the grid, he began to copy every mark onto his slate. Whether it was paint or a scratch or a crack in the rocks, he made no distinction: this would be a drawing, not a transcript of words. The result was a beautiful facsimile that preserved all the confusion and complexity of the original.

Once he'd filled the slate he emerged into the daylight, took out a stick of charcoal, and copied every line of his sketch onto a fresh sheet of paper.

Then he wiped the slate clean and started again, moving to the next square of the grid. By the end of the day he'd filled seven pages, and his sketches covered almost half of the wall.

Chapter Forty-Eight

"Milady, there's a gentleman named Malachi here to see his lordship."

Ailith got to her feet, straightening her skirts. "I assume you've told him there's only me, today."

Thurstan frowned, almost imperceptibly. "I have said what I always say — that he may wait, and I will enquire as to when his lordship might be available."

"Why? You know he's not available."

"I think his lordship would prefer that no-one outside this room knows that."

"Still, I should see him. Is he waiting in the Lower Hall?" That was the usual place for unexpected visitors, just large enough to feel imposing, while clearly giving only a hint of what the castle could offer.

"Milady, if I may be so bold as to offer a suggestion?"

She nodded. "Of course."

"A woman of your status should take her time getting ready. Allow me to go and express his lordship's apologies that he is indisposed, and not well enough to receive guests. I will advise the visitor to expect you at your leisure."

Ailith wasn't sure she held with that kind of deception, but if she'd learnt one thing in Leofwin's absence it was that Thurstan knew more about the business of running a castle than she did. She could just about accept that he also knew more about how castle-dwellers should manage their interactions. For herself she wouldn't have bothered, but she didn't want to completely ruin Leofwin's image by the time he returned.

"At least have him wait in the Drawing Room," she said. "A man of his age shouldn't have to stand."

She picked out a clean dress that was colourful but plain, and had Frida put a plait into her hair. Malachi knew where she'd come from; there was nothing to be gained by wearing silk and jewels. Then, as she was sure she hadn't used up enough time by these simple preparations, she read a couple of pages of Swein's *Treatise on Uncommon Metallurgy*. The slim volume contained nothing but a passing mention of gold, but she was still convinced there were lessons to be drawn from the secrets of copper and silver, if only she could find them.

Once she'd wasted enough minutes to satisfy propriety, she made her way down to the Drawing Room.

"Ailith." Malachi beamed at her, levering himself awkwardly out of a stuffed chair. "A charming surprise. How are you, m'dear?"

She allowed him to kiss her hand, and took the seat across from him. "His lordship apologises," she said. "He's indisposed to visitors."

"Of course. I'm no stranger to a little indisposition myself." Malachi's bright eyes flitted around the room. "Tell me, m'dear. Does his indisposition keep him to his bed? And what of the servants?"

"You can speak frankly," Ailith said. "No-one is listening."

"I'm glad we understand each other."

"Perfectly."

"I was worried about you when you didn't take your usual walk on the full moon. I feared you'd become his lordship's latest prisoner."

Ailith studied him for a moment. Not for the first time, she suspected there was more than there appeared to be going on behind those half-blind eyes, and she wasn't quite sure how far she could trust him.

"I'm no prisoner," she said. That period hadn't lasted long. "But it seems to me that if you can call on Leofwin like this without anyone thinking it odd, you might have called on me without all this cloak-and-dagger full moon nonsense."

"Ah, but we didn't want to raise any suspicions. Not when you were just pretending."

"Pretending?"

"To be his lordship's student. If you're receiving visitors on his behalf, these days, and calling him by his first name — well, then I take it you've properly established yourself."

"I have a real apprenticeship," she said. "If that's what you mean. It's more than I could have hoped for in Bracklea, with the Guild the way they are. And Leofwin seems to have forgiven me for that ill-advised incident with the poison."

"Garrick wanted to feel useful." Malachi had the decency to look a little embarrassed. "Perhaps I should not have allowed it to go so far."

"What's done is done. Tell me what brings you here today."

"As you're safe, nothing. Had you been in trouble, I would have had more business to attend to."

"That's good of you."

"Since I have your attention, however," Malachi smiled, "I think it's important that you know some things. I'm not sure if Leofwin has trusted you with his biggest secret yet, m'dear."

Ailith kept her face carefully neutral. If he was trying to trick information from her, she wouldn't give anything away. She owed Leofwin that much. "A secret?"

"I think I mentioned that when Anselm left me, he took a substantial portion of my life's work."

"Yes."

"Those papers included a particular formula of my own devising, which may be the closest humanity has yet come to an elixir of youth, if we discount the sagas. Your new master may appear to be in his thirties, but he was my student some fifty years ago. Think on that."

"What would you have me think of it? My views of what's possible have changed beyond belief these past few weeks; an elixir of youth is hardly less credible than the other things I've learnt. The next thing you tell me, it'll be dragons waking in the Iron Mountains."

"If he doesn't trust you with such things, you need to consider what else he might be hiding. Can you really trust him?"

Ailith shook her head. "You're as bad as Garrick. If I'm thinking about who I can trust, I'm not sure why I'd choose a mysterious old man who's trying to manipulate me. This isn't a saga: being old doesn't automatically make you wise."

"No, m'dear, I quite see your point. But I don't think I've steered you far from the course you would have chosen."

She shrugged. How could she have made any meaningful choices about her future, knowing as little as she did before she came here? At least now she had that luxury. For that, perhaps, she should thank him.

Chapter Forty-Nine

Leofwin stabled his borrowed horse at the coaching inn and went inside to negotiate for food and board. Dressed in a commoner's simple travelling clothes, he'd soon realised that he had to haggle hard and pay in small coins to avoid raising suspicions on the road. Still, he should be only half a day's ride from Watersmeet; one more night in a hayloft was neither here nor there. Gods, but it would be good to be home.

He took his supper in the bar and downed three tankards of cheap ale. It was vile-tasting stuff but if he drank enough it might take the edge off his stiff muscles, or at least ease his way into sleep. It was dark by the time he made his way across the yard and pulled himself up the ladder. He slung his bag into the corner of the loft, keeping his notes from the erdstall tucked safely out of sight in his boot. The inn wasn't busy, but that was the only thing he'd mind losing if he encountered a light-fingered fellow traveller.

He curled up beside a stack of hay bales, but sleep didn't come. By the time the watery beer made its way to his bladder he'd been tossing and turning for an hour or more, and was almost glad of the excuse to get up. He dropped down into the barn and wandered outside to relieve himself against the wall, as a traveller of his supposed means would be expected to do. In the bar, quiet drinking had turned into rowdy singing. He turned to make his way back to bed, and when the shadows seemed to move he assumed it was a fault of his drink-addled brain.

Even as the shadowy form resolved into an approaching man, he didn't understand the threat until the dagger hit his chest.

Then old instincts kicked in before he had time to think, and he dropped to the ground and rolled, coming back to his feet with his own knife in his hand. It had been over forty years since he'd been in a proper fight, but some things weren't easily forgotten.

The attacker moved in close, and Leofwin had to block the next slashing blow with his elbow as he brought his dagger down to stab his opponent's shoulder. The fight was fast and messy like a tavern brawl, no time for polite circling and careful parries. Whoever this man was, he wanted only to kill, and Leofwin had no choice but to respond in kind with whatever clumsy stabs and punches he could manage.

It was a slash across the jugular that ended it, and the man crumpled onto the cobblestones. Covered in blood, Leofwin stumbled as quickly as he could manage towards the stables. His injuries could wait. Such men seldom travelled alone: if he wanted to live, he needed to get out of here, and he could only hope they wouldn't dare to openly pursue him. He could stop and bind up his wounds once he'd put a few clear miles between himself and the tavern. The stablehand had fled at the sound of a struggle, leaving the horses unattended. Leofwin untied the nearest stallion and hauled himself awkwardly across its back, clinging to the bridle with his right hand as his left hung limply at his side.

He'd never liked riding in the dark, but at least he was close to home. He probably wouldn't be recognised at the castle, but the guest-right extended to healing as much as to hospitality. His people knew their duty, even to strangers.

Chapter Fifty

Ailith was woken by a hammering at the bedroom door, and was wiping the sleep from her eyes as Frida ran in with a lantern swinging wildly in her hand.

"There's a man," she gasped. "At the gate. Asking for you. Hurt."

"What?" Ailith rolled out of bed and pulled yesterday's dress over her head. "Who? What's happened?"

"I don't know," Frida said. "I didn't see him myself, but everyone says he's asking for you by name."

Frida fell into step behind her as she hurried down the corridor, straightening the laces of her bodice as she went. Better to be disheveled and prompt, if her unexpected visitor was injured. Her hair hung loose around her shoulders, and the flagstones were cold and rough against her bare feet since she'd stopped to grab a pouch of herbs instead of her shoes.

Worried thoughts flashed through her mind as she ran down the stairs. Had Malachi tried to pay a visit? Was Garrick making another unannounced call? And whoever it was, what in Refah's name had happened to him that she should be roused at such a time? The sky was beginning to lighten, but only farmers and guards should be awake at this hour.

The man was lying prone on the ground just inside the outer gatehouse, surrounded by anxious guards. His grey tunic was soaked with blood, and a ragged gash tore across the left knee of his trousers.

"What's going on?" Ailith asked.

"He's been asking for you, milady," one of the guards said,

prodding at the body with his foot. "When he's with us. Oi! Wake up, she's come."

Ailith moved around so she could see his face. Stunned, her lips began to shape his name, but he shushed her with a finger to his lips and beckoned her closer before she could speak. She dropped to her knees by his side, taking in the ragged clothes and the way he'd tied his hair at the nape of his neck. No wonder no-one had recognised him.

"They don't know who I am," Leofwin whispered, his voice strained. "Let's keep it that way."

"You're hurt."

"A little. Help me?"

"Of course. Here." She handed him a piece of willow bark to chew, something to take the edge off the pain. "Can you walk?"

"Barely."

"Do you want me to send for a proper healer?"

"No. You're good enough."

"This had better not be another test." Ailith turned to the guards who were still loitering nearby. "You and you, help me carry him," she ordered. "Frida, can you fetch some hot water to my room? Rethar, go with her, please."

"Are you sure it's wise to bring a stranger into the castle?" one of the guards asked. "Do you know him?"

Ailith glowered at him. "Just do as I say."

Leofwin groaned in agony as the guards lifted him, but there was little Ailith could do besides making sure they avoided touching the worst of his wounds. Once they'd helped him into the castle, she'd be able to clean him up and get to work. Until then he would simply have to deal with it.

Somehow they managed to get him up three flights of stairs and laid out on Ailith's bed, propped up on a stack of pillows. She instructed Rethar to stand guard and make sure they weren't disturbed, and bolted the door from the inside, too, to make doubly sure.

"Do you want to tell me what happened?" she asked as she

started to ease off his boots. "This looks pretty bad."

He forced a smile. "You should see the other fellow."

"That's not funny."

"My notes… careful…"

"I don't care about your notes."

"You should. Put them somewhere safe."

Ailith nodded. The papers were curled around his leg, only slightly bloodstained along one edge. She shoved them out of sight under the bed. She leaned across to unfasten his belt, which instead of the usual array of pouches, this time held only a simple dagger. Blood from the handle stained her fingers as she set it aside, and she could only imagine how much worse the blade would be within the sheath. She made a mental note to clean it up after she'd dealt with his injuries.

"Did you get mugged on the road?" she asked. As long as he kept talking, he was awake. And though she didn't know much about stabbings, she knew that it was important to keep people awake after a blow to the head.

"No. Attacked."

"Do you know who?"

"No. Nor why."

"Your shirt's ruined." She considered the bloodstained cloth with dismay. "And if that's your blood, we need to get you fixed up as quickly as possible."

"Not all mine." He reached out with his good arm — the other was clearly incapacitated — and flicked the dagger out of its sheath, offering it to her hilt-first. "You'll have to cut the fabric."

Once she'd cut away the tunic and what remained of his trousers, she could finally see the extent of his injuries. The left side of his chest looked to have sustained the worst damage so she started there, fighting the urge to vomit as she sponged gently at the ragged skin. At least his temporary bandages had stemmed the flow of blood. She lost count of the times she had to send poor Frida for fresh water and clean towels.

"It looks pretty bad," she said. "What do I do? Just Payne's balm?"

"Not yet, they're dirty wounds. Raspwine and campenbalm first."

Those weren't formulae she recognised. "Do you keep some made up?"

He shook his head. "Ingredients in the store room. Instructions in Sefled's *Herbal*."

Well, most of the ingredients were in the store room. For a couple of fresh herbs, she had to run up to the garden. By the time she returned with both mixtures made up, Leofwin had slipped out of consciousness again. She stood and watched him for a long moment. In sleep, he looked peaceful.

"I'm sorry," she murmured, stroking his arm. From a scratch on her own finger she knew how much the raspwine stung; it was bound to wake him. "It'll get worse before it gets better, but it will get better."

Besides the stab wound to the chest, he had significant injuries to both legs, his left arm, and his head. She started with the chest wound, which had started to seep blood again. Raspwine was a thin, acrid-smelling tincture that she washed across the skin, causing him to mutter in his sleep, but the campenbalm had to be rubbed into each cut and amalgamated directly into the blood. Then she could slather on Payne's balm, and bind him with bandages to keep the wound clean while it healed. Leofwin mumbled drowsy objections to the pain, but she persisted. When she'd bound his chest she moved on to his arm, and then his face.

She soaked the cloth in raspwine and wiped it across his forehead, squeezing the liquid into the gash that crossed from his brow to his cheek. He jerked upright with a screech of pain, clutching at his face with his good arm.

"What…?"

"It's okay," she said. "It's just the raspwine. I know it hurts."

"No." He shook his head, frantic. "Water, quickly. My eyes."

She grabbed the bowl she'd been using to wash his wounds, scooping the water up with her hands, and hurried to rinse his eye.

Rivulets of water ran down his chest, soaking into the bandages.

"That'll do," he said, rubbing at his still-bloodshot eye. "Gods, that hurt."

"What went wrong?"

"You have to keep raspwine clear of the eyes. People have gone blind."

"But you're not... I mean, tell me I haven't...?"

"I'm not blinded. Things are a bit blurry, but I'm sure it'll be fine."

"I'm so sorry." She bit her lip, fighting back tears. "I should have read more of—"

He shook his head, sinking back against the pillows. "You weren't to know. I was supposed to be instructing you, not sleeping while you did all the work."

"What's the point having an apprentice if she can't even manage one simple task? Gods, you should just send me home and have done with it."

"I'd quite prefer you to carry on saving my life, if it's all the same to you." He smiled, but she couldn't force herself to match him.

"How?" She reached out to touch his face, carefully avoiding the broken skin. "I can't risk making things worse."

"Payne's balm will be fine, that's just a scratch. And you'll make a tonic for the bruises, once you've finished with the bandages."

"Of course." That, at least, was a recipe she knew. She dabbed a little Payne's balm onto his cheek. "Is there something else I should make to soothe your eye?"

"No, it'll heal. You've quite enough to keep you busy."

She patched up his legs and went back to the workshop. The tonic she made up had ingredients to help him recover from the bruising and the blood loss, as well as something for the pain. She was about to take it to him when she realised that neither of them had eaten anything all day. And the tonic would knock him out for a few hours.

"Can you ask Cook to send up some soup — something light that he can drink?" she asked Frida.

While she waited, Ailith started to clear the room. She bundled up the bloody rags and stained towels, dumping everything unceremoniously in the corner of the room, and tucked a blanket around Leofwin's shoulders. In the morning, she'd go to the market and order some new linens.

"What about you?" Ailith asked when Frida returned with two bowls of broth. Her friend hadn't stopped since daybreak, either.

"I'm fine."

"You must be starving, and exhausted. Get some rest — it's been a long day, and there's nothing more we can do."

"Are you sure?"

"I'm sure. I'll see you in the morning."

"Shall I send word to his lordship?"

Ailith glanced back towards the bed. It was something of a shock to realise Frida hadn't even recognised her employer. She shook her head. "He knows where to find me, if he needs me."

She forced Leofwin to drink the broth down to the last mouthful, and then the foul-tasting tonic.

"Told you," he said as he handed back the tumbler, words starting to slur as the drugs took effect. "You know what you're doing."

"But I hurt you." His eye was still red, and he kept scratching at it when he thought she wasn't watching.

"You've been wonderful."

"I'm going to use your room," she said. That seemed easier than trying to move him again before he'd finished healing. "You can sleep here, I'll come and check on you in the morning."

He reached out and grabbed her wrist. "Stay."

"Well, of course, if you need me." The vice-like grip loosened slightly. "But I think I've done all I can for the moment. Some of these are pretty deep."

"Someone just tried to kill me. I don't want you alone in my rooms if they decide to send a proper assassin to finish the job."

"I can use the Blue Room, then."

"I'd rather you not be alone at all."

"Don't worry, you've more than enough guards to keep an eye on both of us. I don't think you'd be much help to me, anyway, the shape you're in."

He squeezed her hand. "Ailith, just… stay. Please?"

"Oh. Alright."

"Better."

"I can sleep on the floor," she suggested half-heartedly, but she knew he wouldn't hear of it. As if to demonstrate, he leaned over and pulled back the covers on the empty side of the bed. He was already quite close to the other edge, where the guards had set him down atop the covers, but he shuffled awkwardly to try and make more space for her. She checked and double-checked the lock on the door.

"More gossip," she mumbled to herself, scrambling into bed without stopping to undress. This was becoming something of a habit: all of the scandal, with none of the sex. And she gathered from her friends that a lot of the servants, who knew nothing of Leofwin's studies, already thought she'd moved in for old-fashioned reasons.

"For you, maybe," Leofwin said. "And for the mystery man. Not for me, since as far as anyone knows I'm safely tucked up in my own bed."

It was all she could do to refrain from punching him in the wounded arm.

He blew out the lamp and slumped back against the pillows. "Sleep well."

Chapter Fifty-One

It took Leofwin a good few minutes to work out where he was and to remember, through a cloud of pain, the events that had brought him to be sleeping in Ailith's bed instead of his own. His chest ached with every breath, and if he used his left eye the world was still shrouded in a thick mist, but he was luckier than he'd had any right to expect. With his left eye squeezed closed, he looked down at Ailith's sleeping form. The part where he'd begged her to stay with him was particularly excruciating, but it appeared that she hadn't minded too much. In her sleep, she'd gripped his right hand and wrapped herself protectively around his arm, her knees tucked in against his side. It was lucky he hadn't toppled from his stack of pillows and landed on her in the night, but she looked comfortable. Her hair was loose, framing her face in a way that was quite at odds with her usually-immaculate braids, and a few stray hairs curled across her cheek.

He started to extricate himself from her grasp and she stirred, mumbling something incomprehensible. Leofwin froze, waiting for her to drift back to sleep, but her eyelids fluttered open and she looked up at him.

"Good morning," she said, a smile playing on her lips until she came round enough to notice where her hands were. She pulled away as if she'd been burnt, rolling from the bed and stumbling to her feet. He realised a moment too late that he should have feigned sleep and given her the privacy to wake up in peace. "Savash and Oelum, I'm sorry! I didn't mean to take liberties. I didn't… it's only… I must have assumed you were my sister."

"No matter." He tried to wave away her concerns, but his arm was stiff and he didn't have a full range of motion, so the gesture came off more jerky than the casual way he'd planned it. "I'm sure I've been mistaken for worse."

"I don't mean… It wasn't that I thought… I wasn't thinking anything at all. I was asleep."

If there was one benefit of being a complete recluse that he'd previously failed to appreciate, it was the avoidance of awkward situations like this. The social niceties hardly mattered when your only day-to-day contact was with servants paid to indulge your every whim. And since he didn't want them to notice his condition, even that had been limited to one or two staff at a time, for at most a couple of years. He'd never been good at working out the right thing to say, especially to women. He was, he felt now, particularly lacking in experience of the right way to soothe the kind of attractive, young, skittish, stubborn, wonderful woman who'd just spent the night in his bed. Or he in hers, as the case may be.

"Did you put my notes somewhere safe?" he asked, opting for a complete non sequitur. It seemed the safest route.

"Oh, yes." She, too, latched on to the change of subject with relief. "They're under the bed. Are we going to work on the saga this morning?"

He noticed the pile of bloodstained rags which had once been his clothes. "I don't suppose you could find me something to wear? Without raising suspicions?"

"I'm sure I can work something out."

"If you can manage it, I think I could hobble to the garden, and we can talk over breakfast."

"I'll do that." She shot from the room like an arrow, leaving him alone to his thoughts. He struggled over to the sideboard and studied himself in the looking glass. The cuts on his face had been shallow, and had all but disappeared in the night. And whatever was wrong with his eyesight, at least it wasn't obvious: from the neck up, he looked much as he always had. It was a different story for his chest and his arm. Ailith had done a good job of keeping him alive, but his wounds went deep and would take some time to heal, even with alchemical assistance. He found a half-empty pot of Payne's balm and collapsed back into bed to tend his injuries.

The fact that someone had risked an attack so far into his own lands came with its own worrying implications. To be robbed on the road was one thing, but that man had been no opportunistic bandit. Such a determined assault implied that someone had recognised him... or followed his tracks from the erdstall.

Ailith was gone for just long enough that he was starting to fear that something had happened, but dressed as he was in nothing but bloodstained undergarments and a blanket there was little he could do besides wait, impatiently, hoping no-one would barge in on him where he lay. She returned with a stack of clothes, and turned her back to give him privacy to change, though he couldn't help feeling it was a little late for him to worry about his modesty.

"Your chamberlain tried to ask me awkward questions," she said. "But I think I'm mastering the imperious tone that gets things done around here."

"You've taken to it much more naturally than I ever did," Leofwin agreed, struggling into a clean pair of trousers.

"You? But you've had a lifetime of practice."

"Not quite." He considered his tunic for a long moment, before deciding there was no way he could handle sleeves without assistance. "Could you help me out here? I'm a little sore."

"Of course you are, you got into a knife fight." She strode over as if it were the most natural thing in the world, and helped to ease him into the shirt. "What do you mean, not quite?"

"Another time. We already have much to occupy our thoughts this morning. You go ahead to the garden, make sure to send Thurstan on some errand to the kitchens, and I'll join you shortly."

Despite his best efforts at evasion, though, Thurstan waylaid him a he was on his way to join her on the rooftop: "Milord, you've returned just in time. There were strange goings on last night."

"Yes?"

"A man turned up at the gate — collapsed at the gate, by all accounts, asking for your young student. She brought him up to the castle."

"Very good."

The chamberlain looked worried. "Milord?"

"I'm sure she knows what she's doing."

"The men are saying she took him to her room."

"So?"

"To her bedroom, milord. To her bed."

"Thurstan." Leofwin gave his most imperious stare, the one he usually reserved for fellow nobles, and then only when he needed to intimidate or frighten them. "If I'm ever wounded, I hope to be fortunate enough to encounter a healer who would put my needs ahead of the diktats of the rumour mill. The gossip-mongers should think about whether they don't feel likewise."

"Yes, milord."

"I'm glad we're agreed. Now, is there any real news, or was that it?"

"Would you like me to make discrete enquiries as to the gentleman's identity?"

"If you hear any rumours, you should inform me, but you needn't trouble yourself over it."

"Then that is all, milord."

The chamberlain bowed and excused himself, and Leofwin walked on in a daze. It troubled him that his little altercation might have repercussions for Ailith's reputation. Most likely the staff already assumed she was his mistress — and he could hardly tell everyone about her studies just to correct them, although Thurstan would be blind indeed if he hadn't noticed by now that the girl was some kind of scholar, and of course her friends already knew.

Usually they sat side by side beneath the arbour, but today Ailith had chosen a chair on the opposite side of the table, and instead of her normal chit-chat she continued to pick at her food in awkward silence as he took up his usual place.

"We have a problem," Leofwin said, hoping that he could again distract her attention with practical matters.

"Yes, we're supposed to trust one another." She jumped in

before he could expand upon his thoughts, surprising him into silence. "We need to, more than ever, if we're under attack. And we can't do that if we have to pretend all the time."

"That isn't the problem I was thinking of."

"But it is a problem, and we need to fix it before we can fix anything else."

"Okay. How?"

"I don't know."

He looked up at her, and found her expression a mixture of fierceness and pleading.

"I don't know," she repeated. "But let's try honesty. You wanted me to stay, so I did. And I don't mind, I didn't want to leave you when you were hurt, but I've always shared a bed with my sisters and we've always held hands in the night. You have to believe that I wasn't getting ideas above my station."

"Is that what you're worried about? Status?"

"You're one of the Twelve."

He reached over and lifted her hand from her lap. "Look," he said, squeezing her fingers. "The world doesn't end if I hold your hand. Savash and Oelum, I slit your palm open the day after I met you. And you've tried to kill me. I think we're a long way past the point of worrying about the social order, but perhaps I should explain, after all."

"Explain what?"

"My background. I was only an advisor, a merchant with a minor title, when the last Lord Baron of Watersmeet died, but he died childless and alone. You must have heard something about it by now, it was quite the scandal."

"But I know better than to believe idle gossip."

"Good. I didn't kill him, as it happens. But the fact remains that I wasn't born to this, and the aristocratic manner doesn't come naturally. Why do you think I'm so antisocial?"

"You're not antisocial."

"I am around the nobility. For some reason, I find them to be mostly insufferable."

"Tell me how you came to inherit, then."

"Avelin adopted me when he realised how sick he was — unfortunately, he wasn't long for this world, and that's just the kind of thing to draw the attention of the gossips. That, and the fact that I wasn't proper, true-born nobility."

"A minor title is still a title."

He studied her for a long moment. "I didn't get that one from my parents, either. My parents... well, I don't remember much about them. I was six when they sold me to Malachi."

"They... sold you?"

"It's not so uncommon in the poorer provinces. You have twenty children because you need every pair of hands you can get in the fields or the mines, but if the harvest fails how do you feed all those extra mouths? And the harvest often fails, in the mountains. It's better for everyone if you can sell one or two into lucrative apprenticeships."

"And you..."

"I was lucky." He could tell she didn't quite believe him. "Really. I had talent, and Malachi was on one of his periodic sweeps of the countryside, and we made it to milder climes before the winter set in."

"And you've never been back?"

"It was a very hard winter. The next we heard, the village had been abandoned, and Malachi wouldn't let me go back to find out if I still had a family."

"That's cruel."

"I thought so at the time, but he was right. I might have spent years searching and still never found a living relation. Which," — he said, holding up a hand to stop the interruption that was forming on her lips — "is not to say I don't miss them. I do. But life is only in the present, and at least now I'm in a position to ensure that no-one in my lands will starve. And I trade very cheaply with Kethsgill."

She nodded, still looking a little doubtful. "So... you're not angry? About last night?"

"Not at all," he said. It would have been all too easy to leave it at that, but it wouldn't be the most honest answer, and she was right: they both needed to stop pretending. "I didn't expect to wake up in your bed, though, and I was embarrassed when I remembered I'd asked you to stay. If I seemed upset, I'm sorry. I was just caught by surprise."

"You and me both." She laughed, and he relaxed into a matching smile. "Could you try to avoid getting attacked again? I don't think it's good for either of us."

"You were fantastic," he said.

"I was scared. And… your eye. I'm sorry."

"You've nothing to apologise for. But I don't think we can assume this will be the last time."

"You don't know who it was, though?"

"I don't know. I can only assume someone followed me from the erdstall."

"Garrick."

He nodded. "It's a reasonable hypothesis."

"But they weren't expecting you to fight back, or they would have sent more people to make sure they succeeded."

"I am quite handy with a blade, thankfully."

"Are there more skills you need to be teaching me, then?"

"That's not the kind of strength you need to be developing."

"You said you'd teach me everything you know."

"I was apprenticed to a nomadic mage, on roads overrun with bandits, and with abilities that made my fellow apprentices jealous. I had no choice but to learn to defend myself — but you have an army to command, should you need defending."

"Your army didn't help you this time."

"Because I'm a fool who thinks he knows best, but I won't make the same mistake twice. I'm doubling my guard, and you'll move into my apartments, immediately."

The words came out of his mouth without much thought behind them, but as he spoke, he knew it was the right thing to do. Whatever he did to increase his defences, she needed to be on the inside.

"But…"

"Immediately," he repeated. "No arguments. I'll have a room prepared for you at once."

As soon as he'd settled Ailith in the library, Leofwin told Thurstan to arrange for her belongings to be moved, and summoned the maid he'd assigned to her when she'd first arrived. It was one thing to move her into the relative safety of his apartments, but he didn't want to remove her from her friends.

He had the girl meet him in the Red Room. She dropped straight into a deep curtsey when he arrived, head bowed, eyes fixed on the floor at her feet. Even when he told her she could stand, she didn't look at him.

"Frida, isn't it?"

She bobbed another curtsey. "Yes, milord."

"Have a seat."

"That won't be necessary, thank you."

"You're Ailith's friend."

"Yes, milord."

"As am I. In that we're equals, so please, sit with me for a moment."

He ushered her over to the bay windows, where they could sit and look out over the river. She perched awkwardly on the edge of her chair, as if prepared to flee at any moment, though he knew she'd never dare leave before being dismissed. She'd been in his service almost her entire life, and though he'd had no personal hand in it, he knew she'd been well trained.

"From tonight the Red Room will revert to its intended function, as an occasional guest room."

That startled her. "Milord, but Ailith…"

He watched in impassive silence as she struggled for words.

"Has she… is she gone?"

"Ailith is moving into an empty suite in my private quarters," he said. "That will be more suitable for the long term. If you're willing, I would like you to continue to attend her."

"Of course, milord, but… in your private wing? Beyond the guards?"

"I'll advise Thurstan that you're to come and go as you please, and you'll have a room adjoining Ailith's bedchamber. Your duties will be entirely at her discretion, and your pay will be doubled."

"Thank you, milord."

"You've been a good friend to her, Frida. I appreciate that. Will you speak plainly with me, now?"

"Milord?"

"A moment ago I tricked you. It was cruel, perhaps, but you were easily led. Do you really think she would leave without saying goodbye? Has she said something to you?"

"She's said nothing about leaving, no."

"But?"

Frida twisted her hands in the fabric of her skirt, and avoided his eyes.

"There's something you're not saying. Is she unhappy? Please. You must tell me if there's something I could do."

"It's not you, milord. She always speaks very highly of you — well, except that verse Ymma made her write, that was a bit rude, but never mind about that. Thing is, she likes you. But she's a long way from home, and she misses her family. And she's in a funny position, isn't she?"

"I see."

"Do you?"

There was a hint of defiance in the question. This was closer to the woman Ailith knew, he was sure. Here was a hint of someone Ailith could be friends with.

"Tell me what I'm missing," Leofwin said.

"I'm not sure you'd know what it's like to be a woman. Most folks that don't know her think she's your mistress. Those of us who know her, we know she's much too proud to settle for that — but she won't give them anything to talk about, so they makes up their own stories. And then there was all that palaver last night with that bloke who..."

Her voice trailed off, she looked up, and for the first time she really seemed to see him.

"It's a funny thing," she said quietly. "But he did look rather like you, the man who was wounded."

"I shan't insult your intelligence by asking you to believe that a coincidence."

"But he… you… had something of the beggar about him, milord, if you'll excuse my saying so."

"I was trying to go unnoticed. If you're to attend Ailith in my rooms, you'll see more of me, and you'll realise that I wear linen more often than silk. In general, I prefer such things to pass without discussion."

"You can rely on my discretion, milord."

"I know. That's why we're having this conversation. Speaking of indiscretion, should I ask you about that verse?"

Frida looked away. "I think you'd best ask her, if you were asking anyone."

"I think I'd better not. At least tell me what tune it was set to."

"It's a little ditty called *Under the Willows*. But it's a common sort of song, milord, I don't suppose you'd know it."

"Oh, I know it well enough." There was a time in his youth when he would have easily sung ten verses to amuse a crowd, and not a one of them fit for polite company. He couldn't imagine Ailith putting her voice to such words, let alone writing new verses of her own.

"She sings it well. You should ask her — as your friend — if she won't do a turn."

She stressed the word 'friend' just a little too long, and Leofwin knew that even in the hearts of those who knew Ailith best, there were still unspoken questions. And, he feared, if that were so then Frida was right. Ailith must feel very uncomfortable in her current position.

He'd have to do something about that.

"Perhaps she knows something a little more appropriate," he said, hoping to divert both of them from the image of Ailith singing bawdy ditties for him. "I'll ask her."

Chapter Fifty-Two

Frida helped Ailith to unpack in her new suite, and by lunchtime she had the rooms set up much as she wanted them.

"There's just one more thing I need to fetch from the Red Room," Ailith said. She'd almost forgotten. "Tell Leofwin I'll be along for lunch shortly."

"I think his lordship is bathing," Frida said. "But if he comes to look for you, I'll tell him."

Ailith ran through the corridors and scrabbled under the bed to retrieve Leofwin's papers. Returning to the workshop, there was still no sign of him, so she spread his notes out on the table. He'd drawn the cave wall in great detail, and she pieced together the sketches until half of the table represented what she'd come to think of as the saga wall. She sent Thurstan for lunch, and started to examine the papers.

Leofwin came in with his hair still dripping down the back of his neck, his skin flushed by the heat of the water.

"You didn't have to rush," she said.

"I'm as keen as you are to pick apart the secrets of this tale," he said, pulling up a chair beside her.

"Well, don't drip all over the place or you'll ruin all your hard work," she said, shuffling the sketches slightly further away. "We should make another copy to be safe."

"I hope we can work out all the words," he said. "Then we'll have an actual story to transcribe, and I can file these drawings away in some dusty corner of the library."

She dipped her pen and waited, nib poised above a clean sheet of paper. "Let's get started, then."

They worked through the manuscript letter by letter, beginning to end, writing down all the alternatives they could think of whenever they encountered archaic spellings that didn't quite correspond to a modern word. On their second pass, they selected the variants which gave rise to the most meaningful sentences.

They worked through the afternoon and into the evening, with only a brief interruption for supper, but by nightfall they had a readable version of the story.

"Let's go through it once more, beginning to end," Ailith said. "And then perhaps we should sleep. You've still got some healing to do."

She straightened the papers, and began to read:

This tale concerns Ealhwyn and the golden elixir.

Long ago, in the age of kings, Ealhwyn was a mage of most celebrated skill. Her name was known across the realm, and her prodigious talent was the envy of all who toyed with magic. Yet none could hope to match her.

For all her fame, she was not a proud woman, and did not like to boast of her successes.

Ealhwyn had an iron will, and the strength of three men, but she did not choose to duel. She amassed great wealth, but would not charge the poor when she cured their ills. And though she could find no-one of sufficient power to become the heir to her work, she trained dozens of students without complaint.

So it was that when she came upon the golden elixir, the draught of unending life, she told no-one of its secret save her husband. Iwain had not the skill to match her achievement, and she laid him in the ground before she was a hundred.

And yet, as she lived for years and generations without ageing, the secret was not easy to keep, and soon enough word spread across the kingdom.

For all her virtues, Ealhwyn was not without enemies. The afraid and the envious plotted against her, and in time she was tricked, and fell into the hands of those who would steal her secrets.

And though they tortured her and threatened death, she could not give the gift of youth to them. For the golden elixir is made only in the action of pure intent and strength of will, and its use cannot be taught.

And though they imprisoned her friends, and she wept, still she could not give them what they wanted. And so it was soon discovered that even the gift of gold is no protection from the sword, and Ealhwyn was buried in her two hundred and seventh year, with her head apart from her body.

"It's a sad story," Ailith said, laying the finished transcript down on the table. "But I'm not sure I'm any wiser."

"No." Leofwin frowned across the table. "I thought as much while I was drawing it, but perhaps it will make more sense in the morning."

Chapter Fifty-Three

It wasn't even murder. Garrick didn't have to concoct a poison or wield a blade. All he had to do was prevent his father from returning to Watersmeet, and it would be as good as done. He needed only to wait, and time would do the job for him.

And with what he knew, the temples would even take care of constraining his father's movements for the necessary number of days.

The temple of Oelum was the obvious choice. The priestesses who served Death had a severe reputation, but this was heresy of the worst kind. No-one could say he wasn't justified in involving every temple in the city, if it came to it.

He introduced himself and was shown to a small chamber within the temple's gatehouse. A young acolyte greeted him, with none of the pomp his rank would usually demand, and waved him into a chair.

"When will your priestess be joining us?" he asked.

She shook her head. "I am to hear your story and take it to the elders."

"This is a sensitive matter," Garrick said. The weight of the purse he laid on the table bore witness to precisely how sensitive, and the temples had never been known to turn down the generous donations of their wealthiest devotees. He could only hope his father had been lax in this, as he was in all other matters of governance.

The acolyte's face was serious beneath the hood of her white robe. "Speak."

When he'd imagined this scene, it had been in earnest conversation with a purple-robed priestess who had been more than happy to hear of his father's misconduct. Explaining himself to an acolyte played no part in his plan. His fingers tapped against his purse.

"I would speak with your elders directly."

She made no move. Garrick leaned forward to meet her gaze.

"Do you know who I am?"

He had dressed, he thought, with appropriate formality, but perhaps she hadn't realised she was speaking to her future lord.

"You haven't introduced yourself," she said.

"My name is Garrick, son of Oeric. I stand first in line to Highfort."

Her eyes widened a little.

"And I would speak with the priestess of my temple."

"Wait here," she said, departing with the merest bob of her head.

She was shortly replaced by an elderly priestess swathed head to toe in robes of the deepest purple.

"Garrick of Highfort." The priestess looked him over. "An unexpected caller, indeed."

"My lady of Oelum." He stood to greet her, pressing the purse into her hands. "Thank you for your time."

"Your beneficence is welcome." She lowered herself into a chair, his donation already vanished beneath the flowing fabric of her robes. "But you have not come merely to show your piety, I think."

"No. I have some... concerns."

"Concerns."

"Forgive me, it is not an easy matter to speak of. It has come to my attention — and you'll see, now, why I'm so cautious — it has come to my attention that my father has been dabbling with forbidden magics."

"All magic is forbidden," she said. "But we are pragmatists, these days. Most lords choose to employ a herbalist or two, and the Temple Law cannot be enforced against every hedge healer. Your devotion is commendable, but you need not fear for your father."

"I do not speak of hedge healing."

The priestess waited for him to go on, and he realised how

ridiculous his words must sound to one with no idea of what he spoke. He needed to make his claims swiftly and clearly... but not *too* clearly. The last thing he needed was to sound like he knew what he was talking about. As far as he knew there was nothing that could be proven against him, but coming here was a risk, and one he had no wish to exacerbate. He had no wish for Oelum's searing gaze to turn upon his own activities.

"My father isn't sick," he said. "This is no healing. He's put himself in thrall to a magician of the vilest kind, and only for vanity. He seeks to preserve his looks from the passage of time."

"Many seek," she said, as if it were nothing. "Fewer find. Being a charlatan is a crime, but it is not the Temple's concern. If someone is defrauding your father, it is a matter for your guards to pursue."

"You have to help me," Garrick said, allowing a pleading note to enter his voice. "Father must visit the magician every month to have the charm extended, and he sickens if he's even a few days delayed. I fear for his very life if the enchantment can't be broken."

"I will take the name of this sorcerer," she said. "Perhaps I have heard of him."

He'd toyed briefly with the possibility of reporting Leofwin's involvement, but Watersmeet was far away, and although the gods were everywhere each temple tended to mind their own local jurisdiction. And for now, at least, he wanted to keep their focus closer to home.

Besides, there were more efficient methods for handling the Lord Baron of Watersmeet.

"I don't have his name," he said. "But no doubt my father can supply it when you question him."

"You would have me invoke the Law against your own father?"

"Please, no." Garrick allowed his head to fall into his hands. "Not that. But if you can just give him enough of a fright, perhaps he'll ask for the help he needs. It's for his own good."

"I will consult with my colleagues," the priestess said and stood, clearly indicating that the audience was at an end.

"He's due to set out two days from now," Garrick said as he, too, got to his feet. "And he intends to call on some of our allies in the riverlands to disguise his true destination. If you stop him before he leaves the Highfort, you should have no longer than a fortnight to wait before he ails, and that should loosen his tongue. Then we can pray for a cure."

But from what Malachi had said, there was no cure. And by then, there would be no need of a trial. It would be too late.

"Hire a messenger if you need me," Garrick said. "I will attend the temple as you require it, but I would prefer my father get no wind of this before you come to speak with him."

She nodded, and opened the door to usher him out.

The fact that Malachi was waiting for him in his apartments did nothing to improve Garrick's mood.

"I thought I'd dismissed you," he said. "Did I not make myself clear?"

"Are you twice as stupid as you look, boy?"

Garrick frowned. That the old man dared speak to him in such a way in Bracklea was one thing. To do so within his own fortress was quite another level of insolence, and he was not in a generous mood.

"Have you really involved the temples in an alchemists' dispute?"

"Are you having me followed, now?"

Malachi shrugged. "You are not subtle."

"Then you should know that this 'dispute' has nothing to do with alchemy, and everything to do with justice."

"Justice?"

"For Ailith, and for Anselm. Without the command of my own armies, how can I save them?"

"Child, you cannot hope to pluck prisoners from a fortress like Watersmeet by force."

"Watch me," Garrick said. "And I'll thank you not to interfere."

Malachi looked at him sadly. "Then you are not just foolish, but mad. Your ill-considered actions will endanger us all."

Garrick was about to warn the old man how very unwise it was to bait him, when he realised Malachi's presence was a blessing in disguise. Here, standing willingly before him, was a mage. Just the very thing the temple had asked for. Never mind that it was a different man. The priestess wouldn't know the difference, and when Malachi denied it? Well, he would do that, wouldn't he?

Summoning his guards was but a moment's work, and if Malachi was surprised, he hid it well as two burly men took him by the frail, bony elbows.

"Are you going to cause trouble, or will you come peacefully to the temple?" Garrick asked.

"If you will not be dissuaded from such a self-destructive course, I will not fight you. But you should know that this cannot end well for you. Oelum is no ally of yours."

"The only people in danger of destruction are those who are actually guilty," Garrick said. "So I'll be fine, thank you. Save your concern for yourself."

Peasants stopped to stare at them as their little procession worked its way through the streets to the temple district, which was annoying but couldn't be helped. At least no-one knew who Malachi was. If any rumours reached Father's ears, they would be so vague as to be meaningless.

Garrick marched straight back into the gatehouse. He wasn't certain whether the white-robed acolyte who came to meet him was the same one, but if she wasn't identical, it was close enough. And they all served the same purpose.

"I've brought the magician," he declared, waving an arm towards Malachi.

"I'll fetch the priestess," the acolyte said, and almost ran from the room. From her nervous manner Garrick guessed she probably wasn't the same one, after all.

The priestess kept him waiting, and when she returned, she did not wear a patient expression.

"This man is a sorcerer and a heretic," Garrick said, quickly, before she could speak. "I present him as proof of my father's enchantment."

"What is the nature of this proof?"

"This is the man responsible for my father's heresy." That much, however indirectly, was true. "And he is under the same enchantment. If you hold him for a moon's turn, away from his tinctures and potions, you'll see the truth of it with your own eyes."

The priestess took a moment to gather her thoughts. Malachi looked as though he might have finally realised that it was his own words that had brought him here, but if anything, that only seemed to amuse him.

"There will have to be a trial."

"It will be a trial by ordeal, I assume, in the traditional manner?" Malachi asked.

The priestess inclined her head in silent assent.

"It is the usual custom, is it not, to give the accused some time to put his affairs in order? I confess I have few enough affairs, but a day or two would be appreciated."

She nodded again.

"Hang on, you can't just let him go," Garrick protested.

Malachi extended his hand towards the priestess. "You may take of my blood, should you require a bond. You and I both know that is worth more than whatever irons the boy would demand."

"You know a little of our ways, then." The priestess frowned. "You should not flaunt such knowledge."

"Fortunately, this one is a fool," Malachi said, causing Garrick to splutter with ill-suppressed fury. "He would not know gold if it landed squarely on his pretty head."

"This man is my prisoner," Garrick said, forcing the words out one by one lest his emotions get away from him. "It is not in your power to release him, save into my custody."

"He is a prisoner of the Temple now," the priestess said. "And he is correct. Tradition demands he be given time before the ordeal, for if he is guilty there will be no afterwards."

She pulled a fine silver blade from a wrist sheath that had been hidden beneath her generous sleeves, and took Malachi's hand in her own.

"You are charged and committed to trial," she said as she carved her sigil into his palm. Garrick flinched at the sight, but Malachi didn't even blink as the blood welled up around her knife. "Until your ordeal is over, you are mine. Your blood binds you to the temple, and binds your words to truth."

She pulled a white cloth from a hidden pocket and mopped the pool of blood from his palm, before causing it to disappear the same way.

"Swear upon your blood that you will return after two nights have passed, that we may proceed with your trial."

"I swear."

"Make him swear he won't do any alchemy while he's gone," Garrick said. "Otherwise he'll undo the enchantment, or extend it, or something."

"I swear it," Malachi said before the priestess could ask him.

The priestess nodded, and Garrick found himself dismissed.

Chapter Fifty-Four

Five unfamiliar men waited in the Lower Hall. Their robes gave four of them away as priests from the temples of Refah and Hasat, Keyif and the Twins, which made Ailith hesitate on the threshold. She forced herself to continue, putting one foot woodenly in front of the other as she walked with Leofwin to greet them.

"Dress well," he had instructed her over breakfast. "And meet me as soon as you can."

He'd refused to answer when she'd asked who was visiting, though he was quite insistent that she should make herself presentable. Ailith had picked out an emerald green dress with flowing sleeves, its skirt slashed with cloth-of-gold. It was a perfectly impractical garment that she could never wear to do actual work, but it suited her and would look nice alongside that green velvet cloak which Leofwin always wore when he was trying to impress. After adding a diamond necklace that she gathered was worth rather more than her father's house, and getting Frida to put a simple braid into her hair, she went to wait for him in the library. She'd tried to use the time wisely, picking up various books on herbs and minerals, but the sudden change of plans had disturbed her concentration.

Now, faced with a group of men who would gladly see her hanged for her abilities, she was even more puzzled. Leofwin's rank gave him some protection from their interference, but surely even he could see it was tempting fate to invite them into his home.

"Have you prepared the necessary documents?" he asked the fifth man, whose clothes were black and plain.

"It is done, my lord." The man proffered a bundle of scrolls. "Is this the young lady?"

"This is Ailith." Leofwin took one of the scrolls, inspected its contents, and returned it to the pile before Ailith could decipher the fancy writing. "Good. Let's not waste time."

They spread the scrolls on the side table, and Leofwin applied his signature and seal to the bottom of each sheet. Ailith waited a few steps behind, praying that nothing about her appearance would mark her out to the priests, but ready to run and dive into one of the castle's secret walkways if they seemed unduly interested in her. The priests, however, were more concerned with applying their own temple seals alongside Leofwin's signature. Ailith couldn't imagine why she'd been brought along to witness this swapping of paperwork, not unless there was some lesson to be brought out later.

Once everyone had made their marks, and the papers had been re-rolled, the dark-robed man took Leofwin's hand and laid it upon one of the scrolls.

"You are Leofwin, son of Avelin, the present and ninth Lord Baron of Watersmeet," he began.

"I am."

He beckoned Ailith to step forwards, placing her hand beside Leofwin's on the scroll. "Are you Ailith, daughter of Godwine, from the town of Bracklea in the province of Eldren, under the barony of Highfort?"

Ailith nodded, too surprised to do anything other than play along. "I am."

"My lord, you have signed this contract and affirmed it with your seal. Before gods and mortal witnesses, do you solemnly swear your intent towards this woman?"

"I do so swear."

Ailith thought she might to be asked to make some kind of promise, as well, at which point she would have had the excuse she needed to ask what was happening. But the men seemed satisfied. Leofwin was given one of the scrolls, the priests took their own copies, and they left her empty-handed. Then they were gone, as suddenly as they'd arrived.

"What just happened?" Ailith asked as soon as they were alone in the hall.

"There are people who want me dead, as you well know."

"Yes."

"Oeric has lost control of Highfort, which can hardly be a coincidence. There are armies on the move, the region is unsettled, and no doubt an assassin or two has been hired. If something should happen to me, I want to be sure that my work is in safe hands. Your hands." He grasped said hands to his chest as though she might run away. "The only way I can do that is to ensure you would inherit the castle and title, as well as my library."

"You want me to inherit your castle." That was one of the strangest things anyone had ever said to her.

"And my title. The way things stand under the Temple Law, there are only two ways to accomplish that."

"Which are?" she asked, a sinking feeling in the pit of her stomach. A potter's daughter had no right to be inheriting castles, but then most potters' daughters wouldn't be standing here, hands clutched by a powerful baron, painfully aware of the strong beat of his heart through his shirt. She feared her life was about to get even more complicated.

"An adoption," he said, "or a betrothal."

"Tell me you chose adoption." Even as she said it, though, she was absolutely sure he hadn't. *Do you solemnly swear your intent towards this woman?* That didn't sound like an adoption kind of question. "Tell me we didn't just get betrothed."

"Why? Was there someone else you were planning to wed?"

He said it so flippantly that Ailith wasn't sure she could trust herself to speak. Eventually, she managed, "It would have been nice if you'd asked."

"You might have said no."

"Exactly."

"I'm afraid I can't afford to be sentimental about these things. This was the quickest way."

"But…"

"It's just a betrothal. This contract binds me, not you; it's not as though I've actually married you against your will."

Until he said the words, she hadn't known that was even possible.

"An adoption would have taken much longer to arrange," he went on. "And with far more serious consequences."

"Such as?"

"Such as making you my daughter," he said flatly. "This way, we still have options. Nothing has changed."

Ailith could feel herself shaking as the shock set in. She prised her fingers away and fled without another word. At the first opportunity she ducked through a hidden door and into the secret passage: her escape plans had come in useful after all. Not that he was following her. Why would he? And if he did, he knew this warren of passages better than she did.

She collapsed against the wall, tears streaming down her cheeks. This was not how she had imagined her eventual betrothal would be. Oh, she knew that any match was as much business as romance, she'd seen it with Hilde and Ingrith and Aidith in turn, but she'd hoped to find someone who would at least try to win her affections. Betrothal to a man who had no intention of ever marrying her had most assuredly not been part of her plans.

And a baron, at that.

Mama, she thought bitterly, would be delighted.

She wiped her eyes and nose on the sleeve of her gown, sobbing into the soft fabric. It was entirely her own fault. Alone in her room, she'd dared to imagine what a future here could look like. Developing her abilities under Leofwin's careful tuition, soon to be standing by his side as an equal… that much she'd felt quite sure of. But she'd allowed her mind to wander on to the idea that maybe, one day, it would be nice if he'd notice that she was a woman as well as an alchemist. She'd forgotten that the gods were watching, ready to make a mockery of such dreams.

She didn't know how long she cried, but eventually the tears dried up, and some time after that she got unsteadily to her feet. If she set aside her ridiculous fantasies she could continue her studies;

that was the most important thing. Of course he'd never fall in love with her, but if today's events proved one thing it was that he truly wanted her to stay, enough to arrange this farce of a betrothal. And being an unwed alchemist was better than whatever loveless marriage Mama would have liked to push her into.

With no lantern, she had to feel her way along the passages towards Leofwin's quarters, but by now she knew the route by heart. She found the peep-hole overlooking the workshop where he sat in silence, almost totally still. Though he had a book open in front of him, it was evident even from the set of his shoulders that he wasn't reading.

Ailith crept to the nearest exit, let herself out of the passage, and made her way back along the corridor. She hesitated at the door, but she would have to face him eventually, and it wasn't going to get any easier.

He turned slowly in his chair. "There you are."

"Yes." She wasn't quite sure what she could say, but they would have to get past this awkwardness. It might as well be now. "Is it time for lunch?"

"Long past. But we should talk, first."

"Must we? You said it didn't change anything — can't we just pretend it never happened?"

"It's true, I suspected you'd say no, that's why I didn't ask you," he said, heedless of her request. "And you can choose whether or not you lay claim to to the status this gives you. But I swear I didn't realise the idea would cause you such distress."

"I didn't... I don't..." She didn't know how to put her feelings into words.

"You don't have to explain. I suppose there's some boy back home? You needn't think I plan to keep you here forever, if we both survive what's coming, but I wanted to put something in place lest anything happen to me."

Ailith thought of the brief kisses she'd shared with Garrick. That was the closest she had ever come to meeting someone back home. She'd felt so stupid when she she found out who he was, yet here she stood, betrothed to a baron after all… while Garrick manoeuvred against them. A lot could change in a few short months.

"There is no-one else."

"What, then? You're not still planning to be the architect of my untimely demise, are you? Because I'm fairly sure that would invalidate any arrangements."

"I wish it were so simple," she said, laughing. Everything would have been so very, very easy if he'd only been the cold-hearted bastard they all said he was.

"It never is," Leofwin agreed. "But I'm no monster. I'll release you whenever you choose to leave. I'll release you now, if you truly wish it."

"I'm just in shock," she said. "I wish you'd asked. If it's really the best way, you could have persuaded me, but at least I would have liked to have the choice. Now, even if you convince me it was the right thing to do, it's still the case that you've already done it."

"Then I apologise." He stood, took her hand, and placed a firm kiss on her knuckles. "I hope you can forgive me, in time, but for now I'd settle for your company over dinner. We have much to discuss."

"Other than… this?"

"Other than this."

Chapter Fifty-Five

Garrick sat in the uncomfortable chair behind his father's desk.

It wasn't that his father's study was any nicer than his own — in fact, since it had almost never been used for studying anything, it turned out to have a significantly worse aspect. But when handling the nobility, symbolism was everything.

The evening was drawing in, though, and the carvings on the chair back were becoming an unbearable irritation. He hadn't even left his seat for lunch, such was the flow of minor nobles coming to offer up their insincere sympathies and swear their renewed fealty to the son of their fallen lord.

Not that Oeric's guilt had yet been established. The priestess had been very clear on that point, even as she had explained to Garrick that she had no choice but to begin a formal indictment.

In theory, until such a time as the judgement was pronounced, Father could return at any point, exonerated. Garrick could not afford to wait on such formalities. Time alone would tell whether Malachi had lied, but meanwhile at least the old troublemaker himself was also safely locked in an ordeal chamber somewhere in the depths of the temple, and Garrick could get on with summoning his tributary lords. So far, not one of them had dared to question his newly-adopted authority.

As they came and went, he had his master-at-arms make discreet enquiries as to the strength and placement of each man's extant armies. His steward had been tasked to uncover the local alliances and alignments. Serving staff had been given strict instructions to gather whatever snippets of news they could from the attendants who'd arrived with the visitors. The collection of details was growing, soon to coalesce into a vibrant picture of the region and its power structures.

Tonight there would be a feast, the greatest the Highfort had seen since the night of Grandfather's funeral. And tomorrow, the serious business would begin.

"Albold of Greytown, my lord," the herald announced.

Garrick generally held a fairly low opinion of Father's drinking-and-hunting companions. He didn't recognise the soft-faced, middle-aged man who now knelt before him, but the red nose and expansive waistline spoke of years enjoying Oeric's hospitality.

"Rise," he snapped, shuffling again on the uncomfortable chair.

"My condolences, young Highfort," Albold said as he straightened. "This must be a difficult time. Is there any assistance I can offer my lord while he waits for his father's return?"

"I will let you know if anything comes to mind," Garrick said, careful not to rise to the challenge behind the words. He had known that someone would eventually draw attention to the obvious, but Greytown was an insignificant enough little place, and his concerns could be brushed aside. "Meanwhile, I assume I can rely on you to support me as you have always supported my father?"

"Naturally."

In truth, a man such as this had offered Oeric little besides his company on the hunt. He had a parcel of land that he struggled to afford, a manor that was slowly falling down around his family, and only a small guard force to watch his back. Those few men could be pressed to join Garrick's slowly mobilising army, but their loss would be no great tragedy. The only thing that was not yet clear was how he aligned with the other lesser powers of the region.

"These are, as you say, difficult times," Garrick said. "And it's important I know who I can rely on. You will let me know if you hear any troublesome rumours."

"Of course, my lord."

"Good. I will not forget those who help me to identify any festering disloyalty."

Albold bowed as low as his girth allowed, and Garrick snapped at the herald to stop before the next visitor could be introduced.

"Who remains?" he demanded.

The herald recited over a dozen names, but only one that mattered.

"I'll see Yutta now. Tell the others to enjoy the feast, and we'll resume the audiences in the morning."

Yutta of Wulfsberg was a towering, red-haired warrior with a sword slung across her back. As the first-born heir to her mother's title she was technically of a rank with Garrick, and her reserved half-bow underlined her confidence in that position. She might have come to build bridges, but she was never going to beg.

Garrick grasped her hand between his and kissed her knuckles as he would any other lady, though her leather gauntlets made the experience rather different. The Wulfsbergs had always favoured a hands-on approach to leadership, on and off the battlefield.

"Have a seat, my lady. I trust the journey has treated you kindly?"

Yutta shrugged. "It isn't far, with a good horse."

"And you left your mother and brothers in good health?"

"My mother fares better than your father," she said, "but that may be attributed to the fealty of her children."

He smiled at her bluntness. He'd met Yutta only once before, when they were both a decade younger and the eight years separating their ages had set them a world apart. Now, he thought, he might rather like her.

"I understand that Helle and my father had some disagreement, and I sympathise. Father can be a most disagreeable man. But I hope in the present circumstances we might put that behind us."

"You mean we should be grateful that you've disposed of an inconvenience. You can speak frankly; I wouldn't be here if I didn't share some of that sentiment."

"Good." Perhaps this would be easier than he'd imagined. "Then I'm at your service. Tell me what's required to mend the friendship between our families."

"A betrothal would be a good start. Your sister will soon be of an age, and three of my brothers are not yet spoken for. Send her to Wulfsberg and she can have her choice of them."

"And for her dowry?" They could hardly afford to lose more ground, but there was no way they had enough gold in the coffers to marry Mayda to one of the Wulfsbergs.

"Don't worry, we're not looking to annex Highfort's ancestral lands. If you succeed in the east, though, Watersmeet has some productive lands south of the Brim."

Garrick nodded. That would keep a neat border between his land and Helle's. "And in exchange, can you offer support in the field?"

"I'll lead the army myself." She favoured him with a broad smile. "It's been too long since I was on a proper campaign."

Chapter Fifty-Six

It was long past the midnight bell, but Ailith tossed and turned, unable to sleep. Every time she closed her eyes, she kept going back to the erdstall saga, and the mystery of the golden elixir. If others — even just one other mage — had been able to make an amalgam with gold, why shouldn't she? It was infuriating.

Applying herself to the biggest challenge she could find was also the only way she'd yet found effective at taking her mind off the bizarre and sudden circumstances of her betrothal. She'd come to her room one evening to find Leofwin's copy of the contract dumped unceremoniously on her bed, with a terse note informing her that she could burn it or use it as she liked. If her mind wandered away from alchemy for even a minute, it wandered there, and then she invariably found herself poring over that document instead. The wording was strangely archaic, and the contents were like nothing she'd ever seen. Amongst its many provisions the agreement guaranteed that if he defaulted he would settle upon her two substantial manors of his fief, amounting to over six hundred acres, and a sum of gold that would see her comfortably through ten lifetimes. Though it was nice to know he trusted her not to take advantage of it, she could think of no reason he'd choose to impose such harsh penalties upon himself.

No, it was much safer to keep her mind on alchemical impossibilities.

She lit a lamp and padded across to the library, where Leofwin's sketches had been safely filed away. She could recite the whole of the saga now, just as easily as she could recite any of the tales she'd learnt in childhood, but perhaps they'd missed something in the pictures. Perhaps the layout of the text or the shape of the wall held some clue. She spread out the pages and aligned the edges.

Closing her eyes, she was standing again in the cold and musty erdstall, breathing in the damp air, trying to pick out the mysterious words. But in her imagination, instead of puzzling over the inscriptions with Garrick, it was Leofwin who crouched beside her and pored over the ancient script. She wished he'd taken her with him. Perhaps there was something more to find, some physical artefact to accompany the words.

She wondered again how Garrick had found out about the site. He'd been so vague in his responses. Had there been more context with the map? Had he kept things from her, even after he'd learnt she was a mage?

She shook her head. Daydreaming wouldn't help. If she was to have any chance of solving this, she needed to be systematic. She would start again, from Leofwin's sketches instead of their transcripts. She hauled a couple of ancient scrolls down from the shelf. If they'd missed or mistaken anything, perhaps it was down to the archaic spellings, so she wanted to compare the lettering to the oldest sources she could find.

She worked until she started to make mistakes, her eyes burning with exhaustion. It was no use. No matter what she wished, there was no chance of making progress when her vision blurred, smearing words across the page. She was about to shuffle the pages back onto their shelf when her tired eyes caught a familiar phrase.

For the golden elixir is made only in the actor of pure intent…

And suddenly, she was wide awake again.

Abandoning the papers on the table, she snatched up the lantern and ran through to the workshop. She scoured the shelves, grabbing the ingredients she needed. Fennel seeds, wolfsbane root, and birch bark. A drop of thrice-concentrated sage oil. A pinch of finely-ground crystalline sulphur, and powders of chalk and arsenic. And gold… where could she find some gold at this hour? She didn't know what Leofwin had done with the chain he'd cannibalised for their earlier experiments, but there was jewellery enough to spare in her wardrobe.

She found a plausible-looking brooch with a flat, plain back. No-one would ever notice if she shaved off a little of the soft metal. She took it back to the workshop and scraped at it carefully with her knife, brushing the resulting flakes of gold into the bowl of the balance until she'd weighed out two grains. That should be sufficient for an experiment. She carefully measured the other ingredients into the bowl, and ground them together until the minerals crumbled and the fennel seeds cracked beneath the weight of the pestle.

The mixture wouldn't amalgamate in the bowl, she knew that much already. The silver elixir was made by a two-stage process, first a preparation over fire to form the amalgam itself, and then a second phase to activate it in the blood. If she was right, though, she would have to do both stages within her own body to be successful. It would never work on the mice.

She slashed the dagger across her arm and smeared the lumpy mixture into the cut. And then, her arm already stinging, she turned her focus inwards and pushed. Blood pulsed in her veins, and pooled around the cut.

She'd practised enough times with the mice, but it wasn't since Leofwin had poisoned her that first day that she'd worked alchemy within her own bloodstream. The pain was an unwelcome distraction, but if her theory was right this would make all the difference.

And they were running out of options: she needed to be right.

She probed and pushed... and nothing happened. Her skin was beginning to tingle as the wolfsbane poisoned her. If she didn't complete the amalgamation soon, she'd have to stop and clean out the wound, but the ingredients didn't want to come together.

Perhaps she still needed a flame.

Frowning, she lit a taper from the lantern, and thrust it towards her skin before she could think better of it. Her skin started to blister, and she dropped the taper to the ground even as she used its energy to fuel the beginnings of the amalgamation. She barely felt her heel blister as she ground out the sparks against the floor.

The formula was a complex one and she had to weave it like a braid, bringing together first the fennel and sulphur, while she wound the arsenic with the sage and chalk, before gradually pulling everything together with the wolfsbane, birch, gold, and finally the blood. This time she could feel the gold flowing, melding into a perfect amalgam with the other ingredients and slowly spreading into her vein…

She froze.

The implications of what she was doing hit her like a runaway wagon, and she pushed back at the newly-formed amalgam, unwinding the bonds, splitting it back into its constituent parts before the effects could take over her body.

It was all very well to prove she could work gold, but she wasn't ready for this. Anselm had shown her that much.

They kept a bucket of water on hand in case of fires, and Ailith plunged her arm into icy water up to her elbow. She rubbed at the cut until the ingredients dispersed into the water, along with no small amount of her blood. Shivering, she shook the worst of the water from her skin, splattering pink drops across the floor. But clearing up could wait — everything else could wait. It was an uncivilised hour, but she had to tell Leofwin at once. She ran down the corridor and slammed open his bedroom door.

Chapter Fifty-Seven

"I did it!"

"Ailith?" He sat up in bed, blinking, and pushed the hair from his eyes as she slammed into the room dressed only in her light under-tunic. In the half-darkness, he had to squint his injured eye closed to make anything out. "Am I dreaming?"

"I did it," she repeated, running across the room and flinging herself onto her knees at his bedside. "I actually did it."

"You did what?" he asked, still sleepy.

"Gold," she said. "What else?"

It wasn't often that he was rendered speechless, but even his usual biting comments had deserted him. What else, indeed? This woman would wake him for nothing less than achieving the impossible. He stared at her for a moment, then yawned, stretched, and rolled from the bed.

"Where are you going?"

"I'm coming back to the workshop with you." He straightened his tunic and reached for yesterday's discarded breeches. "You want to show me, don't you?"

"It's the middle of the night."

"I'm aware of that."

"And… there's not really anything to show. Sit down and let me explain."

She sat on the edge of the bed, pulling him down beside her.

"I couldn't sleep," she said. "I took another look at the erdstall saga, and I realised that if we had just one word wrong, then everything changed. It's not action, it's actor. *The golden elixir is made only in the* actor. You can only amalgamate it in your own body, that's why we haven't managed to use gold before. We've never done it the right way."

"You made it in your own veins?"

The golden elixir.

If he'd been drowsy before, that thought brought him completely awake. The golden elixir, the draught of unending life. The hypothetically perfect form of his — of Malachi's — formula, and she'd made it in her own blood. Gods damn the woman for being so impossibly competent.

"Do you have any idea how dangerous that is?"

He gripped her arm, which was blistered and smeared red with blood where she'd broken the skin. She hadn't even stopped to patch up the wound before running to wake him, so perhaps there was hope. His power flared as he probed her arm, wondering if it was too late to unmake the amalgam; whether it had yet taken its irrevocable hold on her body.

"I know the dangers," she said. "That's why I unmade it again. That's why I've got nothing to show you."

He didn't realise he'd been holding his breath until he exhaled with relief. He hugged her close, beaming into her hair.

"You're brilliant," he said, releasing her awkwardly. In the excitement of the moment it was all too easy to get carried away.

"You could do it, too," she said. "I'm sure of it. We both felt the same thing when we tried it before."

"I don't mean amalgamating gold — although that's pretty impressive." As little as an hour before, he would have said it was the most impressive thing anyone could do. "I mean realising, in time, what you were doing to yourself."

"Anselm was too young," Ailith said, rubbing at the cut on her arm. "I may be a woman by every definition, but I haven't stopped growing yet. I'm not ready to stop getting older."

"No," he agreed. She was getting better by the day, and he didn't want to lose one single ounce of that exuberance. Besides, no-one knew exactly what the consequences would be. He should be the first to find out.

"But I did it." She laid a tentative hand on his arm. "Think about what that means for you. If we're right, if the golden elixir is perfect, you should only have to use it once."

"We don't know exactly what it will do," he said, caution creeping back in to displace some of his initial excitement. "And if it's as irreversible as the silver, I'll need to understand every implication before I use it. As for Anselm…"

"It doesn't help him," Ailith said quietly, tears springing to her eyes. "I know. I've been trying so hard to save him, and this isn't his answer. But it might be yours."

"Thank you," he said. "That's the nicest thing anyone has ever done for me."

She started to sob in earnest at that, and flung herself back into his arms. He wasn't sure why she was crying, or whether he'd inadvertently said something to make it worse, so he didn't ask any of the questions that were pressing on his mind. He just held her, occasionally stroking her hair, until she ran out of tears. Even after she finished crying she stayed where she was, clutching at his tunic without speaking, her chest heaving.

He wasn't sure exactly when she fell asleep, but her ragged breathing gradually subsided into gentle snores and her grip on his shirt loosened. He laid her down on the bed, arranged a pillow under her head, and pulled the covers over her. He probed briefly at the cut on her arm to make sure she hadn't left any toxins behind, and spread a little Payne's balm over the wound so it could heal while she slept. And then, remembering how startled and scared she'd been the one morning they'd woken up in the same place, he took a change of clothes and went to spend the rest of the night in her room.

He woke late, to sunshine streaming through the windows and a cross voice demanding "Why did you sleep here?"

For a moment he had no idea, until the events of the night before came crashing back to him in a wave of memories.

"Gold," he said, not completely sure it hadn't been a dream.

She shook her head. "That does not explain why I woke up in your bed, and you in mine."

"You fell asleep," he said, trying to shake the image of her sleeping form from his mind. Not that she looked any less adorable as she stood before him now, sleepy and disheveled and huffy. "I didn't want to disturb you. Not when you'd been working so hard."

"If you were afraid I'd start bawling like an infant again, you can say it. I know that's not the expected response to accomplishing a so-called impossible task."

"That might have played a part, but you were exhausted. It's nothing to be ashamed of."

"I'm not ashamed."

"Feeling ashamed is nothing to be ashamed of, either," he said, trying hard not to laugh at her bleary-eyed indignation. "Feelings just happen. It's what you do with them that counts."

"Right now I feel like throwing you out of my room so I can dress," she said. "And I have every intention of acting on it."

"As long as you promise to join me in the workshop as soon as you're ready. We have a lot to discuss."

He tried to read while he waited for her but he struggled to focus on the words, and not just because of his damaged eye. Gold. Nothing in any of his books had prepared him for the idea that she might actually succeed. It would take some time to unpick the implications of her midnight discovery, but her intuition was right: it could be exactly what he needed.

The idea made him giddy, almost drunk.

She'd succeeded where every alchemist in recorded history had failed. If she could do that, then what else could they accomplish together? Perhaps they would yet find a way to adapt the method for Anselm's benefit.

Unable to concentrate, he sent Thurstan to request a late and hearty breakfast from the kitchens. The night's events had left him ravenous, and Ailith could hardly be less hungry after the efforts she'd put in.

"Tell me, then," he said as they settled down to eat. "What gave you such a clever idea?"

"It wasn't really cleverness." A slight blush rose in her cheeks as she spoke. "I was falling asleep and I couldn't see straight — I thought I'd misread it, until I realised that that reading gave us a new avenue to explore. So you see, I was just lucky."

"Don't think less of yourself for that," he said. "There's always a little luck in these things, but if you're not putting in the work then all the luck in the world won't help you."

She frowned. "Maybe."

"I promise you, I've seen it enough times. You have to work hard, and then you have to be just a little bit lucky."

"Not lucky enough, though," she said. "Not yet."

"You're not the only one to be disappointed," he admitted. "I thought we were doing this for the good of humanity. What's the point of an elixir of life that can only benefit a few of the world's strongest mages?"

"Maybe it just gives us the time we need to develop something better. Something that works in a different way."

Chapter Fifty-Eight

As his allies' armies converged steadily on Watersmeet, Garrick presented himself at the gates of the castle. It was important to show willing, even as he knew that Leofwin would never meet his demands. The drawbridge was lowered for him, and he was surrounded by guards the moment he stepped into the barbican.

"I've come to offer my terms," he said when Leofwin finally deigned to join him in the hall.

"I don't see that we have much to discuss," Leofwin said. "You've proved yourself quite unworthy of my trust, and we both know you can't take these walls by force."

"Not alone, perhaps, but mine is not the only army marching. Listen, I don't want this war any more than you do. Give up the prisoners, and I'll settle for a few border provinces."

"I have no prisoners."

"That's not what I heard."

Leofwin's mouth curved in a smile that didn't reach his eyes. "Well, if it's rumour that's driving you, that's hardly within my control."

"I know you have Ailith. Give her back to me, and we can talk about resolving this like grown-ups."

Leofwin shook his head. "You wrote one letter, that doesn't mean you own her."

"It gives me a responsibility."

"To see her safe, which she is. Your duty is discharged."

"She won't be safe when the castle is besieged."

"It's for Ailith to choose where she spends her days, whether it's here or elsewhere. I will, of course, be delighted to fetch her if you're interested in hearing her views."

"Do it." He had a feeling it was futile, but he would have one more try. If he could get through to Ailith, he could at least lay siege to the castle without fear of her being caught in the cross-fire.

A messenger was despatched, and a few minutes later she stood in the doorway, arms folded across her chest. "What is it?"

"I've come to negotiate for your safety," Garrick said. "But Leofwin won't deliver you into my custody until he hears you say you want to leave."

"And if you just want to leave, I can spare an escort to take you anywhere in the Twelve Baronies," Leofwin added unhelpfully. "But of course, if you wish to accompany young Highfort, that can also be arranged."

"I'm not going anywhere."

"But you've done your bit." Garrick stepped towards her, but the guards restrained him before he could move more than a couple of paces. "There's no need for you to stay, and Watersmeet is about to get dangerous."

"You really don't understand, do you?"

"What is there to understand?"

"I want to stay. I like it here, and what do I have to go back to? I'm not like you, with an apprenticeship and a barony waiting for me."

"I've explained this before. Come home, and move to the Highfort where you can focus on your studies."

"And who would train me there?" she asked. "You couldn't even find someone to teach you, without taking up a disguise and apprenticing yourself to a commoner. Why should I believe you could do better for me?"

"When I took up my apprenticeship I was only a son," he said, trying not to show how her words stung. "Now I'm the Lord Baron of Highfort. No-one would dare refuse me."

Ailith frowned. "I dare."

"That's because you're a stupid little girl who has no idea what she's dealing with."

For a moment he thought she might hit him again, but she just turned on her heel and left. Truly, the girl was bewitched. But if that was the way she wanted it, he would be more than happy to proceed with what remained of his plan. If she wouldn't come with him, they'd soon see how she liked being besieged along with the castle. His advance forces were only two days' march from Watersmeet.

"I think Ailith has made her wishes clear enough," Leofwin said. "You can see yourself out."

Chapter Fifty-Nine

"How do you feel about military strategy?"

Ailith shrugged, and broke off another piece of bread. She knew Garrick was posturing, making the most of his newly-snatched inheritance, but that still wasn't a question she'd expected to hear over the breakfast table. "I've never really thought about it."

"Me neither, but it looks as though we may have to start."

"Don't you have people for that kind of thing?"

"I have captains who know how best to garrison this castle, or how to keep a unit together when manoeuvring on a battlefield, but traditionally it would fall to me to determine which course to take. I was hoping your knack for Fortunes might apply."

"You always beat me at Fortunes."

"I beat you narrowly at Fortunes, and I've been studying it my whole life. But neither of us has studied for this, and as you've noted before, you have an eye for patterns."

"Go ahead, then. Tell me what pieces we've got on the board."

"We have a rather fine fortress, here. That's our primary asset, but our strength is also what isolates us, and we'll be completely cut off within the week. We have an uneasy collection of allies: Kethsgill, Oakfeld, and the White Marches. Those are the lords whose personal survival presently depends on me."

"The ones you're selling to."

"The same. They won't help Garrick, but nor should we expect them to bring armies to our aid."

"Even though they'll die without your help?"

"Death in battle is every bit as fatal as death from poison. If Garrick gets wind of the situation I expect he'll offer them safe passage to the castle in exchange for keeping out of the war."

"And if they turn up here you can't refuse to treat them, or they might decide to bring their armies out for a bit of exercise, after all."

"Exactly."

Ailith cleared a corner of the table. "So this is us," she said, setting the jar of honey down in the middle of the space. "The rivers run here, and here. Garrick" — she held up the pepper pot — "is already encamped out here, a couple of miles beyond the city boundary. Right?"

"Right."

"And who else do we expect to be joining him?"

"Oeric kept small standing armies in Applegate, Combeford, and Sevenash Square. Those have been mobilised, and joined by a number of minor garrisons from Highfort's tributary forts. Those will all be marching in from the west and the north-west. Additionally, I hear he may have persuaded Helle of Wulfsberg to resurrect their alliance and send one of her armies in from the south."

Ailith arranged jars and bottles as he spoke, forming a gradually closing half-circle. "And on our side?"

"We have a strong guard company, with excellent archers. I command eight more forts along the rivers, which will stop the boy taking control of the waterways, but to do that they need to retain their current garrisons: I can't risk open battle."

"So we'll be utterly surrounded, and no-one is going to help us. Is that what you're saying?"

"That's the pessimistic view. On the bright side, we have a well-stocked granary, and logs enough for two winters' fuel already stacked and seasoning in one of the barns. And the boy doesn't come across as the patient sort."

"Then what can we do, aside from prove ourselves more patient than he is?"

"There are a few things we need to arrange before the armies arrive: evacuating the town; bringing in anything that's ready to harvest; burning and salting the fields so we're not feeding the enemy come the autumn."

Ailith blanched at the idea of destroying crops when they were about to start rationing, but he was right. Anything they left behind would just become an advantage for Garrick. "How many people are we expecting to move in?" she asked. "For that matter, how many people live here already?"

"Presently we've almost a hundred in the barracks, sixty domestic staff, and probably thirty children, half of them orphans."

"Two hundred." She let out a low whistle. "I had no idea."

"We should expect to house four times that number for the duration of the siege."

"Right. You know, this would all be a lot easier if you stopped trying to hide from your own people."

"But…"

She held up a hand to stop his interruption. "I'm not saying you should tell them everything, but no-one is going to expect to see you age in a month or a year. You can go back to invisibility once this is over, but while we're under siege and everyone's crowded within the walls, I think a few rousing words from their lord will be just what people need."

"I'll think about it," he said.

It wasn't much of a concession, but it was more than she might have hoped for.

Ailith nodded. "Can we be ready to open the gates tomorrow?"

"I'll send guards out today to start spreading the news. Some families will be ready to move at once. Will you ask your friends to start preparing for our guests?"

So it was that the next morning, while Leofwin went around the castle introducing himself to the staff he'd spent so many years avoiding, Ailith took control of the incoming crowd of refugees. They came on foot and in carts, carrying sacks or herding livestock. She met each family at the gate to explain what was happening, while Frida supervised the wagons which ran back and forth carrying heavier supplies from the town. Only the temples had refused to evacuate, and even Garrick should be wise enough to leave the houses of the gods in peace.

Food was taken to the pantries, hay and firewood were absorbed into general stores, and animals herded together into the barns. From knives to pitch-forks, anything that could serve as a weapon was stored in the armoury, just in case. Wynflaeth made meticulous records of every contribution so compensation could be arranged once life returned to normal, while Nia — one of the few who could write — made lists of skills and trades and started to assign people to rotas. Whether it was cooking and cleaning, mucking out the animals, or learning to handle a bow and arrow, everyone would have work to keep them occupied.

"Ledric and Godesa, from the bakery."

"Welcome." Ailith smiled at the young couple. "Has Frida arranged someone to fetch the sacks of flour from your stores?"

Godesa nodded. "And a lot of our equipment has preceded us, I think."

"That's great. Pip here will find you somewhere to sleep, and Nia will put you down to report to the kitchens."

The castle's children ran back and forth guiding the newcomers to their new homes. The guest suites could each house one or two whole families, and Ailith had opened up every disused room that could be cleaned and brought back into service. Even Leofwin's own apartments hadn't escaped her notice. She'd silenced his protests by presenting him with keys to every room they actually used, which would remain locked and private. Then she'd moved a number of their most loyal staff into rooms that would otherwise have stood empty, freeing up more space in the servants' quarters and the barracks. The Lower and Upper Halls had been cleared of furnishings and were also available as sleeping areas, as were any empty spots in the hay lofts. Some families preferred to set up camp in the Outer Court, bringing their own tents or constructing lean-to shelters against the walls. Even the dungeon cells could be unlocked and given over to refugees, although Leofwin had drawn the line at interfering with Anselm's space.

By Ailith's calculations that should be enough accommodation, at least until winter set in. That allowed the Great Hall to be kept in its current configuration, which would ease the process of feeding hundreds of extra mouths. The Drawing Room remained in case they needed a more formal space for meetings.

"Endelyn, the potter." The woman who introduced herself was followed by a small team of apprentices and a wagon-load of pots. Ailith indicated where she should park the wagon so Wynflaeth could update her records before it was unloaded.

"What about raw materials?" Ailith asked. "Are those being brought separately?"

"We can hardly move the kiln," Endelyn said. "No use filling the place up with slabs of clay we can't fire."

Ailith nodded, but she was thinking about the abandoned pottery workshop next to the forge. Watersmeet hadn't had its own potter in residence for some time but everything had looked in fair condition, and it wouldn't hurt to have the option. "Let me show you the old kiln, and you can see if you think we might get it running again. Nia, can you hold the fort here? I won't be long."

Chapter Sixty

Leofwin hadn't thought any messages would make it through the siege lines, but if he'd been told he would get one letter, he still wouldn't have expected to see the slanted letters of Malachi's spidery hand.

Malachi never wrote letters.

He had always traded primarily in secrets and whispers, and since Anselm's betrayal it was said that even his formulae were now stored only in his head. Certainly, the old snake was wily enough never to commit anything to writing to which he could later be held. But these were not ordinary days.

The boy who managed to sneak across the lines was a young orphan who squired for one of the lords in Garrick's retinue. That fact alone was enough to raise thrice three hundred questions, and the boy had been picked up by the guards and swept off to a holding cell while the matter was investigated, though the story of long hours and beatings from his master was a familiar refrain. The important thing was that the letter, folded into a tight square and sewn carefully into the hem of his tunic, was genuine. Malachi's script was unmistakable.

Leofwin broke the thumbprint seal and scanned the text, growing more anxious with every word.

Leofwin,
I have been a fool.
As I write this, I await my trial at the hands of Oelum, and it is a situation entirely of my own making. I gave young Highfort information he did not earn, and now he knows our weakness. I did not dream an alchemist, even

one as green as he, would invoke the Temple Law. I must present myself at the temple by midsummer's eve, and I dare not imagine I will survive until the Feast of Hasat.

I can only hope this missive gives you enough time to uncover some fragment of lore that might allow you to escape the clutches of Death, even if she takes your blood as bond.

If not, forgive me.

— M.

It was the most frank communication he'd ever seen from Malachi, and it raised some alarming questions. If the Temple Law had been invoked, it was probably only a matter of time before trouble came knocking at their doors. And the temples could cause a lot more problems than some uppity lordling with his siege engines. No walls were thick enough to keep a priestess of Oelum at bay.

Leofwin tucked the letter into his pocket. There was no need to bother Ailith with the news, not while it remained a remote and unsubstantiated threat, but Malachi's words gave him pause. Their studies had fallen by the wayside under the strain of managing the now-crowded castle, but they had added incentive now to reexamine Ailith's latest discovery.

He'd need to steer her attention back to alchemy without raising her suspicions, but he'd hardly seen her since the influx of refugees. The fact that her bedroom was six doors from his own counted little when she spent half the night organising logistics, checking ledgers, supervising the garrison, and ensuring the kitchens didn't exceed their rations. For his own part, Leofwin had found himself primarily occupied with resolving the minor disputes that were an inevitable consequence of cramming so many bodies into a confined space, in a hurry. It all left little time for poring over scrolls or tending the garden… but there were others who could adopt their more mundane duties. They did not have an excess of alchemists.

Ailith wasn't hard to find, once he set out to look for her. In a corner of the Inner Court she'd strung up a tarpaulin and arranged two dozen chairs in the resulting patch of shade. A group of older children were scratching awkward letters onto slates while Ailith corrected their strokes.

"Wynflaeth needs more help," she explained, stepping away from her students. "But she can't spare the time to teach reading and writing."

He raised an eyebrow. "And you can?"

"No, but it's an investment. It'll make everything easier, in the long term, and these kids are going to teach the younger ones."

"I never imagined this being part of your apprenticeship, you know. I can only apologise."

"Actually…" She hesitated, a smile spreading across her face. "I'm actually enjoying it. There's a lot to do, but it's really interesting. But is everything okay? I'm fitting the teaching in between other jobs, I can stop if you need me."

"Everything is fine, but I hoped you might join me for lunch."

She glanced towards the Great Hall, where queues were already forming at the door.

"In private," he added. "It's been a while since we spoke."

"Oh, of course. Just let me tell Frida not to wait for me, we've been catching up at mealtimes."

"I'll have Cook send something up. Will you join me in the garden when you're done here?"

She nodded, and he went ahead to arrange their meal. The kitchens were bustling and he didn't like to interrupt, so he ended up taking half a loaf of rye bread, a jar of pickles, and a few cold potatoes and chicken legs that were left over from the previous night's supper.

"It's a humble meal," he apologised when Ailith flopped onto the bench alongside him. "But the kitchens were busy."

"As they should be. Anyway, this looks delicious, I'm ravenous." She tore into a piece of chicken with her teeth, while he sliced the bread and loaded his plate. "What did you want to talk about?"

"You've taken on a lot, lately. I know you're enjoying yourself, but it would be a shame for you to completely neglect your studies. I think we should make time to resume our lessons."

She nodded. "That would be good, but the castle won't manage itself."

"No, we'll both have to delegate more of our duties, but that's achievable. Everyone is settling in to the new routine — it won't hurt if you check the numbers weekly instead of daily."

"Look at you," she said, grinning. "I think you're really getting the hang of this trust business. Yes, you're quite right, I can ease up on the reins a little. It'll be nice to get back to work. And maybe once the children have mastered their letters, we can test them for other latent talents."

Chapter Sixty-One

Garrick was as surprised as anyone when the priestess of Oelum presented herself at the camp. He took a deep swig of brandy to steady his nerves before acceding to her herald's request that, of course, he would meet with her at once. How could he refuse? He could only hope that there was no way to prove whatever allegations may have been levelled against him. Unlike Malachi, his own forays into alchemy hadn't left him with a fatal weakness that was open to exploitation.

He'd equipped a large square tent to serve as a reception room while they were encamped, and he found her sitting there, looking tiny as a bird amongst the stuffed chairs and statuary that he'd installed to give a suitable gravitas to the space. At first glance she didn't look like a formidable avatar of Death, and as she stood and straightened to her full five feet he thought they'd sent a child as a messenger, though as he drew closer, the faint lines on her face told a different story.

And then she fixed him with a look that said she had seen through the mists, and would not hesitate to send him to join her Mistress if he made the mistake of crossing her.

He felt himself shaking, and clamped his hands together behind his back to hide the tremors. Since taking his position with Selwyn he'd learnt only one secret of the temple of Oelum: that every acolyte must wield a blade in execution before she could wear the ceremonial sword and take up the duties of the full priesthood. No-one could mediate with Death who had not experienced it firsthand.

"My lady of Oelum," he said, offering the brief formal bow of equals. "How may I assist you?"

"I must be permitted to enter the castle," she said without preamble. Oelum's adherents were not known for their loquacity. "And I must be permitted to leave freely thereafter."

"Naturally," Garrick agreed, feeling a weight lift from his shoulders. "I, ah… if I might ask… has the lord of Watersmeet displeased the temples somehow?"

"That remains to be weighed," she said.

"Ah. Of course."

"You will allow his lordship to pass through your camp in safety, in order that he can face trial."

It wasn't a question but Garrick nodded solemnly, struggling to keep his face neutral as his heart soared. It was better than he could have dreamed. The temple of Oelum would remove Leofwin from the balance, the wool would be lifted from Ailith's eyes, and he would be able to take the castle without so much as unsheathing his sword.

"You will not take advantage of this situation to press your attack," she went on, as if she'd read his mind. "You may maintain the siege, if you must, but you will not attempt to take the castle while the Lord Baron is awaiting our judgement. This may take some time. And if he is innocent, you will allow him to return in peace to the stronghold before you resume your little war games. Do you understand?"

"You have my word."

"Then we are in agreement, and all is settled."

She gave a little bow that mirrored his own, and he wasn't quite sure if she was mocking him. But the servants of Death were not known for their sense of humour, either.

"Will you require an escort to see you safely to the castle gates?" Garrick asked.

She met his eyes, and again he had an uneasy feeling that she might well be capable of pushing him through the mists with nothing more than a stray thought.

"I should be safer without a company of guards around me, I think," she said. "My robes are armour enough. But I thank you for your concern."

"You'll let me know if there's anything else you require."

"I will. And you will be notified, of course, if it is determined that his lordship will not be returning."

Garrick reached into his pocket and drew out a purse full of gold. "To assist with your expenses," he said.

She bowed again, and the purse vanished beneath her robes. "We accept your gift," she said. "Though I trust you are not so naïve as to think the temple can be bribed. Such an insult would demand its own investigation."

The blood drained from his face. So much for securing Leofwin's doom. "I meant no such slight," he said quickly. "I am merely a devout servant of the gods."

She seemed to accept that, though he was sure she could see straight to his heart.

He watched from the edge of the camp until she passed within the outer walls of the castle. He noted that this time she did not send the herald ahead of her, preferring to walk alone. As the gates opened for her, he toyed with ideas of hiring female assassins and dressing them in purple robes… but he could only imagine the retribution that such a deception would invite. Death would be too kind a punishment.

Once the priestess was out of sight he went to pay a visit to the prisoners. Their accommodations were basic but large, more than adequate for the comfort of two commoners. And although they seemed harmless, he'd stationed six guards around the perimeter of the tent. He found them as he had every time he'd dropped by: the old woman paced slow circles around the edge of the tent, while the girl lay on her pallet with her arms folded across her chest, staring at the canvas roof. The girl got to her feet and dropped into a low curtsey as he approached; the old woman refused, as always, to acknowledge his presence. He'd managed to provoke a reaction from her only once, and that was when he'd had the girl whipped on the first day. Now she didn't even respond to that, and he'd learnt it was easier to ignore her in return.

"Things are happening," he told the girl.

"My lord?"

"The eye of Oelum has lighted upon Watersmeet," he said. "I may need you sooner than I thought."

"I'll help you to persuade her," she said, earning herself a hard look from the old woman. "She'll listen to me."

Garrick nodded. She would help him, certainly, but it might not be in the way she imagined. There was no way he was going to let her go free, just on some half-baked hope that Ailith might be won over. But as soon as Leofwin was removed from the picture, the value of holding Ailith's sister hostage would be incalculable.

"Come," he said, extending his hand towards the girl. "It's dinnertime. Eat with me."

Perhaps, if he spent a little more time with her, she'd let something useful slip out of that pretty mouth.

Chapter Sixty-Two

Leofwin watched the slight figure wending her way up from the barbican. She was completely alone, purple robes flapping in the wind, knowing that no-one would dare interrupt her progress. With Malachi's warning in the back of his mind, he wasn't entirely surprised by her appearance. He turned on his heel and made his way back through the castle. He would intercept her at the gatehouse; he would give no cause for her to doubt his piety. Though he seldom attended the temple rites, Leofwin had been impeccably careful in all his dealings with the priesthood.

She reached the outer gate moments ahead of him, and was attending carefully to the guards' directions when he arrived. He bowed low and led the way to the Drawing Room.

"My lady," he said. "To what do I owe the honour of this visit?"

"Leofwin, son of Avelin, ninth Lord Baron of Watersmeet," she intoned, and from her formality he knew that it was bad. She looked over his left shoulder as she voiced the words, as if reading from an invisible scroll. "You have been charged with the gravest of transgressions. Do you know of which I speak?"

"No, my lady."

"You are charged with theft from my Mistress, to whit, the exploitation of unnatural magics to preternatural ends. In simple terms, they say you are a magician, and that by your magic you prolong your life."

"They?"

Her eyes refocused on his face. "It is of no consequence who levels these accusations. What matters is that they are investigated."

"Of course, my lady. What can I do to demonstrate my

innocence?"

It would be a dangerous question to ask, in normal circumstances, but the letter had hinted at a way out. In that alone there was a sliver of hope.

She smiled, then, her face softening from its formal mask. "It is the right question, but one I cannot answer. All will become clear at your trial."

"It's to be a formal proceeding, then?"

"There is no other way, in a case such as this."

"I see."

"As a kindness, I warn you, this could be a lengthy ordeal. You will need time to set your affairs in order for an indefinite absence, so you need not accompany me today, but you must present yourself at the temple by sunset on the night of the dark moon." She met his eyes with a baleful stare. "I can see I don't need to warn you of the consequences if you fail to meet our conditions."

"Quite so. You needn't think I would be so foolish."

"I have made a few small arrangements on your behalf. The boy in the tent is to allow you safe passage, and his armies will not trouble your castle or your people in your absence."

"Then you have bought for my people a moment of peace that I could not have negotiated. My thanks."

"You shouldn't thank me, when I may yet be the instrument of your demise."

She reached her left arm across her body and twisted her fingers into the flowing fabric of her sleeve. Although her robe looked no different afterwards, she came away holding a long, thin triangle of purple fabric.

"Carry this as a pennant when you come," she said. "Then the boy can have no excuse for mistaking your intent."

He nodded, and she gave a half bow before turning to the door.

"I can show myself out. You have eight days."

At the moment the door closed behind her, Ailith materialised from behind a tapestry. "Who was that?" she asked, hurrying to his side.

"Trouble," he said, though if she'd been listening, she could be in little doubt of that. "How much did you hear?"

"Enough to be afraid. Do you really have to go?"

"If I wish to avoid certain death."

"Will a trial be any better? The temple of Oelum is hardly known for leniency."

"It depends. I had a letter from Malachi."

"What? When?"

"Just a couple of days ago. I didn't want to trouble you when there was so much else going on, but the essence was simple: he was arrested on Keyif's Night, and ordered to be tried by ordeal."

She glared at him. "And you didn't think you needed to 'trouble me' with this information?"

"You'd only have wanted to help, and truly, there's nothing we could have done. By the time the message reached me, he was probably already dead."

"That may be so, but if you want me to help you play this game of martial Fortunes, you really shouldn't obscure half of the pieces."

He nodded. "Noted. I won't do it again."

"So can I read it?"

"Later, but I'll summarise. He told Garrick, and Garrick has almost certainly told them, everything about our silver amalgam. In particular, they won't expect me to last longer than a month in their custody."

He watched the understanding dawn in her eyes.

"That might be the best thing he's ever done for us, if it means you can prove your innocence through gold."

"Quite so."

"Come on, then." She tugged at his arm. "What are we waiting for?"

"Patience," he said. "She's given us a few days. We might as well use it to make sure we learn everything we can about this amalgam."

Chapter Sixty-Three

"A siege is one thing." Leofwin was pacing the garden paths, his hands folded behind his back. "We're prepared for a siege. But in my worst nightmares I never dreamt he would be so stupid as to involve the temples."

"Can I help?" Ailith asked. He'd seemed calm enough in front of the priestess, but in the intervening hours he'd grown steadily more agitated. "Should I come with you?"

"You'll help by looking after things here while I'm gone." He stopped, took the signet ring from his finger, and slid it onto her thumb. "If they're using Garrick's information I'll be gone for over a month, and you'll have a lot to do here, not least keeping Anselm alive."

"Of course. You can rely on me, whatever needs doing."

"I know." He nodded, rubbing absently at his damaged eye. "You're already doing most of it."

"So what else? Make elixir for Anselm and the mice, talk to Thurstan and Wynflaeth to keep things running smoothly, make sure we're not getting through the rations too fast…" She twisted the ring as she thought. "Have I missed anything?"

"It would, I think, be useful if you'd allow me to announce our betrothal to the staff."

"Since when do I allow you to do things?"

"I was wrong not to ask you before I brought in the priests. I shan't make that mistake again, so if you prefer that it hadn't happened, then as far as I'm concerned it didn't happen."

"But you think it would help." She just couldn't quite imagine why.

"I need every one of them to obey you without question while I'm gone, and this time we can't just pretend I've taken to my bed for a few days. An announcement might be the easiest way to clarify your position."

She pondered for a moment. "You said you'd try to trust your people. Do you think it's a good idea to start that by lying to them?"

"It's not exactly a lie. For better or worse, we are betrothed."

"But one day you'll have to explain to them why you're not going to marry me after all. Whatever the strict status of our betrothal, it feels like a lie. Won't that undermine their trust, when you have to explain it?"

"There's one obvious alternative."

"Hmm?"

"I could marry you." He hesitated, looking as uncertain as she'd ever seen him. "If you wanted me to."

She stared at him, and when it was obvious he wasn't about to elaborate, she could manage only the simplest of questions: "What?"

"I mean it. Do you want me to marry you, assuming we survive all this?"

"That's not the most romantic proposal."

His lost expression hardened into a scowl. "Sometimes you seem to think we're in a saga just because we're in a castle. I'm not one for poetry, Ailith. Say no, if that's your answer, but don't tell me I need to find prettier words."

"I don't mean poetry. I just mean… I don't think I want to marry anyone for a tactical advantage. That's where I always fought with Mama. She said I could fall in love later with whatever man she found for me, but I've never been sure about that."

"I wouldn't wed someone I didn't care for. Why do you think I haven't made an alliance that way? I could command the eldest daughter of any lord who fears me — which I believe is every last one of them. I wouldn't choose that, though it would gain me a tenth of their lands. But I do think love is another one of those things that's misrepresented in the tales."

"What do you mean?"

"In the stories, like Gisla and Edwyn, falling in love and getting married is an automatic route to a happy ending. The way it's told, you'd think it's as simple as looking deep into each other's eyes. Their story stops there, but real life doesn't end on the day you attend the blessings. It's just like everything else — you choose, and then you have to keep on choosing, every day, for the rest of your lives."

"Like being a hero."

"Like everything. However much you love someone, you still have to make those little choices every minute of every day. Feelings are fickle things. I can't guarantee how I'll feel in ten years' time, or even tomorrow, but I can always promise to make my choices with you. And I've never been happier than in these days since you walked into my life and tried to kill me."

"No… me neither. But…" She toyed with the hem of her sleeve, avoiding his eye. "Sorry, I don't know what to say. I wasn't expecting this."

"You do look a little shocked. I'd been hoping, since you're so good at figuring things out, you might have found some little clue in the fact that I arranged our betrothal."

"I thought the gods were mocking me. A potter's daughter from Bracklea can't marry a baron, everyone knows that."

"Everyone knows you can't use gold in alchemy, but you didn't let that stop you. And they would have you believe that a shepherd's twelfth son can't inherit a minor title, let alone a barony. We're alike, you and I. We stepped away from the well-worn path when we embraced our talents. So leaving aside what everyone knows, what do you think? Would you like to marry me?"

"I don't know." His face fell, and she felt it like a blow to the stomach. The last thing she wanted was to hurt him just as he was about to leave. "That's not the right answer, is it? But it's the only answer I've got."

"It's kinder than a simple 'no', I suppose."

"I'm not saying no." She reached out and laid her hand softly on his. "Gods, I'd be lying if I said I hadn't dreamed of this."

"But?"

"But in my dreams it came with time and courtship, not a question out of nowhere. We have a lot of tomorrows to choose… more than most people, with the elixir. It's too much to think of. Too much has changed lately."

"Then when I return, if you'll allow me, I'll attempt to court you in a more traditional manner. How does that sound?"

"It sounds wonderful." Perfect, if not for the heartbreaking possibility that he might never come home. "But why wait? We have a day or two before you leave."

"Why, indeed?" He flipped his hand over to enclose her fingers. "One day at a time, then."

"One day at a time. And today, I choose to be a woman who might one day marry you. Will that do?"

He smiled, and brought her hand up to his lips, placing a kiss that went on longer, much longer, than the usual, formal brushing of lips over fingers. Ailith fancied it was something of a promise, as if he wanted to show the merest hint of what 'yes' would mean, and her heart thudded in response. She'd given the right answer, though; she had no doubt of that. It was nothing like any romantic ballad, but it was real.

"I think I can settle for that," he whispered, his breath warm against her fingers.

He showed no sign of releasing his grip, so she tugged his hand across and placed a kiss of her own on his wrist. She immediately feared she'd overstepped the mark… but no. If she was even to entertain the possibility of marriage then she had to forget completely that he was one of the Twelve, entitled to have her head off for any reason or none at all. She wouldn't be happy in any relationship where she couldn't say what she thought and do what she felt.

"Since we're beyond social conventions," she said, "you should know that this woman you wish to court is no demure and passive noblewoman, there to be kissed without kissing back."

"Is that so?" He raised one blond eyebrow. "What is she, then?"

"She's a artificer's daughter, so she's good with her hands." She twisted her fingers with his as she spoke, emboldened by the warmth of his smile. "She's a mage, with a will of iron. And moreover, she's an alchemist, so she's nothing if not stubborn about getting what she wants."

"I'm liking her more and more."

"Me, too."

Without giving herself time to think about consequences she leaned in until her lips met his, tangled her hands into his hair, and kissed him with a fierce determination that said she, too, knew exactly how good they could be together. If he was surprised by her boldness, it didn't slow him as he wrapped his arms around her and drew her closer.

After a long moment, she pulled back and looked up at him. "I think I could get used to making that kind of decision."

He reached out to smooth her hair. "One day at a time," he said. "Remember?"

"One kiss at a time," she said and claimed a second one, inhaling the almond scent of his hair, the tang of leather, and the echoes of a thousand herbs that infused his work clothes. She wound her arms around his waist and settled her head against his shoulder. "I think I shouldn't mind too much if you wanted to tell the staff. No-one would expect a wedding before spring, and it wouldn't be too scandalous to wait an extra year."

"Oh, I don't know." He trailed his hand across her cheek. "With a demure and passive noblewoman, such as you are most assuredly not, I might be able to manage a year without scandals. But if you're going to go making decisions like that all the time, I think I may already be in trouble."

Chapter Sixty-Four

He held Ailith's hand beneath the table. It was one thing to get to know her friends, but it was quite another to have them descend all at once on his private dining room with next to no warning. In the thirty years he'd held Watersmeet, this was the strangest social situation he'd had to deal with. Ailith had persuaded him that her friends would be more comfortable if he kept to simple clothes, so he wasn't dressed for feasting, yet she'd asked the kitchens to prepare a meal that befitted the nature of their announcement... within all the constraints of siege rationing, of course. Just because they were celebrating, that didn't mean they could take more than their share.

"Tell me again who's coming," he said.

"You know Frida already. Ymma usually works in the kitchens, though she's been taking on a lot more for me since the evacuation. Lufe and Nia you might recognise, they're the girls who ran after me that day I hit Garrick. Lily works in the scullery, Wig is the baker's apprentice, Ulf is a guard, and Ada's started training as an archer."

"And you haven't told them why you want them to eat with us?"

"I've told them it's dinner, and that I want them to meet you."

"But not why."

"I want it to be a surprise. And I wanted to tell them myself, before you tell everyone."

"I'll leave the explaining to you, then?"

She leaned over and kissed him lightly on the cheek. "I was rather hoping you would. I don't mind you doing the big announcement, but these are my best friends."

"Of course."

He was planning to gather the staff in the courtyard tomorrow, but that would be a brief and formal affair, strictly to ensure everyone was informed of Ailith's new position. This was… different. It was a social occasion, but it had been obvious from the outset that dining with Ailith's friends wouldn't be the same as hosting a feast for visiting nobles. And not least because she'd forbidden him — and apparently them — from any mention of rank or title.

The door opened, and Thurstan showed the eight young people to their seats amidst a lot of murmuring and hastily-exchanged glances. Ailith filled their goblets herself, and once everyone was seated she stood and banged her knife on the table until they were quiet.

"I don't know how this usually works," she said. "With castles and barons and whatnot. I suspect mine isn't the usual way."

"For what?" Ymma asked.

Ailith crossed her arms and stared the older girl into silence. "If you can shut up for one minute, you'll find out."

"Alright, alright. Get on with it, then."

"Thank you. As I was saying, I've probably missed something crucial, but I've never been very good at doing things properly. You've all got wine, that's the main thing, so I've got a little announcement, and then we'll have a toast."

She took a deep breath, and let it out slowly. Leofwin wanted to reach for her hand, to still his own nerves as much as hers, but that kind of gesture would only preempt her announcement. He settled for taking a sip of his wine to steady his resolve.

"I'm just going to get straight to the point. I wanted you to come and meet Leofwin, properly and as friends, because you're all very important to me, and…" She rested a proprietorial hand on his head. "Well, we're betrothed. That's my news."

There was a moment of stunned silence and then everyone started talking at once, their voices rising in a cacophony of sound as each tried to be heard over the others. Then Lily stood up and pulled Ailith into a hug, and everyone realised that hers was the right answer. Before he knew what was happening Leofwin had been pulled to his feet as well, though only Frida was bold enough to embrace him, and then only briefly.

"There is one important tradition, for a betrothal," Nia said once the hubbub had died down a little. A couple of the girls nodded their agreement. "You have to kiss."

"And kiss 'er like you mean it," Ymma added, urging Leofwin into the middle of the impromptu circle that had formed around Ailith.

Only a day had passed since the awkward conversation that had changed everything, and he wasn't yet accustomed to the idea that he could reach out to her whenever he liked without having to first manufacture some excuse to take her arm or brush his hand over hers. And this was something quite different again. He rested his hands lightly on her shoulders, and placed a soft kiss on her lips. Her eyelids fluttered open as he pulled back but he couldn't quite read the expression on her face.

"Like you mean it," Ymma heckled.

He stopped, his nose an inch from Ailith's, and looked straight into her eyes. "Is that okay with you?"

"I should think so," she said, her voice barely above a whisper, her fingers creeping beneath the hem of his tunic to trace a line across his back. "If it's traditional."

He lowered his mouth to hers again, and her lips parted as he pulled her closer. He barely heard the claps and cheers from their audience over the pounding of blood in his ears.

When Ailith let him go — and it was definitely that way round — he kept a protective arm around her shoulders. It was one thing to sneak a kiss or two in the privacy of the garden, but a public display like that would feed the gossip mills for weeks, even if it did come with news of a betrothal.

"Oh yes!" Lily said, clapping her hands and grinning with such glee that the tension in the room evaporated. "You'll do. If you kiss her like that, you'll do nicely."

"I'll say," Nia agreed.

"An' I thought you was just after his money," Ymma said, nudging Ailith in the arm. She whistled a couple of bars of *Under the*

Willows as she returned to her seat.

Ailith picked up her goblet. "I promised you a toast. To us, then. To friendship, and love, and good wine."

"To us," they all echoed before draining their glasses. Ailith passed the flagon round for refills, and signalled to Thurstan that they were ready for their first course to be sent up from the kitchens. As they tucked into bowls of freshwater mussels, which had been cooked to perfection in a light broth of garlic and thyme, the questions started up again.

"How long have you been keeping this a secret?" Nia asked.

"It's a bit complicated," Ailith said, and Leofwin wondered if she was going to tell them the whole painful truth. "But I suppose you could say it was yesterday that we reached an agreement."

"Yesterday!" Lufe shook her head in disbelief. "A kiss like that, it looked like you'd been practising for weeks."

"Oh no," Ymma said with disconcerting conviction. "What you saw there was two people who've been *wanting* it for weeks, but ain't quite got as far as the bedroom."

"It'll be so exciting to have a wedding in the castle," Frida said. "You will have it here, won't you, after the siege lifts? You'll have to send for your parents, and just imagine how your sisters will love it."

"Eddy will love running around the battlements," Ailith said. "I'm not sure Sunneva will be interested in anything aside from whether I can find a nobleman for her, too."

"You picked the wrong baron for that, my love," Leofwin said. "I'm not overrun with brothers and cousins like most of these noble types."

"I've got enough siblings for both of us," she said lightly, but the way she squeezed his knee under the table told him she was thinking of his lost family, too.

They were just tucking into the second course when Thurstan slipped a note into Leofwin's hand. He glanced at it beneath the table, struggling to make out the words in the dim light, and slid it across to Ailith. She frowned as she read.

"We should go," she said, whispering straight into his ear so the others wouldn't overhear. He nodded. She got to her feet and turned to her friends.

"You'll have to excuse us a moment," she said, with impressive calmness. "Something's come up."

"No wonder, with that kiss," Ymma said in a stage whisper, sending Nia into a fit of giggles.

"Well, quite," Ailith said, seizing his hand without skipping a beat. "We might be some time."

As she pulled Leofwin from the room she gave him such a smouldering look that he wished they really were sneaking off for a tryst.

She'd somehow signalled for Thurstan to follow them into the corridor, and spoke to him in hushed tones as they passed. "Keep the food and wine coming. There's no need to ruin everyone's evening, and this is the safest side of the castle."

"Nicely done," Leofwin said as they started up the stairs towards the battlements.

"I think two of us panicking is quite enough for now. Don't you?"

"You don't look much like someone who's panicking."

She shrugged. "You neither, but you'd be daft if you weren't a bit worried."

The siege towers had gone up almost overnight. It had been inevitable: wagons full of logs had been rolling in for days. But seeing the finished structures looming over the camps was still a shock, and the fact that the first boulder had already hit the walls was doubly frightening. Knowing that Watersmeet had been designed to hold off just such a siege was one thing. Watching the castle come under attack would be another matter entirely. He put his arm around her shoulders and hugged her close, the warmth of her body a reassurance in itself.

"They'll wheel those ones up to the wall," he explained, pointing across to two large towers. "And then send men up with grapples to climb over the walls. Those ones, across the river, are clearly designed to fold over into temporary bridges. And there are trebuchets, of course, to fling rocks and burning pitch. Look, they're winding that one now."

The archers had done a good job at keeping the moat clear, raining down a deadly hail of arrows on those who had tried to bridge the rivers. On the opposite bank, though, and in the town of Watersmeet, the builders had withdrawn just far enough to construct their monstrosities out of range of attack.

"Savash and Oelum. She said they were supposed to wait," Ailith said, glowering at the camps.

"She said they weren't to attack in my absence, but I'm not absent yet. If they keep this up, I'll have to go to the temple even sooner than we'd planned. I don't want to leave you a damaged castle."

"I don't want you to leave me at all." She tucked her hand into his. "But you'll come back. You have to."

"You realise that, strictly speaking, I'm guilty of exactly what they charge?"

"I know. So am I."

"On a very narrow technicality. You didn't go through with it."

"No, but... I doubt that's what they care about."

He kissed her on the forehead. "What matters is what they can prove."

"Will you do the gold tonight, then?"

"If you'll come down to the workshop with me, before we rejoin your friends. There's not much we can do up here."

"And the walls will hold?"

"The walls will hold."

Ailith took control the moment they stepped across the workshop threshold. While he was caught in troubling daydreams of his forthcoming ordeal, she steered him into a chair and began to measure out the necessary ingredients.

"You have to do the last step yourself," she said, placing the mortar full of lumpy proto-amalgam on the table. "And it's going to hurt."

"More than the silver?"

"The silver amalgam isn't in your body when you put the flame under it," she said.

He gave an involuntary shudder. It hadn't occurred to him that they'd still need fire to start the amalgamation. But this was what Ailith had done to herself while he slept: if she could manage it, so could he.

"Ready?" she asked. She was holding his hand, but in her other hand she held his dagger poised above his arm.

"Ready."

She didn't hesitate. She drew the blade across his skin in a swift and confident movement, smeared the mixture into the cut, and thrust a flaming taper against his skin without compunction.

Leofwin screamed.

Ailith squeezed his hand, gently but deliberately grounding his attention until he managed to focus on forming the amalgam. He bowed his head, eyes closed, and felt the ingredients shift within his veins. It should have been easy — he'd had enough practice with the silver — but he'd never before needed to work on such a complex formula while fire and poison burned his skin. By the time he finished the amalgamation, sweat was dripping from his brow. But the gold had amalgamated.

Ailith kissed his hand, and fetched Payne's balm to heal his arm.

"What would I do without you?" he asked as she smoothed the ointment across his skin.

"Whatever you did before I arrived, probably," she said. "Without sieges and temple trials. I imagine it was quite pleasant."

"Well, when you put it that way…" He caught her around the waist and pulled her close. "I don't suppose this represents an improvement for you, either, in those terms."

"Maybe not," she said. "But it's been worth every heartbeat. Gods, the draught of life! How could I have imagined that?"

"And is that the only thing worth staying for?" he asked, hugging her tighter.

"It's not that you're not lovely," she said, dragging the word out as her hands wandered across his shoulders. "But if you're asking me to compare being with you to investigating arcane and impossible magics, you might not like the answer. And you said yourself, feelings are fickle."

"I did say that."

"Well, then." She kissed his brow and pulled him to his feet. "I have some deliciously fickle feelings right now… but I don't know. Are you in a rush to get back to the party?"

Chapter Sixty-Five

It was Ailith's turn to feel awkward.

She knew Leofwin had been nervous the previous night, and she'd invited only a few of her closest friends. He was determined to parade her in front of everybody.

She peered out of the window while she waited for him to join her in the Drawing Room. With the exception of the small company of guards who were actively patrolling the walls, every single member of the castle staff had been gathered in the Inner Court, the only space large enough to contain them all now that the Outer Court had transformed into a camp. By the size of the crowd, most of the refugees had also decided to come along and see what the fuss was about. A couple of carpenters had been roped in to knock up an elevated wooden platform from which Leofwin could speak, someone had covered it with emerald green drapes, and a couple of small boys were arranging white ribbons around the edge in an attempt to create a festive air.

Ailith was wearing her favourite purple gown, and Frida had spent over an hour expertly braiding her hair into a design of such ridiculous complexity that Ailith suspected the main goal had been to force her to sit still and stop pacing the room until everyone was ready for them. She had argued with Leofwin about an appropriate level of jewellery, talking him into silence only when she pointed out how cruel it would be to flaunt their wealth when so many people didn't even know if their homes were still standing.

"You'll be fine," Frida said, squeezing her hand. "This is just a formality. Everyone already knows."

"They don't."

"Of course they do, Ymma wouldn't stop talking about it all day."

Ailith shook her head. "It's not just the betrothal. There've been some… allegations. Leofwin has to go to the temple of Oelum for trial."

Frida gaped at her for a moment before she found her tongue. "I'm so sorry. I had no idea."

"It's been quite sudden," Ailith said. "But I'm to take charge while he's away. That's why we wanted to tell everyone what was going on."

"He'll be fine, though," Frida said, a reassuring smile returning to her face. "He's innocent. A trial can only prove that."

Ailith nodded, not trusting herself to speak for fear that all her worries would come tumbling out. There was no way she would get through this with her sanity intact if she couldn't convince herself that he'd be returning safely, and yet the knowledge of his guilt weighed heavily on her. And she was every bit as guilty as he was, now.

"You'll tell me if there's anything I can do," Frida said, and it was the offer of a friend rather than the duty of an employee.

"I'll need rather more from you than hairstyles," Ailith said. "You grew up here. You know how everything fits together in a way I never will."

"I think you're settling in nicely."

"She is, isn't she?" Leofwin stood in the doorway; neither of them had heard his approach. "But she's right, too. You're too smart to spend your life as a chambermaid."

"We'll talk about this later," Ailith told Frida, before stepping forwards and tucking her hand into the crook of Leofwin's elbow. "Let's do this before I lose my nerve."

The walk from the keep to the platform felt like miles, with every curious face turned in their direction. Ailith kept her hand on Leofwin's arm, and her eyes straight ahead. Frida had slipped off to join her friends; the girls had secured a prime spot just in front of the stage, and Ailith was pleased to have their supportive faces to focus on. Ymma winked at her as the gong sounded to silence the crowd.

"Thank you all for coming." Leofwin raised his voice to reach the furthest corners of the yard. "I won't insult your intelligence by pretending the gossip mill hasn't been working all day. You all know that I'm going to make this wonderful woman my wife, come the spring."

He put his arm around Ailith's shoulders, and she smiled up at him, but it felt a bit forced. She couldn't stop dwelling on the reasons why they were having to do this now. The crowd cheered, Frida and Ymma and Lily the loudest of all. Leofwin waited for the noise to die down before he continued.

"That's the good news. The bad news is that the siege engines being built beyond our gates are now operational. The castle was hit last night by the first few rocks from their trebuchets."

This was met by gasps and murmurs; this, apparently, was news. Ailith was glad they'd managed to keep a lid on the night's events until they had time to talk to everyone.

"There's no need for anyone to panic," Leofwin said quickly. "We have the strongest walls in the Twelve Baronies, and rations enough to withstand a year's siege, if not longer. They'll get bored and go home long before Watersmeet falls, but it's important you all understand the severity of our situation. Make no mistake: this is a war. And since we find ourselves besieged, it's essential that orders are not questioned. Ailith's word is to be taken as law, whatever she says. When she speaks, she speaks with the full authority of this house."

Considering how much time she'd spent ordering people around over the past couple of weeks, Ailith wondered if this kind of proclamation was really going to make any difference to anyone.

"This is made all the more important," Leofwin went on, "as I shall be away for a period. It may be weeks or even months, but I know that I leave you in the safest possible hands."

Once the crowd dispersed, Ailith found Frida and Lily at the door to the kitchens. Ymma sat in the doorway hulling strawberries, twisting the green leaves away with her long fingers.

"How did you get those?"

"Chef's secret garden." Ymma grinned up at her. "Some things don't travel well, and his lordship loves 'em, so we grow 'em in the kitchen gardens. Figured we might as well pick whatever's left before he goes."

"Make sure you get some, too," Ailith said. "They smell fantastic."

"Here." Ymma twisted off the last stem and held up the bowl. "Take these upstairs, and don't you dare come back to work before he's gone. We can handle things here."

Chapter Sixty-Six

Ailith walked with him through the castle, holding his hand in silence as they crossed the Outer Court and started down towards the barbican. In his left hand Leofwin carried a small travel bag, and in her right she held the stave to which he'd attached the purple pennant. As the guards began to lower the drawbridge he pulled her aside, into a tiny alcove that had once been used as a weapons store, and set his bag down at his feet. She leaned the staff against the wall.

"Are you ready?" she asked.

He shrugged. "Are you?"

"No."

"Me neither. But I don't think I could ever be ready for this, so it hardly matters."

She looked down, and he followed her gaze to where her shoes were toe-to-toe with his mud-splattered riding boots. "I'm sorry I didn't have a better answer for you," she said, so quietly he had to strain to hear her over the creaking of the drawbridge chains.

"Shhh," he said, reaching out to tuck an imaginary hair behind her ear. "It was your answer. That makes it perfect."

She caught his hand, pressing his fingers hard against her cheek. "I'll think about it while you're gone," she said. "I promise."

"It's my own fault," he said. "If you were the sort of woman to say yes too easily, then I probably wouldn't have asked you. So think, if you like, but not too often and not too sadly."

"I imagine I'll think of little else."

"You'll have more important matters to attend to," he said. "This is your castle, now. You have eight hundred people to worry about."

"Eight hundred people, and you. I fear yours will be the more precarious position."

"It's a trial before Oelum," he said. "It's for the gods to judge my position. At least that brat won't have any further influence."

"Then I entrust you to the gods, and I pray that we have skill enough to outwit them."

"I'm not sure you're supposed to pray for things like that."

"Probably not."

She leaned in and kissed him on the cheek, and then the lips. He tried to commit every detail to memory so he could at least remember the feel of her when he was alone: her soft mouth tasting of the fennel she so often chewed as she worked, her fingers snaking across the small of his back, the way her cold nose brushed his cheek. And a warm, tingling sensation as she mapped every inch of his body with her blood-awareness. Apparently she, too, was gathering up details that had never before seemed worth memorising.

"Come home safely," she said. "Please."

"If it's within my power, I will." He picked up his bag, and the staff with its purple pennant. There were a thousand things he wanted to say, promises and declarations and exhortations, but none of it mattered. He would be exonerated or he would die. That left very little worth saying, so he settled for a simple "I love you," and another gentle kiss.

Ailith wiped the tears from his eyes. "You can't walk out there crying," she said. "You have a fearsome reputation to protect. Remember? Sometimes it even works."

He laughed, which in the circumstances just made the tears flow harder, and pulled her into a firm embrace. "I'm glad it didn't work on you," he said. "Remember that, whatever happens."

Turning away from her was one of the hardest things he'd ever done, but it was never going to get any easier. He would come home. He had to. But if he didn't, he was leaving his people with the best possible leader.

If he'd made the deal with Garrick himself, he would have taken additional precautions, but even the arrogance of young Highfort surely wasn't enough to tempt him to cross a priestess of Oelum. Nevertheless, he felt painfully exposed as he stepped out of the barbican and onto the bridge.

The pennant did its job, though, and he crossed the moat without incident. As he reached the edge of Garrick's encampment, the guards allowed him to pass, but a couple of soldiers fell into step behind him.

"Is there a problem?"

"We're to see you safe to the temple, milord," one of the men explained. "His lordship don't want any trouble."

"That won't be necessary," Leofwin said, but he knew his words would make no difference. Keeping a few respectful paces behind, they trailed him through the deserted streets and up the short hill which led to the temple district. He lost them only at the gates.

He was met by a young acolyte, her white robes trimmed around the hem with a double purple stripe which indicated her position in the temple hierarchy.

"You're Quen's," she said. "Come."

Stepping across the threshold was terrifying, but then the strangeness of the temple awakened his curiosity, and fascination overwhelmed his fear. He'd never before been further than the courtyard where the public rites were held. The acolyte led him through a series of darkened rooms and twisting passages, illuminated only by flickering purple lanterns. He soon gave up trying to keep track of their route; the geometry didn't make sense, and it seemed they must have crossed their own path half a dozen times. Perhaps it was a tactic to disorient the visitor, or perhaps there were subtle slopes and turns he hadn't registered. Either way, he had no intention of trying to escape, so if he were to leave the temple alive he assumed he would be escorted again.

The room where they stopped was a large hexagonal space with doors in three walls and lantern niches in the others. A narrow wooden staircase spiralled up to a gallery which ran around the upper level of the room. Although the sun had been shining brightly outside, there were no windows anywhere.

"Wait here."

The girl disappeared through one of the doors without waiting for him to respond, but he was not foolish enough to wander alone in this labyrinth. Even if his life hadn't depended on a successful trial, he wouldn't have chanced it.

A moment later, the woman called Quen emerged from the door to his right. He supposed he should start to feel afraid, but she had the same calm demeanour as the day she'd called upon him at the castle, and the ghost of a smile that put him at his ease.

"You came early," she said. "You did not wish another night or two with your beloved?"

"Better to get this over with, my lady," he said, although when she framed it in those terms it sounded like he'd made a huge mistake. He didn't think to ask how she knew.

"Your confidence suits you. It is as well I am not judging you, or your conviction might sway me."

"You're not? What's your role, then?"

"Only Oelum can judge," she said. "I am your Administrator. I merely intercede."

He wondered if that was a euphemism for executioner. The priestesses only wore their swords in public on the midwinter feast day, but their blades were clearly more than ceremonial.

He detached the pennant from his staff and handed it back to her. "This is yours."

"Thank you."

She twirled it into the fabric of her sleeve, where it appeared to vanish. Even knowing it must be a trick, he couldn't tell how she manipulated his perceptions.

"This is your space," she went on, her focus shifting away from his face and her voice switching into the rhythmic cadence she adopted when she was reciting ritual words. "For as long as it is needed, it is yours and yours alone. The first door will be locked; it is the way you entered and the way you hope to leave. The second door is mine; I will bring you food and water, and if you wish to confess I will be available to hear you. You need only knock, and I will be here.

The third door is Death; that path is never closed to you."

She met his eyes again.

"Do you have any questions?"

"Why would I choose death?"

"This process may be a long one, and it will be tiring for you. Oftentimes the guilty choose not to persist. Sometimes even the innocent become too weary, and the path of eternal rest is more appealing."

"I'm not sure I understand the nature of the trial."

"That is because it has not yet begun."

"There's nothing you can tell me?"

She shook her head. "All will become clear, in time. Such things cannot be rushed."

"Then I have nothing else to ask."

"In which case, let us begin."

Quen left him alone in the room, returning by the door she'd come in through. The second door. As she'd indicated, he found the first door locked. He wasn't bold enough to try the handle of the third, although he peered in vain through the keyhole. Pressing his ear to the door met with a similar lack of results. Whatever the promised death was, it was silent and black.

Climbing the stairs, he found that the gallery was wider than it had appeared from below, as if it belonged to a larger room. There was a single cot against one wall, and a series of metal exercise bars set into the walls just above head-height. A small niche in one corner led to a privy, and there was a basin with a cold water pump. At a basic level, the room contained everything one might need to survive, but no indulgences. Leofwin set his bag down by the bed. Downstairs, he sat cross-legged beneath one of the lanterns, the door of death to his left, the locked door to his right. It was important to remember which door was which; he had repeated the order to himself two dozen times, anchoring their positions relative to the staircase.

He watched the purple flickering lamps, and waited for something to happen.

Chapter Sixty-Seven

The fortnight since Leofwin left for the temple had passed painfully slowly, but so far at least, the priestess's peace had held. There had been one day's excitement, early on, when Garrick had sent a messenger. He'd suggested to Ailith that she could open the gates and invite him inside to assume command of the castle, since a girl of her background shouldn't be left to struggle with such matters alone. She'd sent the boy back to inform his lord that, should she feel suddenly inclined to suicide, she could think of less painful methods. Then she had instructed her guards to leave the gates barred, even to messengers who came under a flag of peaceful negotiation.

Lily had picked up the duties of chambermaid with only occasional hiccups and Frida, relieved of those duties, was proving invaluable as an advisor. With her extensive network of contacts and friends, and an ear for whispers and secrets, she had the clearest insight into the mood of the castle's staff. She could spot trouble brewing before it got out of hand. Although Ailith suspected that some of the issues she put to her friend for guidance weren't exactly the normal business of running a baronial castle.

Not least because of the alchemy.

First she'd enlisted Frida's help in testing the children for magical ability, taking them aside one at a time. She'd found five with promise so far, although she hadn't yet managed to work her way through every family. For those five, she'd had Nia set aside time in the rota every couple of days, and the little group mixed batches of Payne's balm between writing exercises. It wasn't much, but it was a start, and by keeping to obvious herbal cures she hoped to delay as long as possible the moment that someone noticed what she was doing.

She'd co-opted Endelyn the potter, next, and set to investigating whether shields of copper-glazed ceramic could begin to match the strength of metal. The older woman was a little puzzled by Ailith's insistence on mixing the glaze herself, but she was soon won over by the results, and delighted to have a way of contributing to the defence of the castle.

But it was her inability to help Anselm that was keeping Ailith awake at night.

The golden elixir might have worked for Leofwin — and they wouldn't know for another two weeks whether its effects would truly outlast the silver — but Anselm was still trapped. She regularly stalked the battlements after dark, looking down on the glowing campfires tended by refugees and besiegers alike, and trying to force herself into a new way of looking at the theories. Surely there was some alternative interpretation that would yield a better solution. She usually found herself recounting her nighttime musings to Frida at the breakfast table.

The night that inspiration hit, however, she ran in from the garden and woke Frida in a rush of excitement.

"We've been going about this all wrong," she said as Frida propped herself up in bed and rubbed her eyes. "The golden elixir works like the silver, only better. Right?"

"Right." Frida nodded. Although she didn't seem to be a mage herself — Ailith had tested her with shimmering powder and a couple of herbal preparations, without success — she'd become quite familiar with alchemical terminology over the past couple of weeks.

"And Anselm can't use it, any more than he could make his own silver amalgam, because he can't amalgamate metals for himself. But he took it too soon, so what he really needs isn't a stronger version of the formula. What he needs is a cure."

"A cure?"

"He needs to grow up. Think of the silver amalgam as a poison in his body — a really insidious, creeping poison that will kill him if he goes without his next dose."

"So you need to make an antidote."

"Exactly! We need something that will push every ounce of the amalgam from his body. Will you help me?"

"Right now? In the middle of the night?"

Ailith found herself desperately missing Leofwin, then, with a painful specificity that dwarfed the general ache she'd been feeling ever since he left. He would have been out of bed already, pulling on his clothes as he quizzed her and forced her to crystallise her ideas. He would have been as excited as she was, just *because* she was, before she even explained herself.

Frida just lay there and watched her, waiting to hear if this was really an emergency that required them to work through the night.

"No, you're right," Ailith said at last. "We can work it out in the morning."

She knew she should go to bed, but instead she went back up to the garden and started to weed the borders behind the arbour. In the darkness, with the scent of the night stocks enveloping her, she could almost imagine that Leofwin was about to step out from between the bushes as he'd done so many times before. Always ready to converse with her about even the most obscure corners of alchemical theory, always keen to join her in half-considered experiments, and without a word of complaint when her enthusiasm overreached even their combined abilities.

She realised with a start that her previous longing had been grounded in lust. Certainly she missed the warmth of his hands, and those kisses… she'd dreamt of those kisses every night. But if the gods didn't see fit to return Leofwin to her, it would be in these moments of discovery that the loss would hit her hardest. Even Garrick kissed well enough, but who else would sit up with her, as thoroughly delighted as she was, through a night of ideas and innovations?

She curled up on the bench and wrapped her arms around her knees, twisting the signet ring around her thumb. The hard wooden surface was far from the most comfortable accommodation that Watersmeet could offer, but she felt closer to him here than anywhere. The gold would be enough to fool the temple. It had to be. But she knew she wouldn't sleep properly until the whole ordeal was over.

After a couple of fitful hours, she entirely abandoned the idea of rest and made her way down to the library. She tidied away her notes on the golden elixir, and covered the desk instead with theories of poisons and their antidotes. The silver amalgam wasn't referenced in any of the texts, and certainly not as a poison, but she hadn't expected anything so simple. Somewhere, she was sure, would be something that would point her in the right direction.

Most of the texts — dozens upon dozens of slim treatises — examined natural antidotes to natural venoms. Alchemical cures tended to be more generic in their application, with amalgams such as lemontyne salve that would counter the symptoms of several common toxins. On the treatment of alchemical poisons, there was much less to say: every author accepted that the best solution was to unmake the amalgam. There was little concern for those unlucky enough to lack the necessary abilities. If you weren't a mage, it seemed, no-one cared enough to think about curing you.

Ailith fetched a dozen bottles and jars from the stock room and laid them out in pairs on the table, poison and antidote side by side. There had to be a pattern. She explored each substance in turn, letting the usual flood of sensations wash over her, but there was no system. She couldn't identify anything linking a poison to its cure.

With a sigh, she pulled out her knife. She'd hoped this wouldn't be necessary, but it was the natural next step. Maybe it would be in the interactions that the pattern was to be found. She sliced open the end of her middle finger, and dipped a rod into the first poison.

Chapter Sixty-Eight

Without any daylight to mark the passage of time, days had soon blurred into nights within the temple. Leofwin slept when he was tired, which was often, and ate when food was presented. He had no real idea of the date or time, except that he had just woken up. His eye was bothering him. At first he'd imagined that the mists would clear, in time, but he was starting to suspect the damage to his vision was permanent. And it itched. He'd rubbed and scratched so much that his eyelid bled, but in the confines of the ordeal chamber he had no supplies from which to attempt a remedy. And the more he thought about it, the worse it became.

For the first couple of days he'd tried to distract himself with thoughts of what Ailith might be doing up at the castle, managing the effects of the siege and its flood of refugees, but trying to think of the outside world in too much detail just caused him headaches. It was the same when he dwelled for too long on the details of theories he couldn't check and experiments he couldn't conduct, particularly as he dared not make even a brief note of alchemical significance.

He'd given up asking when something would *happen*, though he felt the constant threat of the ordeal hanging over him.

He lay on the sleeping pallet and watched the flickering shadows cast by the purple lamps. Sometimes he thought he saw movement in the darkest corners, but when he looked closer there was nothing to see. He pressed his palm hard against his injured eye. Perhaps it was causing him to see things that weren't there. And the itch was growing worse with every blink. He tucked his hands beneath his back to try and force himself not to scratch at the raw skin, but a moment later his concentration drifted, and when Quen arrived with his next meal he was surprised to find his fingernail caked with blood again.

She brought him a bowl of barley topped with a mixture of wilted leaves, mushrooms, and beans. The meals that she supplied were always hearty but plain, and whoever prepared them made no obvious distinction between breakfast and supper, presumably to aid the illusion of timelessness. There were always grains and vegetables, occasionally accompanied by a block of cheese or a boiled egg.

He lifted a forkful of beans and mushrooms to his mouth and chewed slowly, savouring every burst of flavour. Mealtimes presented the only variety in his days; every time he'd wolfed down a bowlful without thought, he had been wasting the proffered opportunity. Taking one slow mouthful at a time, he could draw out the experience.

As he set down the empty bowl, he realised he hadn't scratched his eye once while he'd been concentrating on his food.

He knocked at Quen's door, and handed her the bowl.

"May I ask you a question?" he ventured before she could leave. It was the first time he'd spoken to her in days, beyond a murmured thanks for each meal.

She paused, the empty bowl cradled in both hands. "Of course."

"You never bring meat or fish — has Garrick's occupation of the town prevented you from buying such things? Or is it forbidden in the temple?"

"Forbidden is a strong word."

"But it's discouraged?"

"I am no longer an acolyte: I must weigh my own decisions," she said, and he sensed he'd come close to offending her, but she went on with her explanation before he could apologise. "To cause a death is a grave responsibility. Once one realises this, it seems rash to incur such a debt when it can be avoided. To add variety to one's diet is a frivolous cause, and wasteful. Certainly I would not dare it on your behalf."

She waited patiently while he absorbed the idea. He was surprised to find it made sense, although if someone had told him a month earlier that the priestesses of Death avoided causing death, he would have thought it madness.

"Then I thank you," he said. "For your consideration as well as your answer."

"You are most welcome."

There was a smile in her voice, but she turned and was gone before he could see if it had reached her eyes. In the days she had been administering his trial, she had come and gone from his presence with her face a neutral mask. Her voice was always soft and her motions smooth, but the glimpses of humanity were brief.

He got up and did pull-ups on the bars until his arms were burning. It didn't take long, but the effect was much as he'd hoped. While he was thus occupied, he could focus on nothing but his muscles; even the sense of impending doom faded into the background of his awareness. He nodded, understanding slowly dawning. He couldn't help Ailith with the castle, he couldn't do alchemy, but within the constraints of this small room, he could still live. That would be better than waiting to die.

Chapter Sixty-Nine

Leofwin had been gone for three weeks when Hubold, Lord Baron of the White Marches, rode up and presented himself at the gates of Watersmeet.

"Should I make him wait?" Ailith asked when Frida brought her the news.

"This seat is yours, in his lordship's absence," Frida said. "You make everyone wait."

"Even barons?"

"Especially barons. Come on, it will give Lily chance to do something special with your hair."

"Do you know why he's here?" Lily asked.

"One of Leofwin's customers, I imagine." Ailith shook out her plait and sat patiently as Lily started to partition her hair for braiding. "I knew it would fall to me to keep them alive, if this went on more than a couple of weeks, but I wasn't sure Garrick would let them through without asking difficult questions."

"Even a boy of his arrogance wouldn't risk isolating himself from every one of the Twelve," Frida said. She'd developed an impressively low opinion of 'the boy', as the girls all called him now, though they waved away Ailith's protests that she was younger even than Garrick. Younger, Frida insisted, but wiser.

"Well, it's good timing," Ailith said. "I can try out Anselm's cure."

It had been two days since she'd succeeded in displacing the silver amalgam from the bodies of a couple of the mice, but that wasn't long enough for her to feel confident about their long-term prospects. Hubold would make a good human test subject.

"Is this your secret project?" Lily asked.

Ailith nodded, then cursed and muttered an apology as the motion caused Lily to miss her fingering and drop the half-tied braids. "Not so secret any more, is it?" she said. "Now I've told you both."

"Only Frida really gets it," Lily said. "I just know you're trying to save his life, that Anselm."

"It might save this Hubold, too."

Once she was dressed for battle, Ailith sent Frida to fetch the product of her latest experiments while she went ahead to the Drawing Room.

"Where's Watersmeet?" Hubold demanded the moment she stepped over the threshold.

"I assume you mean Leofwin?" she asked, with a smile of practiced innocence. "You will find, I think, that in his absence I am mistress of Watersmeet. Did my people not warn you?"

"You?" He looked her up and down with thinly-veiled disgust. "What bloody good are you?"

She withdrew a bottle of the silver amalgam from her pocket. "You're here for your monthly treatment, I assume."

"You can't just drink that stuff, you know. Can't just swill it down like a shot of brandy and be done, else I wouldn't be here, would I?"

"I'm aware of that. You see, as well as being the heir to Watersmeet, I am in fact an alchemist."

"You? An alchemist?" His scrutiny was more curious this time, but still a little disdainful for Ailith's comfort.

"Will you take me at my word, or would you prefer me to demonstrate my skills in a more direct manner?" She could think of a few painful ways to make her point to a man like this.

"Leofwin told me that no common-or-garden hedge healer could work such magic as this requires. Even my own court alchemists don't have the necessary skill."

Ailith drew back her shoulders and glared straight at him. "Do you really believe Leofwin would have chosen a woman who was less than his equal?"

"Hmph."

"But if Leofwin explained to you the complexity of this amalgam," Ailith added sweetly, "then he surely also explained what would happen if you didn't return for your next dose in a timely manner."

"Bloody swindler. Yes, he told me."

"Would you prefer to take that risk?"

"No."

"Then you have no choice but to trust that I can do as I say. Unless, of course, you'd like me to remove the amalgam from your body entirely?"

"Impossible."

Ailith raised an eyebrow. "You're an expert, are you?"

"Leofwin might be a bastard, but at least he explained what I was getting into. I know it's not reversible."

Frida had slipped in while they were talking, and stood silently by the door with the bottle of antidote in her hand. Ailith waved her over. "It turns out he was mistaken on that front. I've been doing a little research of my own."

"Why should I believe you?"

It was the one question she wasn't really equipped to answer, but she couldn't let him know that. She held up the bottle. "If you brought an alchemist in your retinue, I'd be more than happy to allow them to inspect my amalgam."

He hadn't, though. She'd checked. In consideration of the siege he'd brought only a couple of attendants, and Ailith had still needed to shuffle a couple of families around to free up a suite for the visitors to share.

"And you'll know when it's worked," she added. "You're welcome to retain your room here until you're sure."

"You'd really free me from this obligation?"

She'd been thinking only about testing the formula before she used it on Anselm, but the look on his face told her she'd be making a mistake if she allowed him to leave without paying for the privilege of his freedom. And although she'd examined the books thrice over and persuaded herself that Watersmeet could be sustained on the income from taxes and tolls, it would go some way to making up to Leofwin for the loss of this income.

"For a suitable price," she said.

"Can't hardly be worth as much as that silver potion."

"Then I'll be happy to give you your monthly dose and send you on your way." She smiled politely, and removed the stopper from the silver amalgam. "I don't know how you persuaded Garrick to let you through to my gates, but I hope your luck holds out when you return next month. He's promised us a truce only as long as Leofwin is gone."

"Highfort wouldn't dare to cross the power of the Marches."

"Allies, are you? How nice. You realise, I trust, that the boy reported his own father to the temples."

"I heard Oeric had had trouble."

"Garrick found out about the elixir, and it seems his piety outweighed his filial duty. But perhaps he likes you more than he liked his father?"

Hubold grunted. "How much?"

"I think an amount equivalent to five years' payments should suffice. If you don't have it in gold, I'll accept a writ of debt."

"It'll have to be a writ, for that amount."

Ailith nodded. "Frida, fetch Wynflaeth. We'll have this signed and sealed before I do the work."

"Don't you trust me?"

"You don't trust me."

"But I am Lord Baron of the White Marches. You're just a commoner playing dress-up."

Ailith smiled. It was far easier to deal with open hostility than with Garrick's insincere pretence of friendship. "That's as may be," she said. "But it's also the case that I'm the alchemist with your life in her hands, so we'll do this my way."

Wynflaeth didn't keep them waiting, and within a few minutes Ailith had dispatched her again with an immensely valuable piece of paper to file away in her office. She turned her attention back to Hubold.

"The process might be a little unpleasant," she said. "You'd be more comfortable lying down."

"Now you tell me," he grumbled, but he allowed her to lead the way to his room.

The antidote, once she'd thought of it, had proved to be a simple formulation, at least compared to the silver amalgam. But it took the best part of an hour to administer a high enough dose and Ailith had to transform it, little by little, in the baron's veins. At first he looked on, glowering at her as she worked, but as the process began to take effect the sickness gripped him and he fell into delirium.

"He'll be fine," she reassured Lily, who was standing by with a damp cloth to mop his brow. At least, Ailith really hoped he'd be fine. If not, his death would be on her hands, and that wouldn't do anything to help the region's stability. When she'd done all she could, she left him alone to convalesce.

Chapter Seventy

The fourth week came and went without a word from the temple. Hubold had recovered and left, and Ailith had offered Anselm the chance to start growing up again, a choice he was considering with due solemnity. But there was no news of Leofwin.

As the fifth week drew to a close, she was starting to fear they'd underestimated the powers of the gods. Why would Oelum rely on something so mundane as counting the days? Perhaps the priestesses truly had the uncanny powers that were rumoured. It would hardly be stranger than anything else she'd learnt this year.

It was Frida who reminded her, as she was drowning her sorrows in the kitchens one evening, that she'd come from one of the temples herself. "Maybe they'd listen to you, if you went as a pilgrim," she suggested.

"But the temples all hate each other," Lily said. "Won't that make it worse?"

"That's only the High Priests," Nia said, and as she'd once been a temple orphan herself, everyone was inclined to believe her. "In the town, everyone works together. And they're not totally inhuman."

"I can try," Ailith said. "I don't see how it could possibly make things any worse than they are now."

The next morning, Ailith dug around in her chest until she unearthed Selwyn's armband, and fastened it in place around her left arm. Frida offered to accompany her, but if anything were to go wrong, Ailith would prefer her friends to be safely behind the castle walls. She hoped the priestess's peace would mean Garrick allowed her to leave and return without interference, but she didn't trust him enough to leave Watersmeet without a full complement of guards.

"Halt." Garrick's soldiers stood two deep, blocking the exit from the bridge, and one man stepped forwards to speak with her.

"You're not to attack while the Lord Baron of Watersmeet is at the temple," Ailith said. "That deal was struck with the priestess of Oelum. And for myself, I'm on a pilgrimage for Saaluk and Bereket. You should think twice before impeding my progress."

"We'll escort you to the temple of the Twins," the spokesman said, as the soldiers reformed to surround her little group. "Nowhere else."

Ailith thought quickly through her options. The town of Watersmeet had a temple district, set apart from the now-deserted shops and houses, so heading for the home of the Twin Gods would at least get her into the right part of town.

"Thank you," she said, motioning her own guards to stay close and hoping that they wouldn't do anything to upset her chances.

They made their way through the camp, and into the eerily silent streets beyond. Doors had been smashed and premises looted: it was a chilling reminder of how much was at stake, and her responsibility for everyone currently sheltering in the castle. If she couldn't get Leofwin back… but that was a line of thought she wouldn't allow herself to follow.

They came to the temple of Saaluk and Bereket, but Oelum's compound was a little further up the hill. Ailith instructed her guards to wait outside the gates, Garrick's soldiers still surrounding them. When she showed him her armband and explained her purpose, the priest was more than happy to show her out through the temple's back gate, and she walked to Oelum's temple along a narrow alley which ran parallel to the road.

A young acolyte — probably one of the orphan girls — met her at the gate and led her into a small room.

"Can I help you?" the girl asked as Ailith caught her breath. "Only, if you're a stranger to these parts, you should know that the town is deserted and the castle besieged. This isn't a safe place for travellers."

"I've come from the castle, actually." She unfastened the

armband and pressed it into the acolyte's hands. "You have my lord committed for trial. As you see, I was sent by the Twins to attend his lordship, so I came to see if I could offer any testimony on his behalf."

"And you would speak with his Administrator?"

Ailith met the girl's eyes, searching for the humanity behind the placid mask, and nodded. "Please."

"Wait here. I can't promise she'll come, but I'll ask her."

"Thank you."

The woman who joined Ailith in the antechamber was the same slight, dark-haired priestess who had come to inform Leofwin of the initial summons.

"You wished to speak with me?"

Ailith dropped into a low curtsey. "If you're the one looking after Leofwin? I came to talk about his lordship."

"And you claim to speak in the names of Saaluk and Bereket?"

"No." Ailith shook her head emphatically as the priestess fastened the armband back into place for her. "I would never be so bold; I'm no priestess. But I was sent on a pilgrimage here, from the temple in Bracklea, and I've come to know his lordship better than I'd imagined. I hoped that you might let me vouch for him."

A slow smile spread across the priestess's face. "And do you think I should consider his lordship's beloved to be impartial in such matters?"

She knew.

Ailith swallowed hard.

She *knew*.

She'd risked her life for no reason. How could she expect the priestess to give any credence to her words if she thought her mind was clouded by affection? Part of her wanted to run away, but she couldn't let a little thing like guaranteed failure stop her from saying her piece.

"I'm not here because I love him," she said, once she was sure she could trust her voice to be steady. "I'm here because he's a good person, and he doesn't deserve this."

"But you do love him."

"So what if I do? It wasn't supposed to happen, but the fact that I care for him is a testimony in itself."

"And it truly was Saaluk who sent you to him."

"It was," Ailith agreed. This strange priestess didn't need to know that Selwyn had sent her for reasons more personal than religious.

The priestess nodded. "That is interesting."

"Please," Ailith said, determined to press what little advantage she could wring from the priestess's attention. "You've held him for five weeks now. Isn't that long enough for Oelum to make her determination?"

"These things cannot be rushed." The priestess took Ailith's hand, and allowed a faint smile to crease her eyes. "I cannot force it. But one way or another, something in my heart says it will not be long, now."

"He's a good man," Ailith said. "That's what matters."

"I am only the Administrator," the priestess said. "What will be, will be."

Ailith nodded. She wasn't going to get any further, but at least it wasn't over yet. If the golden elixir hadn't kept him alive, she didn't think the priestess would pretend. "Thank you for your time," she said as she got to her feet.

"Go safely, in Her name." The priestess bowed. "I would not wish to be the one to tell him if you stumbled into misfortune."

Garrick was waiting across the road, leaning against the wall of the temple of Av. She wondered who had spotted her sneaking between the temples. Her guards and his had both moved up the hill, and the two groups eyed each other warily, but thankfully there was no sign it had devolved into violence.

"Come to turn yourself in?" Garrick asked, smirking at her. "I hear they're invoking the Temple Law quite freely these days."

"I heard it differently," Ailith said. "But if you'd like me to go back and tell them what I know of your alchemical dabbling, I'll happily oblige."

"My offer still stands, you know. When you get bored of waiting for him to die."

She glared at him. "Don't you have a barony to rule? I can't see how camping out here is helping you discharge your duties to your people."

"You're one of my people," he said. "And don't you forget it."

She wasn't, but telling him so would only provoke him, so she bit her tongue. But she was very glad she'd brought her own well-armed escort.

"If you've only come here to taunt me, I have business to attend to," she said. "Some of us take our responsibilities seriously."

"No harm will come to the peasants if you give me the castle. That's more than you can promise them if you persist in this folly."

Ailith started down the hill without a word. She hated it when he was right.

Chapter Seventy-One

Usually Quen presented him with his food and then left, but today she sat across from him and studied him as he ate.

"Do you miss her?" she asked.

He looked up in surprise, his mouth full of spinach, and nodded. "Of course. Every day."

"And yet you have managed to relax here. That is no easy feat, even when one is not in the first agony of love."

"It must be worse for her," he said. "She has things to do; people to manage; decisions to make. Apparently my only duty is to live."

"You make it sound simple."

"Isn't it?"

"Not everyone finds it so."

He swallowed another mouthful. He wasn't sure what to make of her suddenly becoming so talkative, but she seemed to be expecting a response.

"It would require more effort to die," he said. "Even when you've put death just a door away. This is easy, somehow, though I'm still awaiting the horrors an ordeal would usually entail."

"You truly mean it," she said. "You have been tried for over six weeks, and you do not even feel the beginnings of it."

"Six weeks?" The gold had worked, then. He knew it had been a while, but with Malachi's note in mind he'd assumed he would be released if he survived beyond the expected month. Not that he could mention that particular assumption to her.

"It has been six weeks and two days," she said. "Less some hours, for it is only lunchtime, and you came to us in the evening."

It should have been nice to know the time of day, but the information felt strangely disconnected from reality. Trying to think about it was disorienting. Such things didn't matter so long as he was here. It would have been painful to cling to such constructs as time.

"Why are you telling me this?"

"I wanted to give your mind a chance to return to the patterns of day and night. You have quite abandoned the rhythm."

"In this place…" he began, but she interrupted him.

"Yes, you are right. It is the easiest way, perhaps the only way to survive here, but now I must prepare you to return to the world."

He hardly dared to draw the obvious conclusion. "Are you saying…?"

"You have displayed remarkable equanimity," she said. "I have waited in vain for this trial to test you; I cannot in good conscience spin this out for longer. If you will finish your lunch, I will escort you from this place."

He set his bowl down. "If I'm free to go, I can eat at home."

"Your home is still besieged," she said. "If I were you I would take this opportunity to enjoy the vegetables. What is another quarter-hour, added to six weeks?"

She was right, of course. He had been prepared to wait patiently for as many more days or weeks as was required. He could spare a few more minutes to enjoy the food that had been prepared for him. But even knowing that, he gulped it down too quickly, the prospect of freedom hastening his actions.

It took him mere moments to pile his few possessions haphazardly back into his bag, and he was ready to leave. He took one last look around the place that had been, however briefly, his home. He still didn't know what made the lantern flames burn purple; even when he'd seemed to be alone in the room, he hadn't dared probe the alchemy of their construction. Nor had he seen the priestess tend the flames, in the whole six weeks of his imprisonment. It could only be alchemy.

"Come, then," Quen said, holding the door open for him. "Let us return you to your beloved."

"What should I tell her when she asks what's happened to me?"

"Tell her the truth," she said. "That is always the best way, between friends."

"Isn't it a secret?"

"I appreciate your concern for our mysteries, but it is different for everyone. Your experience was yours alone. It is yours to share as you will."

The route out of the temple felt shorter and more direct than the way they'd come in, but whether there were fewer tricks, or if it was simply his anticipation of freedom speeding his steps, Leofwin couldn't be sure. He blinked in the bright sunlight, appreciating the warmth on his face in a way he never had before. He rubbed lightly at his eye, but caught himself in the act and tucked his thumbs into his belt.

Quen walked with him to the gates of the castle, and waited as the drawbridge clattered down before them.

"You have been a most interesting subject," she said. "I only regret the circumstances that gave me chance to study you."

"You did what you had to," he said, and she nodded her agreement.

"Perhaps you will come more often to our rites, now you have seen the face of Oelum."

He nodded. "Perhaps."

"Farewell, then. And take care," she said, offering a small bow, which he returned with a smile. The face of the most terrifying of gods could be a friendly one, at times, and he left with a certain fondness for the strange woman who had supervised his trial.

The face he was desperate to see, however, was — he hoped — safely ensconced beyond three layers of thick stone. He strode up to the gatehouse, and glanced at the sundial as he passed through the Outer Court. It was a little late for lunch, but perhaps she would still be in the dining hall. That would be the first place to look. A small boy sprinted across the courtyard, almost knocking his feet from under him, and disappeared ahead of him through the inner gate. Leofwin wished he too could break into a run, but a baron had to retain some dignity.

Ailith apparently felt otherwise.

He was striding purposefully towards the keep when she came flying down the steps and threw herself into his arms, and he had to lift her off her feet to stop them both from crashing to the ground. As he set her down, she hugged him so fiercely that he thought she might crack his ribs.

"You found me." He placed a light kiss on the top of her head. "I was just on my way to look for you. I believe we have a courtship to resume."

"Pip came to fetch me," she said, waving at the boy who was still watching them. She took a step back and tipped her head to the side, considering him. "You look well. Better than well. They took good care of you?"

"I suppose so."

"Do you want to tell me about it?"

"What I really want is to take a stroll through the gardens while holding your hand." He took her hand and kissed her fingers. "You might persuade me to talk as we go."

"You don't have to, if it's painful to relive it."

"No, that's not how it was at all." Her voice was so full of concern that he had to try to explain, even as they started up the steps towards the keep. "No-one did anything to hurt me, it's just difficult to make sense of exactly what happened. They basically left me alone in a room, but saying it like that doesn't really capture how strange it is to be without daylight for weeks on end. They woke me up at lunchtime today and I didn't know what day it was, let alone what time."

"But it wasn't dreadful?"

"I've missed your company, and sunlight and fresh air and freedom, but once I got used to the strangeness it was actually quite relaxing. My position was easier than yours, I imagine, since at least I knew I was safe."

"It has been hard," she said, thoughtful. "But I've kept myself busy. You'll be pleased, I think, with how I've managed your affairs."

"I'll always be pleased with you." He squeezed her hand. "And I don't care about my affairs, so long as the brat hasn't broken his vow? I assumed Quen would tell me if he did."

"Quen?"

"The priestess."

"You're on first name terms with the priestess of Oelum?"

"Only one of them. She's the one who came here; it seems I was her responsibility."

"Oh." Ailith shook her head, frowning as they emerged into the rooftop garden. "I think I prefer to consider her as the avatar of Death, not as a woman in her own right. I'm not sure I'd want to know the name of someone who had me imprisoned."

"It wasn't really like that. Besides, I imprisoned you, after a fashion, and you don't seem to have held it against me."

"Well, I had just almost killed you. It's surprising how firm a friendship can grow from an accidental poisoning. Mama never told me to try that one."

Only one word stuck: "Accidental?"

"Of course." She stopped dead in the middle of the path. "You don't really think that I ever meant to kill you?"

"It was an obvious conclusion."

"I can't believe... How could you think that?" She folded her arms across her chest and stared at him. "Don't you know me at all?"

In truth, it hadn't even crossed his mind to consider an alternative. Now she brought it up, though, he couldn't imagine why he'd been so dense. She was obviously no killer. She was right: he should have known her better than that.

"You hadn't been here that long, I suppose, but I should have known." He gathered her into his arms, relieved when she didn't resist. For a moment he thought he'd offended her. It would be ironic beyond belief if he'd survived his trial only to lose her through his own stupidity. "Why didn't you tell me?"

"I'm not sure," she mumbled into his shoulder. "It didn't seem all that important, when you said you'd already forgiven me. I just assumed you'd guessed."

"And I assumed that you knew what you were doing."

"No… he told me it was a sedative. And, fool that I am, I believed him."

"Apparently we were both being foolish around that time."

"No harm done," she said. "As long as I never believe another word he says. Of course, now you're back, he's free to wind up the trebuchets again. What are we going to do about him?"

"Today?" Leofwin tilted her head until her lips were an inch from his own. "I suggest we ignore him entirely."

Chapter Seventy-Two

Ignoring Garrick was a temporary solution. They'd spent the previous afternoon in defiant denial, playing Fortunes and drinking wine and kissing beneath the arbour until the sun went down. It had been wonderful. But with the morning light came the chilling realisation that Leofwin's survival would make Garrick nothing if not more determined to take the castle by force. And Ailith knew she had to explain about Anselm and Hubold and her antidote to the silver amalgam.

She dressed in a fine green gown and summoned a few young messengers: one she sent to instruct Leofwin to smarten himself up before breakfast, the others to make various arrangements about the castle.

"What's this about?" Leofwin asked as they tucked into bowls of barley porridge, sitting awkwardly in their formal clothes.

"Perhaps I just wanted to see you all dressed up."

He frowned.

"No, even I'm not that bold. I thought we should make an announcement. Everyone knows you're back, of course, the gossip mill hasn't broken, but they'd like to hear it from you. And you need to formally release Anselm."

"I need to do what?"

"It's done already, actually, but he needs to hear it from you. He's the one person around here who won't take my word as law."

"Okay." He took another mouthful, and didn't ask the obvious question.

"Don't you want to know why?"

"I trust you."

"But..."

He reached across and squeezed her hand. "I gave you command of this castle, and I promised myself I wouldn't second-guess your decisions. If we're setting Anselm free, then there's a good reason for it."

"You might not like my reasons, but I've been busy these past weeks. Busy enough that he's just a boy, again, so I don't think we can really justify locking him up for his own protection any more."

"You've managed to reverse the effects of the amalgam? Safely?"

"Safely, if not comfortably. I'll explain it properly another time, but the short version is that I made an anti-venom to suck it from his system. I tested it on a couple of the mice, and one of your barons, before I risked it for real."

"One of my barons?"

"Hubold of the White Marches, to be precise. He was willing to pay quite handsomely for the privilege of ageing again, though I dare say vanity will bring him back for another dose in a year or two. Ceawlin and Maeloc, too. With Oeric's fate becoming known, it's not surprising they were easy to persuade."

"So to summarise, you've lost me all my customers, and you want me to release my one and only prisoner?"

"I'd prefer to say that I've fixed a number of your outstanding problems."

"Wonderful." He kissed her fingers. "I knew I could leave everything in your care."

The atmosphere in the courtyard was jubilant. Ailith hoped people weren't assuming the siege would be broken just because their lord had returned, but he was careful not to give out false hope when he spoke. Everyone still seemed heartened by his return, and there were a few cheers when he reminded them that Ailith's word was still to be obeyed without question.

"I fear you won't like what comes next," Leofwin said, as they snuck away from the crowds.

"Tell me."

"You're half of the boy's excuse for being here, but Anselm is the other part. If he wishes it, now that you've found a cure, we should ask Garrick to grant him safe passage back to Bracklea. And then, while we have his attention, we should see if we can't arrange an end to this nonsense."

"He won't give up."

"Not for nothing, maybe, but a little compensation might change his mind."

"You can't." Ailith shook her head. "You can't bargain with him. Not while the walls hold."

"I told you you wouldn't like it, but what about when they move the towers, and bring grapples, and we have to ask our friends to die to keep us safe? The walls will hold, but at what cost? At least let me find out what his price would be."

"But if you pay him to go away, what's to stop him coming straight back again?"

"There are oaths and contracts to cover that kind of thing, and the temples would send witnesses. It wouldn't be the first or the last time of making such an arrangement."

She wasn't convinced, but she couldn't think of a sufficiently persuasive argument. Besides, it was just a conversation. They could explore the options without committing to anything.

Chapter Seventy-Three

The messenger was unexpected. It had been only two days since Leofwin's sudden return to the castle, and Garrick had been preparing his forces to resume their assault against the walls. Whatever had transpired within the sanctuary of the temple, the last thing he'd expected was for Leofwin to have suddenly developed a taste for negotiations. But then he hadn't expected the baron to survive. Whatever infernal bargain he'd struck with Oelum for his freedom, perhaps this was a part of it.

Of course, he was on the verge of conquering this stupid castle, with or without Leofwin's return. At this stage it would make no sense to settle for anything less than unconditional surrender: even Watersmeet's thick stone couldn't hold him off forever, and they had no way to replenish their supplies. Maybe that was the truth of it. Perhaps Leofwin had returned only to find that his people had eaten their way through his stores in his absence.

"Make them wait," he instructed the man who'd carried the message to his tent. "Tell their boy... no. Wait."

Garrick settled at his desk, laid a clean sheet of paper on his blotter, and scrawled a quick note. Three days should be enough for what he had in mind. He twisted the signet ring from his finger, hesitated, and replaced it before reaching for the full ceremonial seal. He was starting to see why his father had chosen to stamp even the most minor papers with the weighty seal. It did make a very satisfying thunk as it hit the desk.

He turned back to his attendant. "Send their boy back with this, and fetch me a priestess of Savash."

The terms he'd laid out were simple and standard: he was willing to attend peaceful negotiations, but he would meet the Lord Baron of Watersmeet only on neutral ground outside the castle walls, accompanied by a suitable intercessor from one of the temples. A priestess of the goddess of War was the obvious choice. On the surface it was a logical precaution, the only way to be sure he wasn't walking into a trap. In reality, demanding a few days to make such arrangements gave him a little time to make preparations of his own.

He'd seized Malachi's belongings when he'd first taken the old man to the temple. Going through the contents of the cart had been a revelation. Here was someone who evidently embraced all the darker corners of alchemy that Selwyn preferred to pretend didn't exist. There was a significant collection of exotic toxins that could never be traded on the open market. In amongst the old family trees and botanical sketches, there was even a collection of papers which explained exactly how best to amalgamate and use them. If things had worked out differently, Garrick thought, he could have found a better apprenticeship here.

He shook his head. There was no time to waste in lamenting lost opportunities. The old man was gone, and though he was far from concluding his studies, Garrick knew enough to apply some of the lessons from these documents.

If he was going to talk with Watersmeet, he was determined to be prepared for every eventuality.

It took him all day and most of the night to complete the essentials. The priestess had easily agreed to accompany him. He had succeeded in making one of Malachi's poisons on his third attempt, despite the delicacy of the technique. And in the next tent his secret weapon slept peacefully, unaware that she had any part to play.

The next two days passed in a blur of checking and re-checking his strategy. The trebuchets were still, but stood ready; his people and Yutta's were well prepared. If today didn't go according to plan, tomorrow at least would be a success.

The elderly priestess arrived as he was eating his breakfast, and pressed him into making an oath of peace before a temporary altar. It was just the kind of foolish, empty gesture that he'd come to expect of the temples, but he went along with it. He would need her co-operation later.

Leofwin waited at the foot of the drawbridge, alone, although his guards were only a few feet away. Garrick instructed his own men to wait, and led the priestess over.

"Young Highfort," Leofwin said with a nod. "My lady."

"I am the twelfth Lord Baron of Highfort, now," Garrick said, in case the news of his father's death had somehow failed to reach Watersmeet, but Leofwin showed no reaction.

"I was surprised you agreed to talk. Does that mean you're getting bored, out here? Are you ready to be reasonable?"

"I've been nothing but reasonable."

"You took an interest in the fate of a boy called Anselm. You know his father, I think."

Garrick nodded, although Selwyn's family was no longer his concern.

"If I release him to your care, will you see him safely home?"

"That can be arranged."

"And with that done, will you agree to end this silly game?"

"Do you think this a game?" Truly, Leofwin was more stupid than he looked. "It's far too late for truces now."

"Then why are you here?"

"Because you took someone who matters to me, and I've come to take her back."

"Ailith doesn't wish to leave. We established that the last time."

"And how would she feel, I wonder, if she knew that I hold her little sister in the camp?"

Leofwin's pale skin blanched, and Garrick fought to hide his smile.

"Of course, I don't want to involve her," he went on easily. "She's an innocent girl. This is not her war."

"Let her go, then."

"I think not."

"What are you asking?"

"I want you to give me Ailith, in exchange for her sister's

safety."

"No."

"It's what she'd choose, you must realise that. You've always said the choice was hers. How would she feel if she found out you'd made this decision for her?"

"This is blackmail."

"Oh no." Garrick shook his head. "This is war."

"There must be an alternative."

Garrick pretended to think about it, as though this whole plan hadn't been fomenting in his mind since the moment the girl stumbled into his camp. "I suppose, if she's really worth that much to you, we could talk about the river forts and the lowlands."

"I could spare a province or two."

"I'm not talking about a couple of border towns," Garrick said. "I'm talking about the lands south of the Brim for Wulfsberg, and to the west of the Keth for me. We'd permit you to keep the headland provinces."

Leofwin bowed his head for a long moment. "How can I trust you? Even if I gave you all this, how would I know that would be an end to it?"

"We'll swear an oath," Garrick said. "I even brought a priestess so we'd have a witness. We can end this tonight."

"If I agree to your terms, you'd release her sister, as well as lifting the siege?"

"Yes."

"And you'd swear never to tell Ailith the details of what we've agreed, or why?"

"Of course."

"Alright."

He said it so quietly that for a moment Garrick thought he'd imagined it.

"Alright," he repeated, more clearly this time. "Let's get it over with."

Garrick nodded, and beckoned the priestess forwards. He'd already given her a document laying out both sides of the bargain, so it was a simple matter to affix both their seals and signatures, and then it was time for the binding.

The priestess took their two hands and pressed their palms together, looping a blue cord around their wrists. Garrick had practised this manoeuvre on his own hands three dozen times with a blank needle, and he knew the point wouldn't be felt until it was much too late. The priestess pulled the cords tighter and he tilted his fingers, pushing gently until he felt the needle slide in.

Then Leofwin was falling, the cord slid over their fingers, and in the confusion Garrick had just enough time to drop the needle and kick it neatly into a crack between the cobbles.

Chapter Seventy-Four

Ailith watched from the battlements of the barbican as Leofwin stumbled and crumpled to the ground, clutching his head. She hadn't been able to make out any words, but their expressions had been deadly serious. They'd signed something, the priestess had looked about to bind them in an oath… and now this. Garrick stepped forwards as if to help, but the priestess held up her hand and he retreated.

Ailith took the stairs two at a time and sprinted across the bridge.

"What's going on? What happened?"

"It's okay." Garrick stepped forwards and gathered her into his arms, whispering into her hair. "You're safe now."

She pushed back and stared at him, disbelieving, as understanding dawned.

"What have you done? What in Refah's name have you done?"

"You're safe. The castle is mine."

Leofwin lay on the ground, unmoving now, his arms splayed at an odd angle. The priestess bent over him, murmuring a prayer. Ailith wrenched herself away from Garrick and ran towards him, kneeling on the cobbles as she loosed the buttons of his collar. If he died, she didn't care whose castle it was. She pressed her fingers into Leofwin's neck, feeling desperately for a pulse.

"My lady, you must not interfere with the prayers," the priestess said.

Ailith ignored her. The pulse at Leofwin's throat was weak, but his heart was still beating. Just. She pressed her lips to his and breathed a deep breath into his lungs. If she could keep him alive, perhaps she could work out what Garrick had done. There were no obvious wounds, so it was probably alchemical, but in that case why wasn't Leofwin fighting back? She had no doubt who was the stronger mage.

Ailith clutched his hand and reached out with her other senses as the priestess got to her feet. It didn't take long to find the poison. Nightfall was a fast-acting sedative, a familiar amalgam that was already widely diffused into his body. By itself it wasn't particularly dangerous, but it explained why Leofwin's mind was absent from the fight. The priestess pulled her away, forcing her to drop his hand, but she was still in range of her powers. She closed her eyes and set to the task of unmaking the poison, but it was barely a moment before Garrick was fighting her, holding together that which she was trying to force apart. The cold determination of his mind felt like an iron clamp. She thought she was stronger but the amalgam was already formed, giving him a huge advantage.

Then she noticed the second substance.

It wasn't a compound she recognised and it was localised in his hand, drifting only slowly into his blood.

"His lordship's body must be taken to the castle, and the rites prepared," the priestess said. In her mind, then, he was already dead.

Keeping a part of her attention focused on her duel with Garrick, Ailith started to push carefully at the wisps of the unfamiliar poison. Only a few rare formulae demanded this kind of separation of intent, but Ailith had practised on the silver elixir and could split her mind three ways when she needed to, though this was the first time she'd worked two completely unrelated processes. She hoped Garrick might not know the technique, and as long as she kept him focused, fighting her on the nightfall, perhaps he wouldn't notice that she was also trying to dissolve his other poison.

"Summon his guards to carry him," Garrick said, his concentration slipping a little as he spoke. But he knew, as did Ailith, that removing Leofwin from her reach was the surest way to condemn him.

Ailith went to follow as the guards lifted Leofwin's limp form, still ripping apart the poison within his veins. Before she could take more than a couple of steps, two of Garrick's soldiers had stepped up behind her and caught her arms.

"My lady," she appealed to the priestess as Leofwin slipped beyond her reach. She didn't know if she'd yet done enough to save him. "This man has already profaned your oath of peace. Will you let him keep me from my home?"

"That is a serious allegation," the priestess said. "Can you prove what you say?"

Ailith wanted to scream. How could she provide proof when the evidence was flowing through Leofwin's veins? And she could hardly explain to a priestess how she was even able to sense such a thing. "He was fine, and now he's not," she said. "What do you think happened? You were right there."

The priestess bowed her head. "I saw no malfeasance."

Garrick didn't need to be told twice. "Take her back to the camp," he said before Ailith could respond, and she found herself lifted backwards.

"Please," she cried as they carried her towards the row of tents, but the priestess still avoided her eyes. Perhaps Garrick's oath had not covered her, and fool that she was, she'd rushed down without thinking to bring an escort of her own.

Garrick's guards took her to a small tent in the middle of the camp, and didn't let her out of their sight. He arrived a few minutes later and dismissed the men with a wave of his hand.

"Ailith. Can't we clear up this little misunderstanding?"

"You call this a misunderstanding?" She glared at him. "You came under a flag of negotiation, accompanied by a priestess of Savash and presumably under the attendant oaths. This is murder."

"It isn't murder, with barons. It's assassination."

"Well, doesn't that sound far more civilised? It's still killing someone."

"Leofwin hasn't any heirs, you know. Not even a distant uncle or second cousin."

"I'm his heir."

He nodded. "That's what I was thinking. With my help, you can…"

"No." Her stern look silenced him. "I mean, I am his heir. Officially. It's been sworn and sealed in front of all the gods."

"Even better. We'll plan a wedding for the spring, and between now and then I can teach you how to be a lady."

"Really?"

"It will be a challenge, but you've proved that you can learn quickly when you put your mind to something."

"After all this, your first thought is still to change me?"

"What?"

"I know how to run a castle, Garrick, I've been managing this one for months. Remember, when you had Leofwin dragged off to the temple? I don't need you to teach me anything."

"But you're a peasant."

"I'm an alchemist."

She could see that he didn't understand.

"You might be a reasonable administrator," he said. "But you're still a commoner. My wife needs to be a proper lady, and to act as such."

"And that's another thing," she said. "I've no wish to marry you. I'm heir to Watersmeet in my own right. I don't need your help."

Garrick frowned. "I don't think you understand your position. You will marry me, and you will behave yourself."

She folded her arms across her chest. "Says who?"

He stepped briefly outside and whispered instructions to one of the guards.

"I was hoping you'd come to your senses on your own," he said. "But there's something you should know before you decide to cause me any more trouble than you already have."

She stared at him without a word, waiting for him to elaborate. Counting silently in her head, she got to eight before the tent flap was lifted and one of his men pushed the girl inside.

Ailith felt like her heart had stopped.

"Sunneva?"

"Ailith!"

Sun ran across to her, and the two sisters hugged for a long moment before Garrick signalled the guard to pull them apart. Sunneva screamed as he hauled her back to her own tent; Garrick just smiled as Ailith's resolve collapsed. She'd thought that inheriting a castle might be enough to save her, but she hadn't reckoned on this.

"How?" she asked, quietly, staring after her sister.

"Sunneva has been my guest these past two months. So I think you'll be wanting to do exactly as I say, won't you?"

"What do you want from me?"

"I thought I'd made that perfectly clear. You'll hand over control of Watersmeet, you'll present yourself silently at my side whenever I need you, and you'll give me the heirs I need. If you can manage all that, then we can talk about your sister's freedom."

Ailith nodded, feeling like she might be sick, but she had no choice but to play along until she could find a way to get Sunneva out of the camp.

"In the circumstances, I don't think we need wait for a traditional spring ceremony. Watersmeet has priests enough to see to things this afternoon."

"That wouldn't be auspicious timing. It's almost Refah's Day, you can't get further from the wedding season."

"It sounds auspicious enough to me. The sooner you're bound to me, the less trouble you can cause."

"How does it all work?" she asked. "With the inheritance?"

"What do you mean?"

"Leofwin's death hasn't even been announced yet. If you marry me before I've officially inherited, surely that would nullify the betrothal and Watersmeet would pass to someone else."

It took Garrick a few moments to find his tongue. "A betrothal. Right. That changes matters a little."

"And?"

"At least a betrothal isn't as serious as a marriage. I think a three day mourning period should be sufficient, but I'll consult the priests."

Ailith crossed her palm with a desperate plea to the gods. Three days wasn't much of a reprieve, but it was better than being wed tonight. If nothing else, perhaps she could find a way to get Sunneva to safety before then.

She managed, somehow, to hold back her emotions until she was alone in the tent that was to be her prison. Left by herself at last, she curled up on the bed and sobbed until long after she'd run out of tears. It was hopeless. She was surrounded by armed guards and they'd taken her utility knife, but even if she'd had a weapon she couldn't try to escape. Not without a plan to rescue her sister. If she left Sunneva behind, she didn't know how Garrick would take his revenge.

And what did she have to go back to, anyway? Leofwin had been wrenched from her before she could finish unmaking the poison in his veins. Her friends might miss her, but for the people of Watersmeet an end to the siege would be a happy event, however it came about. What did they care whether she or Garrick held the reins? If she gave in, at least they could resume their normal lives and repair the town before the winter set in. And if she could persuade Garrick that she was a dutiful wife, perhaps in time he'd permit her to resume her studies.

She'd been trying to reassure herself that all was not lost, but the thought just made her cry all the harder.

Chapter Seventy-Five

Ailith stared at the canvas wall as the sky gradually lightened outside. She'd spent a sleepless night considering her position, and she'd failed to come up with anything resembling a plan.

Only one thing was obvious: if she was going to come up with something useful, she'd need to get out of this tent.

She sat up, and set her face into a forced smile. For whatever reason, the gods had seen fit to put these obstacles in her path, and she had no choices left. There was no getting around this. All she could do was to get through it: minute by minute, hour by hour, just as Leofwin had survived his time in the ordeal chamber. Eventually it would get easier, or else she would die — but until that time she would have a quieter life if she allowed Garrick to believe she was complaisant.

She'd liked him, once. She could pretend they were still the people they'd been in the spring.

She'd slept in her clothes, so it didn't take her long to get up. She stepped out into the chill morning air meaning to look for Garrick, but the guards stopped her.

"Has his lordship risen yet?" she asked. "I'd like to speak with him, if he can spare the time."

"I'll advise him, milady," the older guard said with a slight bow. "You should wait in comfort, I can't say how long he'll be."

In comfort, of course, meaning where they could most easily continue her confinement. She nodded, and went inside to wait.

The tent was equipped with three chairs set about a low table, as well as a bed which wouldn't have looked out of place in the castle. Evidently Garrick's view of camping differed somewhat from her own. The reed mats were well-worn and moulded to the soft ground underfoot, and she wondered who'd been evicted from their home so she could be caged here.

"Ailith. You asked to see me."

She stood and bobbed an awkward curtsey. It felt all wrong — especially if she was to be his wife, and by definition his equal, any day now — but it was the sort of gesture he'd appreciate.

"I wanted to apologise," she said. "I spoke out of turn yesterday."

"You did." Garrick didn't look to be in a forgiving mood.

"It's no excuse, I know, but I was in shock. No-one expects their betrothal to end with such an unfortunate accident."

"An accident." He nodded. "Yes. I'm glad you see that now."

"Do you think you might ever forgive me?" She reached out to touch his sleeve but he stepped away, his expression not softening. "Do you think we might be friends again, some day?"

"That depends entirely on your behaviour."

She bowed her head, hands folded in front of her. "Tell me what I need to do."

"I'm pressing for the funeral rites to be held tomorrow. You'll be in mourning for three days after that, we'll be wed on the fourth day, and our marriage contract will transfer all Watersmeet lands into my custody. Your part is quite simple."

"And then… you'll let Sunneva go home?"

"Perhaps, when you've convinced me that you'll cause no further trouble."

"I won't."

"Save your words. Time will tell all."

"I'd like to get some clean clothes," she said, afraid he might leave before she even had chance to ask. "Will you let me visit the castle this morning?"

He frowned at her. "Do you think I'm quite stupid?"

"But I'd have to come back, you have my sister. I just… if I'm to start acting a lady, I'd like to look the part." And there had to be a guard who could be bribed, if only she could lay her hands on the jewels of Watersmeet. There weren't riches in the world enough to secure Ailith's freedom, but surely someone could be persuaded to take pity on her sister.

"I'll have your lady-in-waiting pack a trunk," he conceded. "I'm glad you're taking this seriously, at last."

It was after lunch — which she ate alone — that the tent door flapped open and a pair of servants dropped a heavy trunk to the ground. Ailith clicked open the catches, rifling through the fine dresses until her hand settled upon the roll of jewellery that she hoped would buy a way out for her sister.

"What, d'you think a lady can braid her own hair?" Frida's voice floated through from beyond the canvas walls. "Or are *you* going to do it?"

Ailith stilled. She had never been so pleased to hear from anyone in her life. That Frida had chosen to come gave her a flicker of hope, even if she was having trouble getting in. She couldn't hear the response, but Frida's derisive snort of laughter echoed across the camp.

"Gods, if you want her presentable for polite society, you'd best let me through. But go, ask his lordship, if you need permission. I'll wait."

Ailith waited, too, for what felt like hours, until Frida finally pushed her way into the tent, flanked by guards. If anyone could help her to arrange Sunneva's escape, it would be her. She would have run across the tent and hugged her but Frida had dropped into a low curtsey, obviously determined to be a servant rather than a friend so far as any observers were concerned.

"Let's get you into something more appropriate, milady." Frida turned and ushered the guards from the tent. "You need to give her ladyship the privacy to change."

Frida had packed Ailith's trunk with all her finest dresses, and proceeded to pick out a green silk gown and a set of understated emeralds. Ailith eyed the jewellery. It was a fraction of the collection Leofwin had given her, but there had to be enough wealth there to buy Sunneva's safety.

"He's got my sister," she said as soon as they were alone. "He'll hurt her if I don't do as he says… he might hurt her anyway. We have to get her out of here."

"You and her both. The messenger said I'd to prepare you for a wedding."

"If it's me or Sun, though, promise me you'll choose her."

"Ailith, I…"

"Promise me."

Frida shook her head. "His lordship needs you to come home."

Ailith's breath caught. She'd been so busy thinking of herself that she hadn't allowed even a dream that Leofwin might have survived the poison. Perhaps she'd be spared after all. Surely Garrick couldn't force her into a marriage while her betrothed still lived?

"He's okay? Truly?"

"He's breathing, but he hasn't woken. He needs your help."

"I'd have been there yesterday if it was up to me, but you've seen the guards. I'm trapped."

Frida squeezed her shoulder. "I brought something that might help with that. We just need to work out how best to use it."

"What?"

Frida reached into the trunk and pulled out a dark glass bottle. "Quietly," she said. "Draw attention to this and we'll both be killed."

Ailith uncorked the bottle. The scent was familiar, and a brief examination confirmed it. The silvery liquid was exactly as it appeared.

The giver of life — or the ultimate poison.

She threw her arms around Frida's neck and planted a grateful kiss on her cheek. "You're a genius," she said, keeping her voice low and cautious. "An absolute genius."

"I know." Frida smiled. "Put it somewhere safe. We'll only get one chance."

Ailith nodded, and tucked the bottle into the stuffing of one of the chairs.

"Now we'd best get you dressed up, or folks will get suspicious."

Ailith stripped off her smock and tunic, and stood still as a statue to allow Frida to lace her into the silk gown. With her hair braided and jewels in place, she felt ready to go into battle. Leofwin was alive, and she had a weapon. Prayers she hadn't dared voice had been answered... but she still needed a plan.

"You'll be eating with the boy, I assume," Frida said.

"If he decides he can tolerate me."

"He's letting you smarten yourself up. You know what he's like — he thinks he's won, so he'll want to lord it over you."

"So what should I do?"

"You have to get it into the blood, don't you?"

Ailith nodded.

"Then you need a blade. Fortunately, there should be knives aplenty at the dinner table."

"He'll never let me get close enough to stab him. He might think he's won, but he's a long way from trusting me."

"But he'll be thinking of a slash to the throat or a stab to the heart. You only have to nick his hand."

"He'll think of poison."

"Will he? As far as he knows he's broken you, and you've no way of concocting anything here. Does he really think highly enough of servants to suspect me of plotting against him?"

Ailith couldn't help laughing at that. "You could be right. I'm heir to a barony, but I wasn't born noble so I don't think I count as a real person, either."

"Good. That means he'll underestimate us." Frida pulled out the bottle and leaned across to adjust Ailith's skirts. "And this dress is perfect. I've sewn a couple of extra seams so you've got a hidden pocket."

"You've thought of everything." Ailith took a deep breath, gripping the back of the chair as she tried to steady her nerves. She couldn't have asked for a better plan, but it still depended on her ability to convince Garrick she was sincere.

"You can do this." Frida reached out and took her hand. "You can. I swear."

"I know." Ailith set her shoulders and arranged her face into a neutral mask. "I know," she repeated, a little more surely.

Frida smiled, and went to tell the guards that Ailith was ready.

Garrick didn't wait long to summon her. She found herself escorted to another tent, this one a huge canvas pavilion containing a thirty-seat dining table. She was seated across from Garrick; the table was too broad for her to comfortably reach him, but Frida had at least been right about the knives.

"My lord," she said, curtseying briefly before she took her seat. The table was full, but she recognised only Garrick's cousin Wymark. He offered her a brief smile when he thought Garrick wasn't looking; the others stared at her with varying degrees of curiosity and distaste. There was no-one from the Guild.

The food, out here beyond the siege lines, was the freshest she'd eaten in weeks. The conversation was vapid, making it easy for her to keep her promise of silence. But her mind was on neither the plates nor the people. She was afraid someone would notice her distraction, but no-one seemed particularly interested in hearing from her.

During the fish course, she managed to manoeuvre a knife into her lap. As the servants brought out haunches of venison, she doused the blade with thick silver amalgam. Much of the liquid seeped into her skirts, but ruining her dress was the last of her concerns. And at last, when the time came for everyone to toast Garrick's health, he reached for her hand.

She drove the knife into his arm without a pause. If she'd hesitated even a heartbeat, she knew she'd be lost.

The guards were upon her before he could even raise his voice to summon them, while the assembled guests started to panic. She felt the flare of Garrick's power as he examined the wound.

"Wait." Ailith's voice rang out loud across the din as she was pulled to her feet. She looked Garrick straight in the eye. "Dismiss everyone. We need to talk."

"Talk?" His mouth curled into a sneer. "You've had your chance at talking. We'll be wed as soon as the temples allow, and then you'll be hanged for treason."

"You misunderstand me." Ailith forced back the terror that was threatening to paralyse her. "It's not my life I'm concerned for."

"Your sister will hang, too. And your grandmother, and any other stray relatives I can round up in Bracklea."

The guards had her arms clamped tightly to her sides, but she could still reach her skirts. She slid the half-empty bottle onto the table. "You really don't know what this is, do you?"

He waved a dismissive hand. "Some alchemical nonsense, I assume. Certainly not the fastest of poisons, and I've healers enough in my court."

"Not to work silver, you haven't. Or rather," — she smiled — "you had one, and you had him put to death. Now, I think, I'm your only hope."

She fancied she saw a flash of fear in his eyes as he finally caught on.

"Leave us," he barked.

"Milord, is it wise…" one of the guards began, but a look from Garrick silenced him and a moment later Ailith was back in possession of her own body.

"You must have realised I'm not going to marry you," she said, rubbing the feeling back into her arms. "You could have me executed, but you wouldn't have Watersmeet, and you wouldn't live long enough to take your revenge on my family, either."

"I might find another mage."

"You might," she agreed. "But would you wager your life on managing it in the few days available to you? Honestly, I'd much prefer to find a solution where we both walk away from this with our lives and our lands."

"You must have a proposal."

"It isn't terribly complicated. I'll amalgamate that silver with your blood, which buys you a month. You'll use that time to lift the siege, fully and permanently, and to arrange compensation for the damage to our towns and our lands. You'll release my sister, your cousin will come to Watersmeet as a hostage, and you'll swear not to trouble us again as long as you live. The temples will witness our agreement. Do all this, and I'll be happy to cure you."

He stared at her incredulously. "You think you're in any position to negotiate an exchange of hostages? As if you were a noblewoman?"

"Do you think you're doing better, for all your blood and birth?"

"But you won't be able to hold a castle like this for more than a moon's turn, let alone ensure the safety of a hostage."

"I've held it longer than that with your men at the gates, and you're about to send them home. I don't know that anyone else has reason to attack."

She'd have to send a separate missive to Yutta, but they had no quarrel. Ailith hoped, with Garrick's forces out of the way, it wouldn't take much to persuade her to go home. In any event, the Wulfsberg camp was south of the river, and too small a force to uphold the siege alone.

"When the rest of the Twelve hear that a peasant woman has inherited Watersmeet, they'll all want your hand or your life. And don't think they'll stop to ask what your thoughts are. You're nothing to them. Less than nothing."

"Just as I am to you. I know. But I don't think the walls will crumble and fall just because I'm a woman."

Chapter Seventy-Six

His sleep had been troubled with delusions of all kinds, so Leofwin wasn't surprised to find himself dreaming that Ailith sat beside him on the bed, slipping her hand into his.

"Are you awake?" she asked.

He couldn't seem to move, even to speak. His eyes wouldn't open. He tried to squeeze her hand but his muscles refused to obey. Was it possible this wasn't a dream? His mouth was dry and the nausea was overwhelming. Dreams, however bizarre, didn't usually feel this dreadful.

Ailith smoothed a hand across his forehead, and felt for his pulse before sweeping her awareness across his body. What was she looking for? He followed her attention. Was there something in his blood? Was that why he couldn't move? He couldn't seem to concentrate for long enough to find out.

"Oh, gods be thanked!" She threw her arms around his neck, pressing her cheek to his shoulder. "You can hear me, can't you? You just can't speak yet."

Of course. She could feel his power just as he could feel hers. Gingerly, he reached out with his mind to probe her arm, tracing a line from her shoulder to her elbow. She laughed, and hugged him harder.

"I'm trying to work out what's wrong," she said, power flaring again as she examined him. "I must have unmade most of the poison, but perhaps some of the ingredients are still toxic."

Poison. That explained a lot. He'd gone out to talk to the Highfort brat, and then… nothing. He couldn't remember.

"I'll be right back."

She kissed his cheek and then she was gone. He tried again to move, without success. How? By all the gods, how had the boy managed to poison him, even as the priestess of Savash looked on?

But of course.

The oath. The binding. The only circumstance in which he'd ever let Garrick get close enough to touch him.

The memories came flooding back, and he remembered what he'd signed away. How was he ever going to explain all that to Ailith? And he still needed to ensure the boy kept to his side of the bargain.

Ailith tilted his head back and dripped a bitter liquid into his mouth, making him cough as he tried to swallow.

"A little more," she said, opening his mouth again. "Just see if you can manage a little more."

His eyes fluttered open and he tried to speak, but his mouth was too dry.

"Shhh." Ailith stroked his hair. He shut his damaged eye so he could look at her clearly. Her expression was a mix of soft concern and hard determination. "You don't have to say anything. Here, see if you can drink this."

Hooking one arm around her shoulders, he struggled to prop himself up on his elbow, and she held the tumbler to his lips. The peppermint water was sweet, in pleasant contrast to the bitter medicine.

"Thank you," he managed. "For everything. I don't know how many times I can expect you to save my life."

"I quite like you alive."

"I need to tell you—" he started.

Ailith shook her head. "Not tonight. There's nothing that can't wait till morning."

"But Garrick—"

"I've dealt with Garrick, he won't be troubling us again. But that can wait, too."

She stripped down to her smallclothes and climbed into bed beside him wearing nothing but her light cotton tunic. It would have been perfect, if only he hadn't been so recently poisoned.

"You don't have to do this, you know." She wrapped her arms around his waist and pulled his back into her chest. "I'd be more than happy to share your bed without an attempt on your life, first."

"Does this mean yes?" he asked. Her hands were freezing against his skin, but he wasn't complaining.

"It means you should get some sleep."

"I'd sleep better if I knew."

She brushed his hair aside and kissed him lightly on the back of the neck. "It means I love you and I'm glad you're alive, and I'll gladly save your life every time you need me to. If that's reason enough to marry someone then it's a yes."

"That's not the most romantic answer."

She pulled him onto his back and straddled him, her nose against his, glaring straight down into his eyes. "You're lucky you're ill, or I'd make you pay for that."

"I'd say I'm pretty lucky," he agreed, grinning back at her as he slid his hands up to her hips. "And if you're going to sleep here until I'm better, I fear there's a long road to recovery ahead of me. I might be sick for weeks."

"Shut up." She kissed him hard, giving him no option but to comply as her mouth took over his own. Though his tongue still felt thick and heavy, it felt a thousand times better to have her there.

"Maybe even months," he added, the moment she eased back to catch her breath.

"If you think you'll heal faster with me in my own bed..." she said, moving as if to leave, but he caught her round the waist and held her tight.

"You're not going anywhere," he said. "Please."

She settled back against his chest. "No," she said, trailing icy fingers up to his shoulder and down his arm until she was holding his hand. "I'm not."

Chapter Seventy-Seven

Ailith felt a little sorry for Wymark. He was younger than Garrick, she guessed about sixteen, and on the two occasions she'd met him previously he'd always trailed wordlessly along in his cousin's wake.

Now he trudged through the barbican, flanked by Rethar and another guard whose name Ailith didn't know, and soaked to the skin by a sudden downpour of warm autumn rain. Following three steps behind and also well-guarded were the two personal attendants they were allowing him to bring, who between them were struggling to manoeuvre his trunk up the steep, cobbled slope. Watching them only stirred her guilt, so she went instead to change out of her damp clothing and smarten herself up for the evening's feast.

When she'd gone to fetch Sunneva from the camp, Ailith had found Nana there as well, appearing completely unperturbed by captivity. She'd given her bedroom over to the two of them, at least until they managed to free up an extra guest room, but she hadn't yet taken the time to move her clothes into Leofwin's closet.

She considered her sister as she laid dresses out on the bed. "Sun, have you grown? I'm sure you'll fit into my gowns now."

Sunneva cocked her head to one side, and looked up at her sister in a way that made Ailith feel she was looking in a mirror. "You've changed, too."

"I suppose we both have." And she wasn't talking about fancy gowns and hairstyles. "But how in Refah's name did you persuade Mama to let you make a journey like this?"

"I didn't." Sun's eyes sparkled. "Nana was coming to bring that old man's letter, and I borrowed a few pennies and I hired a horse and I rode like the wind to catch her up. Mama has no idea."

"That's doesn't sound like the Sunneva I know."

"It was a quest."

"You told me girls don't go on quests."

"I never wanted to, but you don't always get to do whatever you want." She shrugged, holding a blue dress up against her chest. "You needed our help. And we did help, didn't we? You did get our message?"

"From Malachi," Nana said, catching Ailith's blank expression.

"Oh, yes! You saved Leofwin's life."

Sunneva beamed. "It was worth every bruise, then."

"How did you manage it?"

"He came to visit," Nana said as Ailith helped Sunneva into the dress she'd picked out. "In the days before his trial."

"While Eddy and me were at the farm," Sunneva added. "Nana wouldn't let me come, but I came anyway, and by the time I caught up with her she agreed it was safer for me to stay than to go back by myself. Then we got here and they wouldn't even let us see you, and when I said I was your sister they put us in a tent with guards, but the boy who came to empty the chamber pots was friendly so I got the idea to send him."

"Here." Nana reached around her neck and pulled a disc of carved bone from beneath her dress. "Malachi sent this, as well. For you. Thankfully, no-one looks too closely at an old woman's talismans, and it doesn't look valuable."

"What is it?"

"I don't truly know, but he was adamant it shouldn't fall into the wrong hands."

"The trial," Ailith said, tucking the pendant safely into her jewellery box alongside the treasures of Watersmeet. She'd been so wrapped up with Leofwin's ordeal that she'd almost forgotten. "I don't suppose you've heard about the outcome, if you came straight here."

"No, but he didn't expect to survive. That much was obvious."

Ailith bowed her head quietly and crossed her palm with Oelum's symbol, an instinctive gesture that came surely much too late to placate the goddess, but which felt an appropriate tribute.

"He was very old," Nana said. "You must think of it that way."

She was more inclined to think of the golden elixir, and the weight that their formulation would have lifted from his ancient shoulders, but she hadn't begun to explain all that to Nana yet. How much did she know of what Anselm had done?

"He was already old when you knew him as a girl, wasn't he?" she hedged.

"He seemed older than the wind." Nana took a careful sip of her now-cold tea. "I know, dear. There are mysteries aplenty in this world, knowledge I would have given my teeth for until your mother came along. You don't have to explain it all to me."

"But Anselm…"

"Malachi told me how that must have gone."

"Still, I think it'll be a shock when you see him."

"I don't think I should see him, and I don't imagine he'll want to see me."

"But you were…"

"We were young and foolish, that's all. I think some things are best left alone, especially after all these years. Perhaps, once he's settled back into normal life, we might talk, but not today. Is he going home?"

"That would raise too many questions. He'll visit Selwyn, of course, but then Leofwin has offered to write him some letters of introduction. He's a very talented musician, it won't take him long to find a patron or two."

"But what of your news?" Nana asked.

"Where should I start?"

"We need to know everything," Sunneva said helpfully.

Ailith tried to force her thoughts into some kind of order. It had only been a few months since they'd seen each other, but it felt like the whole world had changed. "Malachi told you I'm a mage, I suppose? He thinks you taught me."

Nana shook her head. "No, dear, that will have been your father."

"Papa's not a mage."

"Of course he is. How else do you think he makes those vivid colours that his rivals can only dream of? Not one of his apprentices has ever matched his skill, but you and Drefan never had that problem."

"But he was furious when I tried to experiment."

"Yes, dear, and he doesn't believe in magic. That doesn't stop it from believing in him, and our Malachi wouldn't have introduced your mother to that boy if he hadn't had a spark of talent in him. But he's the one you learnt your skills from, I'd wager the farm on that, because he's the one who's taught you to make things."

"You taught me letters."

"But nothing else of consequence. No, dear, it was your father — but I don't think you should tell him. I never have."

"Why not?"

"He puts too much faith in the Temple Law. Even if I could show him the truth of it, he'd feel obliged to turn himself in for trial, and how would that help any of us?"

"Are they furious with me?"

"Livid, I'm sure," Sunneva said. "But just wait until we tell them you're living in a castle. Mama won't believe it."

"I thought it was best not to mention that to your mother until I knew exactly what was going on," Nana added.

"And you haven't told them about the alchemy, either."

"Well, dear. I hardly knew if you were a student or a prisoner until Malachi's last visit. Then he made it quite clear you were…" She thought for a moment. "'More at home than I'd dreamed possible,' I think were his words. He said he'd be sorry not to see you again."

"Me, too," Ailith said. She'd barely known the man but he'd steered her firmly onto this path. Whether or not Leofwin was right that he'd acted primarily with his own ends in mind, she'd always be grateful for that particular interference.

"Is it time for supper?" Sunneva asked. "I'm starving."

"Yes, but first I have to welcome Wymark to our halls." Ailith straightened her shoulders, adjusted her dress, and put on her haughtiest expression. "Do I look suitably intimidating?"

Sunneva laughed. "You look strange."

Ailith smiled. She wasn't sure she wanted to terrify the boy, anyway. It wasn't his fault he was being used as a token on a game board. She only needed him to believe that she knew what she was doing.

"Come on, then. The sooner I get this over with, the sooner we can relax. You can go straight through to the hall, I'll join you shortly."

Wymark was waiting in the Drawing Room, as per her instructions, and looked markedly uncomfortable with his damp clothes hanging limply on his frame. He'd been divested of his trunk and his chamberlain, both of which had been sent ahead to his suite. And although his man-at-arms remained he'd been disarmed, rendering the title rather a nonsense. Ailith had given instructions that Wymark's personal supply of weaponry was to be stored in a strong box in the armoury, only to be returned after six months' good behaviour.

"My lady," he said, sweeping into a low bow.

"Wymark." She offered her hand for the customary kiss. "Welcome to Watersmeet. Can I offer you something to drink?"

"A little wine wouldn't go amiss."

Ailith had made sure it was Lufe on hand to fill their glasses. Her placid, supportive smile made the whole bizarre experience slightly more bearable. And with Frida waiting by the door to handle any little issues that might come up, she knew she wasn't alone.

"To your health," Ailith said, raising her glass. "You haven't had a long journey, I know, but I imagine it's been a strange one."

"And wet," he said, combing a hand through his bedraggled hair. "I was hoping to have chance to change before dinner."

"The staff are still preparing your rooms." She tried to adopt a suitably apologetic tone without actually apologising. "This all came about rather suddenly, and until the town can be repaired we're rather full. But perhaps you could clean up in the scullery."

"I would appreciate that, my lady."

"You know why you're here, of course, but we want you to be as comfortable as the circumstances permit. You're a hostage, not a prisoner." Ailith turned to Frida. "Could you have one of the girls fetch water for a bath?"

"Consider it done."

"Will Garrick be eating with us?" Wymark asked.

"No." Ailith took a deep breath, wondering if she could trust herself to say any more on the subject. "I won't give him another chance to abuse our hospitality."

"That's fair. Has his lordship made a full recovery?"

"Yes, he'll be joining us shortly. No harm done."

"Except to the trust between our two families."

Ailith shrugged. "I'm not sure there was much love between Watersmeet and Highfort to begin with. I hope you won't hold such politics against us while you're our guest."

Chapter Seventy-Eight

Standing in front of the fire, Wymark was starting to dry out by the time Leofwin reached the Great Hall, and he'd found a change of clothes somewhere. Ailith stood with her arm slung around the shoulders of a younger, skinnier copy of herself that could only be her sister. The girl was even wearing one of her dresses. And the older woman with them must be her grandmother. They were deep in conversation, sharing smiles and laughter.

Wymark stopped talking as soon as Leofwin caught his eye, and bowed at the waist.

"Wymark."

"My lord."

Leofwin shook his head.

"No, no, we can't have that. Not if you're to live with us until we think of some other way to rein in young Highfort." Not if Ailith had already judged him worthy of smiles and clean clothes.

"Pardon?" Wymark looked up, puzzled.

"You'll call me by my name, as long as you're living here."

The boy adjusted admirably, and by the time he'd given another slight bow and straightened up, he'd almost erased the shock from his face. "Leofwin, then. My thanks."

"And me, as well," Ailith said. "I was trying to be suitably formal, but names are easier."

Wymark nodded. "I can already see that Watersmeet will be rather different to serving at the Highfort."

"And you're already better company than your cousin," Leofwin said.

"This is my sister, Sunneva," Ailith said, steering the girl towards him. "Sun, this is the Lord Baron of Watersmeet, but as he's to be your brother, you should probably call him Leofwin."

"You don't mean…?"

Ailith nodded, and Sunneva let out an ear-splitting shriek of joy.

"She's more excited than you," Leofwin said drily.

"She's more excitable than me," Ailith corrected, spreading her fingers across his back. "She could hardly be happier."

"Wait till I tell Mama," Sunneva said. "Though she won't believe a word of it until she sees the both of you with her own eyes."

"And your mother will have to send her apologies to the young men she's been a-courting on your behalf," the older woman added. Ailith rolled her eyes.

"I'm delighted to meet you, Sunneva," Leofwin said, bending to place a formal kiss upon the girl's fingers. He couldn't overestimate the importance of making a good impression on these, the first of many relatives he hoped would visit in the coming weeks and months. "Welcome to Watersmeet."

"And Mildred, my grandmother."

"Millie, please." Millie extended her hand. "No-one calls me Mildred."

"Come, you must all be ravenous."

"I don't know about them, but I certainly am." Ailith linked her arm through his. Leofwin signalled for the gong, and they went to take their places at the table.

Garrick had already sent two wagon-loads of fresh produce as a token of good faith, so the feast would be a fine one. Over the first three courses — freshwater trout, onion broth, and a rich venison pie — Leofwin and Ailith took turns at questioning Wymark about his cousin and conditions in the camp.

"I don't doubt he'll order the retreat," Wymark said. "For now. But you shouldn't assume his love for me is enough to prevent him returning, if he feels he has a chance of bringing down the walls."

"I don't think Garrick cares that much for anyone besides himself," Ailith said. "But we have good walls. And we wouldn't actually execute you just to spite him, you know."

"You shouldn't tell him things like that," Leofwin said, but he couldn't keep the smile from his voice. Her ways were unconventional, but her approach seemed to work.

"I'll pretend to forget," Wymark said. "If it helps."

"Would you like wine?" Lufe asked, hovering at Sunneva's back with the flagon.

Sunneva turned to Ailith. "Can I?"

"I think we can say you're a grown woman, now, with a quest beneath your belt," Ailith said. "Of course you can have a little wine, if you'd like."

"Oh, it's just like a castle would be in the sagas," Sunneva said as she held up her goblet for filling.

Ailith shook her head. "Not really."

"It is. There's servants and wine and… no, there is something missing. There should be minstrels."

"I'm afraid we've been under siege," Leofwin said. "You tend not to get minstrels wandering in, under those circumstances."

"But, Sun, in the sagas Lufe wouldn't be one of my best friends, and Frida would still be a chambermaid. Real life is much messier."

"Fine." Sunneva took a sip of her wine. "It's close enough. But there really should be music."

"Anselm could play for us," Ailith said. He'd chosen not to join the party this evening, but the chance to play for an audience would surely be enough to tempt him. "Let's have his harp brought to the gallery, ready for tomorrow night."

"And you could sing," Leofwin said, watching her cheeks flush.

"Sun has a good voice, too," she said, recovering admirably and pretending she had no idea what he was hinting at. "We could do a few ballads together, but we don't know anything that compares to Anselm's music."

"Oh yes," Sunneva said, clasping her hands to her chest. "Let's do that, it'll be so much fun."

"Do you play an instrument, Wymark?" Ailith asked.

"I learnt a few pieces on the lyre, but I never really had the patience to be good at it."

"You can play for us anyway," Sunneva said. "We're all friends here."

Ailith beckoned Lufe over. "I was going to come and join you in the kitchens after, but I can't really leave Sun on her first night here."

Lufe glanced over to where Sunneva was now quizzing Wymark about his childhood at the Highfort. "Bring her, then."

"I'm not sure she's quite up to handling the kitchen crowd just yet."

"'Course she is. We're not that bad, and you said yourself, she's a woman grown now."

"Alright, then." Ailith grinned. "It's not that I mind all the feasts and formalities, but sometimes a girl just wants to sing bawdy songs into the night."

"Excellent. I'll tell the others."

Ailith slid her hand along Leofwin's leg beneath the table as Lufe went to do another round with the flagon. "I'm going to join the others for a quick drink in the kitchens after dinner. Are you coming?"

"Will you sing the song you wrote for me?"

She blushed. "That was not for you."

"About me, then. Will you?"

"Not with my little sister there, no!"

He enjoyed watching her squirm, perhaps a little more than was strictly reasonable. "You're only making it worse by putting it off — I already know it's going to be as smutty as any sailor's ditty, and I had all that time in the temple to invent my own lyrics."

"I'm not embarrassed because it's smutty, I'm embarrassed because it was the work of two drunken minutes. It's dreadful."

"When will I get to hear it, then?"

"Maybe once we're married," she said. "Then it's too late for you to change your mind about me."

He shook his head. "I am not waiting six months for a song. If you won't sing for me, I'll just get one of your friends to tell me how it goes."

"They wouldn't."

"They might, after a few drinks. Shall we find out?"

"Promise me you won't."

"If you promise you'll sing it for me later, when we're alone."

"I'll sing, if you can't think of anything else you'd rather be doing," she said. "I'm not planning on letting you sleep alone just because you're feeling better."

Chapter Seventy-Nine

Ailith found Sunneva in the Great Hall, sharing a late breakfast with Wymark.

"You don't have to eat every meal in here," she said, ruffling her sister's hair. "We have more intimate rooms."

"I like it," Sunneva said, glancing up at the vaulted ceiling. "Wymark's been telling me all about the portraits. And I want to make the most of all this grandness while I can — not like you, wearing work clothes when you could have silk."

Ailith smiled. She'd managed to get through the night before without changing out of her fancy gown, but she was happy to be back in more practical clothes now. Sunneva, however, had dressed again in the cornflower-blue silk she'd borrowed for the feast.

"You can come back and visit any time, you know. And you'll have to stay for the wedding."

"I wasn't dreaming, then? You really are marrying him?"

"You weren't dreaming."

"Just imagine: this whole hall filled with dancing, hogs roasting in the courtyard, and proper minstrels in the gallery. You can put flowers in every window, red to match your dress and yellow for joy. It's going to be so beautiful."

"I'll have to ask Leofwin what red flowers bloom in the spring," she said, struggling to think of anything more delicate than tulips. Perhaps he could grow something special in one of the glass houses.

"And you'll get one of your tailors to measure me for dresses," Sunneva went on. "I'll need at least three, for the feast and the dancing and the blessings."

"The feast and the dancing happen at the same time," Ailith said, puzzled, but Sunneva shook her head.

"Not in a castle. Honestly, anyone would think you'd never listened to the old romances."

"Well, I'm not doing everything differently just because the walls are thicker. You can help me with the details, but I want a wedding that feels like Hilde's and Ingrith's and Aidith's. And before you start, I'm definitely wearing the same dress."

"Of course you are." Sunneva rolled her eyes and turned back to Wymark. "Do you have brothers and sisters? Are they as stubborn as mine?"

"I'm the oldest of five," Wymark said. "But I started squiring at the Highfort before the youngest was born, so I don't see them often."

"You'll have to invite them to visit you here," Sunneva said, and Ailith wasn't sure she could face explaining to her sister why that might not be possible. She glanced at Wymark, and realised with heartbreaking certainty that he already knew. He'd been a games token all his life.

"I have a few things to attend to," Ailith said. "Will you two be able to amuse yourselves until lunch?"

"Oh, yes, I wanted to walk the battlements," Sunneva said, then cast an uncertain glance at Wymark. "That is, if you don't have other plans?"

"A walk would be delightful," Wymark said. "The weather seems to have recovered today."

Ailith smiled and left them to it. She couldn't let her guard down for long enough to be a true friend to Wymark, but perhaps her sister would manage it. The gods knew, he would need friends.

She found Leofwin on his knees in the glass house, pinching self-seeded weeds from between his precious cultivars.

"Just you?" he asked as Ailith crouched beside him and started to pluck at the unwelcome seedlings. "Where's the family?"

"They're off exploring. Anyway, I thought we might keep the garden as our own little space."

"Forever?"

"Why not? It's nice to have some privacy."

"Are you afraid they might catch us doing something inappropriate?"

Before she could answer he turned and pulled her close for a kiss. The motion dumped them both unceremoniously backwards onto the flagstones, making her giggle as she realised that — however mystified it left Sunneva — she was much happier in the garden or workshop than she'd ever be in the Great Hall. Leofwin managed to catch one hand behind her neck, keeping her head from the stone as he bent down to kiss her again.

He leaned over her, propped up on one elbow, and traced a muddy finger along her collarbone, making her shiver as his calluses grazed her skin. "Yes, I think you're right."

"About what?"

"Keeping the garden to ourselves. You never know when I'll need to have you all to myself."

"Plus, you grow some things that are less than friendly," Ailith said. "And Sunneva chooses flowers by whether they're pretty. Speaking of which, I had an idea. For the wedding."

"Oh?"

"She was talking about the different coloured flowers we should have, and it made me wonder. Do you think we can make shimmering powder in different colours by using different metals, just the way you would with glazes?"

He kissed her. "You're wonderful."

She slid her hand into his and looked at him quizzically. "More wonderful than usual?"

"I was afraid you'd be bored of alchemy," he said. "Now you've solved everything. I thought we might have to find a new challenge."

"Solved everything? I don't think so."

"The golden elixir and a cure for Anselm's condition within a couple of months? I'd say that's pretty good going."

"I'm not complaining, but we still have to create an elixir that works for people who can't use gold. I don't have any new ideas about that at the moment, though — and coloured shimmering powders sound like a fun thing we could play with while we wait for inspiration to strike."

"Do you want to test a couple of ideas before lunch?"

"I love you." She squeezed his hand and pulled them both to their feet. "Yes, let's. It can't be so terribly different to mixing glazes."

The End.

Afterword

Thank you for reading! If you enjoyed this book, please tell your friends, or consider leaving a review at your favourite retailer.

Acknowledgements

This book wouldn't be what it is without everyone who has supported me along the way.

Particular thanks are due to: Jamie, who knew these characters when I thought they were destined for the stage; Andrew, for endless brainstorming on long and windy walks; and my editor Joanna, for finding loose threads of plot that needed to be woven more tightly.

For reading and commenting on early drafts, I am also grateful to Charlotte, Steven, Jeanne, and my mum.

All remaining imperfections are, of course, entirely my own.

About the Author

When she's not writing books, Rachel conducts research in computational linguistics, works as a vegetarian recipe developer, and blogs about food and travel. She's one half of Strange Charm Books, a project devoted to showcasing women's writing in speculative fiction. She explores the world through the medium of getting hopelessly lost, collects skills instead of trinkets, and lives in the Cotswolds with her husband and adopted rodents. Watersmeet is her third novel.

http://rachelcotterill.com

Twitter, Facebook
@rachelcotterill

Books by Rachel Cotterill

The Twelve Baronies

Novels
Watersmeet

Short Works
The Falconer

Chronicles of Charanthe
Rebellion
Revolution

Recipe Books
Design Your Own Cookies